MW00632464

VEIL
of
DECEPTION

Praise for *VEIL OF DECEPTION*

". . . a Firefox for a new generation. This is one thriller that fans of Cussler, Clancy, and Flynn will not want to miss."

- James R. Hannibal, Author of the Nick Baron covert ops series

". . . hits all the right notes while establishing Lewis among the best in the genre . . ."

- Bella Wright, Bestthrillers.com

". . . a riveting, timely story that will entertain and frighten you at the same time . . .."

--Joseph Badal, Best-Selling Author of Death Ship (Danforth Saga #5)

"A fly by the seat of your pants page turner and not to be missed."

- Manhattan Book Review

Praise for VEIL OF DECEPTION

"A smart, multi-layered thriller . . ."

*- Tom Young, author of The Mullah's Storm,
Silent Enemy, and Sand and Fire*

"Lewis set up quite a tightrope to walk with
Veil of Deception, and with relatively few wobbles, he makes it to
the other side with style."

-San Francisco Book Review

". . . a compelling military thriller . . ."

- Kevin Hurley, Author of Cut-Out

". . . Lewis clearly demonstrates that he has the skills to compete
with some of the top thriller
and intrigue writers of today."

- Anne-Marie Reynolds, Readers' Favorite

By Michael Byars Lewis

SURLY BONDS

VEIL OF DECEPTION

MICHAEL BYARS LEWIS

SATCOM PUBLISHING

VEIL OF DECEPTION

A THRILLER

DISCLAIMER: The views presented in this fictional work are those of the author and in no way reflect the views of the Department of Defense nor its Components.

This is a work of historical fiction. Characters and incidents are products of the author's imagination and are used fictitiously while locations and names of historical figures may be used as reference to ground the reader. Any resemblance of characters and incidents to actual events and persons, living or dead, is entirely coincidental.

Copyright ©2015 by Michael Byars Lewis

All rights reserved. No part of this book may be used or reproduced in any manner whatsoever without written permission, except in the case of brief quotations embodied in critical articles and reviews.

First Printing: April 2016

SATCOM Publishing

ISBN: 978-0-9914764-2-8

Cover Design by Damonza

Printed in the United States of America

To my wife Kim . . .

VEIL OF DECEPTION

1

S HERRI DAVIS APPROACHED THE ENTRYWAY, already regretting her decision. After filling out paperwork and release forms for thirty minutes, she hid behind the filthy curtain covering the doorway, the knot in her belly growing tighter. She pulled a small section of the worn fabric to the side. Colored lights blinked rapidly, and several spotlights locked on the mirrored ball above the stage, creating hundreds of dancing reflections around the large room.

"It doesn't hurt, ya know," a voice said over the loud music.

Turning her head, Sherri spied a girl in her late teens standing next to her.

"You look nervous. It's your first time, isn't it?"

"Yes," Sherri said, releasing the curtain. In the dark hallway, Sherri could barely make out the girl's features, though her heavy eyelashes and straight black hair were clearly prominent. It was the young girl whose locker was next to hers.

"It's not like sex. Doesn't hurt the first time."

Sherri nodded. "Got any advice?"

"Have fun sweetie, that's my advice. Go out there and relax. You'll do fine."

"Relax. Right."

"Honey, once those assholes hand you a twenty to sit on their lap, you'll relax," the girl said. "Now get on out there and bring home the bacon," the girl said as she patted her on the rear. Sherri noticed the pat was a little too soft and lingered a little too long before the girl retreated toward the stage.

Sherri sighed heavily, her hands pressing the pleats of her skirt. She cupped her breasts for a quick adjustment and pulled her shoulders back. The transition from the dark hallway was dramatic. Mist spewed from the smoke machine, burning her eyes, and her ears pulsed as the deep bass vibrated through the speakers. Her steps were short and deliberate, as if she had a choice in these five-inch stiletto heels. She meandered between the tables, dodging a waitress carrying a tray full of beers.

The girl who spoke to her, nineteen at most, took the stage like a veteran and danced around the pole while a variety of clientele watched her every move. The music made her head hurt. Sherri scanned the crowd. Unable to see the two men she was looking for, she worried she might be wasting her time.

"Hey, baby," an overweight, bald drunk said as he reached out and tried to grab her arm.

"Not tonight, sweetie," Sherri replied, pulling away.

While she looked the part—plaid miniskirt and a white button-down tied in front of her push-up bra—she wasn't acting the part. She sensed her awkward movements through the bar. Relax.

Standing by the DJ booth, she tapped her foot to the music and rhythmically swayed her body. Sherri closed her eyes and started a slow, seductive dance. Her hips swayed like sea oats blowing in the ocean breeze. It didn't take long before she noticed the men nearby stared at her instead of the stage, waving twenty dollar bills at her. Feeling more confident, she moved around the bar again. She had to work fast. Her stage debut was in half an hour.

After a couple minutes meandering through the crowded bar and refusing three more requests for lap dances, she saw the first subject. He had come out of the men's room and returned to a table located away from the stage.

His name was Ahmed Alnami, a Saudi Arabian living in and moving around the United States. Now he was in Pensacola, sitting at a table with his partner, Saeed Alghamdi, who was getting a lap dance from one of the girls. Alnami sat at the table where he took a long swig of his beer and flashed his partner a smile. Weren't these two supposed to be devout Muslims? Why were they here?

Sherri approached the table. She leaned toward Alnami, her breasts at eye level, right in front of him. He stared in her eyes, looking fearful. Not the fear of danger. The innocent fear, like a teenage boy about to lose his virginity. "Hey, big boy," she said, "are you lonely?" Alnami continued to stare, clearly unsure what to do.

Sherri smiled and pointed at her eyes. "Honey, you need to change your focus from here, to here," she said as she moved her hands to her breasts. Alnami's face beamed.

"Yes, please to sit," he said in broken English. Sherri sat on his lap. Her breasts were at his eye level. No wonder he was smiling—a blond Amazon had landed in his lap. She reached over and ran her hand through his hair. It was oily and hadn't been washed for a while. Wiping her hand on the back of his shirt, she cringed, yet forced a weak smile. Alnami lunged his face forward and buried it in her breasts. Sherri pushed him back. She wanted to punch him, but that would undo all she'd accomplished.

"Settle down, big boy, we need to get to know each other first."

"This is what I want," he said, pointing at his partner, whose lap dancer was grinding aggressively into him.

"Oh, you'll get that and more," she replied. "We've got to do some talking first."

"What is this talking?" he said in a louder voice. He pulled out a roll of bills. The smile faded and his eyes bulged. "I want boobies. I want the grind-a-grind." The teenage innocence disappeared, and the self-absorbed arrogance of the immature adult surfaced. He started to push her off his lap. Sensing she was losing her opportunity, she grabbed his head and shoved his face back into her breasts.

"Better?" She pulled his face from her bosom, and the smile had returned.

"Yes please."

"Now, before I give you the grind-a-grind, we've got to get to know each other. What's your name?"

"Ahm—" He paused. "Keevin. My name is Keevin."

"Kevin? Okay, Kevin will work for now. My name is Bambi. What do you do, Kevin?"

"I do fine. Thank you, Bom-bi."

Sherri cringed. This was painful. "What's your job?"

"Oh, I train to be pilot."

Interesting. She shifted herself on his lap and ran the fingers of her left hand along the buttons of his shirt. "Are you out at the Navy base?"

He said nothing and his eyes remained focused on her breasts.

"How long are you in town?"

"Two more weeks."

Sherri thought for a moment. The two Saudis had already been in Pensacola for two weeks. Obviously, they weren't students, and they weren't flying with the Navy, but they were there to fly something.

"You must be really smart," she said. "Not everybody gets to fly airplanes."

"I am one of Allah's warriors," Alnami said, his voice rising. "Allahu Akbar."

Sherri studied Alnami. "What is Allah having you do?" She bit her lower lip, realizing she might have pushed the conversation too far, too fast.

His eyes moved from her breasts back to her eyes. His nostrils flared as he bared his yellowing teeth. "No more talk of this," Alnami shouted. "I want grind-a-grind from you." He pulled a fifty out of his pocket and waved it at her. Sherri sighed, realizing she would not get any more information unless she took it to the next level. That was not going to happen. She took the bill and stuck it in her bra.

She rose from his lap and posed in front of him, hands on her hips. He's done talking. It's time to get out of here. She slowly swayed back and forth, running her hands along the sides of her hips up to her breasts. The dancing must have been good, because she noticed his partner staring at her while still getting his lap dance.

Sherri leaned forward, nearly rubbing her breasts from his knees to his head, her body barely missing contact with his. She said in his ear, "How about you and me leave this place?"

Alnami's smile grew bigger. "Yes, please."

Pushing herself away from him, she moved behind his chair and ran hands down the front of his chest. "Okay, I've got to go clock out and change clothes. I'll be back here in fifteen minutes. Don't move."

"I not move. Don't change your clothes. You sexy momma."

Sherri forced a weak smile. "Okay, baby. Whatever you want."

She left the table and headed to the dressing room. Closing the door behind her, she shielded her eyes from the steady light. As her eyes adjusted, she went to her locker and gathered her things. Standing in front of the mirror, she pulled off the blond wig, and her deep red hair fell to her shoulders. Pulling out a brush, she touched it up from where the wig had pressed it down or tangled it. She slipped her tan overcoat over her shoulders and retrieved her clothes from her locker. A few of the other girls watched her.

"Sorry, ladies, I'm not cut out for this," she said. She turned and walked out the back door of the strip club.

The light by the back door was burned out. She clutched her purse tightly and gripped the can of mace in her coat pocket as she approached her rental car, a shiny new red Toyota Celica. She grabbed her keys and cell phone from her purse and climbed in. Kicking off the stiletto heels, she cranked the engine and pulled on to Highway 98, dialing on her cell phone as she drove.

The phone answered on the first ring. "Did you get it?"

"No, I didn't get that far. Alnami was getting a little too friendly."

"I told you this might happen. Did you find out anything?"

"They're here two more weeks, and they'll be flying next week, but I don't know what and I don't know why. Sorry, it's the best I was willing to do under the circumstances."

"Okay," the voice replied. "Get back here tomorrow. I've got something else for you."

"Like what?"

"Our informant in New York wants to meet with you ASAP."

"All right," Sherri said begrudgingly. "I'll see you tomorrow." As she hung up the phone, the car lurched forward. The phone slipped from her fingers, falling to the floorboard as her body slammed into her seat belt. She glanced in the rearview mirror as a car slid back and accelerated toward her again.

"What the hell?"

She put both hands on the wheel and her foot pressed the accelerator as the car made contact with the red Celica a second time. As she reached the Pensacola Bay Bridge, the vehicle tried to spin her car by striking the left rear fender. She accelerated again, making the assailant miss his mark.

The mystery car pulled behind her, two car lengths back. Every time she passed a vehicle, the car followed her.

Who the hell was attacking her? Could it be Alnami? No, she hadn't been gone long enough. He would still be waiting for her inside the strip club, probably constructing ridiculous fantasies in his head.

It was a dark, starless night, and the rise in the bridge was a half mile away. This hump in the bridge allowed larger boats to enter and exit Pensacola Bay from the Gulf. Once on the other side, she would be in civilization again.

Vinyl and glass shards flew everywhere inside the vehicle as bullets pierced the back window of her car and hit the passenger side of the dashboard. She screamed and let go of the steering wheel, her foot coming off the gas for an instant.

Her eyes darted back and forth as her car veered toward the rail to her right. Grabbing the steering wheel, she pressed the accelerator once again as she jerked her car away from the side rail.

"Oh, God," she said, "why the hell are they shooting at me?"

She swerved to put another car between them, then pushed the accelerator to the floor. The innocent car she just passed bumped into the guardrail, sending sparks flying. It spun around as the assailant hit the car from the rear, then continued on. The dark sedan accelerated and closed the distance between them.

Another burst of machine-gun fire. Sherri screamed as the bullets struck the rear of her vehicle. At the bottom of the hump, she checked her rearview mirror. Shattered glass and bullet holes in the rear window were all she could see. Based on the lights in the distance, she estimated she'd reach the end of the bridge in less than a minute.

With a quarter mile until the end of the bridge, the car shuddered. Sherri's gaze shifted to the front of her car, and her shoulders slumped. She beat her fist against the steering wheel as smoke rose from under the hood and the car started decelerating.

The speedometer read 80 mph at this point, but the car no longer responded to her foot pressing the accelerator. She pushed it all the way to the floor, but nothing. In her side mirror, she noticed the assailant closing in behind her. The car had closed within three car lengths when another round of bullets hit her vehicle.

Her heart pounded as she reached the end of the bridge and the Celica slowed through 55 mph.

"Shit . . . If I break down on this bridge, I'm done," she said as she pumped the accelerator. "Who the hell are these guys?"

The Celica slowed to 25 mph now, and other cars quickly caught and passed her.

Glancing in the mirror, she saw the dark-colored sedan make a U-turn at the end of the bridge and head toward Pensacola.

In front of her, red-and-blue lights danced on top of a parked car. Sherri had driven into a speed trap. Her assailants turned and ran.

"Yeah," she said. "Take that, asshole. You'd better run."

A faint nervous smile eased across her face as she glided the unpowered vehicle into the right lane and onto the side of the road.

The car came to a stop, and as soon as she put it in park, her body began to shake as the adrenaline faded. Leaning forward on the steering wheel, she began to sob. She had almost been killed. A myriad of thoughts raced through her head as the police car pulled in behind her. The officer tapped on the window with his flashlight. She lowered the window and covered her eyes as he pointed the light in her face.

"Driver's license and registration," he said.

"No problem." She dug in her purse for her driver's license. When she reached into the glove box for the rental agreement, she glanced in the passenger's side mirror and saw the dark outline of the officer's partner approaching the other side of her vehicle. Why didn't he say something about the smoke coming from under the hood? Or the blown-out back window?

She stopped digging and glanced back at the officer who spoke to her. Is he wearing jeans? With a quick glance back to the passenger-side mirror, she saw his partner approaching the vehicle was wearing—shorts? Wait, how could this guy not have noticed the bullet holes?

"Hey, what agency are you guys with?" she said as she turned back to the cop. Before she could react, he jammed a long stick through the window and pressed it into her neck. The electric shock was fast and intense, then—blackness.

2

April 15, 2001

A SMALL SLIVER of glistening sunlight cut through the dark hotel room, illuminating its small interior. Dust particles danced through the piercing beam like fireflies on a clear summer night. The light pried into his consciousness while the grinding gears of a construction vehicle outside ripped it open.

Jason Conrad buried his face in a pillow and moaned as his head felt ready to explode. He recognized this place, barely. The hangover reminded him that his recent lifestyle choices had their consequences.

It didn't take long for his body to tell him he needed to relieve himself. He swung his feet off the bed and glanced next to him, rubbing the sides of his throbbing temples with his fingertips. The blonde lay nude on top of the sheets. She had every appearance of being attractive from here. He struggled to remember her face. He definitely could not remember her name.

Jason tiptoed to the bathroom, as much to protect his pounding head as not to wake the blonde. After relieving himself, he washed his hands and face and brushed his teeth. When he left the bathroom, she was sitting up in the bed, watching him. *She is pretty. Now, what is her name again?*

"Good morning, sexy," she said. She sounded much more awake than he did.

"Hi," Jason said. She was too bubbly for early morning.

"I can't believe you're up," she said in a strong Texas drawl.

"Yeah."

"Am I still beautiful?"

Jason grinned. "Absolutely."

"You're quiet this morning. You wouldn't stop talking last night."

Vague memories of the night before pushed themselves into his consciousness. He crawled back into the bed, and she leaned over and kissed him.

"Oh, you brushed your teeth. I'll be right back," she said, climbing out of bed.

Jason studied her figure. She had all the right equipment. He could see why he would have been talkative. Now he wished he didn't drink as much. This was a night he would have liked to remember.

Yesterday started off well. As flight lead of a four-ship of T-38s, they'd done a flyover for a Texas Rangers game. It was a great TDY, or temporary duty, to Dallas, with per diem. The flyover during the national anthem at the Ballpark in Arlington was uneventful, and they landed at Naval Air Station Fort Worth, formerly known Carswell Air Force Base, right afterward.

A limousine provided by one of the Rangers' owners, picked them up outside Base Operations. It contained a cooler full of beer and a tray of cheese and crackers to tide them over until they arrived at the stadium in Arlington.

It was a tight fit with eight sweaty, cocky T-38 instructors, but they didn't care. They were amazed at the red carpet treatment and relished every minute of it. The pilots were treated like rock stars in the owners' VIP suite, with all the food and alcohol they wanted. After the game, the limo drove them to the West End in Dallas. Jason and his buddies found themselves in Gators, a piano bar/restaurant with dueling white grand pianos and a rowdy crowd. He remembered meeting her at Gators. *What is her name?*

Jason rolled over on his back and stared at the ceiling. The nameless faces of his women over the years skipped through his thoughts. He felt empty. Like every other one-night stand, *she* crept back into his head. What happened to the one who'd slipped away six years ago?

Whatever happened to Kathy Delgato?

The door to the bathroom opened, and the blonde traipsed back into the room. She took the time to brush her hair and put on lipstick. Posing at the end of the bed, she riveted her eyes at him wantonly.

"Oh, good, you're still awake." She traipsed around the bed to the window and opened the curtain, standing nude in front of the window.

"I can't help it," she said with a wry smile. "I'm an exhibitionist."

"Clearly."

"What time do you fly back?" She posed seductively in front of the window.

Jason glanced at the clock. Red digital numbers displayed eight thirty-three. The pilots planned to leave the hotel at noon. "I need to be at the base at eleven," he lied.

"Oh," she said, sauntering toward him.

"Do I…" He paused. "Do I need to get you a ride home?" He couldn't remember how they made it back to the hotel.

"No silly. I drove us, remember?"

No, and I can't remember your name either, so please don't ask.

"Well," he said, glancing at the clock, "we have some time."

The blonde smiled and crawled back onto the bed. He stopped hating himself as she wrapped her arms around him. Even drunk, he had done very well.

SHERRI SHIVERED from the cool breeze as she lay on her back. Fading in and out of consciousness, she tossed her head from side to side. Various colors edged their way into her brain. She writhed in place, and the ground shifted slightly. Her muscles ached, but the sun on her face was irritating. When she tried to open her eyes, her hand shielded them from the brightness. The smell of saltwater filled her nostrils as waves crashed onto the shore.

She was at the beach.

The sun glared as she struggled again to open her eyes. The sky was a bright blue, and seagulls called out to her as they bobbed and weaved ten feet overhead, floating rather than flying.

Her body ached. Rolling her head to the right, she saw nothing but white sand and sea oats. To the left was more of the same, but with a stinging sensation as she turned her head. Sherri managed to roll to her left side and prop herself up on her elbow. Her joints were stiff and her skin covered with goose bumps. Her head hurt as she tried to figure out how she ended up here, wherever here turned out to be.

Shifting her weight, she managed to sit up on her knees and check herself out. Nothing was broken, and she didn't notice any injuries other than the neck pain, stiff joints, and sore muscles. She still wore the schoolgirl outfit from the night before. Checking her bra and panties, she found everything in place and Alnami's fifty-dollar bill still tucked in her bra.

What the hell happened? Someone chased her on the bridge and shot up her car, but she managed to escape. The cop. He did something to her. When she touched the left side of her neck, the pain shot through her body again. The cop shocked her with something. Only he wasn't a cop.

They had to be working together. She was an easy target and nobody is that bad of a shot to miss her for that long. Whoever it was, they were sending a message. The thoughts hurt her head as she shielded her eyes from the sun, which was inching its way above the horizon.

Sherri rose to her feet. She had no shoes. Rolling off the white stockings, she tossed them in the sand and untied her white shirt to cover her belly. She buttoned her shirt and felt a little more comfortable. She slowly brushed the sand off her thighs, waist, and arms. Placing her hands in her deep red hair, she desperately tried to shake out the sand. It would take days, she determined, if not weeks, to get all of the sand out. She searched her immediate area: no purse, no phone, and no car keys.

When she started on this story, Sherri never thought she would experience something like this. She always enjoyed the sense of accomplishment from hard work. As an investigative reporter, she put herself in many compromising situations, but this had been the worst. Being shot at wasn't something new, but being shot at with automatic weapons was a twist. Even in Sarajevo, she hadn't faced such firepower. There she'd been dodging sniper fire.

Sherri's head ached; she was dehydrated. She scanned the beach. The closest people were an elderly couple using metal detectors a hundred yards to the east. To the west, more people in the distance, the silhouettes of condos and hotels, and the familiar water tower of Pensacola Beach. It was about three miles away. Leaving the solitude of the sea oats and sand dunes of this isolated portion of the beach, she trudged toward the water, then west, toward civilization.

3

JASON DRESSED IN JEANS and a T-shirt, then slid on his flight boots. Stirring a cup of coffee, he sat in the recliner, smiling, watching the striking blonde get dressed. It didn't take her long. She wore a blue jean miniskirt and a white lace bra. When she saw him examining her, she smiled. He could not, for the life of him, remember her name.

"Why are you looking at me like that?" she said, brushing her hair.

"How old are you?"

"You're not supposed to ask a girl that question."

"Oh, no, don't get me wrong. You don't look old. I just want to make sure I didn't spend the night with a teenager," Jason said. "Let me see your driver's license." It was a tactic he'd used before, a quick way to find out a name.

"I left it in my car. I didn't want you to rob me when I finished having my way with you," she said, putting the brush back in her purse.

"Oh," was all Jason could say.

She stopped in the bathroom doorway, half-dressed, frowning at him. Her head tilted to the side. Jason knew he was in trouble.

"What's my name?"

Damn.

Jason squinted at her inquisitively. It was the best he could do in his present physical condition.

"What kind of question is that?" he said, shrugging his shoulders.

"A legitimate one. What's my name?" Her Texas accent was more prominent now. She said she was born and raised in Garland. That one detail didn't bring back her name.

"What do you mean, what's your name? Of course I remember your name. I can't believe you'd ask me that question."

"Okay, then, what is it?"

"Well, what's my name?" Deflecting was the only strategy he could come up with at the moment.

"Oliver."

Jason grinned. "Oliver what?"

"Klosi—something. Hell, I don't know," she said, her voice getting louder. "I couldn't pronounce it. You said last night it was Russian."

Jason chuckled. He'd forgotten they were wearing their "Friday morale" nametags. His bore the name "Oliver Klosov" which, after a few beers, translated to "All of her clothes off." He was pleased he'd managed to stick with his story while drinking so much.

"Well, see, you don't remember my name," Jason said.

"Bullshit. Oliver, what's my name?"

He could see her body tense. Jason had every intention of being apologetic. There was no way out of this one.

"I'm sorry. Candy?"

"Candy?"

"Cindy?"

"Are you kidding me?" she screamed. "You son of a bitch. You had sex with me all last night *and* this morning, and you don't know my name?" She grabbed his shave kit from the bathroom and threw it at him. He caught the bag, but the contents fell on the floor. She started throwing everything she could at him. He was able to dodge it all, or deflect it.

"Look, I'm sorry. I had a lot to drink. You *know* that. You brought me home."

She started crying as she buttoned her shirt. "Why do I always find the assholes? I thought you were nice. You talked to me nice, you treated me nice. You said I was beautiful—"

"You *are* beautiful. And I'm nice. I'm sorry—"

"You're not nice or sorry—you're an asshole."

"I'm not an asshole," he said. "I'm a jet pilot." It was a stupid one-liner from an old joke, but hey, he was hung over.

She grabbed her sandals and headed for the door.

Jason jumped up to follow her. He hadn't meant to hurt her feelings, but it was a little too late.

She marched to the elevator, rode down to the lobby, and headed out the front door. Jason followed her all the way, trying to apologize, but she ignored him. When they reached the parking lot, she stopped. Two guys were leaning on her BMW.

"Carly, what the hell are you doing at this hotel?" the shorter one said, stepping away from her car. "And who's this asshole?"

Carly, that's it. He chose to disregard the asshole comment under the circumstances.

"Why the hell are you followin' me, Billy Ray?" she yelled. Jason watched her disposition change once again as the crying stopped immediately. Jason had pissed her off, but this guy? He lit her fuse.

"You're my girl, Carly," Billy Ray said, as he started to bow up to Jason. He was shorter, but stockier. Not muscular, but a lot of attitude. The sidekick, however, might be someone to worry about. He stood a rather wiry six-four.

"Billy Ray," she said, "we broke up three weeks ago. You've got to quit followin' me." Jason noticed her accent came out naturally when she fought with this Billy Ray.

"But Carly, you're my girl."

"I ain't your girl, Billy Ray. You can't tell me who I can have sex with and who I can't."

Oh shit, here we go.

Billy Ray's eyes grew wide, and his nostrils flared like a bull in the ring. Jason turned to leave. He knew where this was going, and the outcome wouldn't be good.

"Where're you going, asshole? I ain't through with you yet," Billy Ray said. The tall guy moved around in front of him, blocking his path. Jason turned ninety degrees to the right and backed up two steps, positioning the two in front of him.

"Look, fellas, I don't want any trouble. I was just walking Carly to her car," he said, glancing at Carly.

"Oh, great," she yelled. "*Now* you wanna act like you remember my name."

Damn.

Billy Ray glared at her before slowly turning his head back to Jason, his eyes wild and his face contorted. "You screwed my girl, and you didn't even know her name?"

"Look, fellas—"

"And he's a helluva better lay than you, Billy Ray," she yelled. Jason knew she was trying to piss off her ex-boyfriend to get him to start a fight.

It worked.

Billy Ray lunged at Jason and threw a wide roundhouse at his head. Jason deflected it, using Billy Ray's momentum to push him against the car next to him. He immediately turned to focus on the tall guy.

The giant was slow and tried to grab Jason in a bear hug from the front. Mistake. Jason hit him with the heel of his flat palm just below the sternum, and he stumbled backward. Billy Ray turned and charged again. Jason grabbed his wrist and pushed it toward his forearm, and Billy Ray yelped with pain. Jason pushed him on the ground, but now the tall guy grabbed him from behind, lifting him off the ground. His arms were pinned against his body. Billy Ray leaped from the ground and swung wildly to punch him in the stomach. It was a sloppy punch, but he was a captive target. The tall guy grew tired of holding him up and lowered him to the ground.

As Jason's feet touched, Billy Ray moved in closer. Jason lifted his feet off the ground and started to slide out of the tall guy's grasp until he squeezed him again. It was enough, though. Jason kicked his left leg out, slamming his foot into the inside of Billy Ray's right knee. Billy Ray screamed in pain and fell to the ground. The tall guy squeezed him harder and Jason brought both feet underneath him.

Lifting his right leg, he scraped the side of his boot against the tall guy's right shin and slammed his heel into the top of the tall guy's foot. The tall guy yelped and released him. Jason spun around and delivered several quick blows to the tall guy's stomach and a quick right cross to his chin, and the tall guy fell to the ground.

He turned to deliver a quick blow to Billy Ray's left eye as he tried to stand. Billy Ray went back to the asphalt, unconscious.

Jason gasped for breath. Sweat dripped from his forehead, and his heart pounded against his chest. He felt like he was going to vomit. Instinctively, he scanned the area for other threats. Seeing none, he glanced back at the cowboys lying on the asphalt and bent over at the waist, his hands on his knees.

"Oliver," he heard Carly say.

Dammit. He needed to stop pursuing women easily impressed by a flight suit. He glanced at Carly for the first time since the altercation began. She gazed at him like a high-school crush as she stepped over and placed a piece of paper in his T-shirt pocket.

"Call me," she said, kissing him on the cheek.

Jason stared at her and grimaced. He knew it was time to get out of there. Cursing himself, he marched back into the hotel.

4

April 18, 2001

THE T-38 BARRELED THROUGH THE SKY, five hundred feet off the ground at three hundred knots, the morning sun glistening off its canopy. Daylight had pushed its way above the horizon well over two hours ago, making the sky over western Oklahoma clear for miles, though the temperatures still reflected the cold front that had pushed through the Midwest. The jet experienced occasional light turbulence as the morning sun heated the ground, and the two occupants bounced in their seats.

Jason sat in the back seat of the Northrop T-38 Talon. The T-38 had been designed as a trainer for the 1960s Century Series fighters. The T-38 was such a successful design that it had remained the US Air Force's advanced supersonic jet trainer ever since.

The tandem-seat aircraft was sexy. It had the appearance and flight characteristics of a fighter jet, and while the T-38 was a great jet, it had its flaws. The biggest challenge students faced was landing the jet. The small wings required a faster takeoff and landing speed, and that detail often undid many students. They simply could not adapt to the speed needed to think and work in the T-38.

Jason had been an instructor pilot in the aircraft for the last four years. He was what the Air Force called a FAIP (fape), a first assignment instructor pilot. After graduating from pilot training, he went directly to instructor school to return to Vance AFB as an IP.

Teaching someone to fly a supersonic jet was the best way to make a living, period. It was a job he relished, but being required to do it in Enid, Oklahoma, as a bachelor, was a difficult task. He spent as much time out of town as he could, flying student or instructor cross-country sorties. Unfortunately, these trips sometimes ended up like his Dallas trip a few days ago—one-night stands he couldn't undo.

His mind wandered as he considered what his commander asked him over a month ago. "You'll be up for an assignment soon. What do you want to do with your career?" Jason was aware the Air Force was ready for him to move. He needed direction in his life. He'd shown up as a student with no desire to meet a woman, and then *she* stumbled into his life. As quickly as she fell into his life, she fell out of it. Jason had kept Kathy out of his thoughts for most of his time at Vance. But today, for some reason, the vision of her pushed in like a fullback on the one-yard line. Perhaps it was the incident with Carly. Perhaps it was loneliness creeping up on him.

"Okay, sir. I'm coming up on the next turn point in thirty seconds, according to my timing. Fuel checks, altitude, and time are good. Next heading is three-two-zero for three minutes and fifteen seconds. Sir, working big to small, I see the two rivers I want to turn between. Now I'm looking for a farmhouse to the south and the grain silo about a mile north. There's the silo. Confirm?"

"Check, that's the silo," Jason responded to his student in the front seat, snapping out of his daydream. Jason did not need to reference his chart for the turn points. He'd flown this route a hundred times over the years. He'd memorized all the turn points, which was good since it gave him the opportunity to keep his eyes outside the aircraft. Jason cross-checked the stopwatch strapped to his knee board to the time calculated on the chart and nodded silently in the back. His student's times were good.

"There's the farmhouse. Turn point is in twenty seconds. The cows are starting to run away from us."

"Check, Stanley, but those aren't cows, they're horses. The cows don't move—they're used to us. The horses don't like the noise or the speed." Jason glanced at his instrument panel to cross-check his fuel and the Heading Situation Indicator (HSI). Stanley wasn't actually the student's name. It was a generic name all instructors used to identify students: Stanley Student. Jason wasn't sure how it evolved, but it was time-tested and applied to all students, including females.

"Stand by turn," the student said. "Turning in three, two, one, turn now . . . new heading is three-two-zero for three minutes and fifteen seconds." The student rolled the sleek jet into a sixty-degree bank turn and pulled the aircraft to three-and-a-half G's. Their g-suits quickly inflated with air, putting immediate pressure on their legs and abdomens, preventing blood from pooling in their lower extremities. The jet started to lose altitude as the nose tracked below the horizon.

"Climb," Jason said. The command coincided with the student reaching the required heading, rolling out, and raising the nose of the jet. The student rolled the T-38 wings level, and the g-suits deflated. "Remember, just like in the traffic pattern, when you bank this aircraft, you've got to move more than the ailerons. You've got to add a little power and change the pitch."

"Roger," the student replied.

They continued on course for several minutes. Jason kept his own cross-check going, clock to map to ground, bringing his instruments into cross-check periodically. They bounced around more violently as the turbulence increased. He could tell the student had not strapped in well by the way his helmet bounced around.

"Stanley, do you remember in the brief when we talked about low-level turbulence?"

"Uh . . . yeah. Would you mind taking the jet for a moment?"

"I have the aircraft," Jason said, taking control of the jet.

"Roger, you have the aircraft."

Three seconds later the student chimed in, "Okay, sir, I'm back. I have the aircraft," the student said, shaking the stick.

"Roger, you have the aircraft."

"Ten seconds to the next turn point, but I'm not sure where it's at."

"What are you looking for?"

"Uh, it's supposed to be a windmill."

"Do you see it? It's one of the old western-style ones like you see in the movies—not like those wind-power windmills." Jason cross-checked his timing with his chart. His eyes darted from his chart to his instruments, particularly his altimeter, and back to his chart.

"Uhm . . . which one?"

He glimpsed over the shoulder of the student. Five windmills on the right and two on the left. "Huh, that's different," he said. "I guess they put those up recently. There was only one here the last time I flew this route. Turn on time. Turn now."

The student banked the T-38 in a nice, level turn and rolled out on his heading. The jet leveled off, and the student went back to work with his timing and navigation. The two flew in silence for the next four minutes, enjoying the ride. Jason wanted to see how the student would fly with no instruction, and the kid was doing well.

"Fifteen seconds to the next turn point," the student said. "I'm looking for the T-intersection going from north to south. No visual yet, so we'll be turning on timing."

"Checks."

"Three, two, one, turning. Heading one-one-five. There's the turn point to the east. We're a quarter mile off course, sir."

The turn was thirty degrees to the left. Jason cleared in front of the jet for the turn, as he knew from experience that most students glued their head inside the aircraft to the Attitude Direction Indicator (ADI) and the altimeter. Quickly, Jason checked where the student was looking, and his suspicion was correct. Jason was about to speak up when he noticed a black flash in front of the jet.

Uh-oh. Birds. Jason felt the impacts on the side of the jet. He didn't wait for the student in the front seat to react. "I HAVE THE AIRCRAFT!" He grabbed the stick and rolled the aircraft's wings level. He immediately raised the nose of the jet to climb away from the ground. "You okay up there?"

"Yeah, that spooked me," the student said.

"Attention all aircraft, Colt Seven-Two is departing IR-145 at turn point three. Passing through three thousand three hundred," Jason broadcast on the common radio frequency for the low-level route. They were too low and too far away from Vance AFB's approach control to make radio contact with them.

The aircraft shuddered as both J-85 axial flow engines flamed out. Cross-checking his engine instruments, the tachometers, EGTs, and fuel flow indicators were all rolling back, confirming his dual engine failure. The Master Caution light came on immediately. Glancing at the Caution Light panel, he saw the left Fuel Pressure light illuminate instantly, followed by the right Fuel Pressure light. He cross-checked his airspeed, now decreasing through 250 knots indicated airspeed (KIAS). He raised the nose twenty degrees while simultaneously moving both throttles over the hump.

The "Boldface" emergency action procedure for emergency air start is THROTTLE/THROTTLES - MAX. Both throttles slammed into the afterburner range—nothing. He moved the throttles back and over the hump once again.

Still no ignition.

The Left and Right Generator lights illuminated on the Caution

Light panel, followed by the Utility and Flight Hydraulics.

"Mayday, Mayday, Mayday . . . Colt Seven-Two on IR-145. Dual engine failure at turn point three." The jet passed through 6,000 feet at one hundred eighty knots. "Okay, Stanley, I'll try to start these one more time, otherwise we'll have to take the silk elevator to the ground." There was no response from the student. "You still with me up there?"

"Yes, sir. Please start it."

Jason moved the throttles into the afterburner range for the third time with the same result.

"Mayday, Mayday, Mayday . . . Colt Seven-Two, T-38, two souls on board, seventy miles southwest of Vance. Engine failure times two. Crew is ejecting at 7,000 feet."

Jason checked his airspeed indicator one last time. "Okay, Stanley, airspeed's passing through one hundred twenty knots. BAILOUT, BAILOUT, BAILOUT!"

The student left the jet after the first command to leave the aircraft. The eerie silence shattered by the deafening wind blast as the front canopy left the jet. Jason reached for his handgrips and braced his body for the ejection. Placing his knees together, he pulled his feet back, pushed his back straight against his seat, pulled his elbows in, and held his chin down toward his chest. When he pulled the handgrips up, the aft canopy blew off the top of the jet. Everything not welded to the jet left the interior space of the cockpit: checklists, charts, and knee boards all sucked out by the wind.

Less than a second after the canopy left the aircraft, the rocket in his seat exploded and he felt a slight pinch in his neck. The wind blast ripped at his head and body as his seat shot up the rails and pushed him out into the cold blue sky.

5

April 19, 2001

THE VAN CREPT UP TO THE GATE. The two occupants observed the security guard controlling entry into Vance AFB. Ty Nakamura nudged the van forward as each car passed though. A young airman checked the identification cards of everyone entering and glanced at them after every vehicle was waved through.

Dane Robinson, television news reporter, constantly shifted his weight in the passenger seat. Ty, his cameraman and driver, glared at him. "Dude, relax. *I* think you look suspicious."

"I can't help it," Dane said. "I can't believe that after all these years, Jason Conrad has thrust himself back into the spotlight."

"I wouldn't say he 'thrust' himself into the spotlight. He was in an accident."

"An accident he no doubt caused. You can't tell me this wasn't pilot error."

"We don't know yet," Ty said. "Doesn't the NTSB or someone have to review the crash?"

"When I'm done with this story, what the NTSB has to say won't matter."

The guard waved them forward, and Ty rolled down the window.

"Good morning, gentlemen," the airman said. "Welcome to Vance Air Force Base. What can we do for you this morning?"

Ty handed the guard their credentials. "We're the television news crew from WTSR out of Tulsa. We're covering the T-38 crash."

The guard reviewed their credentials, then scrutinized the two men.

"Stay right here, please," he said as he stepped into the small guard shack and picked up the telephone.

"What do you think our odds are?" Ty asked Dane.

"Not a chance in hell. They won't let us in, and no one will talk to the media. Standard procedure. Public Affairs hasn't returned my calls."

The guard continued to talk on the telephone, glancing at the van. Ty strummed his fingers on the steering wheel, and Dane leaned against his door, watching the guard's every move. After two minutes, the guard returned and handed them their credentials.

"Gentlemen, I'm sorry, but the wing commander is not authorizing any media on the base at this time. If you would like, you can move your vehicle over—"

"I know where the hell to go," Dane said. "We'll park over there by the sign and get our cover shot for the news broadcast. We know the drill. What are you people trying to hide in there, sonny?"

The airman didn't flinch, but his eyes narrowed as he glared at Ty. "Sir, I'm going to ask you to move your vehicle right now. Drive forward and make a 180-degree turn. Do you understand?"

Ty slammed the vehicle into drive. "Yes, sir." The vehicle lurched forward, and Ty made the turn, heading away from the front gate. He drove along the entrance road until they reached the open area by the front gate sign that said "WELCOME TO VANCE AIR FORCE BASE."

"Dude, you've got to chill," Ty said, glancing at Dane.

"If I chill, then I don't get their attention. If I don't get their attention, they'll leave us alone. If they leave us alone, this story becomes very boring very quickly."

"Okay, it's boring. So what?"

"So what? Look, I'm the on-air talent here. I decide what we produce for the masses. You just take pictures of what I tell you to."

The comment infuriated Ty. He was the best cameraman in Tulsa. He'd been in this business for seventeen years. Unfortunately, he was the only cameraman who could tolerate the ego of "Dane Robinson, TV News Reporter." Dane Robinson rose to glory covering the story of Jason Conrad six years earlier—a series of unusual events, all with links to Jason Conrad. It started when one of Conrad's classmates died in a T-37 crash. A few days later, Conrad's Mustang crashed and exploded in a wheat field. He claimed it was stolen, but the day after the car explosion, a CIA agent was found dead in a hotel room rented to "Jason Conrad". The same day, another CIA agent was shot at the

Holiday Inn; Conrad made the 911 call.

Dane Robinson tied these events together. He implied Conrad killed and buried the body of a missing classmate at Vance, and then he went after Conrad with vigor. When Dane heard rumors of a Russian spy in Enid, he claimed Conrad was that spy, despite having no evidence. He received national attention and did interviews on a couple of morning shows. When the details of the San Antonio incident came out, and it was revealed that Jason was Senator Jonathan Bowman's long-lost son, Dane went into overdrive. And over the cliff.

Rather than report the facts from San Antonio as they were, Dane tied them together with the incidents at Vance. If Jason was a spy, Dane surmised, his long-lost father must be one, as well. Implying the frontrunner for the 1996 Republican presidential nomination had ties to Russian spies was a bold and outrageous move. He pushed the story, which seemed crazy and absurd, and all of the networks ran with it— initially. Within twenty-four hours, the mainstream media had ostracized Dane Robinson, TV News Reporter and WTSR almost fired him. Now, Ty was stuck with him.

"What do you want to do?" Ty asked.

"Unload our gear and set up over there," Dane said, pointing to the entrance sign. "This is the shot. I'll be facing the sun. There won't be any shadows on my face."

"Okay. What's the story?"

Dane glowered at Ty as if Ty were an ignorant peasant, pissing Ty off further. "Ty," he said, shaking his head, "Jason Conrad, the Russian spy the Air Force is too embarrassed to admit exists, has struck again. He is single-handedly destroying the Air Force's inventory of jets. Sure, he's laid low the last four or five years, but now he's resurfaced. Slowly but surely, he's destroying America and her values. Only this time, Dane Robinson, TV News Reporter, will be there to stop him."

"Okay," Ty said. Ty stepped out of the van and opened the double doors in the back. He gathered his camera equipment as Dane strolled over to the welcome sign.

The few cars entering the base slowed as they passed the television news crew, but no one stopped. Dane slipped his jacket over his paunchy, five-foot-seven frame. He ran a comb through his wavy brown hair, though it didn't need it. Ty set up his camera gear, accomplished his lighting tests, and checked his audio. Dane positioned himself in the grass, the welcome sign positioned over his right shoulder.

"Dude, you ready to do this?" Ty asked.

"Let's go."

Dane adjusted his tie and ran his fingers along his temple.

"Okay," Ty said, hitting the record button on his camera. "In five, four, three, two, one…"

Dane paused for a second. "Six years ago, the sleepy town of Enid, Oklahoma was rocked by disaster. Jason Conrad, son of former Senator Jonathan Bowman, became the most famous personality in Enid since Lee Majors came here to pheasant hunt in the 1980s. A Lieutenant at that time, Conrad was involved in the crash of a T-37 aircraft, a training jet, killing fellow student Lenny Banks. Though Conrad was later linked to the death of a CIA agent, and the shooting of a second CIA agent, he escaped prosecution for these incidents. Could it be his political connection? Did he cut a deal with prosecutors? Who knows?" Dane paused.

"Yesterday morning at approximately nine o'clock, Jason Conrad was involved in the crash of another Air Force jet, an advanced supersonic jet trainer, the Northrop T-38 Talon. After remaining in the shadows for the last six years, Conrad has struck again. He is once again gradually destroying our military arsenal piece by piece. Conrad and his fellow pilot abandoned the jet by ejecting seventy miles west of Vance Air Force Base. While Jason Conrad appears to have survived the ejection unscathed, his student, we are told by sources inside the US Air Force, suffered a broken arm. What did this pilot do to lose control of his multimillion-dollar aircraft? We don't know, and the Air Force isn't talking. We can only hope the true story is told—*before* the Russians and CIA show up. We'll have more on this story as details become available. For WTSR, the Taaaser from Tulsa, this is Dane Robinson, TV News Reporter."

6

CAPTAIN PETE PETERSON shook his head as he drove his metallic blue 1993 Corvette past the news truck at the front entrance. He drove through the gate and straight to the Visiting Officers Quarters (VOQ). Steering his Corvette into the parking spot, he turned off the ignition and walked up to Room 109, carrying a paper sack. He removed his flight cap in front of the door, revealing his bleached-blond hair, and knocked loudly. Moments later, Jason, wearing shorts and a T-shirt, opened the door.

"Hey, Pete, come on in. What's going on?"

Peterson entered the room, tucked his blue flight cap in the right leg pocket of his olive-green flight suit, and set the paper sack on the counter. Peterson was not quite six-and-a-half-feet tall, but his lanky figure, at 190 pounds, made Jason appear stocky and firm. He had known Jason for five years, through unfortunate circumstances. Following the situation in San Antonio, Jason had "washed back" to Pete's class, and the two became fast friends. Peterson flew the F-16 for three years during his first assignment at Luke AFB in Arizona. For his second assignment, he almost went to Cannon AFB in New Mexico, but returned to Vance flying the T-38 instead. He was happy to learn his old friend was still here instructing in the T-38.

"Bro, how you feeling?" Pete said.

"Okay, I guess. My right arm is a little sore with some tingling in my fingers. I've got a little pain in my left hip, running down the back of my thigh."

"You tell the flight doc?"

"Hell no," Jason said. "I'm not risking my flying career for something like this."

Jason gave the same response any young pilot would: ignore your problems long enough, and they'll go away. But ejecting out of an aircraft presents a different set of problems. Pete wondered if Jason's decision was the right one. Maybe he'd bring it up later. Now wasn't the right time.

"Thought I'd drop by and see how you were doing. Tracy packed a lunch for you." Tracy was Pete's wife, whom he'd met in Phoenix when he was at the F-16 schoolhouse. They were a comical couple— he towered over her by more than a full foot, as she barely cleared five feet.

"Thanks. I hate being holed up in this room," Jason said, dropping to the floor in push-up position. "I just want to go home." He began doing push-ups as if to prove he suffered no damage in the crash.

Pete shook his head as he sat in the recliner by the window. "No, bro, trust me. You do *not* want to be home right now. Apparently, someone leaked your name to the press. I drove by your house on the way here, and there are news media all over the place, standing in front of your house two deep. Heck, they kept trying to interview me," he said, grinning, the freckles on his cheeks broadening.

Jason stopped his push-ups and stood up. "Oh, I'm sure you liked it."

"Nah, I told them I'd never heard of you. There's even a TV news van at the front gate."

Jason moved to the counter, opened the bag, and pulled out the sandwich. "Was it a blue truck with electric bolts and the word TASER on the side?"

"Yeah. Friend of yours?"

"Not if it's Dane Robinson, from WTSR, the Taaaser in Tulsa," he said, mocking the reporter's shtick, as he unwrapped the sandwich. "He tried to build a career off my incident several years back."

Peterson nodded his head. "Gotcha. Well, the squadron commander was right to order you to check into billeting so those goons can't get to you."

"Yeah, I guess." Jason took a bite of the sandwich.

"Bro, I need to tell you something," Pete said, leaning forward in the recliner, "but you didn't hear it from me. Rumor has it the wing commander wants to pull your wings."

"What?" Jason replied with a mouthful of food. "Who's saying that?" He set the sandwich on the counter and wiped his hands on his shorts.

Peterson shook his head. "Look, it's just people talking smack. I'm just giving you a heads-up. No one is blaming you for the crash yesterday. You did everything right. I just think the wing commander is tired of being told what to do with Jason Conrad."

"That SOB hasn't liked me from the day he showed up," Jason said. "Doesn't matter. He doesn't have the authority to pull my wings. He needs to convene a Flight Evaluation Board, and he has no cause. I'll fight him on this one."

"I agree. Just wanted you to know the score. Hell, he'll be leaving in a couple of months. All you need to do is ride it out until the old buzzard's gone."

Jason slouched on the bed. "I don't understand this shit! Six years ago, I did the right thing. I never asked for any attention. All I wanted to do was fly jets. I didn't want any international intrigue."

"Maybe it's time to move on."

"What?"

"Bro, I'm just trying to point out you've been here a long time."

Jason slid over to the fridge and pulled out a Coors Light. "You want one?"

"Bro, it's eight thirty in the morning. I've got a flight in two hours."

"Yeah, my sleep cycle is all jacked up."

"Apparently. You don't have to go to the clinic any time soon, do you?"

"No, they took a couple of gallons of blood from me yesterday. Randolph sent up an SIB and AIB. I met with both teams last night." The Safety Investigation Board (SIB) would determine what caused the accident and what could be done to prevent it from happening in the future. The statements made to the Board would not be released to the public or the media, and could not be used against the pilots. The Accident Investigation Board (AIB) would find out if anyone was at fault and could recommend legal action against any individuals involved. Normally, the SIB went first, with the AIB starting as soon as the SIB out-brief was complete. Of course, the two could be run simultaneously, as they had been the night before.

"Damn, the wing king works fast. Did you get a JAG for the AIB?"

"Yeah, but it was uneventful." The military lawyer, or Judge Advocate General (JAG) had advised Jason of his rights throughout the process the previous day during his AIB interview. "They're going to interview the student today. Hopefully our stories match."

Jason returned to the bed, leaned back against the headboard, and took a long swig of his beer.

"I don't understand this wing commander. What the hell did I ever do to him? I had an assignment to Fort Bragg to fly . . . hell, I don't even know what it was. But I had my Top Secret clearance complete, and this asshole turned off the assignment. I even tried to PCS to Randolph to be a PIT IP," Jason said, referencing Pilot Instructor Training where pilots trained to be instructors in the T-1, T-6, T-37, or the T-38. The Air Force was currently phasing the T-37 out of service and replacing it with the T-6.

"Yeah, they're not going to let you do that these days unless you're a fighter guy," Pete said. "Bro, I think the old man is trying to screw you over. You've been a thorn in his side for too long, and he doesn't like it."

"So why not let me go?"

"I guess you've been such an ass-pain, he isn't going to let you do what you want to do."

Jason shook his head. "I love what I'm doing here. There is no better job in the world than flying a T-38."

"Well, it's a nice jet, but it could use some armament."

"Pete, how much time do you guys spend pointing at your watches in your brief and debrief?" Jason said, making the motions with his hands. "How many hours do you spend in the vault studying threats and opposing aircraft, all to log a 1.1 hour sortie two to three times a week? We get to fly two to three hours a day here. We get to do everything the fighters do except the big boom at the end. Quite frankly, I've had enough big booms to last me a lifetime."

"Face it, the Air Force doesn't like guys who homestead. They want you to be mobile. You could always go to the airlines. They're hiring like crazy." Pete sat back in the recliner, observing his friend. "Look, bro, you went through a lot years ago, but it's time to get over it."

Jason looked over at him, stunned.

"I mean it. Get over it. You have to move on. You're a good pilot, but you're wasting your time hiding in Enid, Oklahoma. What are you waiting for?"

"Man, I've tried. I told you, the assignments I want, they won't allow me to do. But I need to do something soon. You're right; it's time for me to move on."

"You know what your problem is? You're not challenged."

"What the hell is that supposed to mean? You think I'm complacent?" Jason said.

"No, not complacent. Content. You've got nothing to work toward, and you've gotten comfortable." Pete walked over to Jason and put his hand on his shoulder. "Look, my friend, you've been through a lot the past twenty-four hours, and you're handling it well. I recommend you rest up and start thinking about what you want to do with your life."

JASON SIPPED THE COLD COORS LIGHT, as Pete walked to his Corvette. Deep down, he knew Pete was right. He'd have to go somewhere soon. The current wing commander now had an excuse to attempt to pull his wings. Jason knew it wouldn't happen, but the wing commander could make his life miserable. The special attention he garnered from several agencies in Washington did not sit well with the wing commander.

Jason enjoyed his job as a FAIP. It was, he knew, a key ingredient in the pilot training puzzle. His counterparts who, like Pete, returned to AETC following their first or second tour in a Major Weapons System (MWS) were the other piece of the puzzle. The FAIPs knew how to get a student through the program, and the MWS folks relayed real-world mission experience to the students.

On more than one occasion, he'd been told he needed to be married because marriage showed a pilot was stable and reliable. Jason said the statement was stupid—his performance should show he was stable and reliable. "How many single pilots ever cheat on their wives?" he'd say. That always ended the conversation.

In his private life, the lack of dating prospects over the past several years led to his self-destructive lifestyle. He was lonely. It was a struggle to maintain the façade of happiness. There was an emptiness tugging at his soul.

Maybe it was time to reevaluate his situation. He believed he could reach any goal he set for himself. His problem was he didn't have any goals at this point in his life. Pete was right. He needed a challenge.

Jason drained his beer, then fell back on his bed, dropping the can to the floor. His mind raced as he struggled with himself, and for the first time he admitted that he did not have a plan for the future.

7

IT WAS TWO IN THE MORNING as Jason drove from the base to his house without passing another moving vehicle. He hated being confined to the VOQ, and he needed some things from his house. Watching TV all day and night had worn on him, and he wanted to pick up Ronald Reagan's autobiography, *An American Life*. The item he *needed* was his cell phone charger. His cell phone battery had died, and they didn't sell the charger in the Base Exchange.

He approached his house slowly in case there was a news truck parked out front. To his relief, the journalists had gone home for the night. No doubt the sensationalism had worn off some, and everyone moved on to something else. He crept inside, quickly gathered the things he needed, threw them in a bag, and left. Jason was backing out of the driveway when he noticed the headlights of a vehicle illuminate.

He stared at the lights in his rearview mirror. Maybe it's just a coincidence. No, it's two in the morning. There are no coincidences at two in the morning. Jason put the truck in drive and headed back to Vance. The headlights followed.

Damn.

He wasn't sure who was following him, but he wasn't about to let them catch him. He was supposed to be restricted to quarters; the last distraction he needed was a reporter catching him off base. Jason sped south on Oakwood Boulevard in an effort to outrun the vehicle, which appeared to be a black Suburban. Should he speed up to avoid the car and risk getting a speeding ticket? If that happened, his superiors would surely know he'd been off base. He kept his speed around forty-five miles per hour. Passing the Oakwood Mall, the black Suburban pulled alongside. This was unusual for a reporter. Gradually, he increased his speed to fifty-five. The Suburban stayed right with him.

Glancing to his left, Jason saw the passenger window roll down. He increased his speed to sixty-five. A man in a suit, with thinning blond hair, stuck his arm out the window, waving at him to slow down. Jason wasn't ready for an interview, but he was glad the suit wasn't hanging out the window with a video camera.

Preoccupied with the black Suburban, he didn't see the vehicle approaching from the opposite direction until the black Suburban slammed on its brakes and slid behind him. In front of him, the oncoming vehicle, now only two hundred feet away, swerved and stopped, blocking both lanes of traffic. Jason slammed on his brakes, and his truck screeched to a halt less than twenty feet from a second black Suburban.

These were no reporters.

Jason wished he had one of his pistols on him as he checked the rearview mirror. Suburban number one blocked both lanes behind him. Scanning the sides of the road, he quickly realized his truck would never make it over the ditch. He was trapped.

The rear door of the front SUV opened, and Jason braced himself for what was about to take place. His body tensed, and his hands squeezed the steering wheel. His eyes widened and his heartbeat increased as a man stepped out of the back, shielding his eyes. Jason moved his right hand to the gear shift, then . . .

He laughed.

The man who shielded his eyes from Jason's headlights was his father, the former Senator Jonathan Bowman. Jason released the steering wheel from his death grip, opened the door, and climbed out of the truck. The two met halfway and hugged.

"Hi, Dad."

"Hello yourself," Bowman said. "I was worried about you when I heard about the crash."

Jason pointed at the black Suburbans. "This is a little dramatic, don't you think?"

"I tried calling, but you don't answer your damn phones."

"Can't answer the phone at the house. They've got me confined to Base."

"Damn good job they're doing there," Bowman said with a smile.

Jason chuckled. "I snuck out to get my cell phone charger. My battery died around lunchtime yesterday, and I couldn't find a charger on base."

His father nodded and put his hand on Jason's shoulder.

"I had my men watch your house in case you came back. When they saw you, they called me at the hotel. I tried to get to your house before you left, but we obviously didn't make it."

"Sorry. Wish I'd known."

"Why don't we go back to your room so we can talk for a little while? We'll follow you."

"Okay," Jason said.

Everyone climbed in their vehicles, and the two black Suburbans followed Jason back to the VOQ on the base. Jason and his dad stepped inside. Walking to the refrigerator, Jason grabbed a beer and handed his father a bottled water. Bowman sat in the recliner, and Jason sat on the end of the bed.

"How are you doing? Are you hurt?"

"I'm fine," Jason said, returning his father's strong gaze. A couple years back, Jason's father told him Jason was one of the few men of his age that looked men in the eyes when they talked to them. Like father, like son. "My fingers are a little tingly, but otherwise I'm okay."

"Tingly? Did you hurt your neck?"

"A little tweak on the ejection, but I'm okay now."

"I'd get that looked at," Bowman said, pointing at Jason's neck. "You could have something in your cervical spine pinching a nerve."

"Thanks," Jason said, taking a sip of his beer. "I'll get it done soon as I can." Jason was ready to stop talking about himself. "How's life as executive vice president working out?"

"Progressing nicely. We have several projects going on right now. I'll be in Yuma in three days to test one of our systems. We'll be closing the sale before the end of the month."

"That's great. How is your new place in Las Vegas?"

"It's not bad. There's no shortage of things to do. And it keeps us close to the DOD at Nellis." Nellis was the base outside Las Vegas that housed the Air Force aerial demonstration team, the Thunderbirds.

"Do you miss being in politics?" Jason said.

Bowman glanced toward the ceiling, then back at Jason.

"Sometimes. I miss having the ability to make things happen."

"I can see that."

"But it won't be a problem for long. The breakthroughs we're making will make us the leader in military technology. If the DOD wants the most advanced equipment available, they'll get it from Century Aero-Bot."

8

April 20, 2001

NEW YORK CITY BUSTLED WITH LIFE during the morning rush. Cars sat bumper to bumper, pedestrians hustled along packed sidewalks, and bicyclists dodged both. Sunlight pushed its way between the buildings, creating an ever-evolving display of light and shadow, giving life to the city as the day wore on. The Port Authority terminal was crowded as people rushed back and forth. The walk from Port Authority to 620 8th Avenue was short. The world-famous *New York Times* logo hung majestically on the front of the building. The spire of gray steel and glass sat isolated on this portion of the city block, displaying its prominence to the buildings around it.

Sherri Davis stood at the front steps of *The New York Times*, a tall, square-shaped building sitting between West 40th and West 41st Streets. Dressed in blue jeans and high-top tennis shoes, a tight white T-shirt, brown leather jacket, and scarf, she resembled any other pedestrian this morning. Her deep red hair was pulled back in a ponytail and her makeup was minimal. She didn't dress up when she was in New York. She found she accomplished more work by dressing casual and avoiding office politics. Sherri loved being an investigative journalist, but after six years, she'd become less and less attracted to the hustle and bustle of New York.

Sherri grew up in a little town in southern Missouri called Hollister, just across the river from Branson. She had two loving parents. Dad taught her farming, hunting, and the outdoors. Sherri became a pretty good shot with the rifle, but grew less fond of hunting as she grew older. Mom rolled in with dresses, books, and etiquette, and the girl in

Sherri started to emerge. She couldn't remember exactly when, but at some point in the eighth grade, she realized she wanted to be a reporter. Blending the skills her mother taught her for research with her father's tenacious attitude, she arrived in high school prepared for her new career.

As a freshman, she scored big by interviewing several top celebrities in Branson for the school paper. She had a way of getting on the inside to get the story she wanted. Her senior year in high school, she did an exposé on the water treatment plant near her home. The plant had excessive amounts of fluoride in the water, which made many of the locals sick.

That summer, tragedy struck when her father died while harvesting the hard red winter wheat in July. The combine he was driving had a catastrophic failure, slinging shards of steel from the cutter bar and reel into the cockpit. An hour passed before anyone realized what had happened. By the time he was found, Walter Davis had bled out. There was no investigation. It was written off as an accident—the officials claimed he'd run over a boulder in the field. Sherri knew different. Her father had harvested those fields for years, and boulders don't suddenly appear. Sherri blamed the manufacturer of the combine, a new company in the marketplace, but her investigation turned up nothing. The company wouldn't return her calls, and the sheriff and the insurance inspector stuck to their stories. That event made Sherri even more determined to become an investigative reporter to bring justice to those who needed it.

Sherri attended the University of Missouri, a beautiful campus an hour and a half outside St. Louis. She flourished there, covering all aspects of reporting, and was promoted to editor of the university newspaper her senior year. It came as no surprise when she landed a job with the *St. Louis Post-Dispatch* as a reporter. Sherri excelled there for three years, breaking stories on political corruption and bribery, before being whisked away to *The New York Times*.

After several relationships and even an engagement at one point, she could not get over the fact that men in New York were different. Sure, they excelled in their environment. But once they were removed from it, there was more complaining and whining than any person could tolerate. She missed the rugged individualist from the Midwest, a man like her father. Maybe that was what she was still looking for in a man.

Pushing her way through the glass doors, she showed her ID badge to the security guard and marched through the sparse lobby to the elevators. She took the elevator to the eighteenth floor and made her way to her desk. The activity on this floor was steady, but not as hectic as others. Sherri tossed her purse under her desk, sat, and turned on her computer. She pulled a bottle of water from her purse as her computer came to life.

"Welcome back," an elderly man's voice said behind her.

Sherri turned and saw her editor, Steven Hollinger, a small man in his mid-fifties, standing behind her with a concerned look on his face.

"Steven," she said as she hopped out of her seat. "It's so good to see you." She hugged him and he wrapped his arms around her, returning the embrace. "I missed you last week when I got back."

"I was hung up in D.C. Are you alright?"

"Of course, other than staying a couple of days longer than I wanted talking to the police."

"When will you start listening to me?" Steven said.

"Steven," she said, plopping back in her chair, "you tell me what you want me to do, then I'll tell you what I'm gonna do."

"I told you the stripper angle wouldn't work," he said.

"I know, I know. But these guys claim to be devout Muslims. I couldn't get them to talk to a female at any point during the day. Women don't exist as far as they're concerned. But, boy, get them to a strip bar, booze and women are number one on their priority list."

"It's called Taqiyya."

"Ta-what-a?"

"Ta-ge-ya. I think that's how it's pronounced. It's a practice Muslim extremists use to pretend to be Christians or any other religion. According to the *Quran*, sometimes lying is accepted or even demanded. That is, if you adhere to Sharia Law."

"I don't understand," Sherri said.

"Well, let's say a devout Muslim is captured by an enemy on the battlefield. If he is given a choice between renouncing Allah or death, the *Quran* says they are permitted to—well, some Muslims say they are required to—lie."

Sherri's left hand went to her mouth, and a thumbnail found its way between her teeth. Her chin rested on her curled-up fingers. Steven always laughed when she struck this pose and he did so now. He called it her "Thinker" pose.

"Okay, so how do we get from there to a strip bar?"

"Apparently, some Muslims interpret this by believing they are 'helping the cause' by doing things the *Quran* says is forbidden to blend in to their surroundings" Steven said. "We've seen the Muslim women from Saudi Arabia get on an airline in traditional clothing, but when the jet lands in Europe, they're wearing makeup and miniskirts. Men going to strip bars, same thing. Taqiyya."

Sherri wasn't convinced by the analogy, but she understood the concept. "Well, it explains the behavior," she said, returning to her computer.

"What did you find out?"

"Not much," she said. "I gave you the data dump over the phone."

"Is that it?"

"Yes." She turned to face Steven. "I had to get out of there or give him 'the grind-a-grind.' I'm not willing to go that far for a story. I'm not sure what kind of plane he was going to fly in. For that matter, Alnami may not have known either."

Steven rubbed his chin. "We spent a lot of money to find out these guys are going on an airplane ride next week," he said, eyeing her sternly.

Sherri stared sheepishly at the floor. "I know. I got what I could."

"You did. And you're onto something. Something big."

Sherri snapped her head up, searching Steven's eyes. "Meaning?"

Steven leaned against the cubicle wall, his hands clasped in front of him. "Two things. One, you're meeting with our informant on Monday at this coffee shop in the Village," he said, handing her a slip of paper. "Two, the assailants who attacked you on the bridge? Well, we had a local reporter find your car in the police compound when you called me from the beach. He was ordered, first by the police, and later, most importantly, by his editor, *not* to publish the story."

"Why? Are tourists being shot at every day in Pensacola?"

"No. But our man did some snooping around and found out what kind of bullets were used. Ten millimeter."

"Okay. What's that mean?"

"The ten millimeter round was developed in the 1980s for use by the feds."

9

April 20, 2001

JEREMIAH WELLINGTON, a retired Air Force one-star general, leaned back in his chair. Wellington was the site manager for the F-2000, the new secret fighter TRENCOR Industries was developing for the Air Force. He had just flown in from Washington, DC on the CEO's private jet and came straight to the conference room.

He watched each member of the group around the table. Their eyes peered at the computer screen integrated into the table at each person's seat. The soft blue glow illuminated their faces, and all of them wore a headset plugged into their console. They watched an audio/video PowerPoint presentation explaining the next phase of the F-2000 development program.

TRENCOR Industries had the room built as part of their new office/simulator facility. The building sat outside of California City, a small town north of Edwards AFB in Southern California's Mojave Desert. The three-story complex, with a total of over 400,000 square feet, sat on 380 acres of isolated desert property. One of the unique characteristics of Edwards Air Force Base, where Chuck Yeager broke the sound barrier in 1949, is the fact that the runway is located next to Rogers Dry Lake bed, which extends the length of the airfield's runways to three times the average runway length.

Wellington sat at the end of the table in a heavily starched Polo button-down and equally starched khaki Ralph Lauren slacks. His blue blazer hung on the back of his chair, and his cigar case lay out on the table containing three Arturo Fuentes, Magnum Vitolla 54s.

To his left sat the Air Force test pilots for the F-2000 program: Major Curt Samson and Major Jennifer Walton. Both were assigned to the 445th Flight Test Squadron but worked with the Dryden Flight

Research Center as part of this secret project. To Wellington's right sat the TRENCOR Industries team, led by Daniel Kirby, electrical engineer and project manager.

The F-2000 was a highly classified test program. It was designed to be the "wonder jet" that would supplement, and then eventually replace, the F-22, which was still under development and testing. The F-2000, the world's first sixth-generation fighter, was light-years ahead of anything in the air, received its numeric designation based on its design being the first jet of the new millennium, representing a new age in aeronautics. The Air Force pilots called it the F2K. Kirby hated the term; so did he.

Building upon the mission-management capability of the F-22, designed to be a game-changer in aerial combat, the F-2000 would eclipse the progress of the F-22. Most of its attributes were conceptual at the time of its initial design, but the technology had advanced exponentially. The single-seat jet utilized a helmet-mounted Heads-Up Display (HUD), advanced stealth capability, memory seat and flight controls, and vertical/short takeoff and landing (VSTOL) capabilities, and soon, hopefully, the revolutionary Integrated Thought Control System (ITCS).

The requirement had been to develop a jet capable of max performance at all speeds, from subsonic to hypersonic. Enhanced Situational Awareness Software (ESAS) was installed in the mission computers, an improvement on the systems developed for the F-22. The exterior possessed the same stealthy material used for the skin of the B-2 bomber, and the dual state-of-the-art scramjet engines reduced fuel intake by thirty percent. Weapons were to be both conventional missiles and guns for secondary weapons, and laser-directed weapons for the primary. Directed Energy weapons would eventually replace the conventional weapons once the technology had proven itself. An Advanced Directed Infrared Counter Measure (ADIRCM) provided a defensive suite against heat-seeking missiles. Traditional chaff and flares were believed to be un-stealthy and were left out of the design.

One requirement TRENCOR still struggled to achieve was the ITCS tying in to the RPA/SIP, the remotely piloted aircraft/sensory integration package. The aircraft requirement demanded the ability to detect when the pilot became incapacitated, at which point the ITCS would automatically take control of the jet and return to base. An earlier requirement to have the aircraft "heal" itself had been explored, at great expense, but was no longer pursued due to severe budget overruns.

His team reviewed the information on the update to the F-2000 simulator. Although the sim had been functioning for more than two months, they had finally finished construction on the TRENCOR Industries building. Building a training facility off-base was abnormal, but the Air Force was reluctant to build a new facility on base. Since this was TRENCOR's first US Air Force contract and their concept was revolutionary and expensive, the government didn't want to raise suspicions. Building it off-base was determined a much more effective method of maintaining secrecy, hiding it in plain sight.

When the PowerPoint presentation ended, the members of the team removed their headsets and turned to Wellington. "Well, Major Samson," the retired one-star said, "what do you think?"

Major Curt Samson looked directly at him. "Gen—uh, Mr. Wellington, I don't think it's ready. Other than utilizing the simulator as a checklist trainer and integrating the memory seat/flight controls to the pilot, it's not ready. The software hasn't progressed any further." Major Samson sounded frustrated.

"What do you mean?" replied Kirby. "The software is very functional."

"Look," Samson replied, "the tactical software is fine, and the graphics are fine. But for some reason, the environmental integration doesn't tie in to the aircraft instrumentation."

Wellington gave a smile of encouragement and nodded as Samson spoke. It was a toothy smile, his pearly whites taking on a personality of their own. He should have been a politician, but there was more money in aerospace. Wellington raised his eyebrows with a questionable glance at Kirby as Samson continued.

"Preliminary testing of this system will be useless if we don't tie the aircraft to its environment. I can run a test at 6,000 feet pressure altitude in the snow, but if the jet thinks it's floating around at sea level in zero-G environment, the tests are a waste of time. Brent O'Malley and I have documented this extensively, and he agrees that we're not ready to start. The tests would be inconclusive."

"Nothing we do at this point will be inconclusive," Kirby said loudly. "Just getting one of you clowns to climb into the sim and turn it on is valuable."

Samson's hands balled into fists on the table.

Wellington leaned forward. "Okay, folks, let's make nice before this gets out of hand. We're all on the same team here. How about this? We start the test cards for the sim tomorrow, and we get what we can get. Meanwhile, our software folks will work on generating the corrections we need to integrate the simulator into the desired environment. Everyone happy?"

Kirby grinned, and the software engineers nodded their heads. Wellington was worried about his program. The Air Force had sunk a great deal of money into it, far more than any other program in history, and they hadn't produced a jet yet. He knew what was riding on this program. Failure meant the Air Force would roll up in mothballs. They would be financially crippled, and their Research and Development would grind to a screeching halt.

"We'll be here, sir," Samson said.

"Excellent. Look, I understand it's not ideal, but we've been kicking this dog long enough. It's time to get this show on the road. Major Samson, we'll see your team here tomorrow at zero eight hundred. Any questions?"

"Only one," Samson said. "We still need to determine a test candidate to validate the requirement for the qualification phase of training. We're months behind on this requirement."

"I know. Why can't we use a test pilot?"

"Because a test pilot won't give us the feedback we need for such an operation. We need a low-time guy with zero fighter experience."

"It'll take months just to get the security clearance," Wellington mumbled. "We'll work it out."

"I hope so. Time is running out."

"Very well. You and your team are dismissed," Wellington said, his smile fading. He often forgot he was now retired and worked as a civilian. "There are some company issues we need to discuss."

Major Samson, Major Walton, and the other Air Force members stood and left the room. Wellington turned to the remaining members of his team. "Okay, folks, what's going on with this software?"

MAJOR JENNIFER WALTON was tight-lipped as the Air Force test pilots left the large conference room and strolled down the long, elegantly decorated hallway leading to the lobby. Their pace was slow as they admired the original oil paintings of historical aircraft lining the walls. Jennifer ran her fingers over the canvas depicting a P-40 Warhawk from General Claire Chenault's Flying Tigers during World War II. The Flying Tigers were key in helping liberate China from the Japanese during the war.

Georgiana Anderson, the program manager for the F-2000, trailed behind them in the hallway. She wore an unobtrusive pants suit that blended into most work environments. Jennifer considered her an odd mix of old-fashioned housewife and career-obsessed woman. Georgiana, now in her mid-forties, had been in the position for over a decade. Jennifer noticed her trying to open each of the doors along the hallway. Every door she tried was locked, except the restrooms.

"What are you doing, Georgiana?" Samson said.

She answered without looking up. "Have you never noticed there seems to be no one working in this building? I mean, it's three stories tall, over 400,000 square feet. Other than the receptionist and security guard at the front door and the simulator operators, no one works here."

"It is a new building," Jennifer said. "Perhaps they haven't moved their people in yet."

"But why is every door in this hallway locked?" Georgiana said.

"Why wouldn't they lock doors in a building containing the Air Force's most classified project since the B-2 bomber?" Jennifer said.

Georgiana shrugged her shoulders, gave up testing doors, and rejoined the two pilots as they walked to the lobby.

"At what point are they going to move their people in?" Georgiana said. "They're supposed to have a grand opening for this facility in two months."

"Well, quit nosing around, Georgiana," Samson said. "You're making me nervous."

Georgiana glanced at Samson and smiled. "Sorry, dear. You know me, I like puzzles."

Jennifer strode confidently past the receptionist and security guard in the lobby. Their gazes followed her as she walked outside. Jennifer had a striking figure. At five-foot six-inches tall, her body had perfect proportions, which never went unnoticed in the tight flight suits she wore. Her sandy blond hair was pulled back in a bun under her flight cap. She had said nothing during the meeting, but once the three of them reached the relatively empty parking lot, she grabbed Samson's arm.

"Look," she said, "I don't understand why you're against starting the test cards. We've flown this simulator through all phases of flight. It works."

Samson scowled at her grip on his arm. Detecting her bad decision, she let go and lowered her head.

"These guys are nowhere near being ready to start this program. Yes, we've flown the simulator. It's an easy jet to operate, but the simulator isn't up to standards yet. To start validating the sim when it's not ready will make things worse when the jet shows up and we've set the standard for cutting corners. TRENCOR is two years behind schedule and I don't know how many dollars over budget. If we start the official test cards, we validate it as a legitimate project, and I don't think the test wing commander is ready to go down this road."

"Curt, I think you're wrong. We need to start this project as soon as we can. Kirby was right—any information we can get from the simulator will be beneficial. I'm ready to get started." She turned and climbed into her Jeep Wrangler. "I'll see you two at zero eight hundred tomorrow," she said as she cranked the Jeep and pulled out of the parking lot.

Driving toward her apartment, she pulled out her cell phone and dialed a number. On the third ring, it picked up. "Well?" a voice said.

"He doesn't want to start the simulator test, for all the reasons we talked about before."

"And you weren't able to convince him otherwise?"

"No. He's solid in his stance. He'll need to be ordered to start."

"Okay, consider it done," the voice said, abruptly ending the call.

10

THE CONDENSATION DRIPPED off the bottom of his glass of Scotch, and he set it on a new napkin. He adjusted the edges of the napkin to align with the small table on which it lay. David Ming looked out the window of the Gulfstream IV as it taxied to the active runway at East Kern Airport District in Mojave. The luxury jet was quiet, but still fell victim to the imperfections in the Mojave airport's taxiway. Ming's Scotch jiggled and shook and spilled over the edge yet again as the Gulfstream bounded its way to the active runway. The lone flight attendant rushed over and wiped up the spill and replaced the napkin. It was late afternoon, but it was never too early for a good Scotch.

He had been troubled since his meeting this morning on Capitol Hill with the House Armed Services Committee. Ming and his site manager, retired Brigadier General Jeremiah Wellington, were grilled for the excessive delay for their top-secret project. Normally, he managed to avoid these hearings by sending Wellington. He was a smooth-talking insider who knew exactly how to approach the powers in the Pentagon and on Capitol Hill. That's why he'd hired Wellington—everybody loved the guy. But with cost overruns excessively high, Ming needed to make an appearance.

Ming chuckled to himself as the Gulfstream took the runway and lifted off for Sacramento. He was flying there to pick up his assistant, Li Zhong, and from there on to a meeting in San Francisco. Ming couldn't get the image out of his mind of last Friday's exchange with the congressman from New York.

"Mr. Ming," the congressman said, "during this era of financial difficulties, I find it incredible the amount of money you've spent on this project. Yet we still don't have anything!"

Ming answered him directly, skipping the titles normally tossed around these meetings. "You do understand what we are developing here? These requirements are for capabilities that once only existed in science fiction. Research and development takes time and money. A lot of it."

"We understand, Mr. Ming, and the requirements have changed to accommodate this issue. But you must admit, we've spent over, what, two hundred billion dollars on this program, yet we don't have one damn jet on the ramp out there."

"The jet prototype is in production and will be delivered next month. The simulator is in full operation, and we are progressing at a rapid rate. Our project will meet the full intent of the government's proposal."

"At what cost?"

Ming lined up the papers and pens sitting on the table in front of him and adjusted the cufflinks on his heavily starched shirt. Leaning back in his chair, he laid his palms flat on the table. Wellington, who sat next to him, started to lean forward to speak, but Ming put out his hand to stop him.

"Members of the committee," Ming said, leaning into the microphone again, "we are making progress. TRENCOR Industries will have the jet next month, ready for flight testing. You are well aware, any project incorporating new technology requires an extensive amount of money up front. When the production line stands up, the average cost decreases."

"Mr. Ming, must I remind you, the jet won't be as advertised," said a congressman from Pennsylvania. "The 'self-healing' surface initiative was scrapped after how many billions of dollars were put into its development?"

"This area of the contract was renegotiated two years ago, congressman," he said. "We will have your jet next month."

"Mr. Ming, I'm not an aeronautical engineer," the congressman from New York said, "but I understand money. I'm here to tell you, your people at TRENCOR Industries need to learn to do more with less. The American people are spending untold amounts of tax dollars on this project that could be spent in other areas."

The exchange had lingered with him for the last two days. The

American people were not spending untold amounts of money on this project—Congress and the Air Force were. If the American people knew about the spending, they would be beating down the doors on Capitol Hill to stop it. But the congressman was right, he thought as the jet leveled off at 24,000 feet. If they don't spend the money on his project, they'll spend it somewhere else—and likely not where it's actually needed.

THE RAMP WAS VOID of people, except himself. Li Zhong stood outside the small terminal at the Sacramento Executive Airport, staring at the sky. The airport sat three miles south of downtown Sacramento and was unusually quiet for the late afternoon. Perhaps the heavily overcast sky and low ceiling kept the general aviation pilots in bed. He waited for his employer, David Ming, to fly in and pick him up.

Li Zhong watched as the Gulfstream punched through the overcast sky like a magician's assistant appearing in a puff of smoke. Ming's jet landed and taxied to the private terminal. The tall Chinese man entered the aircraft, and the female attendant closed the door behind him as he sat across from David Ming.

"Li Zhong," Ming said, "I hope you accomplished what you needed to in Sacramento."

"I did, sir. I appreciate your picking me up. Most employers are not this gracious."

"You have been a faithful employee, Li Zhong. Besides, we'll charge it to the US government," he said.

Li Zhong said nothing as he buckled into the seat and stared out the window. His role was multifaceted: he was advisor, bodyguard, liaison, investigator, sounding board, and enforcer. Li Zhong was surprised to see Ming could be as ruthless in dealing with personal adversaries as he was in handling boardroom acquisitions. Despite the thin veneer of obsessive neatness, Ming was willing to "get his hands dirty" and eliminate opposition when it stood in the way of his objectives. Li Zhong found Ming's traits for business aligned with his own Special Forces background. The two were compatible for the job they needed to do.

"How was your meeting with General Jingguo?" Ming said, adjusting his drink napkin.

"Good. Both his team and the group from Saudi Arabia were in Sacramento to discuss the cloud-seeding initiative."

Ming nodded. "The Saudis have a huge interest in developing agriculture in the desert. I don't understand why Beijing insists on using us for this."

"Perhaps they sense an end to our role here."

Ming fixed his gaze toward him, his mouth downturned. Li Zhong realized he may have misspoken. "I meant no disrespect, Mr. Ming. Was there a problem in Washington?"

"Yes and no," Ming said, adjusting his body at an angle away from Li Zhong. "The House Armed Services Committee wasn't pleased with our cost overruns and the delays in the programs. But they are happy with the simulator progress and the prototype's arrival next month."

Li Zhong nodded and glanced out the window again. They sat in silence for several moments while the aircraft taxied to the runway.

"Why do you think General Jingguo has come to Sacramento?" Li Zhong said, looking back at Ming.

"I don't know. Perhaps the plans are moving forward faster than we anticipated."

"Indeed." *Things are moving forward faster.* Despite Ming's incredible attention to detail, Li Zhong wondered if his employer would be able to keep up.

THE TELEVISION LIT UP the dark bedroom. It had been a long day that was turning into a long night. Jennifer sat up in her bed and pulled the covers over her bare breasts, listening intently to the Tulsa broadcast picked up by the national media:

> "...seventy miles west of Vance Air Force Base. While Jason Conrad appears to have survived the ejection unscathed, his student, we are told by sources inside the US Air Force, suffered a broken arm. What did this pilot do to lose control of his multimillion-dollar aircraft? We don't know, and the Air Force isn't talking. We can only hope the true story is told—before the Russians and CIA show up. We'll have more on this story as details become available. For WTSR, the Taaaser from Tulsa, this is Dane Robinson reporting."

Jennifer bit her lower lip. She remembered when Jason was a student. She'd been a young T-38 instructor pilot at Vance and had tried to seduce him on more than one occasion. Back then, she joked that he was either gay or had incredible willpower.

Jennifer had no illusions about herself. Since she'd been a young girl, she always had to work extra hard to get the boys' attention. She was athletic, which helped, but she was far from the most attractive girl in school. Jennifer was a good math student, and a concerned teacher had convinced her to consider becoming a pilot. After extensive research, she decided the Air Force Academy was the perfect path for her. Jennifer majored in mathematics and had no problem in school, which gave her plenty of time for other activities. She loved the soaring program, flying gliders the Academy offered to prospective pilot candidates. She also ran on the cross-country team all four years. During those four years, she found herself in heaven, though she still found it difficult to date, or at least hold on to a man. She jumped from relationship to relationship, never keeping a steady boyfriend.

When she graduated, she worked as a casual lieutenant at MacDill AFB in Tampa while she waited to start pilot training. While there, she decided to get breast augmentation, a decision her parents vehemently opposed. The change surprised many of her Academy classmates when she arrived at Undergraduate Pilot Training at Vance, but she considered it a good move. She certainly got the boys' attention now, even if Jason stayed away. After graduation, she became a T-38 instructor pilot, then followed on in the F-16. Now, here she was, years later, a test pilot at Edwards.

She climbed out of bed and stretched. The light of the television lit up her nude body as she reached her arms over her head.

The door to her bathroom opened, the light spilling into the room. The manly figure stood in the doorway, leering at her.

"Now, you are a vision of beauty," he said.

"And I'm yours, if you stick around."

"Oh, you know I'd like to, but it's past ten o'clock. My wife expects me to come home eventually."

"Your wife has her arms wrapped around a bottle of bourbon by now—if she's still conscious."

The man ambled over to her and took her in his arms.

"Regardless, I need to get going."

"Your loss," she said, reaching her arms around him and squeezing his buttocks.

He kissed her on the lips, ever so softly, and gazed into her eyes.

"Good night, Major," he said.

She beamed. He liked them referring to each other by rank; it was his kinky obsession. She pushed him away so he could get one last glimpse of her nude body as she slipped on a negligee. She sauntered back to him and ran her finger down the length of his tie.

"Good night, General Wellington."

11

April 23, 2001

THE EARLY MORNING DEW gave the grass weight and density. Gently, the wind blew in from the northwest, and the crisp desert air was cool and fresh as the sun pushed its way up through the horizon. The nearest mountain terrain was the Mojave National Preserve to the west, and the general flatness of the area always made it seem as if morning came early.

Major Curt Samson finished his daily three-mile run. His Monday morning run had taken him out of base housing onto Fitzgerald Avenue, north onto Redmon Avenue, then a left turn on Yeager Boulevard. Yeager intersected Forbes Avenue, which brought him south back to Fitzgerald. The route took him along the outskirts of base housing, and the view left a little to be desired, but he did pass the old man jogging in shorts and combat boots, confirming the rumor his truck had been seen again on the base. The old man lived the life many pilots wished they could have. There was something to be said for being the first pilot to break the sound barrier—you got to jog on a street named after you.

Samson scanned the cookie-cutter base housing surrounding his place. His breathing came in large gasps as the alcohol from last night purged its way through the pores of his skin. He took his shoes and socks off and plodded through the grass in his yard. Grass under his bare feet reminded him of Florida; there wasn't much grass anywhere around Edwards except in base housing and the fairways at the golf course. The previous summer, he played a round of golf barefoot one afternoon with several of the other pilots just to feel the grass beneath his feet.

Samson wiggled his toes in the moist grass as he admired the mountains in the distance. Taking a deep breath, he pulled fresh air into his lungs. He never truly believed he'd get here. Since he was a young boy, he'd worked diligently toward this specific goal. In pilot training, he finished top of his class and received an F-15. He worked harder than anyone in his squadron to earn a test pilot school slot. Now here he was, the lead test pilot for the newest Air Force jet fighter, and he was extremely unhappy.

He was not looking forward to the simulator today.

The program had thousands of issues, and pushing the simulator tests forward was simply TRENCOR's way of proving they were doing something. He had little faith in the aircraft's concept. The technology hadn't reached the level needed for what they were trying to accomplish. Samson was old school. He lobbied hard two years ago to get signed on to this test project, and for the last year, he'd regretted every bit of it. There were some new concepts in Research and Development of the F-2000, but not enough to warrant the absurd amount of money wasted on this project.

Samson gathered his shoes and socks and entered his house. Climbing into the shower, TRENCOR's issues rolled around in his head. He would call General Mark Oglesby, the Test Wing commander, later this morning about the situation at TRENCOR. Because of the classification of this project, Samson reported directly to General Oglesby, who was not happy with the progress of this test program.

As he stepped out of the shower, the phone rang. Samson placed the phone to his ear as he stood dripping wet with the towel wrapped around his waist.

"Major Samson, General Oglesby here."

"Good morning, sir," he said.

"Curt, sorry to bother you this early, but I wanted to catch you before work. It's been brought to my attention that you're reluctant to start the test cards on the simulator. Any truth to the rumor?"

"Yes sir," he said. "It didn't seem wise to start the tests with the environmental characteristics not tied in to the aircraft circuit board. The tests would be invalid and have to be re-accomplished."

"I agree with your thought process. Those folks are nowhere near ready to start this test. They get further behind every day."

Curt was pleased with the general's statement, but there was a pause, as if the general was going to say more.

"I need you to start the test cards today, Curt. Get what you can and make sure your write-up addresses the negative impact of not having the sim up to speed."

"Yes, sir, I'll take care of it."

"Thanks, Curt. I can't get into the particulars right now, but we'll talk. Good luck."

The general hung up the phone, and Samson stared at the receiver in his hand. Odd. Three years of flying test and he'd never gotten a phone call from the wing commander at home.

WELLINGTON SUPERVISED the meeting of Air Force representatives, contractors, and engineers. A fighter pilot fresh out of flight school, He flew the F-4 in the waning days of the Vietnam War, and then applied for test pilot school as a young captain. Most of his career was spent at Edwards as a test pilot and instructor. One of the first pilots in the Air Force to check out on the F-16, he did two tours in the jet. Prior to pinning on lieutenant colonel, he was whisked away to the Pentagon to work in the Checkmate program until he went to Vance AFB to be the wing commander. Two years later, he returned to the Pentagon until his retirement as a one-star six years ago. Following retirement, he signed on with TRENCOR Industries as a consultant and rapidly moved up the chain to site manager for their new classified fighter, the F-2000.

He sat at the head of the table, wearing a freshly pressed suit and tie, relaxed and confident. There were about fifteen extra TRENCOR employees lining the walls. Samson led the discussion on the two sections of the test cards. It had been a long day, and the parts of the test they could complete were benign: the jet could turn on, start engines, cycle through all its basic systems, and shut down. Still, about sixty percent of the data was inconclusive due to software issues.

"We accomplished what we could," Samson said, "but we need to get the simulator fixed. The jet prototype is due here next month, and we'll need to start testing immediately." He turned to Jennifer. "Major Walton, can you describe for the engineers what you experienced in the cockpit? Your input may help them troubleshoot the problem."

Jennifer straightened in her seat. "While accomplishing the after-landing checklist, the main LCD touch screen inexplicably changed from the systems monitor for the checklist to the weather radar. It wasn't the functioning full-color weather radar, either. It was a monochromatic picture running a test pattern."

Samson, Jennifer, and the engineers discussed potential solutions for the problem. The discussion dragged on, going in circles.

"All right, we've seen this before," Wellington spoke up. "Let's get it fixed and move on to the next set of tests on Tuesday. Back in my day, we didn't have these problems. And the problems we did have, we worked through them and got the job done."

"Excuse me?" Samson said, looking up from his computer terminal.

Wellington gave Samson an apologetic glance. "I'm not saying you two are not good test pilots."

"You just did," Samson replied. "Where the hell is this coming from?"

"Major, your test program is way behind schedule. You can blame it on software and the contractors all you want, but in my day, we'd have completed this phase months ago."

"Months ago, we didn't have anything to complete!"

"You two have been flying this simulator through different profiles for months! It wasn't until we needed to start the test cards that you decided to get picky about the software."

"I beg to differ, sir. We've brought up the software from day one. But the Air Force can't accept an aircraft of this cost without ensuring everything is by the book and up to spec. You, of all people, should know that."

"I know, Major. I was flying test when you were picking your nose in high school JROTC," Wellington said. He glanced around the room and noticed everyone appeared tense. Most sat up straight in their chairs and shifted their gaze away from him.

"Well, you'd never know from the way you talk about running this test," Samson said.

"I'd fly circles around you, Major, so don't get cocky with me."

"I'll take that challenge."

"Major," Wellington said, his voice getting louder, "if you're wondering who the best fighter pilot in the room is, don't worry . . . it's not you."

Georgiana Anderson, the US Air Force's program manager for the F-2000, reached over and touched Samson's arm. He acknowledged her move with a slight nod, and leaned back in his chair.

Georgiana spoke up. "Mr. Wellington, I think you're forgetting who you work for."

"Excuse me?" Wellington replied.

"You work for TRENCOR Industries, who is contracted by the US Air Force."

"I know who I work for."

"Then stop talking to your employer as if you are doing him a favor." Her glare said it all.

Wellington leaned back in his chair and grimaced. He'd spent his evening hours in the simulator and knew what it was capable of doing. He was frustrated because Samson was a strictly by-the-book test pilot. If everything wasn't perfectly in order, he would not proceed.

"My apologies, Georgiana," he said with an appealing smile, his eyes wide. "I think we're all feeling the pressure. Me included. The consequences of not succeeding will result in the crippling of our beloved Air Force. Major Samson, I encourage you to understand I'm from a different generation of pilots. We did things different back in my day. I apologize if I was out of line."

Samson nodded as if forgiving his misstep. Wellington scanned the rest of the room. Everyone was a little more relaxed, returning his smile as he looked at each of them.

"Are there any alibis around the room?" he shifted his tone to address the rest of the team. A broad smile came across his face when Jennifer raised her hand. "Yes, Major Walton?"

"We've been discussing the actual flight test of this jet. While Major Samson and I will be the two primary test pilots, we've been searching for the ideal candidate for our 'simulated student'—someone who can fly but doesn't have the experience of a fighter pilot."

Wellington turned to Samson, who still fumed over their last exchange. "This was brought up, what, two days ago? What are your thoughts on this, Major Samson?"

"I think it's a good idea to identify this person early," Samson said. "The secondary intent of this jet is to develop a user-friendly weapon system that will drastically reduce training time. It makes sense to see how a less-experienced pilot adapts to the jet. My training program is built and ready to go."

"Okay, so who do you two have in mind?" Wellington said.

Jennifer beamed. "Captain Jason Conrad. He's a T-38 instructor at Vance."

"The guy who crashed a jet earlier this week?"

News of mishaps traveled fast, and the test community always received information first.

"Yes, sir. He sucked birds in both engines on a low-level route. Both he and the student ejected safely. Preliminary safety reports show he executed a perfect application of emergency procedures."

"Is he the right man for the job? He's a FAIP, isn't he?"

Jennifer reached into a folder in front of her, pulled out several sets of paper, and slid them across the table.

"I contacted Vance's stan/eval office this morning to get his Flight Evaluation Folder faxed to me at the squadron," she said. "During lunch, I slipped over to the base flight records office to get his flight information. He has over twelve hundred hours and a clean evaluation record. I would call him experienced, but not too experienced. Enough to trust him with a multibillion-dollar airplane."

Wellington noticed the numerous heads around the room who nodded in agreement.

"But better than his experience"—she paused—"he has a TS/SCI security clearance."

Wellington dropped the papers on the table.

"How the hell does a FAIP have a TS/SCI clearance?"

Everyone stared at Jennifer as she glanced around the room. "He, uh … he was going to a classified assignment, but his current wing commander turned it off."

Wellington was interested in what he was hearing, but this Conrad character sounded like he was not a good fit. "He's too experienced," Wellington said, shaking his head, reviewing the sheet. "One of the main objectives of this sixth-generation fighter jet is to eliminate Fighter Lead-In altogether and reduce the schoolhouse by fifty percent. How am I going to tell if the jet can support a student straight out of pilot training if my lab rat has six years of flying experience?"

"Sir, correct me if I'm wrong, but doesn't it make sense for the initial runs to consist of a relatively experienced pilot in the event something goes wrong?" Jennifer said. "Whether it's Jason Conrad or someone else, each pilot we use to simulate a student will be less qualified than the previous one until we find the spot where our beta-trainers bottom out."

"I understand what you're saying. And you're right, the pilot needs to be able to manually fly and land the aircraft in the event something goes wrong—like the weather radar coming on when it's not supposed to," he said, glaring at the software engineers, "but I was thinking of a guy about a year out of pilot training. A new guy with a little bit of flying time under his belt—but not too much. This Conrad is too experienced."

Jennifer leaned forward. "Sir, do you remember the San Antonio incident around the presidential election?"

"Yes, the assassination attempt on Senator Bowman."

"Correct. Senator Bowman is Jason Conrad's father."

A slight grin started to show on Wellington's face. His mind was working faster than his mouth could spit out words.

"And the former Senator Bowman is the executive vice president of Century Aero-Bot," Jennifer said with a slight grin.

Wellington sat back in his chair, a toothy grin stretched across his face. Century Aero-Bot was a private contractor developing the Remotely Piloted Aircraft technology with the Integrated Thought Control System. TRENCOR Industries had been trying to purchase this system from Century Aero-Bot for the past three years. Bringing in Bowman's son might just be the leverage he needed to acquire this technology to meet the design specs in the initial proposal. The timing couldn't be better. Bowman was arriving next week to negotiate the deal. Having Bowman's son on their team would help.

"Okay," Wellington said, "I'll call the Pentagon and pull some strings. It may take cashing in a few favors, but I think a FAIP will do. Jason Conrad it is."

12

April 23, 2001

STEVEN HAD SET UP THE MEETING with an informant in Greenwich Village. The informant wanted to meet Sherri at his mosque, but Steven wasn't willing to let her go there. While it sounded like a good idea for her to show up in a hijab to hide her face, Steven didn't like putting her in that position. Neither did Sherri.

She sat at the coffee shop sipping a latte, wearing a scarf over her hair and large sunglasses. A baby started to cry behind her, and she winced. Not that she didn't like babies, but they were a reminder her own biological clock was ticking. She was thirty. Most of her friends from college had already married and were raising families in the Midwest. She had always wanted a family, but her career came first. Coupled with some bad decisions about men in her life, and she was a little gun-shy about relationships.

As a result, she dove deeper into her work, putting all her focus there. And the gym. She realized she was an attractive woman, and when attractive women ask questions, they usually find answers. For the last ten years, she had adopted a solid exercise and dietary regime that kept her looking years younger than her age. It paid off. Dozens of blondes and brunettes could be found anywhere, but tall, fit, olive-skinned redheads? Not that many.

She drew attention everywhere she went. Often it could be a problem. There was the correspondents' dinner in Washington several years back and the drippy reporter who wouldn't leave her alone. And the ESPN function in New York, when the quarterback gave her his phone number—in front of his wife. That one didn't go over so well. But while she appreciated being desired, she hurt inside. She had chosen a lonely career. If she wasn't so damned good at it, it would be easy to walk away.

Ten minutes after the scheduled meeting time, a Middle-Eastern-looking man around age thirty entered the coffee shop and approached her table.

"Ms. Davis?" the man asked in halting English.

"Yes. Who are you?"

"My name is not important." His voice wavered as he crawled into the seat across from her. Perspiration poured down his face and his hands shook. He barely glanced at her as his eyes continuously scanned the area.

"The men you are looking for—they constantly move around the country?"

"Yes. Who are they and what are they doing?"

"There are many of them. They are doing much training and surveillance. There are many meetings. Today, they are in Las Vegas. Meeting with defense contractor. Century Aero-Bot. Not all, but some. Then they split up. Some go to Denver, some to Venice, Florida, and some to Mojave."

Sherri's curiosity piqued. "Who exactly—"

The informant's eyes shifted beyond Sherri, and his lower lip trembled. His hands fell in his lap, and he started rocking back and forth. Softly he mumbled, "Allah, Allah, Allah" as he stared across the coffee shop behind her.

Sherri turned to see what he was looking at, and the informant bolted from the table and out of the coffee shop. Two men watched him leave but didn't move. They appeared Middle Eastern as well, and one of them caught her attention. His hair was thick and curly, but she focused on his eyes. He had strabismus, or crossed eyes, which made it difficult to tell where he was looking. Sherri learned about the disease while reporting on war refugees from Sarajevo. She continued to watch him because she wasn't sure if he was watching her or looking elsewhere.

The informant ran into a bicyclist in the street as soon as he stepped outside, and the two fell to the pavement. He pushed himself off the ground, his shirt torn and bloodied. Blood oozed from his cut hands. Ignoring his injuries, he ran in the direction he'd been headed before he hit the bicyclist.

Sherri watched him until the street echoed with the sound of machine-gun fire. Her eyes darted back and forth along the street. The stranger who sat across from her not twenty seconds before, lay face first in the middle of the street.

Her mouth fell open. Did that just happen in broad daylight? Sherri backed away from the table toward the coffee bar and stood behind the counter, her eyes scanning the street through the plate glass window, unable to locate the shooter.

She glimpsed back at the two men she saw prior to the gunfire. They sat unshaken, watching her every move. The man with the crossed eyes grinned a wicked grin, baring his yellow, crooked teeth.

A white Cadillac raced up to the curb. The two men slipped out of the coffee shop, climbed in the car, and peeled away from the scene, the sound of police sirens wailing in the distance.

GEORGIANA ANDERSON STEPPED out of the women's restroom into the long empty hallway. She had grown frustrated with TRENCOR Industries and their inability to be forthcoming. This building had been called complete three weeks ago, but the grand opening wasn't for another two months. They had been having meetings here for the last two weeks. The only portions of the building they had seen were the lobby, the conference room, the simulator bay, and the hallway connecting them all. As she walked back to the conference room, she turned and stopped at the elevator. The light above the elevator said "3." Georgiana pushed the up button, and the elevator promptly made its way to the first floor and opened its doors. Georgiana scanned the hallway, and seeing no one around, quickly stepped into the elevator. She pushed "2," and the elevator doors closed.

Four years before, TRENCOR Industries made their bid to produce America's sixth-generation fighter aircraft. Georgiana had been a GS-11 assigned to Quality Assurance and was given the task of reviewing TRENCOR Industries. Her research spawned more questions than answers. TRENCOR had been heavily invested in agriculture, genetic engineering, satellite communications, and energy. Aeronautics and aircraft manufacturing were relatively new additions to the company, but they put forward the most realistic bid, with an impressive laundry list of conceptual capabilities that were decades ahead of any of their competitors'.

To top it off, they managed to hire recently retired Brigadier

General Jeremiah Wellington. A former test pilot and influential player in the Air Force hierarchy, Georgiana found him to be an attractive and compelling speaker. He had a way of making you do what he asked—except when he dealt with pilots. Then it was always about who had the bigger johnson. Regardless, his voice as the advocate for TRENCOR Industries' F-2000 gave the company and the project credibility—so much so that many questions that should have been answered were never asked.

Georgiana argued the Air Force moved too fast on this project. TRENCOR had too much of the project ready to go before they received the contract. But that never bothered them. In fact, TRENCOR used it as a selling point, saying that it demonstrated how committed to this project they were. The aircraft acquisition process had grown obscenely long, and this project was sold as a concept that would shorten everything: acquisition, production, and training. The money was needed up front. Lots of it.

Her parents always told her that if something sounded too good to be true, it probably was. That was why TRENCOR Industries interested Georgiana. To her, it was like a huge jigsaw puzzle—all the pieces were in front of her. Now, it was her job to put them together.

The doors opened and she entered the second-floor reception area. Georgiana searched for any signs of life. The empty reception area was beautiful, with terrazzo flooring and wood paneling halfway up the walls. Original oil paintings of various aircraft hung on the walls, and large potted plants were strategically placed.

She wasn't necessarily a brave woman, but she was curious. Cautiously, she stepped to the right, her footsteps clicking softly on the terrazzo floor. Georgiana rounded the corner to the right of the elevator and suddenly, out of nowhere, Li Zhong stepped in front of her. Li Zhong was the silent member of the TRENCOR Industries team.

"Mrs. Anderson, you look lost," the towering Li Zhong said, positioning his body in front of Georgiana.

"Yes, I am," Georgiana replied. She strained to see beyond Li Zhong and saw what looked to be an unfinished, dark hallway. In fact, the entire floor appeared unfinished when viewed from this angle.

"Please," Li Zhong said, putting up his hands, pointing back to the reception area. "The elevator is this way." He herded Georgiana back toward the elevator. "We still have some construction occurring. It is too dangerous up here."

"Yes, certainly. I thought TRENCOR had completed all the construction for this facility? What's going on here?"

"Mrs. Anderson, you are Quality Assurance on your base, but you are in our building. I am Quality Assurance here. You don't ask questions." Li Zhong gently nudged Georgiana all the way to the elevator. "You go back to conference room and stay off higher floors. Bad things can happen around construction."

"I'll keep that in mind, Li Zhong. You know, there's always something we can learn simply by looking, or ask—"

"Good day, Mrs. Anderson."

She got it. He wanted her to leave.

"Goodbye," Georgiana replied and stepped into the elevator. She pushed the button for the first floor, and Li Zhong's expressionless face watched her every move. The doors closed, and as the elevator began to move, it hit her. Her heart raced and her palms became sweaty. A creeping feeling of dread overcame her; Georgiana sensed her body's reaction to the encounter with Li Zhong.

13

April 24, 2001

JASON STEPPED OUT of the VOQ at Vance AFB in his olive-green flight suit and black leather flight boots, and with a big sigh, plodded to his truck. The old Ford F-150 blended in perfectly with all the other vehicles in the region. The paint had faded long ago and begun to chip in several places. It wasn't neglect; he wanted an understated vehicle. Jason liked to remain anonymous, at least as much as possible.

The cool Oklahoma morning air stung his face, as he slipped on his leather flight jacket. He hoped his commander would let him fly soon. The flight surgeon had medically cleared him the day before, and the investigation was the only stumbling block to get back in the jet.

The sky had been overcast all morning, and it didn't appear to be getting any better. A thick gray cloud cover hovered overhead. It was a solid deck in all directions, the top of the base water tower disappearing into the wispy abyss a little over a hundred feet above the ground. The wind had subsided to a calm five knots, but the low ceiling would prevent any flights for the time being. Jason studied the sky as he drove to the wing commander's office. He'd received a phone call to get there right away, and he worried the Accident Investigation Board might have found him at fault for something.

Jason parked his truck in a visitor's spot at the 71st Flying Training Wing Headquarters, entered the building, and headed upstairs. He found the wing commander's suite and entered. "Hey Bill," he said to the executive officer whose desk sat outside the colonel's office, "I got a call—"

"Yeah, hang on and have a seat," the exec said, picking up his phone. "Sir, he's here."

Jason chose to remain standing. He hated situations like this, when things were out of his control. Perspiration developed around his hairline and his palms grew sweaty. He took a few deep breaths and methodically checked all the zippers on his flight suit.

"Go on in, he's waiting for you," Bill said.

Jason entered the office and saw Colonel Andy Birmingham sitting behind his large mahogany desk. The spotless office contained several model airplanes and plaques from previous assignments. Vance's wing commander had a reputation for being a neat freak, which was okay until he started sharing his philosophy with the rest of the base. It started with increased inspections of the student dorms and quickly migrated to the operational squadrons. A few subtle comments to the squadron commanders and suddenly keeping the flight rooms spotless was a bigger priority than flying jets. Jason approached the desk and saluted, and Colonel Birmingham slowly returned the salute.

The short African-American wing commander motioned to the chair in front of his desk and said, "Sit down and relax."

Jason sat in the chair. While his stress level dropped slightly, he was not about to let his guard down. His fingers wrestled with the zipper on the right thigh pocket of his flight suit.

"In case you're wondering, the AIB and the SIB both came to the same conclusion: you did a textbook job with the emergency procedure. Good work."

"Thank you, sir," Jason said. He noticed the colonel remained expressionless. Jason looked him right in the eyes, and the wing commander flinched. He glanced back at his stack of papers.

"My flight safety folks will get with you later today about putting together a briefing for lessons learned. They'll give you an opportunity to tell everyone what goes through a pilot's mind when he realizes he has to eject from his aircraft."

"Yes, sir." Jason fought to withhold a smile. Perhaps he had gotten a reprieve in the "one-mistake" Air Force.

"But that's not why you're here," the colonel said.

"It's not?" Jason was confused—and curious.

"You've been reassigned to another base."

"Sir, if there's any—"

"There's no getting around this one, Captain Conrad. This one has come down from folks with more stars than you and I have."

Jason started to speak, but paused.

"You're going to Edwards Air Force Base to fly the T-38. Makes no damn sense to me— you're a FAIP. Hell, I don't know what you're supposed to do out there that those test guys can't do themselves."

"But sir, I've got a business degree. I'm not qualified to go to test pilot school."

"You didn't listen, Captain. I didn't say you were going to test pilot school. I said you were going to be a T-38 pilot at Edwards. That's what your orders say," the colonel said, handing the paper to Jason. "This is probably better for you. I'm not sure you'd be very successful at fighter lead-in, anyway."

What the hell was that supposed to mean? He took the paper from the colonel. Reviewing the paper, he noticed the Report No Later Than date.

"May 7? That's two weeks from now. How am I going to move all my household goods? How will I get out of my lease? That's not enough time."

"Don't worry, Captain. I have a little pull in this town. Your lease has been coordinated, as well as your utilities. The movers are coming on Tuesday to box up your house. That gives you Wednesday through Friday of next week to close out your out-processing checklist. Most of your particulars are taken care of. If you have any problems, let young Bill out there know."

Jason pondered what had happened. Wing commanders didn't get involved in a captain's out-processing, but Colonel Birmingham had mapped out Jason's schedule for the next two weeks. To Jason, it spoke volumes. He knew where he stood with Colonel Birmingham.

"Thank you, sir," Jason said, slowly rising, still trying to process everything. "I guess I'm moving to California."

14

THE MANSION SAT NESTLED IN THE foothills west of Rosamond, California, overlooking Castac Lake to the south. Sunlight glistened off the still lake, the breeze not enough to ripple the water. The property encompassed more than sixty acres surrounding the eight-thousand-square-foot, two-story house, which had been built four years ago. A separate building, a guest house, sat behind the main house. Next to that was a four-car garage, a tennis court, and a swimming pool. A helipad was located a hundred yards from the back of the house. In the main house, there were eight bedrooms and three full baths. The twenty-by-forty-foot kitchen had a brown-tinted granite countertop and travertine floors. Next to that, the dining area was larger, sixty by thirty. A huge dining table capable of seating twenty-two, made from maple with custom chairs to match, perched on dark wood flooring.

The four-feet-tall by six-feet-wide fireplace was the focal point for the sitting room. Its ceiling reached twenty feet, and the windows to the north and south stood eight feet in height. Combined with the light-colored wood and paint in the room, it had a light, airy feeling. Displaying original artwork from the Impressionist period, the elegance of the room could not be overstated. Two men sat opposite each other on the plush couches, deep in thought.

David Ming sifted through the papers in his hand. He had reviewed Captain Jason Conrad's dossier for the last hour. The stack of paper was two inches thick, consisting of his Air Force records, Officer Performance Reports (OPR), Flight Evaluation Folder (FEF), flying history, medical records, and security clearance. Wellington had his Air

Force counterparts compile this data. Jason Conrad was a most capable pilot; his records spoke for themselves. His evaluations were excellent, with a few downgrades scattered throughout his history. The OPRs were very good until you reached the additional rater, which for him was always the wing commander. Some wing commanders obviously didn't like him, and their feelings were reflected on his Officer Performance Reports.

But those were not the records that interested Ming. It was the package Li Zhong had received from Beijing. This information would not be given to the Air Force, since it might prompt too many questions on how and why it was obtained. This information explained Jason Conrad's personal history: his education, his mother, his marriage and divorce, his relationships with the OSI and CIA—and more importantly, his relationship with his father, the former Senator Jonathan Bowman.

Wellington was correct in his belief that Jason Conrad was the right man for the job. Acquiring him would give them the leverage they needed to obtain Century Aero-Bot's Remotely Piloted Aircraft technology. TRENCOR Industries had given Century Aero-Bot some off-the-books seed money with no strings attached, other than the right of first refusal. It was their fault, of course. No one had been aware Bowman would come on board as Century Aero-Bot's VP as quickly as he did. The company had been composed of "tech-heads" who knew little of the art of negotiation. Maybe that was why they'd brought Bowman in—to help the company grow and acquire. Clearly they needed help, and they quickly recovered after he came on board. Ming knew it was obvious to Century Aero-Bot that TRENCOR Industries needed their technology. Without it, the F-2000 was another tremendously expensive jet with no new capability.

It would be a tough fight, but Ming was confident that with the addition of Jason Conrad, his father would eventually give in and sell the tech to TRENCOR. Ming read with great interest about the situation in San Antonio when Jason's father ran for the Republican nomination.

His eyebrows raised as he set the file on the coffee table. "Jason Conrad had never met his father until this incident?"

Li Zhong nodded, rubbing a finger across his chin. "Correct. He knew who he was but had not seen him since early childhood. His mother chose to protect him from the complications of American politics."

"But it turns out the boy ended up protecting the father?"

"Yes."

Ming nodded and went back into the file. He read through the ten-page report on the San Antonio incident twice. "His relationships with federal agencies . . . does this complicate things?"

Li Zhong rested his elbows on his knees. "No. The OSI agent is not an issue. He has since retired, and they haven't made contact in over two years. The CIA agent, however, could be. They contact each other regularly. It is safe to say they are close friends."

"But he won't be a problem? We can keep the CIA from digging into TRENCOR for the next year?"

"They won't be a problem. They are focusing on other areas right now. We do have a potential problem, though."

Ming stopped reading Jason Conrad's file and looked at Li Zhong. "Go on."

"I found the Air Force program manager, Georgiana Anderson, on the second floor."

Ming's body tensed. "Did she see anything?"

"I'm not sure. She came off the elevator and before she was able to fully round the corner, I stopped her."

"If she becomes a problem, you know what to do."

"Yes, Mr. Ming."

Ming returned to the files. His eyes danced across the page. "This file is fascinating. The assassin, he was a Russian agent?"

"Yes," Li Zhong said. "He was killed. He . . ." Li Zhong paused, thinking of what to say next. "We believe he was a mole activated to kill Senator Bowman."

Ming looked up and started to speak, but stopped. Returning to the file, he continued to sift back and forth for more information. "There is a mystery girl mentioned. Do we know who she is?"

Shaking his head, Li Zhong said, "No. There is no evidence she existed. Some speculation in the media, but nothing concrete. If she did exist, she's been wiped off the map."

Ming nodded and rose from the couch, walking over to the bar on the other side of the room. He opened an eighteen-year-old bottle of single-malt Glenlivet Scotch and poured three fingers with ice. Silently, he offered one to Li Zhong, who shook his head. Ming took a small sip, and the elegantly sublime whiskey rolled over his tongue and down his throat. Smiling, he lifted the glass to observe the translucent caramel liquid clinging to the sides of the glass and pooling back at the bottom until he took his next sip.

"There is a significant risk in bringing such a high-profile individual like Jason Conrad into our plan," Ming said, "but I'm afraid it is my only course of action right now. What do you think?"

Li Zhong looked back at Ming, "The risk is high. But in the interests of TRENCOR Industries, it is a risk we must take."

"But what if he starts to nose around? What if he starts to ask questions he shouldn't be asking?"

"That's why I'm here," Li Zhong said. "If he becomes a problem, I know what to do with him, too."

15

HIS FOOTSTEPS ECHOED on the marble floor of the empty corridor. There were never many people in the Dacha Complex, a small building west of the main building at Yasenevo, the old KGB headquarters southwest of Moscow. Nikolai Gregarin breezed past his secretary and stepped into the large office he occupied as the Chief Directorate of Illegals. This Directorate also contained Section Nine, the secret section of the GRU that specialized in training moles as assassins.

Putting on his round spectacles, he placed the DVD in the machine and turned on the television in his spacious office. Having just returned to Moscow, it had been the first opportunity to review the recording since his intelligence team found it days ago.

The face on the screen caught his attention. Dane Robinson, TV news reporter out of Tulsa, Oklahoma. The man who, in the aftermath of the failed assassination attempt on Senator Jonathan Bowman, had unwittingly helped cover up Section Nine's involvement.

Nikolai watched the television with great interest. Captain Jason Conrad was back in the news again. Six years ago, Section Nine had targeted Senator Jonathan Bowman for assassination. Bowman had been favored to win both the Republican nomination and the presidency. Russia wanted to keep the incumbent in place for another four years because Bowman would have interfered with the overthrow of Russia's capitalist leadership.

The son of Senator Bowman was the key reason their plot had failed. Jason Conrad had somehow discovered their mole and tracked him to San Antonio. At first, Nikolai suspected it was sloppy work on the mole's part, but in retrospect, it had been blind luck. No one knew He was the senator's son, and the odds against the target's son being friends with the assassin were astronomical. Nikolai's mole in America did a poor job keeping him informed of the situation as it developed. Thankfully, he had an observer in place, and as the plan fell apart, the observer was able to terminate the assassin and return safely to Mother Russia.

The secretary walked into the office and handed him a glass half-filled with vodka.

"Thank you," he said as he took the glass, his gaze not moving from the television.

His mind raced, fighting ghosts of the past and contemplating the future. Jason Conrad had essentially dropped off the radar for the past five years. While he'd proved himself to be a thorn in Nikolai's side, he ceased to be a priority as the realities of geopolitics overcame his anger.

The broadcast ended; Nikolai gazed at the floor, deep in thought. A strategy was forming in his mind. He walked to the door and poked his head through, looking at his secretary.

"Yes, Comrade Gregarin?"

"Have Major Vodianova come to my office."

NIKOLAI STEPPED IN THE DOORWAY and looked at his secretary, then did a double-take at the couch, where Irena sat wearing a brown skirt and tan-colored blouse.

"Major," he said, "I did not know you were here. Please come in." He shot his secretary a stern glare, but she never looked up from her computer screen. Irena walked into Nikolai's office, ignoring her as she passed.

"Please, come sit," he said, motioning to a leather chair in the room. "Can I get you a drink?"

"Nyet."

Irena sat in the leather chair, and Nikolai sat behind his desk.

"How have you been? Has your schedule kept you busy?"

"I've been fine, Comrade. Bored since the Philippines job, but I understand my inactivity was necessary." The job in the Philippines was her most recent hit, over a year ago. She had posed as a missionary's wife and had barely escaped the island nation following the assassination of an IMF deputy secretary.

Nikolai stood and moved over to her. He pointed his finger and poked it against the side of her head.

"I need to know what's going on in there," he said as she stared straight ahead. "It's important, because if this isn't working," he said, "you cannot control this."

He moved his hand from her head and laid it on her breast, over her heart. Irena did not flinch. Nikolai was such a pervert. He'd taken every opportunity to grope every woman in the section since he'd taken over. He even flew all the way to Manila last year just to try to bed her there.

"The heart must be kept in check in this line of work," he said, now cupping her left breast. "Are you capable of doing that Major?"

"Yes, Comrade. You know what I am capable of."

"Very good," he said, removing his hand from her breast, but brushing his thumb across her nipple in the process. "I have a special assignment for you. I want to be sure you can handle it."

"I'm ready, Comrade Gregarin. I've never refused an assignment before."

"This is true," he said. "I'm pleased with your attitude because Jason Conrad is back in the news. More importantly, he's received an assignment to the Edwards Air Force Base Flight Test Center in California."

Irena's heart fluttered, and for the first time, she slowly turned her head and gaped at Nikolai. Images flashed through her mind like an old, silent movie, only in vivid color. Over the years, she had been able to compartmentalize this part of her life. But suddenly, thoughts of the man she fell in love with years ago burst back into her consciousness. Could he be asking what she thought? The two sat in silence for a few moments studying each other.

"Yes, my dear," Nikolai said, "it is time to raise Kathy Delgato from the dead!"

16

April 24, 2001

J ASON SAT ALONE in the Officers' Club, sipping on a beer with
stacks of paper spread across the table. He'd made two phone calls.
The first call had been to his father to seek advice on his new
assignment. Jonathan Bowman was patient with his son and interested
in this new development in his career. They weren't able to talk long.
His father was boarding a plane from Las Vegas to Arizona.

The second call was to an old friend. The phone rang three times
before it picked up.

"Jason, how are you doing?" Caldwell said.

Jason grinned when the familiar voice of Aaron Caldwell came over
the line. Caldwell was the CIA agent who followed a Russian spy from
Moscow to Enid six years ago. Caldwell's partner had been killed, and
Caldwell himself had been shot but had survived, thanks to Jason. It
must have been fate because he met his wife in the hospital. Nancy
had been his nurse his entire time in the hospital, and they hadn't been
apart since he'd been released.

"Great! I wanted to give you a heads-up. I'll be leaving Enid
veryshortly."

"How soon?"

"Next Friday."

"Wow! You piss somebody off, or are we just the last ones to
know?"

The waitress brought Jason another beer. She set it on the table as
he talked on the phone.

"Neither. I found out Monday. Some of the guys are having a going
away party for me at the O Club Wednesday night."

"Is this move a good thing?"

Jason explained how he got the assignment.

"Isn't that kind of odd?" Caldwell said.

"Yeah, but there have been these kind of assignments before."

"I mean, you're going to the home of the Air Force test program, but you're not going to be a test pilot. Just seems strange."

Jason said nothing. The way Caldwell put it, it *did* sound kind of strange.

GEORGIANA SAT THROUGH the meeting at the 445th Flight Test Squadron most of the morning, but couldn't concentrate. Her curiosity had been wreaking havoc on her mind for the last several days. She had not stopped thinking about her run-in with Li Zhong on the second floor of the TRENCOR facility five days ago. What happened to the second floor? The building was supposed to be complete. Was there a design flaw causing them to gut everything and start over? Was it a safety issue? Water? Electricity?

It was odd—the reception area was pristine and finished, yet as soon as she rounded the corner, the entire floor seemed incomplete. When the meeting ended, Georgiana stood, gathered her things, and headed to her office.

"Georgiana, you want to join us for lunch?"

The deep, raspy voice belonged to Brent O'Malley, the aeronautical engineer for the F-2000 project. She remained fascinated by his voice. It was inviting, confident, and friendly, which usually conflicted with the nervous and inconsistent words that came out of his mouth. She smiled at him warmly as he pushed his black horn-rimmed glasses up the bridge of his nose. Brent had been a project of hers for years. It had taken a full year to get him to stop wearing concert T-shirts and sandals to work. He'd now resigned himself to an unbuttoned flannel shirt over a Star Wars or comic book T-shirt and beat-up tennis shoes. Georgiana sighed to herself as she noticed his uncombed hair hanging over the top of his glasses.

"Thanks, Brent, but I'm in the middle of something I need to finish."

"Yeah, I've noticed you're busy lately," Brent said, eyeing the stacks of folders on Georgiana's desk.

"I've got some questions about something. It's not a big deal—I just need to wrap my head around it."

"Okay," Brent said, rubbing his fingers along the sides of his beard.

"I made cookies for you boys," Georgiana said, pointing to a plate

of cookies on her desk. Georgiana had become the self-appointed
mother hen of the civilian branch of the 445th. She was always baking
or babysitting, contacting spouses, or, in Brent's case, assisting with
self-improvement.

He reached over and grabbed two. "Thank you, Georgiana. You're
a sweetheart. This is my pot of gold at the end of the rainbow."

"It's my pleasure, Brent. Someone has to look after you boys."

"I'll see you later. We'll get the rest of the cookies after lunch."
Brent left the office grinning as he munched on a cookie. She moved
behind her desk and dug through the stack of folders. Finding the one
she searched for, she riffled through it and pulled out several packets
of paper. Unfolding one of the stacks, she saw the floor plans for the
TRENCOR facility in California City. Spreading the first plan across
her desk, she opened the other two, and placed them on top. Grabbing
a box of tacks out of her desk, she pinned the floor plans to her office
wall.

She stepped back and studied each set of plans. Something wasn't
right. Clearly, the second floor didn't match the plans. What about the
third floor? Her instincts kicked in. Why were they only allowed in
certain parts of the building? Why did they say construction was
complete when the second floor was barren? What were they hiding?
Faulty construction? Corporate secrets? What could be more secret
than the project they were working on? The official walk-through was
scheduled for two months from now. Contractually, TRENCOR
didn't have to let them see anything, despite the fact that the US
government paid for this building. Another move that made her mad
at her superiors.

Never pay in advance.

Carefully, she processed what she knew about each floor and how
much she had not yet seen. Based off her rough visual calculations, the
Air Force had accessed maybe fifteen percent of the building. Why?
What would they want to hide from the Air Force? The more she
studied the plans, the more questions came up. She reviewed the
contracts between TRENCOR and the Air Force. After hours of
relentless research, the corners of her mouth began edging upward.
The puzzle pieces started to take shape.

She needed to get back into the building.

SAMSON SAT ON THE COUCH in his home. Surrounded by
large pictures of the numerous jets he'd flown, he lay back in his
recliner, clutching a small picture frame containing his wedding

picture. Samson watched the television, half paying attention, half sipping on a bottle of Jeremiah Weed. "Weed" is the preferred toasting whiskey of F-15 pilots everywhere. It is an acquired taste, but no respectable Eagle driver would be caught without a bottle of Weed in their freezer.

Samson married his college sweetheart before he went to pilot training, but she left him when he moved to Edwards. The truth was he loved his jet more than he loved his wife. They had different goals, and rather than fight about it for the next twenty years, she cut him loose. It was for the best. He'd gotten to the point where he was marginalizing her, and it ripped their relationship apart. She made sacrifices, she said; now, it was time for him to make a few. He refused. His goal was to be a test pilot, and her sacrifices didn't change that. The divorce was as fast and uncomplicated as their marriage.

His problem was that he began to realize what it was like to be lonely. Meeting women wasn't as easy as he remembered in college. Samson chose to solve the problem through the bottom of a bottle. It didn't talk back, it didn't leave him, and it didn't make him stop flying.

Distraught with the loneliness consuming him, he turned off the television. Curt Samson, F-15 Fighter Pilot and Test Pilot, sat in the darkness of his living room alone, swigging from a bottle of Weed.

SHERRI SLAVED AWAY at her keyboard. For days he watched her search the Internet, make phone calls, and follow up on leads. Her cubicle looked like a bomb had gone off inside. Scraps of paper were tacked to the sides, and she had strings running from pictures to articles and back again.

Steven meandered up to her desk, shaking his head. "I like what you've done to the place," he said, reviewing her display of seemingly unrelated information.

"Don't tease me. It breaks my concentration."

"Why the obsession with this again?" he said, more for conversation than for an answer.

"I don't know." She stopped pecking at her keyboard and turned to face him. "Aside from watching our informant get gunned down in broad daylight in New York City two days ago, it strikes me odd these men show up in our country and bounce from place to place.

"More concerning is when they start showing up around flight schools, simulators, and military bases. They get 'training', but never get 'fully trained.' It's more personal now that I've been shot at while doing this investigation."

Steven understood the last comment. Sherri had a nose for these types of stories. It was what brought her to *The Times*. He'd been her editor for five years and had grown attached to her. Too young to be a father figure and too old to be a romantic interest, Steven settled on being a mentor. In this role, their relationship blossomed. But as her mentor, he also felt like her protector, and this story was getting dangerous.

He put his hand on her shoulder. "It's not too late to consider that TV news bit FOX offered you."

Sherri shook her head. "I want to be an investigative journalist. While I appreciate the compliment, it's not what I want to do. I want to find and write the stories, not read someone else's work on camera."

"I understand," he said. "Any follow-up on the bullets from Pensacola?"

Sherri swung back around to face her computer screen and clicked on an article. "The 10 millimeter was designed in response to a shootout in Miami where the cops were outgunned by the bad guys. It was initially used by some cops and feds, but eventually fell out of favor as more and more folks moved to the .40 Smith & Wesson. Apparently, the 10 millimeter had too much kick for the average shooter."

"Anything else?"

"No. You can buy 10 millimeter weapons and ammo anywhere, but it's not a weapon of choice."

"Is it still in use in any inventories?"

"Can't tell. I'll need a serious data-dive of each specific agency to find out."

Steven moved to the side of her desk, where she could see him.

"Well, in the meantime, I have an assignment for you," he said, handing her a piece of paper. "Some of our Saudi targets purchased a plane ticket to California this morning. You leave for Los Angeles on Tuesday."

Sherri smiled. "Now you're talking."

Steven smiled back, but his heart wasn't in it. He felt like he was putting her in danger again.

17

SEVEN YEARS AGO, Irena/Kathy had embedded herself in America, awaiting activation. When the mole ordered to assassinate Jonathan Bowman was deemed unstable, the Russian leadership grew nervous, and Kathy was activated to take him out and stop the assassination.

Now she sat outside of Nikolai's office, ready to go over her next mission. Who was the target? Nikolai had only mentioned Jason Conrad, and the Section Nine team had spent days re-establishing the life and existence of Kathy Delgato. For six years, she had been able to bury her feelings for Jason. She'd fallen in love with him, but their romance was cut short when she was activated to save his father's life. Of course, she had to disappear afterward, and she had been convinced their romance was never to be. Yet here was Nikolai sending her on a mission that reignited those feelings. Was this on purpose? Nikolai had pursued her for years, but she successfully deflected his advances.

Nikolai directed her to wear something Conrad would like. Irena knew what he meant. Sexy. The miniskirt, tank top, and high heels were a start.

The phone on Nikolai's secretary's desk rang, and she turned to Irena. "Comrade Gregarin is ready to see you now," she said, going back to her computer screen.

Irena nodded and marched into Nikolai's office. He glanced up from his desk, a look of joyful anticipation on his face. It wasn't a "happy to see you" smile, it was one of those smiles a man has when he sees something he wants and is willing to do whatever it takes to get it.

"Sit, Irena," he said, motioning to the leather chair by his desk. He swiveled in his chair and watched her sit, smiling the whole time. "You are beautiful. Jason Conrad will not be able to resist."

Irena sat in the chair with her hands clasped in her lap. Not wanting to play Nikolai's games, she took the initiative.

"And how long after I seduce him will I have to kill him?" she said.

The smile fell from his face momentarily, then crept back on.

"Oh, my dear, fear not. Jason Conrad is not your target. Not your ultimate target. You only need him to reach your target."

She bit her lower lip slightly and looked up inquisitively. Nikolai, done with his drooling, leaned back in his chair and sifted through papers on his desk.

"Your ultimate target, my dear, is Jason's father, former senator and presidential candidate Jonathan Bowman."

Irena's eyes grew wide, but she said nothing. Her target was now the man she saved six years ago. The father of the one man she'd loved in her life.

"I don't understand, Comrade," she said. "We went to a great deal of trouble to save his life in San Antonio. I was almost killed."

"Jonathan Bowman is currently the executive vice president of Century Aero-Bot, a leading innovator in aerospace technology. His company is developing technology twenty years ahead of the rest of the world."

"But he's no scientist—he's a politician."

"Yes, but he has turned a struggling defense subcontractor into the most profitable defense contractor in the world over the last two years. They are leading America's resurging military industrial complex."

"Why involve Jason Conrad? Why don't I simply kill Bowman?"

"Your mission, Irena, is twofold. First, you gather intelligence. The KGB has picked up conversations from low-level Aero-Bot employees on something called the 'Lima Project.' We're not sure what the project entails, but it is extremely sensitive and highly classified."

"Perhaps it's a red herring to ferret out informers," she said.

"Possible, but not likely," Nikolai said. "When you've gathered the information on this 'Lima Project,' you are to kill Bowman."

Irena/Kathy stared blankly and nodded, the complications of killing the father of the man she loved swirling in her head.

THE BLISTERING SUN BEAT down on the flat, deserted runway. The heat wasn't as unbearable as it was insidious. In the distance, the horizon rippled back and forth, nature playing tricks with the eye. The sky was a clear blue, and the twelve men and three women were the only human beings for miles. This was the beauty of the Yuma Proving Grounds—perhaps more isolated than any other test area outside Area 51. The Yuma Proving Ground, over 1,300 square miles of empty desert and airspace, sat thirty miles northeast of Yuma, Arizona, with nothing but the mountains on the horizon and the numerous cacti to keep them company.

Not that the small team had time to take in the sights. They worked feverishly underneath a group of canopies pulled together. Several large generators hummed as they provided power to the large array of equipment set up under the canopies. A lone F-16 with no tail flash or markings of any kind sat on the ramp. Its pilot rested in a fold-out chair under one of the canopies, his flight suit unzipped to his waist, sipping on a bottle of water.

One of the men looked up and stopped his work. He stepped from his desk and shuffled through the soft sand toward the jet, searching the far end of the runway. Despite wearing sunglasses, he needed his hands to shield his eyes from the sun, the reflection on the desert sand making his Ray-Bans futile. In the distance, dust whirled against the ground, and slowly, the shape of two vehicles started to form. "They're here!" the man said as he jogged back to his desk.

The pilot rose from his chair, zipped up, and proceeded to put on his g-suit. Several electrodes protruded from the top of his flight suit. Grabbing his helmet bag, he stepped to the F-16, followed by three other members of the team. The pilot reached the jet when the two vehicles were within a hundred yards of their position. The two dusty Chevy Suburbans pulled off the runway and moved near the other vehicles parked by the canopies.

A portly gentleman with scraggly hair and a matching beard left the canopy's shade and headed toward the SUVs. Doctor Brian Foster was the lead neurologist for the project and had worked for Century Aero-Bot for the last four years. The heat of the sun hit him at once, and he looked forward to retreating back under the canopy.

Four men climbed out of each of the vehicles, but seven of them moved behind the well-dressed man who stepped out of the first vehicle. He was older, perhaps in his mid-fifties, lean, and stood about six-two. One of the men behind him handed him a bottle of water, which he drank quickly. The man the team had waited for to start their test was the executive vice president of Century Aero-Bot—former senator and presidential candidate Jonathan Bowman.

Doctor Foster approached the men as they walked toward the canopies. "Good Morning, Senator Bowman. How was the trip from Vegas?"

"Good morning, Doctor. It was a fine trip," Bowman said. The former senator shook hands with the portly physician. "What's our status?"

"We're ready to begin."

"Then let's get started." The group moved under the canopies as the pilot climbed up the ladder and strapped into the jet. "This could be a major step in the evolution of Century Aero-Bot," Bowman said.

"We have several tests to run today, sir," Doctor Foster said, paying less attention to the guests and more attention to the computer monitors on his desk.

"I'm aware of all the tests, doctor. You know which one I want to see."

"Yes, sir. That comes fifteen minutes into the flight."

"Excellent. It will put Century Aero-Bot on the map for military aviation."

"Yes, sir," Foster said. Typical executive. There was a lot of money riding on this test today. Company insiders were aware that if this technology worked as advertised today, they would be heading to Edwards AFB to integrate it into a top-secret project in development there . . . if the money was right.

Remotely Piloted Aircraft had been around for decades. Century Aero-Bot's was different in the sense that the RPA could accomplish two feats not yet developed by anyone else. First, the ground controller could take automatic control of the aircraft, overriding the manual pilot. This technology was relatively easy to integrate; the uniqueness of it was they could now fly the aircraft from anywhere on the planet. The second test, which was more valuable to the company, was the Sensory Integration Package (SIP). The SIP could detect a pilot who had g-locked or was otherwise incapacitated and internally activate the RPA control and fly itself back home. A device called the Integrated Thought Control System, or ITCS, was responsible for that aspect of the jet.

The engine on the F-16 came to life as the pilot continued with his preflight checks. Five minutes later, the crew chief and other personnel moved away from the jet.

"CAB Zero One is ready for takeoff," the pilot said over the radio, which was broadcast over a speaker system under the canopies.

"CAB Zero One, you are cleared Oscar/Charlie, surface to 40,000 feet. Cleared for takeoff," the radio operator sitting under the canopy replied.

The pilot waved to his crew chief, looked at the end of the runway, and released the brakes. He pushed his throttle into afterburner, and the engine exhaust widened as the fuel system dumped more jet fuel into the engine. A flame shot out ten feet behind the jet. The pilot would get the "kick in the pants" as the jet leaped forward and rapidly accelerated on the runway. The group under the canopies watched the jet leave the ground, raise its gear, and level for several seconds at about fifty feet. Suddenly, the pilot pulled the nose of the jet up, and it shot through the sky to around 10,000 feet.

"Okay, people," Doctor Foster said to his test team. "As soon as he's done showing off, let's get this started."

18

April 25, 2001

THE LEAD ATTORNEY STOOD on the back porch reviewing the contract for the twentieth time, her two associates standing silently behind her. It had been a long, hard negotiation with Caleb Nelson, but they'd eventually reached a compromise. The ink was still wet on the contract, but she was satisfied. This was a great deal of money for a single farmer from Haskell County, Kansas. Caleb Nelson was a pencil-thin, forty-eight-year-old divorcé whose wife left him four years prior, taking both of his children and their entire life savings with her. The only thing he had left was the farm and his equipment. Caleb had not seen or heard from them since.

He did not have enough money to lease the service his family had used to plant and retrieve their corn. Most of his employees had left and found work elsewhere. Caleb had missed the entire season that year, mainly due to depression and drinking. Close friends worked with him and managed to gather enough money for Caleb to plant his corn the next season. He managed to make enough to repay his friends, cover his expenses, and set aside enough for the next season. But he no longer loved his life as a farmer.

Caleb Nelson's family had held this property for over a hundred and fifty years, and he'd just sold it to total strangers. The lead attorney observed Caleb sitting contentedly on the porch, rocking back and forth in his grandfather's rocking chair for the last time. Caleb had a subtle grin hiding under an untrimmed mustache. As he stared across the empty field, he reached into his shirt pocket and pulled out a worn pack of Camel cigarettes. His wiry fingers removed the last cigarette, and after he crumpled up the pack, he tossed it over the small table next to his chair. Reaching in his pants pocket, he removed a faded Bic lighter and lit the cigarette on the third click. Acrid smoke filled the air as he puffed away on the cigarette, content with this new direction in his life.

The attorney, who represented the buyer, slipped her copy of the contract in her briefcase. Her clients had made Caleb a multimillionaire. They'd purchased 2,500 acres of land for fifteen million dollars, an obscene amount of money for unirrigated farmland, roughly six times what it was worth. It was an all-inclusive price for the land, the house, and the farming equipment, but Caleb didn't care. He wanted none of this. Caleb was ready to move on—south, to the Bahamas.

The buyer was more than generous; the only stipulation was payment would be via electronic transfer to an account set up for Caleb Nelson in the Cayman Islands. Caleb had gone into Dodge City and acquired an attorney himself to oversee his portion of the transaction. Dan Fitzpatrick, Caleb's attorney, stood to his right, his coffee-stained teeth bursting out of his smile as he tucked away his copy of the contract. Fitzpatrick, still smiling, glanced up at Caleb.

"Well, Caleb, you're a rich man," he said, slapping him on the back. Fitzpatrick placed his copy of the contract in his briefcase and clicked the clasp closed.

"Mr. Fitzpatrick, I just made you a rich man, too," Caleb said without changing his gaze.

"Fair enough," Fitzpatrick said, reaching to shake his client's hand. Caleb looked toward him briefly and stuck out his hand.

"Ms. Rieffelming, it's been a pleasure doing business with you." The two attorneys shook hands. She didn't care for Dan Fitzpatrick. He was a small-time shyster and a crook, but he was the best Caleb could find. Amanda Johnston Rieffelming and her team had done the legwork. They'd written the contract, established Nelson's Cayman account, and guided Fitzpatrick and Caleb through the entire process. Caleb didn't want his ex-wife to find out about the sale until he was in the Bahamas, and Fitzpatrick had no reservations about signing the confidentiality clause. Not for this kind of money. The hundred-thousand dollar bonus he received beforehand helped.

"I won't miss that son of a bitch when I move to the Bahamas," Caleb said as Fitzpatrick slithered off the porch.

Amanda said nothing as she watched Fitzpatrick saunter to his car and drive off the premises. She noted the long line of construction equipment lining the highway—all unmanned except for one. The lone backhoe's diesel engine roared to life as Fitzpatrick drove off, and the yellow Caterpillar lumbered toward the field in the back of the house. Overhead, traces of clouds dotted the empty sky as a wall of nature's fury pushed its way from the west.

She handed the contract to her associate, a plain-looking Asian woman who wore no makeup and had hair straight past her shoulders. Amanda moved over and stood by Caleb Nelson in his rocking chair. She buttoned her jacket across her waist, covering the slight pudgy roll pushing its way over her skirt.

Caleb stood from his rocking chair and watched the backhoe move into the field. He glanced at Amanda. "Is this real? Is this really happening?"

"Yes, Mr. Nelson, it's real. Congratulations."

"Who do you work for?"

"I'm sorry, Mr. Nelson—you know I can't disclose that information. Rest assured your money is in the bank."

Caleb took a long drag of his cigarette, blew the smoke over his head, and bit his lower lip with a nervousness he could not hide. "I'm not sure I did the right thing."

"Mr. Nelson, we just put fifteen million dollars in your account in the Cayman Islands. Trust me, you did the right thing."

Caleb took another drag of the cigarette and flicked the remainder into the yard. "I always said I'd quit smoking these one day."

Amanda observed him without much sympathy. "It's a tough habit to quit."

Caleb reached into his coat pocket, withdrew a Monte Cristo cigar, and bit off the tip. "I've always wanted to smoke a fancy cee-gar. Now I can afford 'em," he said, lighting the cigar with the faded Bic.

"If you are going to smoke expensive cigars, Mr. Nelson, I would invest in a trimmer and a torch."

Caleb looked at her, crossing his arms. "A what and a what?"

"Never mind," she said. Amanda remained standing, as did her two associates, watching the backhoe make its way across the lawn. The loud motor squealed like a sick sow as it crept on its treads.

The backhoe stopped in front of the family burial plot about a hundred yards from the back of the house and started digging. Amanda watched Caleb Nelson tense up. "What the hell is that guy doing? You folks ain't supposed to dig around the family plot! It's in the contract!"

Amanda replied stoically, "It's not your property anymore, Mr. Nelson." The backhoe dug another scoop of dirt and dumped it to the side.

"Well, it's a damn violation of the contract," he shouted. "Do something!" Nelson was fuming as the backhoe scooped out several more buckets of soil. Amanda didn't budge. "What about one of you damn robots?" he said, staring past Amanda at her two associates. "One of you two want to be my lawyer so I can sue the hell out of Ms. Rieffelming's client?" The male associate moved into the house and opened his laptop on the kitchen table. "What the hell are you doing? Get the hell out of my house!"

"It's not your house, Mr. Nelson. It's not your property. If you feel there's a violation of the contract, have your attorney contact us. We'll see you in court . . . in about three years. And after your ex-wife knows where to find you in the Bahamas."

Amanda was no longer smiling. She gazed at the backhoe while Nelson yelled at the male associate in the kitchen. After a minute, Nelson came storming back onto the porch, carrying a portable telephone.

"Three years, my ass! I'll take care of this right now. I'll call the damn sheriff. We went to school together from kindergarten through high school. He'll shut down this operation right now." Nelson dialed feverishly several times with no luck or dial tone. "What the hell did you do? You cut off my phone?"

"It's not your phone, Mr. Nelson," Amanda replied. "The service was disconnected as soon as the contract was signed."

Nelson threw the phone at the window on the porch, shattering the glass into tiny fragments. Amanda stared at the broken window for a moment and turned back toward Caleb. "That's not your window either, Mr. Nelson."

"I'll buy you a new one," he screamed. "What the hell are y'all doing? The damn ink isn't even dry on this contract, and y'all are violating it. I'm no damn lawyer, but I'm smart enough to know you can't do that."

"Why do you care, Mr. Nelson? You're moving to the Bahamas. You have no family here. There's nothing that should concern you."

"What concerns me is my family burial plot that your guy is digging up. The family burial plot that was supposed to be left alone according to the contract. Screw the Bahamas. I've got fifteen million dollars I can play with before I go. I'll expose your whole damn company to the media. No, ma'am. You stop this right now, or I'll blow the lid off of whatever you folks are doing here."

Amanda looked at him with a blank expression. "What do you

mean, Mr. Nelson?"

Caleb stood in front of Amanda and took a long draw on his cigar. He glanced at Amanda's associates and then at the backhoe digging near the cemetery. "I know I look like an ass-backwards redneck who doesn't have a lick of sense, but I'm no fool. And when some city slicker comes and offers me more money than my land is worth, I start to wonder. And I did some checking. You folks are buying up all kind of land around here. That's why I asked for more money. Didn't think I'd get it, but hell, here we are."

"We know, Mr. Nelson," Amanda said. "We've been following your investigation for some time now."

Caleb paused and searched her eyes. Amanda stared back expressionlessly, tired of the conversation. "Mr. Nelson, you made a good point. You *are* an 'ass-backwards redneck.' You're not *smart* enough to take down my clients, and you're not *man* enough to stop my construction team."

His eyes bulged from their sockets, and the sullen man from the last four weeks of negotiation no longer existed. "I don't need no damn sheriff. I'll stop this crap myself." Caleb Nelson leaped off the porch and marched out toward the backhoe. Amanda watched the skinny millionaire stride out to the noisy diesel, throwing his Monte Cristo cigar into the grass, and she slid to the doorway. "Go ahead," she said to the male associate who sat behind his laptop in the kitchen. He grabbed another bag from the floor, removed a small umbrella-shaped satellite link, and plugged its cord into his laptop.

Amanda heard the diesel engine shut off, and she moved back onto the porch. She stood next to the female associate, who had said nothing up to this point. "It is better this way," the Asian woman said in halting English. "He has found out too much information."

Amanda said nothing as she watched Caleb wave his arms and yell at the driver of the backhoe. She hoped it wouldn't get to this point, but her team had concluded early on that Caleb was a lit fuse. She watched the driver climb down the large machine. The driver stood at least a foot taller than Caleb, whose hand motions stopped once he recognized the size difference. The two stood there for a several moments. The driver pulled out a pistol and shot Caleb twice in the chest. He staggered backward, wounded and confused. The driver took aim and fired another shot in his forehead. Caleb was dead before his body fell into the hole the driver had been digging. The driver climbed back onto the backhoe and fired up the engine. Methodically, he filled the hole, covering the body of Caleb Nelson.

Amanda walked into the kitchen. The male associate typed a few more keystrokes into the computer. "It's done," he said, unplugging the satellite link and flipping the laptop closed. "The program will begin a gradual deduction of his account to a myriad of our front companies starting tonight and continuing over the next two months. By the time someone starts to notice Caleb Nelson is missing, he won't have a cent left in his account."

The lead attorney nodded and inclined her head to the Asian associate. The woman pulled out her cell phone and made a call, muttering words that could only be heard on the other end of the phone. The male associate joined them at the door.

"Here you go, Mr. Nelson," Amanda said, handing him Caleb's plane ticket. He would fly to the Bahamas and check in to the hotel as Caleb Nelson. He'd spend a lot of money for two weeks, then he would simply vanish. "Enjoy your trip to the Bahamas. Okay, let's get this place locked up."

The three of them moved through the house, securing the doors and windows and gathering any paperwork relating to the purchase. Amanda instructed the driver to place plywood over the broken window before he left the property. It was a precautionary measure; in three weeks, they would burn the house to the ground. The official story would be that vandals set the house on fire before the new owners had a chance to move in.

They moved out onto the back porch, where Amanda gazed across the field at the backhoe filling in the impromptu grave. The Kansas farmland darkened rapidly as the afternoon sun gave way to clouds, like sheets of gray-blue cotton balls pulled overhead. A wall of streaking, dark gray rain developed on the horizon and steadily marched toward the farm once owned by Caleb Nelson.

19

April 27, 2001

THE SUN HOVERED over the peaks of the southern edge of the Sequoia National Forest, the small mountain range to the west. Gloria's Mexican Restaurant in California City was empty except for two men who sat at a table far from the entrance. The lunch crowd had come and gone, and it was too early for supper. Jeremiah Wellington sat at the table nursing a frozen margarita. Daniel Kirby had accompanied him to the meeting and chose to have a margarita on the rocks as he nibbled on chips and salsa.

A large black Suburban pulled into the parking lot, and three men stepped out, moving toward the front door. "They're here," Wellington said. The three men entered the restaurant, and one of the younger ones stayed by the door. Obviously a bodyguard.

Wellington and Kirby stood as the two men approached the table, and Wellington extended his hand. "Senator Bowman, welcome to Southern California. I hope your trip was reasonable." Bowman shook hands with Wellington. "This is Daniel Kirby, project manager for our jet."

"Good afternoon, Senator," Kirby said, shaking hands with the former presidential hopeful. The three men sat down. Bowman's second man positioned himself ten feet from the table.

"Senator, I'm not sure if you've heard, but your son has been assigned to our test team," Wellington said.

Bowman's eyes squinted, and his lips tightened. "Is this an attempt to sway my position on this sale?"

"What? No, no. He's a fine pilot. Hand-picked to come here as our test candidate."

Wellington had a hard time reading the senator. He leaned back in his chair and took a sip of his margarita.

"I'll be brief. We know why I'm here. The test results at Yuma were successful. The RPA systems exceeded our expectations."

"That's great news," Wellington said.

Kirby leaned forward and in a hushed tone asked, "What about the Sensory Integration Package?"

"It worked fine. Keeping the electrodes connected to the pilot has its challenges, but the software integrated itself into the aircraft very well."

Wellington beamed. "So, do we have a deal? TRENCOR Industries would like to purchase the RPA/SIP package Century Aero-Bot has developed. The ITCS is key to our sixth-generation fighter jet."

"We have a deal, but we aren't selling you proprietary rights to the RPA/SIP. We own it. We will provide ten separate units for the test program. Century Aero-Bot will service it in your aircraft and simulators. The two companies can sign the contract tonight, and I'll have my people deliver the units tomorrow. We'll have the system installed in your simulator over the weekend, and you'll be up and running on Monday. If not, I have another buyer."

Wellington winced and leaned back in his chair. He knew Ming wouldn't be happy about this. Century Aero-Bot had built a unique system. Compact, easy to install, and easily integrated into the digital thrust and control system contained in the F-2000. The system would simply be mounted in the electronics bay, installed via cannon plugs between the digital control system and the aircraft mission computers. The largest portion was an additional satellite dish for uplink, which integrated into the jet's GPS system.

"That's not the idea my superiors at TRENCOR had in mind. A technology this advanced needs to be kept secret. You can't be selling this to anyone in the aerospace industry. *We* need to own this!"

Bowman leaned forward. "Mr. Wellington, I served as a US senator. I ran for the Republican nomination for president of the United States. Don't attempt to lecture me."

"Senator, don't take this wrong. I'm trying to sort this out in my head." It was time to re-engage the charm offensive. Bowman's demands threw him off his game. The trademark toothy grin returned as he leaned away from the table in a less aggressive posture. He started to speak, but Bowman beat him to it.

"The reality is, Mr. Wellington, your company has already been paid by the government for this technology. You've promised something, and now you've got to deliver. Your project is two years behind schedule. I'm not sure how many billions of dollars your company is over budget. I quit counting the last time you added another zero. You need this technology." He pulled out a piece of paper and slid it across the table. "Here's the terms and the price. The lawyers have drawn up the paperwork and are ready to send it to your new office building." Bowman stood and buttoned his sport coat. "Good day, Mr. Wellington. Mr. Kirby, it was a pleasure meeting you."

"Likewise," Kirby said.

Bowman turned to leave, and the bodyguard who stood by the table followed. When they reached the door, Wellington said, "Senator, your son is part of our team now. He'll fly this jet one day." It was a weak attempt at a veiled threat. Wellington regretted the words as soon as they came out. He had been defeated and was lashing out. It was a poor technique.

Pausing, Bowman turned back to the two men who still sat at the table. "I know. And you should be aware, Mr. Wellington, that his welfare will be your responsibility."

Wellington took a sip of his margarita and said, "Don't worry, Senator, we'll take good care of him."

Bowman's eyes locked on to Wellington's. "Yes, you will."

Wellington felt a twinge of dread as he watched Bowman and his bodyguards leave the restaurant and climb into the SUV. Bowman was sharp and didn't waste the opportunity to let Wellington know he'd spoken inappropriately. He turned to Kirby. "Well, that didn't go as expected."

"Mr. Ming won't be happy," Kirby replied. "I mean, the project will move forward, but he won't like them sticking their noses everywhere."

"Yeah," Wellington said. "Something about that exchange seemed too odd. Let's follow them. I've got a hunch."

THE PUDGY ATTORNEY sat across from him in the private conference room at Love Field in Dallas. Chris Maddox had worked in the drilling business for twenty years and had never come across a deal like this. This woman represented a corporation that wanted fifteen different water wells dug on properties sprawling over 200,000 acres across northwest Texas. His first thought had been, why the hell do they want to do that? He made a bid for the job, and it wasn't cheap, but they accepted it without any attempt to negotiate better deal. His attorney reviewed the contract, looking for errors, loopholes, anything that would ultimately screw his client out of money. Nothing. The contract was clean, and Chris Maddox changed his focus from the "why" to the "how."

The contract was for fifteen wells dug with manual pumps, irrigation systems, and storage systems. His company was the driller, but they subcontracted the pump and irrigation systems out. His standard was the American-made Aermotor windmill pump systems. They were time-tested and proven, with the highest quality metallurgy. The large-capacity Aermotor Windmills could pump up to 1000 gallons of water per hour for virtually nothing since the pumps were wind-powered. The hot-dipped galvanized steel towers would last decades through all four seasons.

Chris Maddox took the paper from his attorney and scribbled his name on the bottom line. "Here you go, Miss Amanda. I'm not gonna try to pronounce your last name." He slid the paper across the table, then opened a bottle of water in front of him. She scooped up the paper and placed it in her briefcase without looking at it.

"Rieffelming. Like the gun. Rifle."

"Oh, hell," he said, smiling, "why didn't you say so? We're big firearms folks around here."

Amanda deadpanned. "We like firearms where I'm from as well, Mr. Maddox. I want to ensure that you understand the importance of speed in this project."

"Well, Miss Amanda, we understand your client wants these wells drilled as quickly as possible. My boys want to earn the bonuses the contract mentions as much as I do." They were to get a one percent bonus for each week the project finished early. By his calculations, if everything went as planned, they would finish five weeks early. "But speed is based on which drilling method we use."

"Is this going to be a problem?" she said.

Chris shook his head. "We should be able to bore our way down to the nearest water level. Shouldn't be too deep in most places, less than one hundred feet, I imagine."

"What about the areas deeper than one hundred feet?"

"We've got that covered, too," Chris said. "If we have to go deeper than one hundred feet, we'll do what's been done for a hundred years.

Process called 'mud rotary drilling.' It's a lot slower than air drilling, but it—"

"Will it get the job done?" Amanda asked, too busy to hear about the finer points of drilling.

"It'll get the job done, ma'am."

"Good. When can you start drilling?"

"Next week. No need to pull a permit in those counties. I'll get my team together. They're finishing up other jobs this week."

"And you'll be able to finish the job on time?"

Chris leaned back. "I'd say we'll be completely done in four months."

"Can't you get it done any faster?"

He shook his head as he took a swig from his water bottle. "Not without increasing the cost. I only have one drilling team. We drill the well, and then my contractor—"

"Four months will meet our timeline, Mr. Maddox. But if you can finish early, we'd appreciate it."

Chris Maddox rubbed his chin with his arms cradled across his chest. He contemplated the pudgy attorney. This project, although perfectly legal and well compensated, didn't make sense to him. "What exactly are you folks trying to do here in northwest Texas?"

"I'm not at liberty to discuss my client's plans, Mr. Maddox. My client is paying you very well. Is there a problem now that you've signed the contract?"

"No, ma'am." He was being paid three times what the job would normally pay out; he realized he'd better shut up rather than compromise the biggest score his company ever came across. Ms. Rieffelming had grown increasingly unfriendly as the conversation continued. "We appreciate your business. We'll get started as soon as we can."

Amanda Rieffelming stood up from the table, gathered her briefcase, and walked to the door. She stopped, turned, and glared back at him.

"I know you will, Mr. Maddox. If you don't, I'll be back."

20

April 27, 2001

THEY FOLLOWED BOWMAN'S SUV about eight car lengths back. The SUV pulled into the Best Western located on the eastern side of California City. Wellington pulled his vehicle to the far side of the parking lot where he could see Bowman.

As soon as Bowman stepped out of his vehicle, an elderly, silver-haired gentleman in a seersucker suit and a Middle Eastern man emerged from the back seat of a limousine. The silver-haired gentleman introduced Bowman to the Middle Eastern man, then backed up and pulled a cigar out of his coat, snipped off the end, and lit it. Shaking hands with Bowman, the two men smiled. The Middle Eastern man gestured back to the limousine and Bowman nodded and motioned for the men still in the car. Two other Middle Eastern men exited the limo and joined the small group. Bowman's bodyguards cautiously eyed the men and the surrounding area as the group ambled into the lobby of the hotel, followed by the silver-haired gentleman, his cigar billowing smoke behind him.

Pulling the car out of the parking lot, Wellington headed to TRENCOR. Neither man spoke. Both tried to decipher what they had experienced. Wellington silently replayed the meeting with Jonathan Bowman. Century Aero-Bot obviously knew the difficulties TRENCOR had fielding the F-2000 and brought Bowman on board to negotiate the contract.

He parked at TRENCOR and they entered the expansive lobby. Wellington and Kirby walked the long hallway to the executive conference room. The meeting was already in progress. Twelve people sat on the sides of the table; eleven of the twelve were TRENCOR employees. Georgiana Anderson was the only representative for the Air Force. The small Chinese woman who sat at the head of the table looked up at them.

"The contract is in order," she said. Those who sat at the table nodded their heads in silent agreement. "Mr. Ming wants you to bring it to him to sign."

"Where is he? I thought he was here," Wellington said.

"He is at home," she replied. "Your transportation is waiting for You outside." She handed him a package identical to the one everyone had in front of them.

"Does he know the results?" Wellington asked.

"No," she said.

Wellington took the package and headed for the helipad in the back of the facility. That bastard Bowman worked fast. Wellington didn't like the fact that the wheels were already in motion while he was meeting with Bowman. It was . . . disrespectful.

When he stepped out the back door, the black Bell jet helicopter was waiting for him, rotors turning. Sand blew everywhere as he shielded his eyes and scooted to the helicopter. Crouching over as he approached the helicopter, Wellington climbed in, and no sooner had he buckled his seat belt than the helicopter lifted off and headed west.

It was a twenty-minute flight to Ming's home in the foothills to the west, and Wellington took the opportunity to relax and review the paperwork. He didn't speak to the helicopter pilot; that would be socializing with the hired help. Besides, Wellington was a jet pilot, a fighter pilot, and a test pilot. In his mind, helicopter pilots were at the bottom of the food chain.

The helicopter landed on the pad a hundred yards behind Ming's mansion. Wellington always marveled at the opulence that did not seem pretentious. Li Zhong met him on the back patio without shaking hands and led him inside.

GEORGIANA GRIT HER TEETH as she left the meeting. TRENCOR Industries was dumping *more* cash into a jet program that had yet to produce a single jet. Regardless of how well the final product was supposed to work, TRENCOR's fiscal constraint was lacking. The man she needed to talk to about this had just left in the company helicopter.

Approaching the executive suites at the front of the hallway near the lobby, Georgiana popped in to make an appointment with Mr. Ming for later in the week. The lights in the executive suite were still on, but no one was in the office.

"Hello?" she said. There was no response. Georgiana stepped in and closed the door behind her. As she approached the secretary's desk, she saw the computer was off, and apparently everyone was gone for the day. She knew Ming was at home.

She started to leave, but paused. *Oh, no, I'm impulsive, but not that impulsive.* Georgiana turned around and looked at Ming's office. *Yes, I am.* She slid to Ming's office and knocked loudly on the door. No one answered. She pressed her ear against the door, but there was no sound from the other side.

Her eyes darted back to the secretary's desk and toward the entrance to the office. Holding her breath, she edged her right hand toward the doorknob to David Ming's office.

Slowly, she turned the doorknob. It was locked. She reached in her purse and pulled out a credit card, sliding it between the door jamb and the lock. After a few seconds of manipulating the lock, she heard an audible click. Her heart started beating faster as she pushed the door open into the dark office. She entered quickly and shut the door behind her. The room was unlit except for the computer on Ming's desk.

Sliding behind his desk, she questioned what she was doing. What if she were caught? Her career would be over. But what if she found information on TRENCOR? What if she uncovered the secret of the incomplete second floor? Georgiana suspected TRENCOR was intentionally delaying this project in an effort to milk more money from the US government, and she needed proof. She'd debate how she found the information later.

The computer was password protected. Georgiana positioned herself behind the keyboard and typed *TRENCOR* and hit enter. PASSWORD ERROR. She paused for a moment and then typed *TRENCOR Industries* and hit enter. PASSWORD ERROR. Leaning back in the chair, she bit her bottom lip as she stared at the screen. She glanced around the dark office and could make out pictures of aircraft hanging on the wall. Positioning herself behind the keyboard again, she typed *TRENCOR F2000* and hit enter. The computer buzzed and whirled as it came to life.

Georgiana suspected something sinister about TRENCOR, and

after her run-in with Li Zhong, she was sure of it. She was pleased with herself for breaking into Ming's computer, and her lips pursed and the corners curved upward. But the smile faded rapidly because she was fully aware she could go to jail for this.

The desktop page was very clean for an office computer, and Georgiana found Ming had everything extremely organized and in order in the document section. She clicked on the icon and discovered at least forty files, each of them containing information she might want or need. Georgiana reached into her pocket and pulled out her favorite new toy. Trek Industries had recently created this amazing new device called the "ThumbDrive." When plugged into the USB ports on newer computers, the small device could easily store vast amounts of data to move the data from one computer to another. Once she inserted the ThumbDrive into the USB port, Georgiana started downloading every file in Ming's documents section. Nervously, she ran both hands through her hair as the downloading proceeded. After ten minutes, the download was complete. She logged off the computer and slipped out of the office, past the secretary's desk, and into the empty hallway.

Once in the hallway, she realized how tense she was as she squeezed the ThumbDrive. Slipping it into her pocket, she took a deep breath and scurried out of the building to her car. She didn't see anyone else in the building or the parking lot. Picking up her pace, she broke into a slight jog on the way to her car. She fumbled with her keys to unlock the car, climbed in, cranked the engine, and headed to her office at the 445th Flying Test Squadron.

On the drive back to Edwards, her heart beat rapidly. She took deep breaths and tried to relax.

Georgiana reached the base and drove through the gate with ease. Hustling straight to her office, she shut the door and slipped into her chair, booting up her computer. She plugged the ThumbDrive into the USB port, opened the computer icon, and waited for the ThumbDrive to show signs of life.

Surely she'd committed a crime, but she wasn't sure which one. She grimaced, focusing on the computer screen while the computer read the folder. When the ThumbDrive showed up in the external port, she clicked on the drive to verify what she had copied to it. Her screen suddenly filled with the mass of files from Ming's computer. It'll take forever to read through all of these files.

There was a knock at the door, and Brent stuck his head in the doorway. "Oh, you're here. We've got a meeting with the commander in three minutes."

"Oh, dear, I forgot," she said, looking at the clock on her screen. "I'll be right there."

Brent paused and stuck his head farther into the doorway.

"Is everything okay? You seem kind of . . . distracted," Brent said.

Looking up for the first time, Georgiana felt the tenseness in her face, but had no way of covering it up.

"I'm sorry, I'm . . . I'm working on something."

"Okay, well, we're getting ready to start," he said as he left, the door still open.

Georgiana closed the file on her computer and removed the ThumbDrive. She stood and shut the door, then knelt down at the mini-refrigerator next to her desk. Reaching in, she pulled out what appeared to be a can of Coke. She looked around to see if she was being watched. It was more of a reflex than a precaution. Unscrewing the top of the "Coke can" safe, she placed the ThumbDrive inside and screwed the top back on. Placing it back in the refrigerator, she left her office for the meeting.

21

D AVID MING SAT ON THE COUCH, discussing the current status of the F-2000 with his wife. She had been on the road the last two weeks and just drove in from the airport. Ming turned to Wellington when Li Zhong escorted him into the vast room. Wellington set his briefcase on the coffee table sitting between the two couches.

"Well?" Ming asked, running his finger around the bottom of his glass.

Wellington looked insulted, but Ming didn't care. "Well what?" Wellington replied tersely.

Ming was perturbed by the arrogance of the man. "Did we get what we want?"

Wellington sighed. "Yes and no."

"What do you mean, yes and no?"

"I mean, yes, we'll get the technology. And I mean no, in that they won't sell it to us."

"What? Those bastards took our seed money to develop this device for our jet and are going to keep it proprietary?"

"The seed money was a goodwill gesture. No strings attached, other than right of first refusal and a two percent return on investment, regardless of who the tech was sold to," Wellington said. "I know this is nonstandard, but no one else bought in to their cockamamie scheme. They are willing to lease this technology, but insist on remaining the primary subcontractor. They'll supply us with ten units for the test phase and increase the units as we go operational. We've got to use their people and their maintenance."

Ming was furious. TRENCOR wanted as few people and contractors involved in this project as possible, but the RPA/SIP capability was a major requirement for the sixth-generation fighter. "Did Bowman say how the tests went?"

"Other than that they were successful, no. They must have gone well because he was very confident. I kind of like the guy. Shame he is such a quitter—he might have made a good president."

"What is the fee for this 'leasing' plan?" Ming asked.

"For the RPA package, five hundred million for the test phase, both simulator and flight, and another seven hundred and fifty million for execution of the first one hundred jets. We are to negotiate after that."

"What? One and a quarter billion dollars? For partial tech on a secret program? Most of the tech is in development or operation," Ming said.

Ming's wife spoke up. "Mr. Wellington, it's not the RPA tech we are specifically looking for. How did the testing go for the Sensory Integration Package with the Integrated Thought Control System?"

"Bowman said it went fine, as well," Wellington said, his brow furrowed, pulling out the package and handing to Ming. "I think there are some issues contractually. We're going to have to bring them into the fold. Our plan for buying the tech outright is dead, that's for sure. The bottom line is, we're two years behind schedule. We need this tech to meet one of our primary design specs, and we've already been paid for it. And there is no one else working on it—or if they are, they can't make it in time. Bowman's got us."

No one said anything for several minutes. Ming was deep in thought.

"We'll accept their offer," Ming said, nodding his head. "Bowman is right—no one else can help us at this time, and we are behind schedule. But being behind schedule is not uncommon when creating something light-years ahead of the rest of the world. Make it work. That's why I pay you the way I do, Mr. Wellington."

Wellington nodded. "I understand, Mr. Ming."

MING UTTERED SOMETHING in Chinese, and his wife gathered the contract paperwork Wellington brought. Wellington glanced around, perplexed. *That's it? I busted my butt to get back here for this? No hello, no stay for dinner, no drink?* He shifted his weight in his seat, awaiting further discussion. Ming glanced in his direction and did a double-take.

"That will be all, Mr. Wellington."

"Okay, Mr. Ming," Wellington said, picking up his briefcase from the coffee table as he stood. Wellington hated the way Ming ended his conversations. He let you know he was done with you. He was amazed Ming had been as successful as he had, being so impersonal. His chunky wife wasn't much better. He didn't know what the hell he saw in her. Brains over beauty that's for sure. Wellington nodded farewell, and Li Zhong escorted him outside to the waiting helicopter, which still had its engine running. Wellington strapped in and the helicopter took off, heading back to TRENCOR.

It was times like these he regretted accepting the job at TRENCOR Industries, but once a month his paycheck made the bad feelings go away. Wellington never questioned his salary when they made him the offer. Salary and bonuses totaled over four hundred thousand dollars a year. He was worth it; he did his job, and he was good at it. And his contacts in Air Combat Command and the Pentagon proved quite beneficial. But things like this made him wonder if David Ming understood who he was dealing with—or if he cared.

The helicopter landed at TRENCOR Industries, and the pilot shut it down this time. Wellington unbuckled his seat belt, grabbed his briefcase, and headed inside for the simulator bay. Coordinating with the simulator operator, he arranged to fly the F-2000 simulator for thirty minutes. He chose not to use a helmet for the F-2000, using a set of Dave Clark headsets instead. Running through the basic checklists, he started the engines and taxied for takeoff. The VSTOL characteristics of the F-2000's design were flawless. The aircraft took off in less than 800 feet. He lowered the nose, and the aircraft accelerated rapidly to supersonic airspeed. Pulling back on the stick, he climbed until he had the nose seventy-five degrees nose high, and the jet climbed up to 60,000 feet.

He was playing. There was no reason for his flying in the multibillion-dollar simulator other than the fact that he could. After fifteen minutes in the simulator, the number one engine stopped operating. He pushed the throttles into the after-burner range, attempting the emergency air start. Nothing. Shutting both engines down, he then attempted a normal start on each engine with no success. It wasn't a flameout due to maneuvers. Beating his fist against the canopy of the simulator, he cursed out loud. The simulator operator called him over the headset and told him what he already knew. The simulator software had failed again.

Wellington powered off the simulator and returned all the switches to the appropriate position to set up for the next test session. The motion to the simulator stopped and the large hydraulic arms brought the device back to its static position as the ramp lowered for Wellington to climb out.

When he opened the canopy, two technicians waited, ready to climb in and start working the problem from the cockpit. Three other techs worked on the problem from the computer room. Wellington climbed out and approached the simulator operator. "Let's get this fixed ASAP. I don't want to give Samson anything else to gripe about."

"Yes, sir," the simulator operator replied.

Wellington strolled out of the simulator bay toward his office on the other side of the lobby. Not being located in the same suite as his boss had its pros and cons. Quick access due to close proximity was always less desirable to distance from the boss. At the executive level, it wasn't quite "out of sight, out of mind," but it was about as close as you could get.

His secretary had left for the evening, and the office area was deserted. When he cracked the door, he noticed the lights from within. A hundred different situations raced through his mind as he pushed the door open, bracing himself for a potential confrontation.

Jennifer sat behind his desk, her flight suit unzipped to her waist, wearing nothing underneath but a black lace bra. Her legs were propped up on his desk, but instead of flight boots, she wore black high heels. Her right hand held a half-empty glass of Chardonnay.

She looked enticing, and his mind wandered back to how they began this . . . relationship. He was the wing commander at Vance and had to fly to Randolph in San Antonio for a meeting with the four-star. She was the IP scheduled to fly with him. On the flight to Randolph, he thought she was a good pilot. Procedurally sound, not bad hands, and strong radio calls. The meeting lasted longer than he planned, and neither of them had the crew rest required to fly back. They had to stay the night. After they checked into billeting, they headed to the Officers' Club for dinner and went downstairs to the Auger Inn for a drink. They sat at the bar for a couple of drinks as Wellington talked to old friends. Jennifer sat quietly to the side.

Eventually the old friends left and Wellington and Jennifer sat alone at the bar. The alcohol must have kicked in as he started to let her know what he thought of her flying skills and what she could do to improve. Wellington realized he might have had too much to drink. She looked like she was going to cry, which made him worry he might have gone too far. Without warning, she said she was good at something and grabbed his crotch and said she could make that thing think it was twenty-one years old again. They left the bar and went back to his VIP quarters in billeting. The next day, he called Vance to let them know he had to extend his TDY another day due to more meetings.

Wellington shook his head as he recalled his fall from grace, but he felt it was worth it. Jennifer made him feel young again. He closed the door and locked it behind him as he stared at her behind his desk.

"I thought you'd never get back here," she said.

Wellington grinned. "You're out of uniform, Major."

Jennifer set the wine on the desk as she moved her feet to the floor and stood up. "Not yet, General," she said, sauntering over to him, "but I will be in a minute."

22

TRENCOR INDUSTRIES and the Air Force test team had been very successful the last several days. The software engineers solved the environmental issues, and the testing of the simulator moved at a rapid pace. Likewise, the Air Force doubled their efforts, as they were well aware of the test program's problems. A sense of urgency to get the sim testing finished radiated throughout TRENCOR's facility. The operational prototype would be delivered at the end of the month, and the test team wanted to get started as soon as possible.

Today was an important day. Century Aero-Bot's team installed the RPA/SIP package into the simulator over the weekend and were ready to test the system. The conference room filled, and Georgiana realized this would be her best opportunity to explore the building.

The first file she read on the data from Ming's office referred to the construction of the facility. While nothing was overtly stated, it was clear construction had stopped after the first floor was complete, though there was no answer to "Why?"

When the pre-brief ended, Samson and Jennifer left for the simulator bay along with several Century Aero-Bot employees. Samson looked part robot with the electrodes stuck to him, and he'd have more before they placed his helmet on his head. The engineers used the computer displays at the conference table to monitor the aircraft instrumentation, the pilot's visual cues. It also displayed video of the pilot and the pilot's vitals.

Excitement permeated the building this morning, as this integration test was one of the big steps to accomplish before flying the jet next month. Everyone was preoccupied with the event. Georgiana kept wandering back and forth from the sim bay to the conference room. She wanted to establish a pattern of moving around the building, at least the parts where the Air Force was allowed access.

It took almost an hour after the pre-brief to get Samson wired up and plugged into the simulator. Georgiana decided that once the test began, she would explore the building. She stood in the conference room, watching Brent's computer monitors while he worked. "I'm going to walk to the sim bay," she told Brent.

"Okay, but you'll get a better view if you stay here."

"They've got monitors there, too. I can look over the shoulder of the simulator operator."

"Yeah, you and ten other people."

Georgiana chuckled. "Hey, it's more exciting that way."

"Suit yourself," Brent replied, never looking up from the monitors.

Georgiana patted Brent on the back and walked out of the conference room. Casually, she glanced around to see if anyone observed her movements. She had established a pattern of getting up and down, leaving and entering; her action now seemed normal. She left the conference room and entered the empty hallway. Scanning back and forth, she confirmed she was alone as she meandered to the bathroom. A quick inspection showed no one there, and she headed into the hallway and moved to the stairwell door. Locked. She briskly walked to the elevator, pressed the button, and, when the doors opened, stepped inside.

Georgiana pressed "2". The light illuminated, the doors closed, and the elevator started to move. The elevator settled on the second floor, and the doors opened to reveal the same empty reception area she saw last week. She stepped out of the elevator as the doors closed behind her. She tiptoed over to the stairwell door and tested the doorknob. It was unlocked. Georgiana opened the door and peered into the dark and empty stairwell.

Closing the door, she crept through the finished reception area. The last time she was up here, she turned right and ran into Li Zhong. Stepping softly and deliberately, she paused between each step to listen for any activity on the floor. Nothing. Rounding the corner on the left side of the elevator, she entered what should have been a hallway. Instead, Georgiana crept along the framework of a hallway. There were no offices built—only steel support beams maintaining the structural integrity of the ceiling. Windows ran on all four sides of the building, except where the walls of the simulator bays extended up to the third floor. The glass windows still contained the paper attached to the inside. The paper effectively blocked out at least eighty percent of the sunlight and was not seen from the outside due to the reflective nature of the windows. There were construction supplies stored throughout, though certainly not enough to finish the interior of the second floor. She stood in the unfinished shell of a building, wondering what the hell was going on here.

She continued to reconnoiter the second floor. Despite the sheet-rock dust covering the floor and a few, nuts, and bolts scattered around, there were no signs of any ongoing construction. If they were still doing construction, they had the cleanest, most efficient construction crew she had ever seen. Looking closer, she noticed there was no electrical wiring for future office spaces anywhere on this floor except in the reception area by the elevator. There was also no plumbing, which meant no restroom on this floor.

Georgiana found herself at the farthest point from the reception area possible when she heard the *ting* of the elevator echo through the empty floor. Not wanting to get caught twice where she wasn't supposed to be, she searched for a place to hide. Finding a stack of sheet rock leaning against the wall in the shadows, she crawled behind it. She barely fit.

Voices carried along the empty, open corridor, but she had trouble understanding them. Georgiana stayed curled up on her knees, feeling like a childish fool. Glancing at her footprints on the dust covered floor, her stomach tightened. Sometimes, being a rebel and defying authority to follow a "bright idea" was really stupid. How could she have allowed herself to get in such a position? Her back and knees started to hurt, but she dared not move.

Two men crept toward Georgiana's hiding place. They were studying her footprints. Fortunately, her path had wandered back and forth but the two continued to move slowly toward her. Georgiana became gripped with fear. Had she made a noise? Did she lead them on a path straight to her? She retreated into her hiding space as best she could, hoping and praying she would not be discovered.

BRENT LOGGED OUT of his computer station and went to the

sim bay to help Samson out of his electrodes. He couldn't help but grin as he looked at the simulator. Despite its flaws, it was the greatest thing Brent had ever been associated with. Fascinated with aviation since he was a young boy, Brent had excelled in school growing up in Downey, California. Downey had a strong Irish community, and Brent's upbringing was relatively conservative. Downey had the pleasure of possessing the oldest McDonald's restaurant in the country and the very first Taco Bell. As he grew older, Brent questioned whether growing up in the bastion of the fast food industry had had any impact on his unhealthy body frame.

Socially awkward as a youth, Brent buried himself in his schoolwork, comic books, and science fiction movies. Brent's father left his job as a hospital administrator with the Downey Regional Medical Center and moved the family to Phoenix when Brent was a teenager. Initially, Brent was upset about leaving Downey, until he found out Embry-Riddle Aeronautical University had a campus in nearby Prescott. Brent excelled in high school with straight A's and received a scholarship that allowed him to attend Embry-Riddle. Majoring in aeronautical engineering, he excelled as an undergraduate, and one of his professors recommended him to a friend in the Department of Defense. Two years after graduating, Brent found himself at Edwards AFB, an aeronautical engineer at the Air Force Test Pilot Center. Life couldn't be any better.

Brent watched Samson peel off his flight suit. He resembled an android with the number of electrodes attached to him. During the process of "disconnecting" the pilot from Century Aero-Bot's Sensory Integration Package, he counted at least thirty electrode leads measuring his heart and brain waves. The key, he knew, was the brain wave aspect of the package. It was more advanced than anything ever placed on an aircraft. It was similar to an EEG, except the electrodes were permanently encased in the pilot's helmet. The special skullcap under the helmet was a conduit for the brain waves.

"This skullcap is a pain in the ass," Samson said, peeling the remaining electrodes off his forehead.

"You look like Brainiac," Brent said.

"Who?" Samson said, pulling off his flight boots.

"Uh, never mind," Brent said. It was a waste of time trying to explain Superman's nemesis to the seasoned test pilot. He decided to keep things scientific. "Not a fan of electroencephalography, huh?"

"Electro-what?"

"Electroencephalography, better known as an EEG. It measures the voltage fluctuations from the neurons of the brain caused by ionic current flows within the neurons. This is an advanced system. It ties all of your body functions into the computer to access your ability to function."

"I'm functioning fine. We need an EEG to monitor the jet."

Three different technicians surrounded Samson to remove the electrodes from his body. Brent chuckled as Samson tried to play it cool every time the sticky sensors were ripped from his flesh.

"Well, how'd it go?" Brent asked Samson once they peeled away the last electrode.

"The tests went fine. All the electrodes communicated correctly, or so they tell me. We self-induced the ITCS to take control, and it worked as advertised. But again, this is the simulator. No telling how it will work in the jet. But from what we saw today—so far, so good."

"That's good news. At least we're making headway."

"The next test should be interesting. Century's engineers are concerned that the amount of hair on the pilot's head could interfere with the helmet electrode readings. Jen's test should answer that question this afternoon," Samson said, pointing at his fellow test pilot. Jennifer stood in her underwear, her face beaming as the technicians placed electrodes all over her body. Normally, a test pilot wore a more modest ensemble, but in her typical style, Jennifer wore a pink, French-cut T-back with matching lace bra.

"We should probably be somewhere else right now," Brent said.

"Yeah, let's go," Samson replied. "Hey, where's Georgiana?"

Brent glimpsed up at Samson, as if thinking. "Haven't seen her in a while. I guess she went back to the base."

CRAMPED IN HER HIDING PLACE, Georgiana trembled in fear. She could hear the two men heading in her direction, talking to each other in Chinese. Sweat poured down her forehead, more from nervousness than heat or exertion, the mascara stinging her eyes. Georgiana silently cursed herself. She would get fired. Or arrested. Or both. It would be humiliating, and she was furious at herself for letting her imagination run wild. How could she have allowed her childish curiosity to ruin her career?

The two men continued in her direction. She heard their voices get closer, their footsteps louder.

When they were ten feet away, Georgiana heard the *ting* of the elevator again. A voice from the reception area called out, and one of the two men answered. The two talked back and forth as they walked toward the elevator. Georgiana breathed a sigh of relief as her forehead rested against the dirty floor. She heard the elevator doors open, close, and then silence. She crawled from her hiding space and stretched in the shadows. Her body ached, and she had to go to the bathroom, as she crept toward the elevator.

23

May 1, 2001

MING HUNG UP the secure telephone sitting on the corner of his desk. He didn't understand Beijing sometimes. It was no secret that China's population had grown exponentially over the years. Their "one-child" policy was viewed unfavorably by the rest of the world. With their natural resources running out, China had mapped out a plan to position themselves globally, acquiring the world's resources and sending them back home.

For decades, the Soviet policy against the United States had been one of meeting force with force or weapon with weapon. China had a different approach. Their long-term strategy was to destroy the United States from within. Ming understood his role was different. He knew the consequences if his operation was discovered. The purchases he had been directed to make over the years made sense, but this latest directive stoked his curiosity. Originally, TRENCOR Industries was designed to acquire various resources for eventual return to China. It didn't take Beijing long to realize how simple it was to infiltrate America's economic structure.

Ten years ago, after watching the fiasco of the F-22 procurement, the Party developed the idea of selling America its next fighter jet. The concept was fleshed out rapidly and became a priority in the secret halls of Beijing. Using a plan for a future fighter jet the Chinese had been working on for years, the F-2000 was born. TRENCOR Industries was the ideal candidate to make the bid, as they had already established themselves as a legitimate conglomerate. TRENCOR's new objective: drain DOD's financial resources through the F-2000.

Tying up US resources in a jet incapable of reaching its advertised potential was ingenious. Using the money from the project to then buy up America's natural resources was better.

Why would they send General Jingguo and his team here? What modifications could they make to the jet that Ming's engineers could not? The adjustments to the F-2000 to install plumbing for a cloud-seeding scheme didn't make sense to him, but he was a businessman, not a scientist or politician. Why use a state-of-the art fighter jet for cloud seeding? They wanted to do it in secret, no doubt, and the stealth capabilities of the jet made it possible. TRENCOR purchased an additional 100,000 acres in southern Nevada for the project, but he didn't understand why Beijing didn't conduct the test in China. There were plenty of uninhabited areas in need of water. Perhaps it was for political purposes. He didn't care; his job was to make and move money, and he was very successful at both. He followed his orders and would be glad when this operation was done.

SHUFFLING TOWARD THE reception area, Georgiana heard the elevator moving again and darted for the stairwell. Locked. She turned and ran around the back side of the reception area to hide as the elevator opened. Crouching in the shadows out of view, she heard the now-familiar voices of the Chinese men as they exited the elevator. The voices trailed off as they moved across the empty floor. Creeping out of the shadows, Georgiana peered around the corner.

The men moved away from her, shining flashlights around the far end of the building. One of them was talking excitedly. It was obvious they were searching for something. Or someone. Georgiana pulled behind the corner of the wall, desperately searching for a way out.

The wall she hid behind ran to the ceiling. The walls on the other side of the reception area aren't so tall. Except the portion that housed the elevator. Sliding along the wall to the right, she peeked around the corner. In front of her stood a different door. She slid to the other end of her hiding place, pushed the door slightly, and it moved inwards. There it was, another stairwell.

Her heart pounded like a high-school drumline, and she took a deep breath. The voices of the men searching for her grew louder as she pushed the door inward and silently stepped into the stairwell. When she shut the door, her eyes struggled to adjust to the black void enveloping her.

THE TWO SECURITY GUARDS marched across the dust-filled floor. Jung was sure he had seen something moving in the darkness on the second floor. He had gone to investigate when his supervisor called them on the radio for another useless task. Ten minutes later, Jung convinced his partner they needed to go back to investigate. They both picked up a flashlight and returned to the second floor.

They approached the dark portion of the floor where Jung thought he had seen motion. Leaning against the wall were several large pieces of sheetrock. Jung shined his flashlight on the floor and saw the dust surrounding the area was disturbed. Clear handprints and footprints were visible on the floor. Women's prints by the size and shape of them.

Shining their lights in the immediate vicinity, their chatter increased as they flailed their lights around the walls, unsure what to do next. Convinced no one was in their immediate area, they headed back to the elevators. It's time to call the boss, Jung thought.

LI ZHONG'S CAREER began in Beijing in the Ministry of State Security, the MSS. He served as a signals analyst until he joined China's Special Forces when China stood up its own version in 1988. Ten years later, he traveled to Estonia with the Special Forces team to compete against other SF teams from around the world. His team did well and was named "Team with the Most Outstanding Performance." Shortly after this competition, Li Zhong shifted back to the MSS. A year later, the premier ordered him to work for Ming at TRENCOR Industries. Li Zhong had a way of getting things done that other people couldn't or wouldn't do.

Li Zhong entered the office, walked to Ming's desk, and bowed. Ming motioned for him to have a seat, and Li Zhong sat in the soft chair. He struggled with how to tell Ming his office had been broken in to. The security cameras picked up Georgiana Anderson sneaking in to his office a few days ago, but Ming had no cameras in his office. Li Zhong didn't know what she did in there. Security was his responsibility and Li Zhong was furious Ming would not invest in the manpower to get the job done correctly.

Ming adjusted the papers on his desk. "Beijing is sending General Jingguo," he said.

Li Zhong nodded.

"I need you to make arrangements for their pickup. They will utilize the laboratory while they are here. It should have everything they need," Ming said. He handed Li Zhong a sheet of paper. "They will stay on the complex grounds. Ensure the living quarters are suitable and stocked."

Li Zhong nodded again. "Is the general traveling alone?" he said.

"No, he's bringing his team. Beijing will have an exact number tomorrow."

Li Zhong started to bring up the break-in when his cell phone buzzed. He pulled it out of his pocket and glanced at the number. "Excuse me, Mr. Ming," he said.

"No, please, it is business," Ming said. "Answer."

"Yes," Li Zhong said into the phone.

"Sir," the voice said in Chinese, "we have a problem on the second floor."

GEORGIANA FELT ALONG THE WALLS until she bumped into one of the stair rails. Holding on to the rail, she found the first step and cautiously proceeded to climb down two flights of stairs. As her confidence grew, she increased her pace. At this point, all she wanted was to go home and see her husband. She planned on baking a cake for the F-2000 team tonight, but decided that if she got out of this mess unscathed, she would take a hot bath and enjoy a glass of wine instead.

Reaching the bottom of the stairs, she felt her way along the wall again until she found a door. With a deep breath and worries about what she would find, she pushed the door open, and bright fluorescent light poured in. Her eyes squinted and it took a moment for them to adjust. The hallway had doors at each end. Tall, opaque windows were on either side of the hallway. She entered the sterile white passage and closed the door behind her.

LI ZHONG STEPPED off the elevator onto the second floor. Jung walked him toward the sheetrock where the second guard was waiting. The two security guards argued and were not making sense. Li Zhong took Jung's flashlight and examined the area himself and saw the disturbed dust and the clearly visible handprint. Now, he understood what the guards were trying to say. He scanned the vast emptiness of the floor. Handing Jung his flashlight, the two guards looked at each other, confused, as Li Zhong walked to the second floor reception area without saying a word.

GEORGIANA CHECKED THE SIGN on one door. It led to the executive office suite. Not the direction she thought she should go. The sign on the other door said "Laboratory." Why would TRENCOR have a laboratory in a simulator building? The executive suite wasn't an option. They were searching for her on the second floor, making the lab her best choice. Turning the handle on the door, she gently pushed it open. The lights were out.

Finding a light switch on the wall, she turned it on. The room appeared to be the stereotypical laboratory, complete with Bunsen burners, test tubes, sinks, you name it. There were a variety of chemicals in beakers and several work stations. Across the room was another door, hopefully her way out.

As she move to the door, she glanced around the room. None of this made sense. Why is this here?

When she reached the far side of the room, she found a large Pelican case on the floor. She unclasped the sides and raised the top. Gazing at the contents, her head tilted to the side as she leaned closer. Her lips quivered, then she gasped in horror, slamming the top back into place and sealing the lid. Resting her hand against her heart, her breathing was short and sporadic. As she turned to leave, Li Zhong entered the room and blocked the door.

"Uh, uh, I, uh . . ." The words weren't coming out. Sweat dripped from Georgiana's forehead and rolled along the side of her face. Her first fear was that he would hold her until the police came. She worked through several scenarios. In the worst of them, she ended up in jail and fired.

Li Zhong pulled a pistol from his shoulder holster and reached into his coat pocket, pulled out a long cylindrical object, and screwed it onto the pistol.

"I told you exploring here is dangerous, Mrs. Anderson," Li Zhong said. "You have just made my day much easier." And with that, he pointed the pistol at her.

24

VARIOUS PILES OF PAPERS and notebooks covered the desk where Samson sat. There was a reason and method to his piles, but as with most intellectuals, no one else could figure it out. All of the material was related to the F-2000. This jet had been a pain in his rear since he'd been assigned to be the lead test pilot. His initial excitement waned as he became familiar with TRENCOR Industries' inadequacies. If the concept of the jet weren't so promising, he would have asked to be removed long ago. Had it not been a black budget and high on the president's priority list, it would have run out of funding shortly after it started. He didn't know how much money had been dumped into the jet, but he was sure it was more than any program in the history of manned aviation.

Pouring the contents of a half-empty bottle of Jeremiah Weed into a cup of Coca-Cola and ice, Samson knew the biggest problem in this program was with himself. He wasn't generating any results and found it difficult to maintain a positive attitude. But he took pride in his hard work and constantly reminded himself that this was a marathon, not a sprint.

Samson picked up the folder Jennifer had built on Jason Conrad and casually flipped through it. Nothing impressive. Conrad seemed competent enough, but he'd make an unofficial call in the morning. It pissed him off that she'd pulled this move before discussing it with him. Regardless, it was a done deal now and one less thing he needed to work on. He was sure if Jennifer was pushing for Conrad, there was much more to it than his flying skills or his father's connections.

BRENT STEPPED INTO Georgiana's office and looked around. He pulled his hands out of his pockets and placed them on his hips. There was nothing unusual on her desk—government contracts, building plans, tour schedules. Nothing out of the ordinary as far as he could tell. He stepped out of the office and bumped into Samson, who ambled toward him, rolling up the sleeves on his flight suit.

"Hey, Curt. How are you?" he said.

"Not bad. What are you up to?"

"Uh," Brent replied, rubbing his bearded chin while staring at the carpeted floor, "I'm trying to find Georgiana. I haven't seen her since yesterday morning."

"Maybe she's home sick."

"No, her husband called. She never came home."

Samson paused. "Really? That's unusual. Wasn't she at TRENCOR yesterday?"

"She was," Brent said. "She was there for the ITCS tests. Her husband drove out there last night to see if her car was still there, but it wasn't. Parking lot was empty. At first, he said he was angry she was late coming home. Now he's worried something might have happened to her." Brent continued to stroke his beard, gazing at the floor. "You know, this was an issue when TRENCOR first said they were going to build in California City."

Samson tilted his head. "What do you mean?"

"Well, this was before your time. When talk about TRENCOR building in California City first started, the Air Force objected because of the crime in the area. TRENCOR discussed all the security they would have, and the double fence with razor wire on top was the first thing to go up." Brent sighed and his shoulders slumped. "Of course, now that the facility is built, security is nonexistent, and Georgiana is missing."

"The question is, what do we do about it?"

"I don't know. I've searched around the squadron. I checked with scheduling to see if there were any meetings or tours she might be on. The commander's secretary had nothing for her schedule either. No one has seen her since yesterday."

"What about the orderly room? Maybe she went on a last-minute TDY to DC or something."

"I haven't checked," Brent said. "I'll head over there now."

"Has her husband filed a police report? Missing persons?"

"Not yet, but he's headed to the sheriff's office to file one now. They won't officially do anything for twenty-four hours. From what I can tell, I was the last one to see her around twenty-three hours ago."

"Understood. I'll talk to the commander and ask around."

"Thanks. I don't know about this. The last time she was seen was in TRENCOR. I think the place needs to be searched. Maybe she hit her head in a corner of the building somewhere and no one knows she's there."

Samson nodded. "It's possible. I'll get in touch with Wellington and let him know what's going on. His people can search the building."

"Thanks. Let me take care of this other stuff. I figured I'd be done with work early and ready for a pint, but it's going to be a long day."

THE VANCE OFFICER'S CLUB was packed inside and out. Plenty of the wing's field-grade officers were present to ensure the younger pilots didn't get carried away with drinking on a work night. Most of the pilots there would be flying in the morning, and the twelve-hour "bottle-to-throttle" rule always applied. Jason had a couple, but wanted to stay sober to say goodbye to his friends.

There was a brief but informal ceremony at 8:00 pm. Lieutenant Colonel Menendez, the squadron commander, said a few words and handed Jason a plaque thanking him for his service. Menendez talked about Jason becoming an institution in the 25th Flying Training Squadron. As one of the senior instructors, he was well-liked. His ability to communicate with a struggling student would surely be missed. Pete presented Jason with a lithograph of a four-ship of T-38s, signed by most of the T-38 pilots in the wing.

After the presentations, everyone filed by Jason, shook his hand, and said their goodbyes. When it was over, Jason found a table with old friends who had come into town: Aaron Caldwell and his wife Nancy. Pete and his wife Tracy joined them, and the five ordered dinner and a round of drinks.

"So did you find anything else out about this job in California?" Caldwell asked.

"No," Jason replied flatly.

"Would you be an instructor there, too?"

"I'm sure I would. I mean, here, I teach students who have never flown the jet. I'm not sure what I'll be doing out there. Getting test pilots current in the jet, I guess, flying chase aircraft for test jets. I'll find out soon enough."

"Are you excited about moving?" Nancy asked.

"Yeah," Jason said without hesitation. It was something he hadn't taken the time to think about since being told he was leaving. "It'll be a change from Enid. Socially, I imagine my prospects will be much better in California. Career-wise, I'm not sure if it's a good move, but I anticipate the challenge."

"What do you mean, not a good move?" Caldwell said. "Edwards is the pilot mecca. It's got to help your career, doesn't it?"

"I don't know. I'll be coming up for promotion soon without ever having been in a major weapons system. It may impact how the Air Force views my ability to contribute."

"How can they not promote you? Hell, every other pilot seems to be leaving for the airlines. Someone has to stick around, don't they?" Caldwell said.

"Jason has a natural habit of pissing off his bosses," Pete said.

"I guess," Jason replied to Caldwell, ignoring Pete's comment, which didn't mean he disagreed with it. "Sometimes I feel like my career is over before it's started. Teaching guys to fly a supersonic jet—it can't be beat. But everyone says I should be out in the 'real Air Force,' expanding my horizons. I don't know. I guess I felt safe here."

"Jason," Nancy said, placing her hand on his forearm. "Sometimes being safe isn't always the best course. Look at what you do. You fly jets. That's not exactly safe, but you do it. And you do it very well."

"What are you trying to say?"

"Maybe it's time you live personally like you do professionally," Nancy said. "Take some risks. Maybe this new job will nudge you in a new direction. California's not a bad place to live."

"That's what I said," Tracy said.

"Don't get me wrong, I'm excited about the prospects," Jason said. "And the job. I'm just worried how it will impact my career. Where will I go after Edwards? Can you believe the wing commander said to me he didn't think I would be able to learn a new weapons system?"

"I've done some checking on him. He's not a fan of yours," Caldwell said.

"I'm well aware of that. He's turned off assignments for me twice now."

"Do you think he'll turn off this one?"

"Not this time. Hell, he's done most of the work for me. He wants me gone," Jason said with a chuckle.

The waitress brought four plates of steaks and French fries and set them on the table. The hickory aroma enveloped the table and attacked their nostrils.

"Oh, my God! I am so hungry," Nancy said.

"Are you sure you don't want to order anything?" Pete asked Nancy.

"No, I'll pick off Aaron's plate," she said. "Calories don't fall off as easy as they used to."

Aaron grinned and cut a piece of steak, pulled some French fries off his plate, set them on a smaller plate, and handed them to his wife. Nancy simpered and kissed him on the cheek. It was obvious to Jason the two of them were happy. Pete and Tracy engaged in small talk with themselves as they ate. Jason stayed quiet, dousing his French fries in pepper. His two best friends were grounded and secure in their relationships. He wished he was capable of finding happiness himself. The right one will turn up.

"Have you told your father about the move?" Caldwell asked.

"Briefly. We haven't had the chance to talk much lately. He's been on the road quite a bit working on a big project. He said to call him this weekend."

"He's at Century Aero-Bot, right?"

"Yeah," Jason said, taking a bite of steak.

"What's he do?"

"I don't know. He's an executive vice president, I know that much. He finds customers for his company's technologies."

"I hear he's been making the rounds in the defense contracting world," Caldwell said.

Jason stopped chewing and glared at his friend across the table. "You heard, or you looked into?"

"I asked around. Just looking out for you, my friend. Your father could still be a target, which makes you a target."

Jason chose to ignore the last comment as he stuffed a piece of steak in his mouth.

He and Caldwell finished eating their dinner as Nancy filled Jason in on what it was like raising a child, Tracy glued to her every word. Jason listened patiently and reevaluated his decisions of the past several years. It was time for a change.

The five rose from the table, and Jason walked around the club, telling the stragglers goodbye and thanking them again for showing up. He joined the Caldwells at the front door, and they stepped outside. Nancy carried Jason's lithograph, reading the comments written on the mat surrounding the photo.

"Conrad," a feminine yet demanding voice called from across the street.

Jason looked up. He hadn't noticed her when he first stepped outside, but when she called out, he stopped dead in his tracks. Her stance was seductive, yet demure. Long brown hair cascaded past her shoulders. The features were familiar. He recognized the beautiful woman standing in high heels and a form-fitting dress across the street. Jason was oblivious to anything or anyone else around him as his plaque slid from his fingers and hit the ground. His head tilted to the side as he opened his mouth.

"Kathy?"

25

May 2, 2001

CALDWELL AND HIS WIFE stood several feet behind Jason, unsure what to do. They watched as he shuffled toward the street. Instinctively, Caldwell scanned the area for trouble. Nancy stepped over, picked up the plaque, and moved back to Caldwell. She squeezed her husband's arm. "Is that her?" she whispered.

"I think so. I've never met her. I've only seen pictures, and he doesn't have that many."

"She looks beautiful from here. If she's as nice as he said, I can see how she broke his heart."

Caldwell observed Kathy, taking in every detail. "She's grown her hair out, and she's not dressed as conservatively as she was before."

"It's been six years. People change."

"I know, honey. Something just seems strange."

"You think everything is strange," Nancy said, watching the events unfold before them as if watching a movie.

"No, darling. I don't believe in coincidences."

"Well, this isn't a coincidence. She obviously came here to see him. She was outside waiting for him to leave."

"True," Caldwell said, wrapping his arm around his wife. "How did she get on base?"

"Aaron," she said, still watching Jason and Kathy, "this is Enid, Oklahoma. A pretty lady can always get on base." He peered at her as the corners of her mouth turned upward.

"But why here? Why now?"

Nancy gazed into her husband's eyes. That's the exciting part isn't it?" He gave her a quick kiss on the lips and they turned their attention back to the star-crossed couple.

"He really likes her," Nancy said. "He has totally forgotten we are here."

"Shh."

Nancy softly punched her husband in the arm. "Don't shush me," she said with a smile as radiant as a summer morning sunrise.

JASON CROSSED THE STREET in a fog and stood in front of Kathy. She glanced at the ground, then sheepishly back at him. She appeared not to notice the two people who walked outside with him.

When Kathy looked up, his heart raced faster. It was like finding someone who died and somehow come back to life. A ghostly spirit manifested in the human embodiment standing before him.

It was her. He tried to rationalize it was someone else, but he couldn't. Her hair was longer, she was much more toned than before, and the dress and high heels were . . . amazing. Slowly, he moved across the street. Delving into her eyes, he could see them start to water. Jason struggled to move each step, but he made it to the other side, a mere two feet from her.

"Hello, Conrad," she said softly, and Jason put his finger to her lips. Leaning forward, she wrapped both arms around him, and he instinctively responded in kind. It was her. She fit right back into his arms. Breathing in her intoxicating scent, he smiled for the first time as he realized she still wore the rosy-smelling perfume. It was if she had never been gone. They embraced for over a minute before she pulled back slightly to admire him. Kathy drew his face toward hers and kissed him hard. It was a long, sensual, inviting kiss. Kathy pulled back and looked into his eyes again.

"I missed you," she said. "Did you miss me?"

"You have no idea," he said before she engaged him in another kiss. They continued their embrace for what seemed like hours. Jason had no sense of time as his head swirled. "Can you drive me home?" he asked.

"That was my plan."

Somehow, Jason remembered Caldwell and Nancy behind him. He looked back across the street and saw them walking toward the front door. "I think I've got a ride," he hollered across the street. Caldwell waved as he and Nancy retreated into the Officers' Club.

Jason turned back to Kathy, his head spinning with a million questions. "You grew your hair out," he said.

"Too long or too short?" she asked.

"No, it's good. Just different. I wasn't sure it was you."

Kathy smiled. "Thank you. It's me."

"I see you've been working out," he said, admiring her toned arms.

"Are you saying I was fat before?" she said, laughing.

"No, no. I can tell there's been a lifestyle change. I like them both—the old and the new."

"You're still sweet."

Jason searched her eyes, studying her reactions. "What happened? Where did you go?" He was expecting her to move away, but she leaned forward and wrapped her arms around his neck. She didn't say anything for at least a minute, then leaned her head back, her left eyebrow raised as she gave him a flirtatious smile.

"Not here, not now. I have so much to say to you. But we've got some unfinished business first. Let's go to your place"

"Okay," he replied as she led him by the hand to her car. "I'm staying at the VOQ."

"I know."

"I have a new assignment."

"I know."

"I'm moving to California on Saturday."

"I know."

Jason's brow furrowed. "How do you know these things?"

"Come on, Conrad. You know how resourceful I am."

Jason grinned; now it was starting to feel normal. The last several minutes had been too surreal for him, and he appreciated some sign of normalcy. They reached her car, a brand new Pontiac Firebird convertible and she unlocked the passenger side, opening the door for Jason.

"Nice car."

"It's a rental," she said with a nervous smile. "I was trying to impress you."

"You didn't need the car for that."

They drove in virtual silence the short distance to the VOQ. Jason stared at her longingly the entire way. Kathy glanced at him periodically, smiling. Her hair curled past her shoulders, and she wore more makeup than before. Not in a trashy way, but more sophisticated.

The dress didn't hurt; it accented her toned body, and he couldn't remember her wearing high heels more than twice, maybe. They reached the VOQ and climbed out of the car. Kathy scooted close to him and held his hand while looking up at him. Jason fumbled in his pocket for the key as they approached the door. He was glad he didn't drink too much tonight—otherwise she would be carrying him back to his room, like she had when she first came to meet him at the O Club six years ago.

He opened the door, reached in, and turned on the light. The lamps on each nightstand lit up. No sooner had the door shut than the two embraced in a deep, desperate kiss. Kathy backed him against the bed and stopped kissing him. She pulled back slightly, then pushed him onto the mattress. Stepping away from him, she reached behind her back. Jason propped himself on his elbows. Slowly, she unzipped the back of her dress. She reached up and unclasped the straps going around her neck. The dress loosened on her body, and she grasped it in her arms. Bit by bit, she slid the dress down her breasts until they were fully exposed. The dress fell to her feet, and she kicked it to the side. Kathy stood in front of him for a moment, completely nude except for the high heels. Sauntering toward him, she leaned over, turned off the light on the closest nightstand, and climbed on top of him.

Gazing into his eyes, she whispered, "Like I said, Conrad, we've got some unfinished business."

SHERRI HAD ARRIVED in town yesterday afternoon following the flight from New York. She once again overcame her fear of flying thanks to her good friend Jack Daniels. Steven sent her north of L.A. to the East Kern Airport District in Mojave, and Sherri sat in her car, frustrated. The airport had become almost as famous in aviation circles as Edwards AFB. It was home of famed aircraft innovator and designer Dick Rutan and his Scaled Composites Company, as well as the civilian National Test Pilot School. Watching the sun fall toward the mountains, she pulled out her cell phone and dialed.

"Hello, Sherri."

"Steven, I'm at the airport, but I'm not sure what I'm supposed to be doing here," she said, scanning the deserted parking lot outside the terminal. The only other people were two men sitting in a pick-up truck across the parking lot.

"I'm glad you called. My contact says the Saudis will show up any minute now."

"Fine, but if this one's a dead end, I'm going to Vegas to check out that lead. And I might be there a couple of weeks."

"Funny. You might be going there anyway."

"Is this someone I'm supposed to talk to? The last guy I met didn't fare too well, and I'm starting to think the same could happen to me."

"No, there's no one to talk to. Just follow them and see what's going on."

"Just follow them," she repeated as she tapped her fingers on the steering wheel. "What am I looking for?"

"A group of six Saudis should be arriving at the airport in a white van. My source didn't say what they'd be doing there. That's up to you to figure out."

"Thanks," she said. "Anything else?"

There was a slight pause. "No. That's all."

"Okay, I'll call you back," she said as she hung up the phone.

Sherri wanted to reach through the phone and grab Steven by the neck, at least until she saw a white van driving toward her on Airport Boulevard and come to a stop in the parking lot. She bit down on her lower lip when six Saudis climbed out of the vehicle and walked toward the two men sitting in the small, beat-up Dodge truck.

26

May 2, 2001

DAVID MING POURED A GLASS of Glenlivet at the bar in his office, returned to his desk, and placed the drink neatly centered on the coaster. His Brooks Brothers suit was meticulously pressed, his shirt heavily starched, and his shoes polished to a high sheen. The phone call to Beijing had been a troubling one. Ming was well aware of his role here in the United States. He had spent his entire career developing plans to acquire US resources. China had long recognized their need for more energy, food, water, and precious metals. Their long-term plan for power was under way, which many believed indirectly led to their imperialist expansionism.

Currently, two-thirds of China's population lived in rural areas and were capable of providing a significant portion of food for their own tables. In ten years, that number would drop to fifty percent. When dealing with 1.2 billion people, a twenty percent swing toward urbanization would put a significant strain on food and water. Hence their efforts to secure means to produce food and water in the United States and ship it back to China. The plan was well under way, though Ming had realized decades ago he was only a small piece of the puzzle. The procuring phase was proceeding nicely, but the shipping phase was still in development. That wasn't his concern; it was the responsibility of another piece of the puzzle. In three years, all of their farmland and wells in the central US would be fully operational, and he would be back in China, totally removed from the project. The wells and irrigation had as many opponents in China as they had proponents. Opponents were in favor of solely building desalination plants along China's coastline, but Ming was one of the factions that believed they needed to explore and pursue all avenues. In addition to irrigating land to grow and ship food, they were in the process of building a bottling plant to send water back, as well. He built the infrastructure and coordinated with a certain billionaire who owned a railroad to ship the water via railcar to San Francisco. From there, the water and food would be placed on a ship to China. America was paying him to ship their food and water to China. Ming loved the concept.

He noticed, however, that over the last four years, he'd had more contact with Beijing than in all the other years combined. The acquisition of the aerospace division attracted attention, and when they'd won the bid for the sixth-generation fighter, the attention doubled. He was concerned when they sent Li Zhong to be his assistant, but he had worked out well.

But now, Beijing insisted General Jingguo and his team come to TRENCOR to work on the cloud-seeding project. Ming knew what that meant—his time here was limited.

SHERRI WATCHED as the six men approached the Dodge truck. The two white men, in their late forties, stepped out and moved toward the Saudis. Casually dressed, they didn't look like anyone special. They all shook hands and started talking. One of the six moved forward and spoke. The conversation continued for about five minutes, and the lead Saudi pulled an envelope out of his pocket and handed it to the taller of the two Americans. The man opened it up, nodded his head, and handed it to the other, who also reviewed the contents.

The two groups shook hands and parted ways. Sherri watched as the Saudis climbed back in their van, and the men they'd come to meet headed toward their truck. She had to think fast. It would be too obvious to follow the Saudis at this point. Sherri quickly unbuttoned the top two buttons on her shirt, popped the hood on her car, and climbed out. Raising the hood, she found the wire from the distributor cap to the spark plugs and disconnected one. She glanced back at the two men, who were now in their truck pulling out of their parking spot.

Bouncing up and down, she franticly waved at them. The men pulled their truck over and climbed out.

"Everything okay, ma'am?" the taller one said. "I'm Bob, and this is Jimmy."

"Hi, guys. I don't know. My car won't start, and I don't know what to do," Sherri replied. She laid on a little bit of a ditzy tone. "Do you fine gentlemen know anything about cars?" she said, her right hand twirling her red locks around her finger. Both men stared at her ample cleavage.

Jimmy, the smaller and stockier one, moved forward to check under the hood.

"Miss, if anyone can fix a car, it's me," he said. Sherri noticed the taller one still stared at her chest.

"Here's the problem. The spark plug wire from the distributor cap is disconnected," he said, reaching under the hood and reconnecting the spark plug. "That should do it."

"I don't know if I understood all those big words," she feigned.

"Climb in and see if she'll crank," he said.

"What?"

"Start her up."

"Oh," Sherri said, thinking she might dye her hair blond after this performance. She climbed in her car and turned the ignition, and the engine roared to life. Jimmy shut the hood, and Sherri turned off the ignition and hopped out of the car.

"Thank you soooo much," she said as she gave Jimmy a big hug. She let him go and saw a big smile on his face. Turning to the taller one, she gave him a big hug, too.

"Our pleasure, ma'am," Bob said with a grin.

"I wanted to ask you for help sooner, but I got scared when that van full of Mexicans pulled up," Sherri said.

Jimmy laughed. "Them's not Mexicans, miss, they're Saudis."

"From Saudi Arabia? What are they doing here?" Sherri said, her fingers of her right hand spread apart, touching her collarbone. She moved back to the smaller one and placed her left hand on his forearm.

"Payin' us lots of money," he said with a smile.

"Oh," she said with a look of concern.

"Jimmy, you've spooked this fine lady," he said as his eyes continuously glanced at her cleavage.

Jimmy edged closer to Sherri. "I'm sorry miss. You see, these fellas are working on behalf of their wealthy benefactor. He's wanting to buy an airplane, and these guys are here to check it out and see if it meets his needs."

"But they just left," Sherri said.

"Yeah, we finalized the deal and got their requirements. We don't control the dry storage area. Our jet is parked on the north side of the runway. They're coming tomorrow to see the airplane."

"Are they buying your jet?" Sherri asked.

"No," Bob said. "They just want to take measurements and photographs. They're payin' us a lot of money to examine the airplane. Easy money for us."

"What do you mean?"

"All we've got to do is hook up power and make sure it works. Raise the shades, stuff like that. It's gotta be safe for them to come in and look around."

"What kind of plane is it?" Sherri asked.

"A Boeing 767."

SAMSON STIRRED THE CUP of freshly brewed coffee as he reflected on his phone call earlier in the day. Wellington said he'd look into Georgiana's disappearance, but Samson gauged his concern as disingenuous at best. Samson could visualize the phony grin and pearly white teeth as they spoke over the phone. The insincerity of his response started to make him worry about Georgiana. Brent wasn't around when he finished the call earlier but he'd let him know that TRENCOR was searching the facility.

Sliding behind his desk, Samson closed his eyes and smelled his coffee before taking a sip. The scent of Dunkin Donuts coffee with a shot of hazelnut made him smile. He took a sip and the coffee breathed new life into his fatigued brain. Uncertain whether his efforts were in vain, he dove back into the pile of paperwork. After four separate tests, they continued to have problems with the jet's software. TRENCOR's software engineers could not decide if it was the simulator interface software, a hardware integration issue, or a flaw in the jet's software. Earlier today, Samson decided he would investigate himself.

He knew the initial problem had been in the simulator interface software. The jet did not recognize the exterior environment, but that proved to be an easy fix. Now the malfunctions seemed to be more systems related. But the malfunctions on the first and subsequent sorties appeared to be related to the jet's software, not the simulator interface.

Licking his lips, he continued to scan one of the tech orders on the computer when something caught his eye. He grabbed one of the previous documents he had been reviewing, homing in on an obscure algorithm randomly appearing around every malfunction. A slight grin formed on his face as he cross-checked various documents. After checking and re-checking his hypothesis, Samson dropped the stack of papers on his desk, jumped to his feet, and left his office.

Samson's excitement might not have been obvious had anyone been watching him. A seasoned fighter pilot and test pilot, he controlled his emotions. Too well, sometimes. His ex-wife accused him of being an emotionless robot during their marriage, which was usually met with an emotionless response. "Be careful what you wish for," he'd tell her. "You just might get it."

But now, even he couldn't contain himself. A shout of joy replaced the slight grin. He needed to share the news with his friend. Leaping down the hallway, he saw the empty office and realized Brent had gone home.

Samson returned to his office, his adrenaline rush in full force. Grabbing his phone, he dialed Brent's number. The answering machine picked up and Samson said, "Brent, I think I figured out the problem with our jet."

27

S HERRI SPENT LAST NIGHT preparing to stake out the dry storage area at East Kern Airport District. Earlier, she had gone to a sporting goods store and purchased an ice chest, a pair of binoculars, and a nylon chair that folded up and fit into a sheath. She anticipated sitting there a while, and comfort would be a necessity. She'd spent the night at the Mojave Desert Inn, an old motel close to the airport that looked like it was straight out of a slasher movie. Jimmy and Bob told her the jet was parked on the northwest portion of the field. Using a map she'd picked up from the airfield office, she had a good idea where the jet should be parked.

The temperature was expected to drop to a low of fifty-three degrees from the current high of sixty-nine. She arrived at ten in the morning and drove to the west side of the field to set up surveillance. West of the airport, Aerospace Highway made a forty-five degree turn to the right. Sherri followed the road, and a couple of hundred yards after the turn, she left the highway and followed a dirt road about a quarter mile to the fence. There were a couple of railroad tracks between her and the fence, and Sherri had a good view of the western portion of the dry storage area, affectionately known as the airport graveyard.

It was an incredible sight. Aircraft, hundreds of them, spread across the area surrounding the airfield, jam-packed next to each other. Most were covered with some kind of white cloth, while others sat exposed. Her eyes scanned the area for ten minutes before she found a Boeing 767 with workers moving around it at a hectic pace. A staircase was moved to the jet, and an electrical power cart put in place. This had to be the jet.

She drove her car halfway back to the highway and parked facing the airport on the deserted dirt road. From her position, she could clearly see the 767. It would be best to stay in her car until the Saudis showed, then move in closer. Sherri grabbed her briefcase and pulled out her files, taking advantage of the time to go over her notes. Who was interested in buying a jet? Was this why some of the men she had been tracking were going to flight school?

The sun beat down on her car for the next seven hours, providing some warmth inside. This sucks. She was tired, bored, and thirsty. Did the Saudis change their mind? Is she in the right place? She'd gotten over the humiliation of having to urinate behind a sagebrush several hours ago. Now it was routine. Thanks Steven.

Sherri rolled down her windows to allow some fresh air to circulate and wished she'd brought a novel to read. She checked her watch; it was five-fifteen. One guy was left at the 767, waiting on the Saudis. Bob and Jimmy were nowhere around, and she wondered if the Saudis were going to show up at all.

Reaching in the back seat and grabbing a bottled water from her cooler, Sherri took a long swig of the cool water, then her eyebrows raised when she saw it.

The white van drove along the fence, heading for the 767.

THE SKY WAS DAZZLING ORANGE and red as sheets of darkness loomed overhead in Enid as Jason sat on the steps in front of his VOQ room. Something wasn't right. Kathy left a couple of hours ago to run an errand and drop in on a couple of friends. When she returned, they would order a pizza. He wanted to go to Chicaros for one last order of ribs and so Kathy could say hello to everyone, but she was adamant about not going there.

Something seemed odd, but he couldn't put his finger on it. Kathy seemed different. The longer hair; the toned body. Clearly, she'd been working out. She looked fantastic, but something was different. She was acting strange, but how?

He contemplated their past relationship. What was it that attracted him to her? Was it so long ago he'd forgotten? Was he confused? Did he create an idealized version of her in his subconscious mind to avoid other women by holding them to this perfect standard?

Maybe that last one. Still, that didn't change the nagging doubt that something about her was different. She was very . . . aggressive. The sex was fantastic, but it wasn't some beautiful event that simply happened. She came there to have sex with him. She was dressed for it. She initiated it. There was no foreplay. Sex was the goal.

And there was no innocence. That was it. Kathy had been a kind, caring, and thoughtful friend six years ago. It was those characteristics that pulled him into liking her. She was fun, energetic, and quick with a joke.

But in the last twenty hours, he hadn't seen any of the Kathy he knew before. Perhaps his mind was clouded with the excitement of her return. That was it. He shook his head and laughed at himself. He was happy she was back. Now he needed to make sure she didn't leave again.

Jason back inside. Grabbing a bottled water from the refrigerator, he sat in the recliner and turned on the television. No sooner had he found a movie to watch than Kathy walked in.

"Hey, Conrad," she said, shutting the door behind her. "Miss me?"

"For years."

"Oh, don't get all sappy on me. I'm starving. Let's order that pizza."

Jason muted the television and leaned forward in his chair. "Are you sure you don't want to go to Chicaros? The ribs are still the best in town, and I'm sure there are lots of people there who would like to see you again."

"No, thanks. I told you before, I didn't come back here to see them, Conrad. I came back here for you."

"Okay," Jason said. "Pizza it is." He noticed she didn't hesitate with her decision. She had a plan and was sticking to it.

Moving to the kitchen, she unloaded the plastic bags she'd carried inside. "Have you talked to your father lately?"

"No."

"How much have you guys talked since . . . the incident?"

"More than you and I have," he blurted out without thinking.

"Funny, Conrad. Sometimes you can be an asshole."

"I'm not an asshole—" Jason stopped himself. Not the time or the place for that line. Plus, she was giving him a look that said, "Oh, yes you are."

"No really, what kind of relationship do you two have?" she said. "It must be agonizing knowing you two have been separated your whole life and to finally meet after you saved his life."

"After *we* saved his life. You were a part of it, too."

"I know. But he's your father. Don't you guys talk? Send birthday and Christmas cards?"

"Yeah, we do." He didn't want to tell her his father had stopped by a couple days ago. But why didn't he want to tell her? It was an odd question for her to ask at this point. They hadn't been back together twenty-four hours, and she was asking about his dad. Was it a coincidence, or simply small talk? She was pushing boundaries he hadn't known existed, and it made him . . . uncomfortable.

"You should call him and let him know you're moving."

"Yeah," he said, leaning back into his chair and turning the volume on the television up.

Kathy marched into the bathroom and closed the door. He didn't sense anger. It was more like indifference. Jason wondered about her attitude and their short conversation. Six years ago, Kathy would have insisted on seeing everyone.

One statement she made stuck in his mind. He wondered what she really meant when she said "I came back here for you."

THE SUN DESCENDED TOWARD the small mountain range to the west as Sherri shuffled closer to the jet. She settled for sitting behind some sagebrush about one hundred yards from the fence. From there, she could easily see the 767 about a hundred fifty yards on the other side. The jet stairs sat in front of the open front crew entrance, and she could hear the hum of the external power cart supplying electricity to the jet.

Sherri sat in her nylon chair and peered through her binoculars. She could see the overweight man who worked for the Americans standing by the power cart. Five of the Saudis left the white van and scurried up the stairs, each carrying a backpack and a few other bags about the size of a duffel bag. The sixth talked to the fat man by the power cart, who appeared to be showing him how to operate it. After ten minutes, they shook hands and the fat man drove off. Sherri sat behind the sagebrush and tried to make herself comfortable. Occasionally, one or two of the Saudis would leave the jet and go to the white van, then go back up the stairs. What the hell are they doing? Are they really trying to buy one of these jets? She watched the activity for another hour and fifteen minutes when one of the Saudis walking back up the stairs stopped and looked in her direction for a couple of minutes.

They'd spotted her. The Saudi was yelling, and two more came out of the aircraft as the first one pointed directly at her. Two of them raced down the stairs and into the van. Sherri began to realize it was time for her to go.

A fourth man appeared at the top of the stairs, brandishing a rifle. Where the hell did that come from? The van spun around and raced toward the gate. The man at the top of the stairs pointed his rifle at her, as Sherri turned and bolted back to her car. Several shots rang out and dirt kicked up around her as bullets impacted the hard ground.

Reaching her car, Sherri cranked the engine, threw the car in reverse, and shoved the accelerator to the floor. The car reached Aerospace Highway the moment the white van burst through a gate and headed toward her. Sherri placed the car in drive and sped off, leaving the hard-packed dirt for the asphalt of the highway. Sherri sped north, away from the airport. She wanted to go south, in a direction she was somewhat familiar with, but the white van changed her plan.

Damn. I feel like I'm back in Pensacola. She'd learned from that incident and wasn't about to let the van get any closer. Sherri floored the accelerator, and the distance between her and the white van increased.

She approached the exit for California City and began to slow. Two semi-truck trailers hauling tractors blocked the exit, plodding along at twenty miles an hour. A quick glance in her rearview mirror showed the white van closing in. Instinctively, Sherri steered her car out of the exit lane back onto the main highway and headed north.

Screw that. There should be another exit eventually.

Heading north on Aerospace Highway, she desperately searched for a way out. To her left in the distance, the small mountain ranges trailed off the southern portion of the Sequoia National Forest. To her right, flat desert. Backtracking on the two-lane highway would be just as dangerous; they'd never let her pass. Her only alternative was to continue north.

The white van slid farther back as she kept the accelerator near the floor. She had less than a quarter tank of gas. Where the hell could she get gas out here? It would be a long hike to a gas station.

After about ten minutes heading north, she approached a side road. She considered getting off the highway, but decided against it. She needed to find a town with people, a safe place to avoid the Saudis following her. Sherri continued north, the van barely visible in her rearview mirror.

Her gas gauge looked as if it dropped by the second, and she began to worry more about her fuel situation. Easing off the accelerator, she reached in her glove box and pulled out her map, fumbling to open it one hand. Her eyes scanned the map and within ten seconds, she found the East Kern Airport District and the road she was currently traveling. Tracing her route north, she found the safe haven she was searching for—the Naval Air Weapons Station, China Lake, about thirty minutes away. It sat north of the town of Ridgecrest. She knew she would be able to shake the white van there.

Sherri kept her foot on the gas, driving ninety miles per hour until she reached the turn to take her to China Lake. She hadn't seen the white van since a few minutes after she made the decision to continue north past California City Boulevard.

It was dark when she pulled onto West Inyokern Road and drove into Ridgecrest. She followed the signs to the Naval Air Station and breathed a sigh of relief when she saw the static display of the F-4 Phantom at the front entrance to the base. Her elation turned to frustration as her car chugged and gasped as she realized she'd forgotten to get gas on the way through town.

She cruised into the visitor's center lot and coasted into a parking spot. Climbing out of the car, Sherri stretched and focused her eyes on the road she'd taken into town. No doubt the white van turned around at some point. Only two Saudis climbed in to chase her; they must have gone back for the rest of them. Regardless, she had lost them. Who the hell are these guys? Why would a Saudi interested in buying a 767 have men with guns inspecting the jet? Once again, she'd been shot at while investigating Saudis.

28

May 4, 2001

CALDWELL STOOD in the backyard of his in-laws' home on the outskirts of Enid. Jason arrived earlier to say goodbye. The two men spent the last hour shooting various weapons in the back of the property. Jason had become a voracious learner in shooting, cleaning, and breaking down as many weapons as he could get his hands ever since the San Antonio incident. He'd adopted a lifestyle of self-defense, well aware he wasted most of his youth on movies, TV, and parties. Jason had taken several hand-to-hand combat courses. Those were a little harder to stay proficient in, and he had to settle for an aikido course in downtown Enid. He never wanted to be caught unprepared again.

Caldwell was shooting his father-in-law's M1-Garand. Jason owned both an AR-15 and an AK-47 battle rifle. For pistols, he owned a Berretta 92F 9mm and a .40 caliber Glock 22. All the weapons would go into storage until Jason had a better understanding of California gun laws. It was nice to cycle a few rounds through each of the weapons before he began the long drive to California. He even managed to impress Caldwell with his marksmanship.

Jason was glad to have one last opportunity to spend time with old friends before the move. He would leave for California after lunch, drive to Albuquerque today and complete the trip on Sunday. Caldwell and his wife had to catch a flight back to Virginia this evening.

Kathy had left town again with a promise to meet him at Edwards next Wednesday. She told him she was here to stay this time, but Jason wasn't so sure. He also wasn't sure he wanted her to.

"So, what are you working on at Langley these days?" Jason asked Caldwell as the two men headed back to the table where the rest of the weapons and cleaning supplies sat.

Caldwell's eyes drifted to the ground and then off into the distance. "Well, I'm kind of in the penalty box."

"What do you mean?" Jason said, breaking down his AR-15 for cleaning.

After the San Antonio incident, Caldwell had been promptly removed from his post in Moscow and returned to Langley. All of this was done while he recovered in the hospital in Enid. The CIA moved Caldwell out of Operations, and when he made it back to Virginia, he found himself in a less desirable position.

"I've been doing deskwork for the last two years."

"Is that bad?"

"Well, not in this case. Nancy and I have had a chance to nurture our relationship, get married, and have a baby. If I'd gone back to Moscow, that never would have happened."

"Painful?"

"It took some getting used to."

Jason threaded the cleaning brush on the brass rod. Opening the bottle of Hoppe's No. 9, he dipped the wire cleaning brush in the solvent and cleaned the barrel of his rifle.

Caldwell looked back at Jason. "I'm still chasing commie bastards in my spare time, but the rules have changed."

"Yeah, the Russians are everywhere these days."

"The Russians and the Chinese."

"Chinese?"

"Yeah, they've learned quite a bit from the Russians' mistakes. The Chinese are imbedding themselves into the fabric of our society. It's been gradual since the previous administration. They're using our own laws and system to defeat us."

"How come we don't hear anything about this?" Jason said, his eyebrows squishing together. He was a military officer and had never heard anything about China being a major problem. Jason removed the brush from the end of the cleaning rod and replaced it with an eyelet holding a small cotton cloth. He thrust the cleaning rod back down the barrel of his rifle, and the cotton cloth emerged covered in black gunpowder residue and oil. Jason replaced the cloth with a fresh one and rammed the rod through the barrel again.

"You'll hear bits and pieces, but no one ever links all these stories together. Everything happening on the international stage happens for a reason. We have to find out what that reason is."

"I've had my fair share of 'international' issues. It's taken six years to reach some kind of resolution. With Kathy back, I . . ."

Caldwell grinned and shook his head. "Really, I'm happy for you, Jason. The timing couldn't be better."

"I know. I'm glad I took care of all of my out-processing checklist earlier in the week. We stayed in bed all day yesterday."

"Did you two ever discuss anything?"

"We talked about getting pizza."

"Jason—"

"Just kidding," he said, replacing the small cotton cloth with another one and ramming it through the barrel again.

"I get it, but this is serious," Caldwell said. "What happened? Where did she go? Why did she come back? Why now?"

Jason fidgeted. "We talked some. She asked about my relationship with my dad. She said following the San Antonio incident, she got scared and bailed. She stayed with various family and friends and kind of bounced around for a while."

Caldwell gave him a stern look. "That's convenient. What does she do for a living?"

"Sales, I think," he said, looking at the ground. "Look, I know this sounds terrible, but we weren't focusing on the 'getting to know you' part of our relationship. We've done plenty of that in the past."

"I understand—"

"We were focusing on catching up on those aspects of our relationship we didn't reach before."

"Jason, I get it—she's a looker. I'm just watching out for you. I want you to be careful. She broke your heart once before, and you don't know why she's back."

"What are you, my dad?" Jason said, wiping the exterior of the rifle.

"No, I'm your friend. I guess it's the spook in me asking the questions others tend to overlook. I'll be honest with you—I don't have a good feeling about this. Wednesday night when she showed up, I said the same thing. It doesn't make sense."

Jason looked at his friend, nodding his head. "I know. I've asked myself 'why' over and over again. I'm not sure if this is what I want. She's different, but hell, I'm different now, too. Part of me doesn't care. The other part is screaming for answers. I don't know what to do."

Caldwell laid his rifle on the table. "Well, you're getting ready to leave town. What's your plan?"

"I'm leaving town. That's the plan," he said, stuffing his hands in his jeans pockets. He glanced at Caldwell, then back at the ground, and crossed his legs. "Kathy said she had things to do, but would meet me in California on Wednesday night."

"And that sounds normal to you?"

"No," Jason said. He paused for several seconds. "None of this sounds normal . . . but she made me happy once. We've been through a lot together. I'm going to see where this goes for now."

"I understand," Caldwell said. "That's your style. You meet things head on and call 'em like you see 'em. Just be careful."

Jason nodded, then turned to pack his cleaning supplies and weapons. The two men walked around the side of the house to Jason's truck in the driveway. Jason opened the door and climbed in, leaving the door open. "Aaron," he said, reaching out his hand, "I appreciate you and Nancy coming out here. It was good to see you both."

He shook Jason's hand, then pulled him in for a man-hug. "We're happy to see you again, and look, my friend, I'm glad your career is starting to take shape. Be careful on the long drive to California."

"It's taking shape, but I'm not sure how good it will turn out."

"Well, don't hate me if I look into Kathy's background."

Grinning, Jason replied, "I guess, deep down, I would be disappointed if you didn't." He cranked the engine as Nancy came rushing out of the house, carrying the baby.

"Let me get a hug in before you go!" she exclaimed. She leaned in, baby and all, and hugged Jason, giving him a soft peck on the cheek. "It was so good to see you. I'm happy for you!"

"Thank you, Nancy. I'm happy for you, too," he said, rubbing the baby's head.

"Be careful. It's a long drive out there," she said. Nancy then stepped back and shut the door of the truck, and moved next to her husband. He put his arm around her as they watched Jason back out of the driveway. Waving as he drove off, Nancy glared at her husband. "You're going to look into this, aren't you?"

"Yes," he replied, watching Jason drive off in the distance.

"Damn it, Aaron!"

"Honey, I talked it over with Jason. I'll do a quick background check. Nothing extensive, nothing too personal. I just want to know why here, why now?"

"If you ruin this for him, I'll cut you off," she said, smiling.

Caldwell hugged her harder. He didn't want to ruin it for him. Jason had saved his life; that was how he'd met Nancy. He wished Jason all the happiness in the world, he just wasn't sure that Kathy Delgato was the route Jason needed to get there.

29

THE SUN CREPT over the desert horizon and began its climb to the height of the morning sky. The cool temperature started to rise, and more signs of life appeared on the remote desert road. Last night, Sherri had sat in the Visitor's Center parking lot of the Navy base, until the sun went down. She spent several hours watching for any sign of the white van. When there was none, she began searching for a gas station. The guard in the Visitor's Center told her to head east and turn left at the intersection; there was a Chevron station a quarter mile down the road. She walked to the station, but was discouraged when she found out they had no gas tanks for sale or loan. The last guy to borrow the loaner hadn't returned it.

It was another two hours before an elderly couple came along who had a gas can they let her borrow. They were nice enough to give her a ride back to her car so she could put some gas in it. She thanked them profusely and gave them twenty dollars for their trouble. It was late by the time Sherri filled her car with gas, and she was starving. She found a quaint 24 hour diner and grabbed a salad and iced tea. When she finished, she decided to check into the Hampton Inn, take a shower, and collapse on the bed. She was asleep in minutes.

Sherri rose early and drove south out of town on China Lake Boulevard until she hit Highway 395. Thirty minutes after leaving her hotel, outside the town of Johannesburg, several emergency vehicles flashed their lights on the west side of the road. She counted four sheriff's vehicles, an EMT, and a fire truck. Sherri slowed her vehicle as she approached, scanning the scene to see what happened. There were no vehicles wrecked on the side of the road; no debris on the highway. She saw the EMTs about a hundred yards in the desert with a hand-carry gurney. Her reporter's instincts kicked in, and she pulled over to the side of the road.

Considering some of the strange events she experienced yesterday at the airport, nothing was off the table. This was something worthy of an inquiry.

No sooner had she shut off her engine than one of the sheriff's deputies stepped over to her vehicle, waving her to move forward. Sherri rolled down her window as the overweight deputy approached. Her eyes darted around as she subconsciously recalled what happened in Pensacola the last time the law approached her car.

"Ma'am, I'm going to have to ask you to move forward and keep going," he said, waving his arms as he approached the car.

Sherri handed her credentials to the deputy. "I'm Sherri Davis, *New York Times*. What's going on here, deputy?"

The deputy took her credentials and reviewed them thoroughly, then handed them back to Sherri. "You folks sure work fast."

"I'd like to think so, but this one is simply timing. What's happened here?"

The deputy stared blankly at her. "I'm not at liberty to discuss this, ma'am, but if you would continue driving through, we'd appreciate you not blocking the traffic."

Sherri turned and glanced behind her at the desolate road, and her bullshit detector kicked into overdrive. She looked back at the deputy. "You're kidding, right?"

"Uh, no, ma'am. I'm going to have to ask you to turn your vehicle back on the road and drive through."

Sherri looked beyond the deputy at the EMTs in the desert and saw them place a figure draped in a white sheet on the gurney. Overhead, the vultures were literally circling, waiting to see if anything was left behind. Someone had found a body, and the police did not want anyone to know about it . . . yet.

"You ever hear about something called the First Amendment, deputy?"

"Yes, ma'am, and—"

"Good, because I'm about to exercise my First Amendment right to freedom of the press."

Sherri opened the door to her rental car and stepped outside.

"Ma'am—"

"Is this going to be a problem, deputy? My attorneys are much better at this than yours, I'm sure."

"Well, uh, no, ma'am."

"Good," Sherri said and walked toward the EMT's ambulance. When she approached the back of the ambulance, another law enforcement officer stepped in front of her.

She held up her credentials. "Sherri Davis, reporter, *New York Times.* What happened here?"

The man was older and dressed different from the deputy. "Good morning, ma'am. I'm Sheriff Alvin Whatley." He looked over Sherri's shoulder at the perplexed deputy trailing her. "It's okay, Taylor, I got this." The deputy nodded and wandered back to his position directing the non-existent traffic.

The sheriff was a tall, lanky man with an unkempt mustache growing a little long in the front and reaching down the sides of his mouth. He sported the regulation shirt and jacket, but he wore blue jeans and cowboy boots instead of the regulation uniform his deputies wore. The brown cowboy hat displaying his sheriff's badge sat on top of his gray hair.

Sherri crossed her arms and watched the EMTs bring the body across the desert toward the ambulance. Several deputies remained where the body had been found, taking photographs and searching for more evidence.

"So I take it this wasn't a death by natural causes," Sherri said.

The sheriff studied her, searching for something.

"Off the record?" he said.

"Off the record," she replied. "For now."

The sheriff grinned and placed both hands on his hips, scanning the field where the body had been discovered. "No weapon was found, so I don't think it was suicide. Unless someone stumbled upon the body and took the weapon. We'll verify it with forensics. Until then, we'll leave that on the table. It's possible the subject expired elsewhere and was moved here. We've found drugs in the area. EMTs estimate she's been out here a couple of days, tops. The coyotes and buzzards must have found her recently, but they didn't destroy the corpse too badly. We'll be conducting the autopsy tomorrow if you'd care to sit in."

"Thanks, I think I will," she said. "Who is it?" Standing in her "Thinker" pose, her eyes absorbed everything and stored the data in her brain. The location, the distance from the road, terrain features, everything.

"There's no ID on the victim but she matches the description of a missing persons filed a few days ago. A lady named Georgiana Anderson," he replied as he watched his men work. "She's a government contractor with the fancy test programs out at Edwards Air Force Base. Her husband filed a missing person report two days ago. We'll run fingerprints as soon as we can. I suspect it'll be a match but I want to be sure before I bring in the husband to ID the body."

"Too soon for any motives or suspects, I imagine?"

"Yep. I talked on the phone with one of her coworkers yesterday regarding her missing persons status. Last time anyone remembers seeing her was at the TRENCOR Industries' facility three days ago."

"TRENCOR Industries?" Sherri exclaimed. Her heart raced as a nervous tingle shot through her body.

She noticed the sheriff looked puzzled by her response. "Yep. They've got a fancy new facility over in California City. Several hundred thousand square feet. They were supposed to provide a ton of jobs for folks in the area, but when they built it, they brought in a bunch of . . . well, I'd call 'em Chinamen, but you might call me a racist. Let's call 'em laborers from out of town. They only used local folks when required for code. Not much going on there lately."

"Thank you, sheriff," Sherri said as her mind sorted through this new information. "And I wouldn't call you a racist—I'd call you a big help."

Sherri smiled as she returned to her car with plans to go to California City.

30

May 4, 2001

BRENT STARED AT HIS now-cooled leftover corned beef and cabbage, unsure of what to do next. He had heated the leftovers in the microwave before the meeting, but suddenly was no longer hungry. The sheriff's department had contacted the base command post, who contacted the wing commander, who in turn contacted the Squadron Commander, who started the recall roster to bring everyone in. They were briefed on what was known about Georgiana Anderson: she'd died and her body was found in the desert northwest of Edwards. The sheriff didn't say if it was murder, suicide, or death by natural causes—only that it was still under investigation. Brent knew what that meant. He moved to the doorway, glancing down the hall toward Georgiana's office. The security police had already been to the squadron and placed police tape across her door.

Samson rounded the corner and approached him. "You doing all right, Brent?"

Brent stared at the floor as he shuffled his feet slowly. "Good as I can be, I guess."

"You've been kind of quiet since the news broke. I know it's tough. You guys were pretty close, huh?"

Brent paused. "Yeah, we were." His eyes focused beyond Samson, unable to look him in the eye, fearing eye contact would cause a swell of emotion over his lost friend. They'd been good friends, not in the romantic sense, but in the team-member sense. Brent had been to her house several times for dinner. "I thought something was wrong ever since the last sim test we did at TRENCOR. She'd been acting kind of since the last sim test we did at TRENCOR. She'd been acting kind of strange. Nobody saw her after that. When her husband called . . ."

"Were they having problems at home?"

"No. No way. These were the two happiest married people I know. Neither of them were able to have children, so their relationship was based on love, friendship, and mutual respect. It's sappy, but it was real. I can't believe she would commit suicide. This . . . this TRENCOR thing. It's sucking the life out of all of us. She's been obsessed with this company for years, and now that the simulator facility is open, she was asking more questions than ever before."

Samson said nothing else, which Brent appreciated. Brent wanted to talk, not listen. Looking back at Samson, he said, "I got your message yesterday. Sorry I didn't get back to you. We were at Georgiana's talking to her husband."

"That's all right. We'll talk next week. I've got to work on the training program for our new pilot."

"Oh, yeah, the Conrad kid. He gonna work out?"

"He's a friggin' FAIP and Jennifer loves the guy." He shrugged. "Sounds like it will be great."

Brent noticed the sarcasm and chuckled. "I guess you've got your hands full. Just keep an eye on your partner. Her reputation precedes her. She was a little overzealous in pushing this guy into the program."

Samson lowered and nodded his head. He appeared embarrassed by what Brent said. "I am not responsible for my colleague's actions, but you're right—she may need to be monitored when this guy gets here." Samson placed his hand on Brent's shoulder. "Look, I need to run, but if there's anything I can do, please let me know."

Brent nodded, "Thanks, Curt." They would talk when they had more time. There were too many unanswered questions about TRENCOR Industries and Georgiana's death.

SHERRI MULLED OVER THIS MORNINGS events. A dead body in the middle of the desert with a bullet hole in the eye—not the normal entry point for a suicide. No vehicle in sight. No weapon found anywhere near the crime scene. No blood splatter. The victim was a government employee working with TRENCOR.

Sherri felt a knot in her stomach as she relived the most significant tragedy from her past. TRENCOR Industries. The company had some shady projects back in Missouri when she was younger. Sherri's father died using a TRENCOR combine. Her mother sued TRENCOR for negligence of quality control in their equipment manufacturing. She lost. Sherri felt they couldn't pay enough. They never could.

Sherri reached California City and immediately spotted the TRENCOR facility. The large complex seemed out of place, dwarfing everything in town. Why? What could they be doing in there?

Pulling her car into the entrance, she noticed the empty parking lot. Eight cars. She counted eight cars in a parking lot built to hold one hundred times that many. She parked in the farthest location she could from the entrance and turned off the engine. Focusing on the large facility, she still held onto the steering wheel in the ten and two o'clock position, tapping her thumbs on top.

She sat there for several minutes, thinking, watching. Sherri pulled out her cell phone, flipped it open, and dialed.

"Sherri, darling, I was wondering if I was going to hear from you. What did you find out?"

"Hi, Steven." She smiled at hearing her friend's voice. "The Saudis were here looking at a 767. I'm told they work for someone who wants to buy one. They were taking measurements and didn't want me hanging around while they were doing it."

"Please don't tell me you were shot at again."

"I was shot at again."

"Dammit, Sherri!"

"Not a big deal, he was a lousy shot. I'm okay. But listen, I stumbled onto something else."

"What could be more important than what you went out there for?"

"I didn't say it was more important. I said I stumbled onto it."

"Stumbled onto what?"

"A dead body."

"Oh, well, that changes things. It *is* California, dear; there are dead bodies everywhere. It's like New York without all the concrete and skyscrapers."

"I know, but this is different. I'm going to dig into this a little deeper," she said, staring at TRENCOR's huge building. "I'll be staying out here longer than expected."

31

May 7, 2001

WHEN HE DROVE THROUGH the gate the night before, it had been too dark to see his surroundings, and so Jason toured the small base at sunrise. It was flat. He thought he would never find a place flatter than Oklahoma, but he found it. Edwards resembled Oklahoma without the wheat fields. The dry desert went on for miles in all directions until it hit small mountain ranges far off in the distance.

The rumbling noise somewhere on the flight line sent a tingle up his spine as a jet pilot engaged the afterburner. Jason paused to reflect on his life as a pilot. Six years ago, flying supersonic jets was a dream. He was a pedestrian with a narrow perspective on the world. Now he was standing in the hub of jet aviation, marveling over the mere dumping of excess fuel into the afterburner, visualizing the nozzles expanding and contracting.

His eyes searched the horizon for the pilot living the dream this morning. Eventually, he caught a glimpse of the lone F-15 thrusting its way into the sky and heading northwest. So much history here, and now he would be part of it. While he was sure he wouldn't make history, he was confident he would see something significant during his tour of duty at Edwards AFB.

After returning to the VOQ and grabbing a cup of coffee and a granola bar for breakfast, he spent most of the morning accomplishing his in-processing checklist. He stopped by the personnel center at Wing Headquarters and started the painful steps of in-processing himself into the base. Surprisingly, he finished quickly, and headed to Wing Flight Management to drop off his flight records. Arriving at the

445th Test Squadron at 0930, he checked in with the orderly room and went to the commander's suite to make an appointment to meet with the squadron commander. The secretary said the commander was booked for the next two days, but there was a time slot on Wednesday. Leaving the commander's suite, he went to the stan/eval office to drop off his FEF.

Next on his list was to check in with his flight commander. Jason noticed the name on the list and did not look forward to this meeting. Major Jennifer Walton had been one of his instructors in T-38s back at Vance and had been very interested in his celebrity following the San Antonio incident. She annoyed him by constantly fawning over him and trying to get him to go out. She'd been very explicit in what he would get at the end of the evening. He was glad she received her F-16 before he returned from instructor training, or his time at Vance would have been miserable. But now here he was working for her. He'd simply have to deal with it.

Jason walked to her cubicle. Jennifer sat at her desk, working on her computer. He sighed softly and knocked on the metal edge of the cubicle. Jennifer stopped typing as she looked back.

"Jason Conrad," she exclaimed, "I'm so glad you're here. What in the world have you been up to?"

She leaped out of her seat, and Jason stuck out his hand to shake. Jennifer ignored his hand and slid next to him, wrapping her arms around his waist. Burying her head in his chest, she squeezed him as if they were two lost lovers who had finally found each other.

"Hello, Major," he said, pulling her off. "I'm here for my in-processing checklist. I'm supposed to check in with my flight commander. It says that's you."

She gave him a smirk. "Of course it's me. How did you think you got this assignment?"

Jason nodded his head. He didn't know whether she was responsible, but he wasn't surprised she was taking credit for it. "What exactly will I be doing in this assignment? I'm not qualified to be a student at the test pilot school."

"You'll get the required briefings once you're in-processed into the squadron. There's a stack of nondisclosure agreements you need to sign right away, and several quick briefings." Jennifer returned to her desk. "I'll also introduce you to our lead test pilot. He's kind of a stick-in-the-mud and a little uptight, but he's nice enough. You're going to love it here. We are the future. There are so many exciting projects taking place here, and now you're part of it."

"Thanks, I guess," he said, handing her his in-processing checklist. He had thousands of other questions, but he figured there was always someone else who could fill him in. He knew from experience that the more he spoke to Jennifer, the more attached she became. "Can you initial off my checklist? I'd love to stay and chat, but I've got to knock out the rest of this checklist."

Jennifer took the paper hesitantly. She seemed to take a long time perusing it, but at last initialed her block and handed it back to him. "Do you have a contact number?"

"I'm in billeting right now."

"No, silly, I mean a phone number. You don't have a cell phone?"

"Oh," Jason replied. "Yes, sorry." He reached in his pocket, pulled out a business card, and handed it to her. "Disregard the address, but this has my phone number, emergency phone number, and personal e-mail."

She took the card with a look of disappointment. The less talking the better.

"The test team would normally start your mission in-brief tomorrow, but we're standing down for the day," she said, spinning her chair around to face her computer monitor. "One of our Government Service personnel died last week, and her funeral is tomorrow."

Jason's head perked up. "Died? What happened?"

Jennifer spun her chair back around quickly. Her eyes widened as she spoke quickly. "We're not really sure. The sheriff's office is releasing bits and pieces. The scuttlebutt is it was a drug deal gone sour. Her body was found in the desert about thirty minutes north of here. It's a shame. She seemed like such a nice lady. Had a husband. It's so sad."

"Wait, it doesn't sound like she just 'died.' It sounds like she was murdered."

"Died, murdered, whatever. She's no longer living. The sheriff isn't sure whether it's suicide or murder, but she had a bullet in the head and cocaine on her body."

Jennifer's callousness troubled Jason.

"Wait—were the drugs *on* her body or *in* her body?" Jason said.

"I don't know. Go to the funeral tomorrow if you're so interested.

You can find out everything about the murder."

"Well, trust me, things are not always what they seem."

Jen giggled. "Yeah, you would know, right?"

Jason noticed her demeanor change from giddy to somber back to giddy. Her insensitivity to the issue made his skin crawl.

"I need to run. It was nice to see you again. I guess I've got you to thank for my being here." He stuck out his hand from a distance. He was leaning over, doing everything he could to give her the impression she didn't need to stand up again, but she did anyway. She slid right back to where she started, pressed against his chest, and Jason liked it less than he did the first time.

"I'm soooo glad you're here, Jason. Look, I need you to sign the nondisclosure statements so I can take you to TRENCOR Industries this afternoon."

"That's on my in-processing checklist. It's in California City, right?"

"Jason, please," she said with a haughty tone, "the locals refer to it as 'Cal City.' You don't want to come off as the frickin' new guy. Come back here at 1430, and I'll drive you to TRENCOR. You'll love it! But it's classified, so don't tell anyone we're going there. Later tonight we'll get together and have dinner. No excuses. We've got a lot of catching up to do."

"Uh, I hope I can get everything done before tomorrow, Major."

Jennifer placed her hands on her hips and ogled him. "Okay, *Captain.*" She grinned like a schoolgirl. "Don't be silly. I'll see you this afternoon."

Jason sort of smiled, turned, and walked rapidly toward the exit. As uncomfortable as the encounter was, he knew it could have been worse.

PILES OF PUBLICATIONS littered the office, performance charts spread out, and dry-erase boards propped up against the walls, making the room crowded. Samson and Brent were on a mission this morning: identify the flaws in the F-2000. Samson was aware he would be the first to fly the aircraft and was concerned about the quality of the new jet. The two men worked feverishly all morning gathering information and building a database to track the various problems they'd experienced.

Brent glanced at the clock on the wall. "Damn," he said. "I need to get to the sheriff's office."

"Sheriff's office? What for?" Samson said.

"It's about Georgiana."

"Okay, but before you go, I think I've compiled everything I can from the simulator. Here's the bottom line. Our mission computer has self-corrupting software."

Brent stopped hanging his performance charts and looked up at Samson. "What?"

"Something has gone wrong with every mission we've flown in the sim. And it's never the same problem."

"Could be a problem in the mission rehearsal database."

Samson shook his head. "Can't be. We flew the first four sets of test cards without linking into it."

"Oh, yeah."

"The software keeps getting corrupted. We have a problem, we stop, reload the software, and continue the mission—then something else goes wrong."

"Maybe it's the mission computer itself."

"Well, I thought so, too, but it's the same model as the F-22. I had maintenance swap it out last week with one I procured from supply. That's the mission computer currently in the sim, and we're still having the same issue."

"It has created substantial delays."

"Yes, it has. Almost as if it were designed to do so."

"Samson, I never pegged you for a conspiracy-theory guy."

Samson moved to the dry-erase board on the side wall. The board had a chronological listing of the software issues the team had experienced since testing of the F-2000 began.

"I'm not so sure it's conspiracy theory so much as conspiracy fact. Look at these data points," he said, gesturing along the list of at least forty different problems. "None of them related. The timing of each is about forty-five minutes after the other. Some of them are big problems, some of them small. Every single system is affected. Even the armament suite, which we haven't activated yet, indicates errors."

"Is the mission computer getting too hot? Or are the mission management systems overheating?"

"Brent, you've been in the sim bay. It's like an icebox in there. Besides, it's one of the first items the simulator operator checks every time we have a malfunction. It helps them troubleshoot whether it's a hardware problem or a software problem. We have yet to have a single hardware issue. But look at this algorithm. It's in the code every time we have a failure. I can't figure out why it's there. It just pops up."

"I think you're onto something," Brent said as he stepped to Samson's desk, placing his chart on the table. "I've been cross-checking the structural integrity of the jet with the performance charts."

"And?"

"Not sure yet," Brent said, rubbing his bearded chin. "It's going to take more research, but I'm starting to have serious questions about this jet."

THE KERN COUNTY Sheriff's Department was the main law enforcement office for the county, with several annexes spread across the vast desert. Isolated on the north side of the street, the one-story cinderblock building sat south of the airport in Mojave. The trapezoid shaped parking lot surrounded by trees stood out in the barren landscape. Inside the building, the young, overweight deputy working behind the duty desk was surprised when the door opened after one pm, and the tall, gorgeous redhead he'd seen at the crime scene three days ago walked into the building. He bragged to Deputy Hayes about this woman he'd talked to, but Hayes didn't believe him. The fool would wish he was here now.

Deputy Taylor stared at her, his mouth partially open. The redhead strode confidently to the counter wearing blue jeans, a thin white T-shirt, hiking boots, and a faded brown leather pilot's jacket.

"Is Sheriff Whatley in?" she asked.

"Uh, no ma'am," the deputy replied, eyeing her figure. "He's at the base, meeting with the wing commander."

"Damn," the redhead said as her thumbnail found its way between her teeth.

"Is there something I can help you with? I'm Deputy Taylor, and I'm in charge of this facility for the time being."

"I was supposed to meet the sheriff here at one o'clock and go to the base with him. I guess I just missed him."

"Oh, no, ma'am. The sheriff has been out since ten this morning. He called in about fifteen minutes ago when he arrived at the base."

"Oh."

"Why were you going to the base with him, ma'am?"

The redhead relaxed her posture, which made Deputy Taylor smile.

She was beautiful, with an incredible figure. Taylor couldn't help staring at her.

"I'm sorry." She reached into her pocket and pulled out a business card. "I'm Sherri Davis, a reporter for *The New York Times*."

"I remember. What are you doing way out here?"

"I was in California City working on another story when I stumbled upon the murder scene. I understand the victim was a government employee with ties to TRENCOR Industries."

Taylor was caught off-guard. His mind wandered for a moment as his fingers rubbed nervously over her business card. Clearing his throat, he shifted his posture and attempted to display some type of professionalism. "Ma'am, that incident is still under investigation."

"I know, Deputy Taylor, and I'm still gathering facts myself."

Taylor wasn't sure, but he felt like the beautiful woman was flirting with him. It must be the uniform, they all dig the uniform.

"I was with the sheriff and the medical examiner Saturday when he conducted the autopsy and determined this was no suicide. No gunpowder residue on the victim's hands, no murder weapon at the scene, and no evidence of drugs in her bloodstream. The sheriff very kindly invited me to join him this afternoon to visit with the wing commander when he reported the findings."

"Oh, okay. I gotcha," Deputy Taylor replied. "Yeah, I'm gonna apologize on his behalf. We had another issue pop up this morning, and he had to go take care of it. I'm betting he forgot about you . . . I mean, not that you're easy to forget . . . because you're not . . . I mean, I'm not going to forget you . . . I mean, I'll tell him you were here."

The redhead smiled. "Thank you, Deputy. Please tell the sheriff I'll get in touch with him."

Taylor gulped and blinked twice. She sauntered towards the door and he could tell she was adding a little extra 'swagger' for his benefit. She stopped at the front door and took off her leather jacket. It was like slow motion to Taylor and he was oblivious to anything else going on. The sunlight pushed its way through the doorway and the thin white t-shirt. Her back-lit figure showed perfectly through the t-shirt and when she turned sideways, Taylor almost fell out of his chair. He caught himself on the counter and looked back at the door but she was gone.

Taylor stared at the door for a moment then sighed. He looked to the right and saw Deputy Hayes standing there with a cup of coffee.

He no doubt had witnessed the whole event. Taylor started to say something and Hayes just shook his head and said, "No . . . don't even think about it."

32

DANE SHIFTED UNCOMFORTABLY in the passenger's seat. The drive took over three-and-a-half hours from Tulsa on Highway 412, through Enid, and on to Woodward. He knew his producer had sent him on a wild-goose chase, punishment for the piece he recently did on Jason Conrad. Ty drove without speaking as they passed through Woodward. The directions said their destination was another fifteen miles away. Dane could not understand the point of sending a reporter and cameraman across the state for such a story.

The two rode in silence for the next fifteen minutes. Dane noticed Ty did not converse much since the broadcast from Vance. He knew Ty had squawked to the producer when he assigned them this story. It embarrassed him that the veteran cameraman insisted on being assigned something else. He tried to apologize, but Ty wasn't interested in hearing it. He said he'd had enough.

Dane leaned forward in his seat as they approached the address. His mouth fell open and his face contorted in the initial confusion, but seconds later it was followed by jubilation. What he saw wasn't what he expected: Dozens of giant windmills dotted the landscape. Dane considered this a fluff piece, but what he saw changed his mind. A heavy metal gate blocked the road, and a double fence surrounded the property, twelve feet high with razor wire on top of the outer fence.

"Holy shit," Ty said, turning his head to Dane. They grinned as they realized they were both wrong about this story. Ty followed the road farther west for two miles until the fence stopped and turned south. Driving along the exterior fence, they continued south for another mile until they saw what they had traveled all this way to find. Ty stopped the van, and Dane leaped out and ran across the road toward the twelve-foot-high fence. He grabbed the chain-link fence with both hands. His eyes darted across the horizon, counting the windmills as best he could. He expected two or three, but there were at least two dozen. Somebody was planning something big. Now, he just had to find out what.

SHERRI STOOD BY HER CAR, typing a text message to Steven in New York. Texting was something she still needed to master. It took excessively long to find the key with the right letter, mistakes happened way too often, and it was too difficult to correct them. As a professional writer, mistakes bothered her, and as an editor, they must have driven Steven nuts. She hoped one day someone would invent a phone with a typewriter keyboard. Sherri, frustrated the sheriff had gone to the base without her, gave him the benefit of the doubt that it was not intentional. While she stood there texting, a car pulled up next to her. Sherri noticed DOD and Edwards AFB stickers on the window.

The man exited his vehicle as Sherri strolled toward him. He appeared rather disheveled, wearing a wrinkled flannel shirt with a *Star Wars* T-shirt underneath, faded blue jeans, tattered sneakers, and uncombed hair.

"Hi," she said, reaching out her hand. "I'm Sherri Davis."

He looked at her strangely, as if unsure he should know her.

After a pause, he reached out and shook her hand. "I'm sorry, I'm Brent O'Malley. Please excuse me. I'm a little distracted today."

She noticed his pleasant voice. He'd be good on the radio. They released hands, and Sherri gave him a solemn look. "Are you here about the woman whose body was found last Friday?"

"Yes, she's a friend of mine."

She noticed he did not say *was* a friend. "Brent, I'm sorry for your loss. I'm a reporter for *The New York Times*. Friday, I stumbled upon the sheriff's department recovering the body in the desert."

"Oh," he said. "I've got to speak with the sheriff."

"The sheriff isn't here."

Brent shuffled off, ignoring her, and went in the front door. Sherri watched him enter the building and waited by his car. If he truly went to see the sheriff, he'd be back soon, and sure enough, several minutes later, he came back out, scratching his right cheek and running his hand toward the back of his neck.

"I tried to tell you he wasn't here," she said.

He looked at her as if he noticed her for the first time. "What did you say you do again?" His head tilted to the side.

"I'm a reporter for *The New York Times*," she said, handing him her business card. "I was in the area, investigating another story. Driving around the desert Friday morning, I stumbled upon the crime scene. I—"

"What crime scene?" Brent moved closer to her. "What do you know? We were never told this was a homicide."

Sherri recognized she now had the upper hand. "We know who I am. Who are you again?"

"I'm Brent O'Malley. I'm an aeronautical engineer at Edwards. Georgiana and I worked together."

That caught Sherri's attention. "Do you work with TRENCOR, too?"

Brent stammered for a moment, "How—how do you know about that?"

Sherri slinked over to Brent and placed her arm around his shoulders. "I think I need to buy you a drink. We've got a lot to talk about."

JASON MET JENNIFER at 1430 for a ride to TRENCOR Industries. The squadron commander was gone for the day, as was the lead test pilot. He'd have to meet them later. They headed outside, climbed into her Jeep, and drove north to California City. Earlier, he filled out a stack of nondisclosure statements and was briefed on the jet, the F-2000. If everything they said about this jet was true, it was going to be the most revolutionary design in high-performance aviation in decades. And he was going to fly it.

The compound sat to the southeast of Cal City and dwarfed everything in the area. The double fence with razor wire across the top made it resemble a prison more than a simulator facility.

When they reached the main entrance, Jason noticed the guard shack was not occupied. As they approached the facility, Jason was impressed with the contemporary architecture of the three-story complex. The glass windows at the entrance went up the entire three stories. The building looked like it belonged somewhere else—Los Angeles or Miami, maybe.

When they walked in, he was immediately overwhelmed with the change of environment. The air was set at a perfect temperature. Soft elevator music played over a hidden sound system, and the scent of fresh lilacs permeated the air.

Jennifer introduced him to the receptionist, who checked his military ID and took him to the security office for his TRENCOR ID. He filled out the appropriate paperwork and was told his security badge would be ready by the time they left. The receptionist gave him a visitor's badge for movement around the facility until then. Certain areas were off-limits to Air Force personnel, she explained, as she pulled out the map of the facility and handed it to Jason.

Jason thanked her and studied the expansive lobby. It was breathtaking. Fresh lilacs were placed throughout the lobby, along with numerous other plants. Original artwork hung throughout the lobby. The artwork was the type any pilot would love—original oil paintings of airplanes throughout history. Jason gently ran his finger across the canvas of a Sopwith Camel engaged in aerial combat, exploring the rough yet delicate texture of the painting.

He caught up with Jennifer, who was looking at him oddly from ten feet away. "Why'd they build this in Cal City?" Jason said.

"The land was cheap, I guess. Come on," Jennifer said, "let's check out the briefing room." They walked along the hallway and into the main conference room. A huge table sat in the center of the room. Built into the table at each seat were integrated computer displays, with the interior of the room decorated as exquisitely as the lobby.

Jennifer led him from the conference room to the simulator bay. The simulator bay itself was like any other: a large, enclosed bay with a thirty-foot-high ceiling, one attached room for the computer banks, and another where the simulator operator sat. Only one simulator occupied the large area at this time, but there was room for two more. The F-2000 simulator sat twelve feet off the ground on a series of hydraulic arms used to provide motion for the sim. They climbed the stairs and lowered the walkway to reach the cockpit.

She opened the cockpit, and he peered inside the state-of-the-art simulator.

He let out a low whistle. The interior was impressive. Glass cockpit, but much more streamlined than the T-38C upgrade for Air Education and Training Command. This consisted of nothing but flat panels. He could see the oxygen system and where the anti-G harness system connected. Several cannon plugs for electrical devices were visible, as well as three separate circuit breaker panels. He opened his mouth to ask a question, but decided against it.

"What the hell are you two doing up there?" a voice said from the ground.

They both turned to face the commanding voice.

"General," Jennifer said. "I'm so glad you're here," Jason noticed there was a little too much excitement in her voice as he looked down at the man in the civilian suit who stood with his arms folded across his chest. If this was who he thought, maybe the stories of the old wing commander were true.

She grabbed Jason's elbow and marched him toward the stairs, only letting go as she scurried down the steps to the floor. Jason lagged several feet behind, mainly to observe her reaction to the general.

By the time he reached the floor, Jennifer was standing in front of the general in a modified attention stance. The general leered at her. Jason couldn't make out what they were saying, but it made his stomach hurt thinking what it might be.

"General Wellington, I'd like you to meet Captain Jason Conrad. Captain Conrad will be the beta test for our simulated student pilot."

Jason stuck out his hand, "Nice to meet you, sir."

The general grunted as his smile went away and he shook Jason's hand. "So you're the FAIP? This is a multibillion-dollar program. I hope you don't screw the pooch."

Jason had a witty comeback, but chose to keep silent and nod his head.

The general looked back at Jennifer. "Has he signed the nondisclosure agreements?"

"Yes, sir."

"Has he been briefed on his role here?" Wellington said, ignoring the fact that Jason stood right in front of him.

"Yes, sir," she said.

The general nodded and stared at him, expressionless. "Good. A fucking FAIP will be perfect to play the part of a dumb student pilot."

33

May 7, 2001

JEREMIAH WELLINGTON left the two pilots in the simulator bay and sat outside David Ming's office, fidgeting. Normally he did not act this way, but the death of the Air Force program manager attached to their project made him nervous. He caught himself constantly rubbing his hands on his pants. Taking a deep breath, he focused on his objective. He needed Ming to understand the severity of a government investigation into the Georgiana Anderson situation.

He tried to speak to Mr. Ming several times that morning, but the CEO of TRENCOR Industries had a busy schedule. Wellington often questioned himself and his relationship with TRENCOR. They paid him extremely well to be the intermediary between the corporation and the US Air Force; some would say he was paid *too* well. He brushed it off as something he had earned. He sacrificed for thirty years as an Air Force officer, and the time had come to reap his rewards.

The phone on the desk buzzed, and Mr. Ming's secretary picked it up and spoke softly into the receiver. "Mr. Ming is ready to see you now," she said.

Wellington glided through the doorway. He had been in here many times, but it never ceased to impress him. The contrast of the huge office was immediate. Aesthetically, the interior design conflicted with the architecture and design of the rest of the building, but as a stand-alone room, it was exquisite. Fine mahogany bookshelves lined the walls on three of the four sides of the room. Custom crown molding adorned the ceiling, seamlessly integrating into the bookshelves.

Expensive, hand-carved furniture seemed over-the-top, but Wellington never mentioned it.

Ming sat behind his desk, reviewing papers. "Mister Wellington," he said, looking up from his work. "Please come sit." Ming motioned to the leather wing-backed chairs in front of his desk. "What can I do for you today?"

"Mr. Ming, I'm concerned about this death in the desert last Friday."

"Ah yes. Mrs. Anderson. Most unfortunate. How was she involved with the F-2000?"

"She was the program manager for the Air Force. Due to the nature of her job, someone might try to link TRENCOR Industries to her death and start digging deeper into our operation."

"How so?"

Wellington shifted in his seat. "Her job was to make sure we are on the up-and-up. With the problems we've had, I'm concerned someone may think she found something TRENCOR has to hide, so someone here had her eliminated."

"Is that what happened, Mr. Wellington?" Ming said, leaning forward, placing his hands flat on his desk.

"I don't think so. I mean no, of course not. I can't imagine anything like that taking place. But I don't want anyone from the outside snooping around here. This program is behind schedule and over budget by billions."

Ming picked up the phone and spoke in Chinese. Wellington hated when he did that. He didn't understand any of the language. They gave him the Rosetta Stone Mandarin Chinese course when TRENCOR hired him years ago. He was not required to learn it, so he never did.

"Had Mrs. Anderson been to our facility?"

"Yes, absolutely. That's why I'm concerned. She was last seen here on Friday during our sim test."

"I see."

"Mr. Ming, my sources tell me the sheriff is meeting with the wing commander as we speak. I'm not sure what is going on or how this lady died. But she was found in the middle of the desert with a bullet in her head. Whether it's suicide or murder, a lot of folks we don't want will be poking their noses under the TRENCOR tent."

"What do you think they might find?"

"Well, sir, I mean . . . nothing to do with her death, of course, but we are substantially behind on this project. We have taken most of our money up front. Quite frankly, have very little to show for it. I don't want anyone else from the Air Force nosing around."

Ming's glare cut into Wellington's consciousness. He was uncomfortable with the mood change.

The door at the back of the office opened. Wellington turned and saw Li Zhong standing in the doorway. Ming motioned for him to come to his desk.

"Mr. Wellington, thank you for your perspective. We will investigate this as soon as possible."

Wellington was stunned as he realized he was being asked to leave. "Mr. Ming, I—"

"That will be all, Mr. Wellington."

Wellington rose and slowly shuffled toward the door to the office, passing Li Zhong, who ignored the fact he was in the room. Reaching the doorway, he turned to see Ming stand and start talking softly in Chinese to Li Zhong. Sometimes he couldn't understand why Ming did some of the things he did. Moments like this frustrated the hell out of him. He wished he had taken that position with Lockheed-Martin.

SHERRI AND BRENT sat in a booth in the Voyager Airport Restaurant overlooking the runway at the airport in Mojave. It was past two o'clock in the afternoon and the restaurant, which served breakfast and lunch, would be closing soon. Sherri divulged to Brent her father's death in a TRENCOR combine, and Brent seemed to relax when he understood her interest in the company. She continued to explain everything she learned about TRENCOR Industries in the last three days as she stirred her coffee. When she finished, Brent talked about working with Georgiana and their incidents with TRENCOR. Sherri grew frustrated as Brent constantly talked about something, then stopped, before changing the subject and talking about something else.

"Brent, you're all over the map. What's going on?"

"I'm sorry," he said. "Sometimes I just get so much information bottled up, it's like a Bernoulli tube when I start talking."

Sherri leaned back in her chair, her face blank and eyebrows raised. "A what?"

"A Bernoulli tube. Bernoulli's principle is what the theory of lift is based on. That's how wind lifts an aircraft off the ground."

"Brent—"

"If you have a tube with fluid running through it and you compress the tube in the middle, the tube is narrower in that section. Fluid passing through the narrow section travels faster at a greater pressure.

Sometimes I get like a Bernoulli tube with things in my head. I start talking fast about too many things."

Sherri reached out and touched his arm. His eyes shot up and glanced at her briefly, then shot back to the table.

"Brent, I need you to stay focused. When you get too technical, it goes over my head."

"I'm sorry. I don't mean to come off as cryptic, but this project is highly classified. I can discuss TRENCOR because you've done your homework and all the information you've given me is obviously from an open source. But please don't ask me what we've been working on."

Sherri nodded. "I understand. You tell me what you think I need to know."

"I've told all there is to tell. Everything about Georgiana. What her job entailed— unclassified, of course. Everything I can think of about TRENCOR."

"What other areas does TRENCOR Industries work in?"

"Say again?"

"Um, there's probably a better way of asking this," Sherri said, shifting in her chair. "TRENCOR Industries is a huge conglomerate. Aviation research and development is one of their newer endeavors. Are you familiar with their corporation across the board?"

"Of course not. I'm an aeronautical engineer, so that's what I focus on. Georgiana did the data dive on TRENCOR's overall picture. Even then, she only scratched the surface. I believe most of the detailed research was done at Wright-Patterson Air Force Base. That's where the company liaisons are primarily based. There's a couple of folks at Warner Robbins in Georgia and a cell at the Pentagon. Wellington was part of that on active duty, but he retired and was hired by TRENCOR."

"Who is Wellington?"

Brent took another sip of coffee. "Jeremiah Wellington is TRENCOR Industries site manager. He's a retired one-star general. He was a test pilot back in the day. Spent most of his time in the test community. He was headed for bigger and brighter things as a young officer, but then stepped in it."

Sherri leaned in curiously, "How so?" she asked.

"Well," Brent stroked his beard as he started to grin. He leaned forward and lowered his voice. "This is all hearsay now. Rumor has it that when Wellington was a major, he pulled one of the greatest practical jokes in the history of Edwards Air Force Base. Only some folks didn't think it was such a practical joke."

"What happened?"

Brent searched the restaurant to see if anyone was around them, as if whatever he was about to reveal was far more important than what they had already discussed.

"This happened when the B-2 program was still top secret and no one had any idea the program existed. The facilities were being constructed and refurbished on the south side of the main runway, and someone pulled the greatest practical joke of all time. Between the hangar and the main building, there is a patch of grass, which is unusual for this area. But in the middle of it is a recreational area. You know, picnic tables, grills, those kind of things."

"What's so unusual about that?"

"Nothing. Unless you're a couple of thousand feet overhead. The picnic area is almost to scale the exact dimensions of the outline of the B-2 bomber."

He let Sherri digest that for a moment.

Brent continued as he stroked his beard. "It wasn't obvious to anyone what the design was until several months after the public announcement of the B-2. Some intelligence agency picked up chatter somewhere. The Russians were talking about a sidewalk shaped like the B-2, how long it was there, and why didn't they make the connection sooner."

"How was Wellington involved?"

"It was his idea. Or at least he took the fall. No one is really sure. Shortly thereafter, he was sent to the Pentagon, but he continued to make rank. That happens when you're protected. Anyway, it's a great story, whether it's true or not."

The waitress came by their table and poured them both more coffee. Sherri took a sip and brushed the red bangs from the front of her face. "Let me ask you something. How many people work at TRENCOR? I drove by the facility Friday afternoon and this morning. It's a ghost town. Why?"

"Georgiana was always asking that," Brent replied. He started to come alive, as if reminded of a topic he meant to discuss but had forgotten. "She wanted to know why TRENCOR had this huge facility, but very little staff."

"For future expansion, right?"

"Yes. We've been told that after the welcome banquet this Friday, the rest of TRENCOR's employees will migrate into the facility."

"What welcome banquet?"

"It's not really a welcome banquet. It's probably more like a reception. TRENCOR wants to spend money on a party, I guess. They'll add the cost to the bill, no doubt."

"What's the purpose of this event?"

Brent took a sip of his coffee and set the cup on the table. "That's the day the first prototype of the F-2000 arrives at Edwards."

Sherri's eyebrows rose as she leaned toward Brent.

"What's the F-2000?"

34

May 7, 2001

THE SUN HAD SET on another beautiful Southern California day, and the temperature dropped several degrees with nightfall. Jason returned to his billeting room to review the stacks of in-processing paperwork he'd received. He was frustrated with how long everything took and realized it was his first time changing assignments since he joined the Air Force. He would probably move several more times over the years, which meant even more paperwork. His cell phone rang and he picked it up, glancing at the incoming number as he flipped it open.

"Hey Caldwell, how you doing?"

"I'm doing fine, Jason," replied the CIA agent. "How was the trip out?"

"It was fine. I made good time. It's beautiful country out here, and the view on the road was fantastic. I wish I could have taken more time and enjoyed the sights along the way, but obviously I was in a hurry."

"I understand what that's like." Caldwell paused. "Are you alone out there?"

Jason grimaced. "Yes, Mom, right now, I'm alone."

"Hey, it's a legitimate question. You said she was coming out there."

"Damn, Caldwell, I've only been here two days. She should be here Wednesday."

Caldwell paused. "It's taking her that long to get out there?"

"She had loose ends to tie up, then she's flying out."

"Loose ends? Flying? What's she going to do with her car? What does she have to tie up? Is she working? Jason, there are so many unanswered questions about this girl. I'm sorry, but the counterintelligence hairs are standing up on my neck."

Sighing, Jason shifted in his chair. He knew what Caldwell was trying to say—something about Kathy didn't add up. "I understand. I don't know what she's been doing the last six years, or what kind of job she has now. She could be married for all I know." Jason hesitated for the next statement. "You said you'd look into her background. Can you do that for me?"

There was a brief pause on the other end of the phone. "I've already started."

"I figured as much. Hey, I know you're trying to help. Don't be in too much of a rush, though. Our reunions are incredible." He grinned as the memories whirled through his head. There was a knock on the door, and Jason turned his head, wondering who it could be at this time of night. "Hey, I've got to run. Someone's at the door."

Caldwell laughed on the other end of the phone. "Fair enough. Be careful out there, Jason."

"I will. Tell Nancy hello. I'll talk to you later," Jason said and closed the flip phone.

Jason moved to the door and grabbed the doorknob. Who knew he was here? Then, he caught himself. Every time he talked to Caldwell, he reverted to "trust no one" and "everyone is the enemy." He shook off the negative vibes and opened the door.

Standing in front of him was Major Jennifer Watson, civilian style. He had forgotten she mentioned dinner. Insisted on it was more like it. She was wearing four-inch navy blue high heels and a royal blue miniskirt. A skin-tight, light blue T-shirt cut off several inches below her bra-less breasts exposed her bare midsection. In her hands she carried a tan overcoat. It was cold outside, the temperature in the low sixties and dropping. She lunged for him with her arms out.

"Oh, Jason," she exclaimed, "it's sooo good to see you!"

Jennifer pressed her breasts into his ribs. This wasn't a hug, it was an invitation. No, not an invitation—a demand. Two weeks ago, he would've taken her. Now, with Kathy back in the picture, he wasn't so sure.

"Hi, Major," he replied. "I forgot you mentioned dinner earlier today."

"Cut the rank. It's Jen to you."

"Okay, Jen. I'm just trying to maintain professional decorum."

"I forgot—Jason Conrad, consummate professional. Get dressed, we're going out."

Jason scratched his head. "Jen, I appreciate it, but . . ." He hesitated. If he went out, he knew what would happen. Dinner, drinks, and then she'd either want to show him her place, or she'd insist on coming back here. He knew her tactics; she had a reputation at Vance among the instructor cadre, and was very much despised amongst the spouses.

"I see you hesitating, Jason. Don't worry—there is no work you've got to get done before tomorrow. We've slowed to a crawl this week because of the memorial service on Wednesday. Your first academic courses won't be until Thursday morning, and you won't get access to your pubs until then."

She approached him again, placed her left forearm against his right shoulder, and stared up into his eyes. "So come on," she said softly. "Let's go have a good time tonight."

Jason wondered how he could get out of this. At a new assignment, the last thing he wanted was to show up on day two and have a bad reputation.

"Maj—uh, Jen, I'm kind of in a relationship right now."

"How are you *kind of* in a relationship? You either are or you aren't."

"Okay, I'm in a relationship."

"How? With who? You lived in Enid. There's no one there to date."

"Well, there was—"

Her eyes went wide as she reached out and playfully punched his bicep. "NO! That girl? The one from Chicaros that everyone drooled over? What's her name, Karen?"

"Kathy."

"She came back?"

"Yes, last week."

Jen laughed. "Oh, her timing is perfect! A lot of good she did you the last six years." Jen sauntered close to him and ran her finger up the buttons of his shirt. She gazed at him with a glimmer of hope as she pressed her hand against his chest. "Well . . . she's not here, once again."

35

May 7, 2001

THE LONG DRIVE to the Texas Cattle Company restaurant in Lancaster went quickly. From the outside, the Western aura made him feel like he was entering a saloon. The interior was nicely decorated with wood-paneled walls and ceiling fans. They bypassed the line for a table and took a booth in the bar. Jason noticed Jennifer garnering a lot of attention from most of the male patrons.

The waitress arrived and took their drink order and gave Jennifer a dirty look. Jennifer seemed not to notice as she ordered a Chardonnay and Jason ordered a Coors Light.

"So Jason, tell me what's going on with you since I last saw you in Enid."

"I've stayed busy. I've done the things I'm supposed to do. Filled all my squares. I've done Squadron Officer School in correspondence and in residence, and finished my master's degree. I've been a check-pilot and flight commander, and worked in stan/eval for a while. I've kind of done it all."

"That's smart. So many pilots don't do what they need to do to get promoted."

"That's because the airlines are hiring like crazy. We have guys at Vance separate from the Air Force the moment their initial commitment is up and walk across the street to get hired by the Reserve Squadron. They don't skip a beat. They're already current and qualified. Hell, the ones that don't have airline jobs yet get picked up by a civilian contractor to be a simulator instructor. It's a great gig for those guys."

"Interesting. What are your plans?"

"Uh, I just got this assignment. I'm not sure what I'll be doing. I thought I was going to be a T-38 pilot, but obviously there's much more to it."

Jennifer nodded and started to respond when the waitress arrived with their drinks. Jason took a swig of his beer when Jennifer raised her glass for a toast. "To old friends," she said. Jason acknowledged by clinking her glass.

"This job is highly classified," she said, peering from side to side. "Your position is listed as a T-38 pilot because we didn't want to raise any suspicions by listing it as classified."

Jason nodded as his gaze shifted to the table. He was familiar with these types of jobs. Usually they were "by name" requests. Things were starting to become clear.

AS SHERRI LEFT THE AIRPORT meeting with Brent, Steven called with a possible contact for the Saudis. Sherri headed south on Highway 14 toward Palmdale. When she arrived, the tip turned out to be another dead end since the contact didn't show.

Heading back to Cal City, she was tired and hungry and needed a drink. She stopped in Lancaster for gas, and the girl behind the counter recommended a friendly restaurant a couple blocks away.

When she entered the Texas Cattle Company, the hostess offered her a table, but the wait was going to be thirty minutes. She slid into the booth by the bar.

It wasn't long after she starting sipping her Jack and Coke before the first male suitor began the hunt. Sherri politely insisted she was there for dinner. It must have become an event to hit on her. Over the next ten minutes, four more men came by her table.

Once her steak arrived, she was left alone. Sherri ate quickly because she didn't want to stay much longer. As she finished her second Jack and Coke, two men at the bar stood up, yelling and pushing each other. Another man walked by them as the two pushed more aggressively. The innocent bystander was pushed off-balance, stumbling and half landing on the empty bench in her booth.

She started to smile, but caught herself. The bystander watched the two men fight while she studied him. He was handsome enough— sandy blond hair and fit. And he looked like her type, the rugged individualist—confident in himself and not afraid of a challenge. But she wasn't in the mood for conversation. The man watched the two struggle for a moment until two employees broke up the incident. Finally he looked at her and grinned.

"Nice entrance."

"Thanks," the man responded. His eyes locked on hers. "It wasn't planned, although I might've planned something like this in a previous life. I'm Jason Co—"

"Thank you, but no," she said forcefully. She fought the urge to talk to the handsome stranger with the nice smile. "I'm here for dinner, which I am about to finish. I came here alone, and I plan on leaving alone." Sherri glanced across the bar and a half-naked dirty blonde stared daggers at her. "Besides, I think your wife objects to you sitting here."

"Oh, she's not my wife." The man chuckled.

"Your hooker?"

"No." His smile faded, and she realized she might have gone too far.

"Fine. Look, I'm not interested. Every asshole in this place as approached me since I sat down. I just want to go back to my hotel and get some sleep."

He gave her a quirky look. "You did see this, right? I didn't just hop over here. Those two clowns knocked me off-balance and I fell."

"Yeah, and so did every other asshole in here," Sherri said in a Bronx accent.

"I'm not an asshole. I'm a jet pilot," he said.

"Is there a difference? I thought the whole *Top Gun* thing died out years ago. Let me guess. I'm supposed to 'take you to bed or lose you forever'".

He shot the same daggers at her that his date had moments ago. Sherri, internally jumping victoriously, watched with a blank expression as he stood and walked off.

36

JENNIFER AND JASON didn't speak much on the drive back to the base. Not that there was anything wrong. Jennifer struggled with her feelings. She had wanted to sleep with Jason since the first time she saw him. When it was revealed his father was running for president, she wanted him more. But she had a pretty good thing going with General Wellington. True, he was older, and she had seduced him, but her feelings were genuine. He charmed her right out of her pants and didn't even know it. She loved everything about him, except his wife. He assured her he would leave her soon, but Jennifer was reluctant to put all of her eggs in that basket. Other men had made the same promise and never delivered.

She was well aware that she had been the subject of gossip in the wives' network. It was partly earned in her days as a lieutenant when she dabbled with the enlisted force. She still had a bad habit of flirting with them. It was a power trip, making some poor sweaty think he was going to screw an officer. The reality was that her sexual liaisons were limited, and the last three years she'd only been with the general. But how does a single woman with a body like hers lose a bad reputation? What could she do except get married? Jennifer saw she had a limited window, which could go one of two ways: she could sleep with Jason tonight and hope he left his girlfriend, or she could return to the general tomorrow and hope he left his wife.

"Don't you think you need to slow down?" Jason said loudly.

"Huh?" Jennifer said, snapping out of her thoughts.

"You're doing seventy in a forty-five."

"Oh, thanks," she said, letting off the gas. "I need to stop by my apartment to check on something."

She had to think quickly.

"I think I left my stove on, and I don't want my apartment to burn down because I drove past it to take you home."

"Okay." She could sense the skepticism in his voice.

Jennifer grinned like a Cheshire cat and put her eyes back on the road. Ten minutes later, they pulled into her apartment complex in Rosamond. Jennifer turned off the ignition and climbed out of her Jeep. She glanced at Jason, who was still buckled in.

"Don't you want to come inside?"

Jason hesitated.

"Don't worry, I'm not going to jump you. Unless you want me to," she said wryly.

"I—"

"I'm kidding, Jason. Geez. Come on in and let me show you my place. Once your dream girl shows up, you'll probably never come over here again."

Jason smiled slightly and nodded. "Okay, but I don't want to stay too long. I've got a lot to do tomorrow, and I need some rest."

Jennifer rolled her eyes and grabbed him by the hand.

He followed her up the stairs to her second-floor apartment. When they entered, Jennifer marched straight to the kitchen and pretended to check her stove. "Oh, good," she said, "it's off." She turned slowly and leaned against the stove with her legs crossed at the ankle and her hands behind her back. Jason stood by the doorway, glancing around the apartment. "Well, come on in and make yourself at home."

Jennifer proceeded to give him the tour of her apartment. She didn't linger around the bedroom too long because she didn't want to spook him. It was a good call because Jason perked up as soon as they moved away from the bedroom. They wandered around in no particular order, and she talked about how different items in her apartment related to different assignments. It was awkward, and she struggled with ways to seduce him. He paused at the mantle over her fireplace and picked up her small, gold-colored model of the F-2000. The model was about five inches long and rested on a pedestal about three-and-a-half inches high. It wasn't a shiny gold like you see on a trophy; it was more yellowish, as if it tarnished slightly by all the hands that no doubt had touched it over time.

"This is nice," he said. "Where can I get one of these?"

"There aren't any more of those around," she said. "General Wellington said there were only ten of them made, and they were only given out to certain people."

"Is this gold-plated?"

"Of course not," but his question made her wonder. She'd never asked the general what it was made of. He told her there were only ten of these made and she was never to lose it because it would be valuable one day. "When have you known the government to buy a gold-plated model to give away?"

"Never." He set the model back on the mantle.

"Jason, don't mention the model to anyone. Curt Samson, the lead test pilot, didn't get one, and neither did anyone else on the Air Force team." She started to worry maybe she was revealing a little too much to Jason.

"And you did?" he said, a hint of accusation in his voice, as if she had done something unethical to earn it.

"Yeah," she said as she placed her hands behind her back, pushing her breasts slightly forward and she swayed back and forth. "Perks of having these, I guess."

"Clearly."

Jason's phone rang, and he pulled it out of his pocket. "I've got to get this." He flipped it open. "Kathy, hi . . ." he said, turning away to speak. Jennifer's shoulders sank as she realized her opportunity was lost.

IT HAD BEEN A LONG DAY in the office for Wellington. He was frustrated with his boss, who basically ignored his concerns for protecting the company. Wellington was convinced the death of the Air Force project manager would somehow be a thorn in their side.

Jennifer had shown up with Jason Conrad at TRENCOR earlier today. She had feelings for Conrad, he was sure of it. She was too giddy when they were at the simulator. He became more suspicious when, after work, he drove by her apartment and she wasn't home. Where the hell was she? Normally, she was at home or with him.

Wellington knew he ran the risk of losing her. She'd pressured him several times about leaving his wife. He kept promising her he would when the time was right.

But now this Conrad character was in the picture, and Jennifer was nowhere to be found. He sat in his BMW fifty yards away from her apartment, his eyes on her building. After an hour sitting there watching her apartment, Jennifer showed up with Conrad. She practically dragged him by the hand upstairs.

He pulled away from the side of the road and drove to his house. The images of the two having sex weaved through his mind, and it pissed him off. He'd brought this guy on board to secure the technology they needed from his father's company. Well, they'd acquired the technology. He could get rid of Jason Conrad just as easily as he brought him in.

THE SMALL, TWIN-ENGINE AIRCRAFT landed at an abandoned blacked-out airfield north of Helendale. Ten dark figures exited the ramp in the back of the plane, each carrying large cases. Four black SUVs were parked nearby to pick them up. No sooner had the vehicles started to wheel away than the aircraft turned around on the runway and took off south, toward Mexico.

The small parade of black SUVs drove on back roads south toward Helendale, turning west until they reached Highway 395, and then north. The deputy sheriff's vehicle met them where Highway 395 hit Highway 58. He was out of his jurisdiction, but that was irrelevant. The deputy took the lead as the formation headed west toward California City. The deputy didn't use his flashing lights or sirens—his mission was strictly to escort and run interference in case anything unusual happened.

Making a right turn onto California City Boulevard, the entourage drove north to the compound entrance. The deputy stopped at the gate, and the four black SUVs raced through toward TRENCOR Industries. Darkness enveloped the industrial compound like a thick leather glove. The moon's illumination was less than five percent, and the overcast sky washed out the stars. Electrical power to the streetlights had been cut, as had all exterior power to the building, from the parking lot to the doorway.

TRENCOR Industries sat in total blackness.

The four vehicles stopped at the front entrance of TRENCOR. Armed men leaped out of the front and rear vehicles and took defensive positions, scanning the area surrounding the building. Simultaneously, the men from the middle two vehicles spilled out of the right sides of the vehicles and moved quickly into the facility. Seven guards took position around the outside doorway.

David Ming stood in the dimly lit lobby with Li Zhong standing behind him. Both bowed as the entourage approached.

"General Jingguo, welcome. I hope your trip was comfortable."

"Mr. Ming," the general replied in Chinese, "our comfort is irrelevant. Shall we get started?"

The two men entered the TRENCOR facility and watched as General Jingguo's men unloaded the SUVs.

"I'm concerned about this Jeremiah Wellington," General Jingguo said without looking at Ming. "What does he know?"

"He knows nothing," Ming said. "The self-corrupting software has been a most ingenious design. He is not capable of detecting it."

General Jingguo nodded his head slightly, his arms crossed behind his back. "What about Operation Dragonfly? Does he suspect anything?"

"No. The spray system has been integrated into the jet seamlessly. Our engineers have replaced the original aircraft schematics, and no one is the wiser."

"Good."

"General," Ming said, "help me understand Beijing's thinking. We've designed a plan to steal billions of dollars from the Department of Defense, and it's working. Why do they insist on using this jet for Operation Dragonfly?"

Ming noticed Li Zhong turn his head toward him briefly, and General Jingguo turned to face him.

"It is not our place to question Beijing, Mr. Ming. Perhaps this chemical is too experimental for use in China. If we are to taint an area and make it unsafe, better it be in America and not our home."

Ming absorbed the last statement. He had been told his operation in the United States would be coming to an end in the fall, and he was to return to China. Now he knew why. There was a much bigger plan in place.

AFTER GENERAL JINGGUO'S MEN finished unloading and the SUVs drove off. Outside, Ming's helicopter flew overhead and landed on the pad.

"General Jingguo, my ride has arrived. You are welcome to stay at my residence in the mountains if you like."

"Thank you, but no," General Jingguo said. "My place is with my team. I understand your accommodations here are more than adequate."

"As you wish. Li Zhong, please ensure the General and his men are taken care of."

"Yes, Mr. Ming," Li Zhong said, bowing.

General Jingguo watched Ming step out the door to the waiting helicopter.

"Does Ming know the true extent of Operation Dragonfly?"

"No sir," Li Zhong said. "He believes we are testing a cloud-seeding formula to produce rain."

"How do you explain our interaction with the Saudis?"

"They live in the desert. Rain would give them a stronger agricultural base. It makes sense."

"Good."

"David Ming is too focused on the financial aspects of TRENCOR Industries," Li Zhong said. "He doesn't examine the scientific or technical details of the company."

"We must make sure it stays that way. If he were to find out the true objective of Operation Dragonfly, he might pose a problem."

37

May 9, 2001

JASON SAT IN THE CLASSIFIED VAULT at the 445th Flight Test Squadron. The air was stifling, a tabletop fan across the room providing circulation. The room itself was about ten by fifteen feet, with a row of classified file cabinets at one end and an airman sitting in front of them at a desk. The airman spent most of his day reading a book since he couldn't surf the Internet in the classified vault.

Having no flight publications of his own, Jason had to come to the vault to read them or go to TRENCOR's simulator facility. Jennifer had brought him to the vault earlier to show him how he could access the manuals on the F-2000.

Surprisingly, Jennifer wasn't angry with him. She had come on to him pretty strong on Monday night, but he had been able to deflect her advances with stories about Kathy. It had been a long, slow week, and the funeral for Georgiana Anderson yesterday had occupied everyone's thoughts.

Leaning forward in his chair, Jason poured over the stack of pubs on the classified fighter. He skimmed each book, reviewing the table of contents and flipping through every page. The Dash-1, the aircraft manual, was incomplete, with every page watermarked "DRAFT." Section 3, the Emergency Procedures section, was blank. There was an Emergency Procedures supplement in a separate notebook provided by TRENCOR Industries, but it had not been tested and put in the Dash-1 yet. The Air Force test team made additions to this section after every simulator sortie.

The door to the vault opened and a bearded, paunchy civilian wearing black-rimmed glasses and a Spider-Man T-shirt entered the vault. "Hi," he said, "you must be the FAIP."

Jason tilted his head with an inquisitive slant. "Yes, I guess I am. Jason Conrad. Nice to meet you," he said, shaking hands.

"I'm Brent O'Malley. I'm an aeronautical engineer for the F-2000, or F2K as we like to call it. Welcome aboard. You're going to be our lab rat, I hear?"

"I'm not sure what my role is."

"Curt Samson is the lead test pilot. He's running this show from the Air Force side and will fill you in soon. We have been having our issues with the contractor, but you'll learn about them in due time."

"I've been skimming these pubs, but most of them are incomplete. I admit," he said, raising his hands in defeat, "I'm in over my head. I can't make sense out of this material."

"It'll come. Major Samson will have a training program set up for you. I'd stop studying this information for now. You were brought here to test the concept of this aircraft."

Jason leaned back in his chair. "What do you mean?"

"Well," Brent said, taking a seat across from Jason, "the F2K is supposed to be *the* sixth-generation fighter. There are several technical advances making this jet light-years ahead of the F-22, and it's not even in production yet. The concept is to have a jet that is 'user-friendly' and trains pilots in minimal time. There's state-of-the-art nonlethal weapon capability, but you'll be dealing with the flight portion.

"Because they've had a lot of problems with the sim, this test program has been ass-backwards. They want the Air Force to fill out the test cards to say they've done it. The jet arrives in two days, and they'll start the taxi tests next week and get it airborne sometime after that. Anyway, you probably shouldn't be studying these yet, mainly for the integrity of the test program. The test requirement calls for an inexperienced pilot to go through the training program to validate the concept."

Jason closed the Dash-1 he had been reading. "Is this a problem? Did I get myself in trouble?"

"No," Brent said, laughing, "I don't think you've had enough time to compromise the program. What do you say I take you around and introduce you to some folks? I hear you already know Major Walton," he said with a grin.

"I know her," he said defensively. "I don't *know* her."

Brent chuckled, "I got ya. She can be aggressive, I hear. You seem like a nice fella. Just so you're in the loop, she's the one who brought up your name for this. So if anyone looks at you kind of funny, that's probably why."

"Swell. Never get a second chance to make a first impression, huh?"

"Nope."

"Hopefully it's obvious why I'm hiding in here."

"It's a good start."

Jason closed the books on the table, returned them to the airman, and followed Brent out of the vault. They walked to the Command Suite, but the Squadron Commander was across the base at a meeting with the wing commander. Jason rescheduled his appointment for Friday, and the two left the office.

When they stepped into the hallway outside the commander's office, Jason was pushed to the side by a short, balding old man wearing a flight suit rushing toward Life Support.

"Hey," he said to no avail. Perturbed, he turned to Brent, who laughed.

"Don't you know who—? Never mind," Brent said as he turned and continued walking, Jason several feet behind him.

At the end of the hallway, Brent stopped at an open door and knocked. The major sitting at his computer didn't move.

"Curt, have you met Jason Conrad yet?"

Major Curt Samson looked up from his computer screen at the two men standing in his doorway.

"No, I haven't. Come on in," he said. "You must be the FAIP."

"Yes, I get that a lot."

"Welcome aboard. I take it Major Walton has ensured you're getting settled in?" he said with a similar grin to Brent's.

"We're not that close," Jason rebutted. "Let's just say I'm in a committed relationship elsewhere."

"Noted. Enough said."

Brent spoke up. "I found him in the vault reviewing the pubs. I figured you wanted him to start at a specific point when we would be calculating his study time."

"Yeah, nice save. Sorry, Jason, you've been brought here for a specific purpose. You're part of the test team, but you're our 'monkey in a space capsule.'"

"Say again?" Jason said, unsure of what he implied.

"The F2K is a state-of-the-art, sixth-generation fighter. We take a kid straight out of advanced jet training and stick him in the jet. Minimum training, both on the ground and in the air. We don't want to test our program with a brand-new pilot, so someone like you seemed to be the next best thing. Major Walton recommended you, and I guess because of your father, you are the lucky candidate."

"My father's not in the Senate anymore," Jason said. He didn't appreciate the implication he rode his father's coattails.

"No, he's not. But he *is* the executive vice president for Century Aero-Bot. It was a business decision rather than a political one. Mr. Wellington decided it would help TRENCOR acquire the RPA/SIP system, which Century owns. I don't know if you were a factor, but you're here and we got it. All I know is that your FEF says you're a good pilot. That's good enough for me."

Jason calmed down slightly, but he grew tired of having his father's clout being pushed in front of him. He thought he had distanced himself from this, but apparently not.

"Thanks," he said.

"Look, Jason, we'll get together tomorrow and discuss your training. It's going to be fast-paced, and I want you to be ready. I've spent a lot of time on this syllabus, and I think it's a good plan. In the meantime, take time to explore the base. There's a ton of aviation history here. Learn your way around, enjoy yourself. Once we start working, you won't have time for any of that."

Jason nodded. "Okay, sounds like a good idea." He was noncommittal. He would save his opinion of Major Curt Samson for another day.

KATHY'S PLANE LANDED at Los Angeles International Airport two hours earlier. She retrieved her luggage, acquired a rental car, and headed for the interstate. Weaving her way through the congested traffic, aspects of her mission played in her mind over and over again. What was Nikolai up to? She was supposed to kill the father of the man she loved. A man whose life she saved six years earlier.

Could she kill Bowman and defect to America? How could she do it and keep Jason from finding out? Maybe she and Jason could find a way to make it work. She could defect and not kill Bowman, but Section Nine would kill her if she didn't follow through. How would Jason react if he knew her secret? There was no telling, but she suspected he wouldn't take it well.

Pulling off a random exit, she drove through various streets, being mindful of the direction she needed to drive to return to the interstate. Kathy needed to contact Nikolai, well aware the Americans monitored his phone. Meandering through the cluttered streets of East L.A., she realized this portion of the city was somewhere she didn't want to stay.

She pulled over and placed the car in park. The shiny new rental stood out in the decaying neighborhood. Locking the doors, she scanned the surrounding area. The only people she could see were a couple of kids playing up the street. It was still early, but as the morning dragged on, the night-stalkers would rise and meander the filthy streets of East Los Angeles. Kathy reached into her purse and pulled out the third-generation Glock 19. She checked the magazine, put a round in the chamber, and set the pistol in her lap. She pulled out her disposable cell phone with the newly activated account. Dialing a number from memory, she waited for the line to pick up on the other end. A woman's voice answered.

"I need to speak to Mike."

There was pause on the other end. "Good morning, Ann," Nikolai said. "How is your trip going?"

"It's going well. I'm in a better position now. My boyfriend was very happy to see me."

"I suppose you had a happy reunion?"

Kathy sneered; she knew what he asked. "Oh, yes, we've had many happy reunions. In fact, when I see him this afternoon, we'll have another happy reunion." She liked pissing him off. "My situation has changed. I sent you an e-mail with an update." Nikolai had a special e-mail account bouncing through several servers around the globe to make it difficult to track his IP address. Kathy sent the e-mail the day before, explaining the reunion with Jason Conrad in Enid, his new assignment to Edwards AFB, and what she considered her next step. They had another account through which he would give her follow-on instructions, so there was no way to match the two e-mails to each other.

"Stay on the line," Nikolai said. He had not taken the time to follow protocol for communications with an agent in the field. This worried Kathy. For the last six years, Nikolai had experienced a gradual decay in efficiency. The power had gone to his head, and he made decisions based on his ego or his crotch.

Kathy scanned her surroundings again. The children who had been playing now stood on the corner with a teenager, pointing at her car. She touched the Glock in her lap and continued the scan her position.

"Okay, I have your e-mail. Okay . . . uh, yes . . . OH! This is most fortunate! You are quite the risk-taker. Continue with your course of action. Clearly the two of you were meant to be together."

She looked again at the small group on the corner. The onlookers continued to grow as two men arrived, one carrying a baseball bat and the other a crowbar, both of them staring at her car.

"Yes, Co—," she caught herself. Was she getting sloppy also? "Yes, Mike. I look forward to hearing from you."

Kathy hung up her cell phone, pulled out a handkerchief, wiped the phone thoroughly, and dropped it out the window on the street. The two men carrying the bat and crowbar were heading her way at a steady pace. She reached into her lap and wrapped her hand around the Glock.

Without warning, a young Hispanic gangbanger popped up on the passenger side of her vehicle, pointing a semiautomatic pistol at her through the window.

"Buenos días, señorita. Please step out of the car. You can leave the pistol on the seat."

38

May 9, 2001

THE DESKTOP COMPUTER whirred to life once again as its parent computers covering the back wall of the office systematically collected vast amounts of information. It had been fifteen minutes since Nikolai Gregarin, head of the GRU's Section Nine, had received a phone call in Europe. The Communications Division of the CIA at Langley desperately attempted to find out who called him. The wall-based computers were cumbersome but perfect for converting the analog signals older European phone systems still used into a digital format. Four different systems with large disks attached in the front, resembling the old reel-to-reel stereo systems, worked to break the signal diversions. The desktop computer took those inputs, running them through a database, and attempted to match them with a particular area code. It was laborious, and Section Nine's communications team was very skilled at hiding their calls.

Gregarin's phone call came from a woman, an agent based somewhere in the US. The technician had difficulty tracking the signal. Whoever devised the pathway did an excellent job. Nikolai was in Norway, but the signal traced to Paris, London, Florence, and now Barcelona.

Carl Smith, impressed with their work, continued sorting through the data. He was old-school CIA, a relic from the Cold War. Tracking cell phones was one of the latest areas of expertise he had acquired. Carl, as a true professional, admired good work, regardless of which side did it. It forced him to rise to the occasion. If they did good work, his work had to be better.

KATHY CURSED HERSELF for her own sloppiness. Cautiously, she placed the pistol on the passenger seat and slowly raised her hands. The Hispanic with the crowbar rushed over and motioned for her to come out. Kathy methodically exited the car, keeping her eye on the young man with the pistol.

As soon as she stood up, the man carrying the baseball bat grabbed her by the hair, pulling her away from the open door. The muscular Hispanic, in his late twenties or early thirties, shoved his face within six inches of hers, his breath reeking of stale beer. He wore baggy pants and a muscle shirt about two sizes too small. A variety of tattoos covered his arms and shoulders. Two-week-old stubble covered his face; Kathy figured shaving—or bathing, for that matter—were not part of his personal hygiene.

He spun her around, pushing her forward. Her reflexes still in place, she caught herself with her hands against the car. The unshaven thug dropped his bat, kicked her feet apart, and began to crudely search her for weapons. It was more likely he was feeling her up. The thug spent a long time on her breasts, her crotch, and rear. Then he worked down each leg of the tight blue jeans to her tennis shoes.

He held a switchblade up in her face and pushed the release, the blade swinging out with an audible click. It was meant to intimidate her, but Kathy ignored it as she continued to study her situation. He spun her around again, ripping open her blouse with the knife, one button at time, exposing her beige bra. The unshaven one grinned sadistically as he moved his face close to hers. His tongue wet his lips as he stared at her breasts. He placed the switchblade near her waist, digging the sharp blade into the surface of her skin. The blood from the wound oozed down her hip, soaking the top of her jeans.

Kathy returned her focus to the teenager with the pistol. He moved to her side of the car, most likely to get a better view of what his partner was doing. He appeared to be about seventeen, thin, wearing baggy black pants with an oversized black shirt. A bright red bandana was wrapped around his head, in contrast to the all-black ensemble. The man with the crowbar still stood behind the open driver's-side door. He had a pudgy face, and his exposed forearms showed no indication of muscular development. Kathy noticed he was more interested in his friend's actions than grabbing her Glock from the seat.

The unshaven thug reached up to grab her bra. Kathy looked at the one with the pistol, who seemed both confused and excited. She gave him a wink with a seductive smile, which confused him more. The unshaven one struggled with the snap on Kathy's bra, which was fine with her. Placing both hands on the shoulders of her assailant, she swiftly drove her knee into his crotch.

Kathy held onto him as he doubled over in pain, quickly turning her attention to the kid with the pistol. He hesitated as he saw her standing half naked, holding his partner. Raising the pistol in her direction, he squeezed off three shots.

Shielding herself with the grimacing, unshaven thug, Kathy felt his body convulse two of the three rounds struck his body. After the third shot, Kathy heard a familiar click. Looking past the limp body of her assailant, Kathy saw the slide on the young Hispanic's pistol in the aft position, indicating his magazine was empty. He stared at the pistol, as if unsure of what happened.

The chubby one stood behind the door, holding his crowbar loosely. His dirty skin glistened as the perspiration gathered on his pudgy face and forearms.

Kathy and the teen both looked at the empty gun, then at each other. He took two steps toward her before throwing his gun at her. The pistol hit the thug's shoulder and clattered on the dry pavement. Kathy tossed her assailant to the ground and pounced on the shooter as he turned to run. Wrapping both arms around his head, she snapped his neck effortlessly, his body falling to the ground.

The ping of metal on concrete caught Kathy's attention. She turned to the chubby one and saw the crowbar had slipped out of his hands. He slammed the door and ran toward the corner where the small crowd stood.

Kathy reached across the seat and grabbed her Glock. She stepped back into the street and took aim at the fleeing hoodlum, now twenty meters away. As she squeezed the trigger, he turned his head slightly. In a moment, the 9 mm round impacted the side of his skull. Blood, brains, and bone fragments spewed into the air as his body ceased moving forward, falling toward the ground.

The whole incident took less than ten seconds.

Pulling the pistol to a ready position, she scanned each quadrant, searching for the next potential threat. The abandoned streets were silent, except for the noise from someone's stereo in an apartment. Scanning every window nearby, she deftly moved back to the other two hoodlums lying on the pavement. The one shot by his partner lay bleeding in the street. He wasn't dead yet, but he would die before any type of medical help arrived as the blood pooled under his body. His glazed eyes stared lifelessly as blood dripped out of his mouth.

Climbing into her car, Kathy grabbed the paper napkins on the console and pressed them against the knife wound on her hip. It wasn't deep and would require no stitches. Kathy pulled her shirt together, covering herself. She buttoned the one button left on her blouse and closed her door. The adrenaline pumped through her system as her mind struggled to keep up with the rest of her body. Her reactions had been based on training and instinct—now she needed to think.

Remembering her phone on the ground, she picked it up and tossed it onto the passenger seat. She didn't want the dead bodies tied to the phone, which most likely would be linked to Nikolai. The phone would have to be ditched elsewhere. Placing the Glock in her lap, she started the engine, pulled away from the curb, and raced up the street.

Kathy found her way back to I-210, which tied into I-5, and she took the exit north to the Antelope Valley Freeway. Traffic slowed her progress, and she applied constant pressure on the knife wound to stop the bleeding. The freeway forked as she approached the edge of the mountains, and she turned due north onto Aerospace Highway.

She stopped at a convenience store near Palmdale, grabbed one of her bags, and went inside the store. Searching the shelves, she found a tube of Krazy Glue and entered the women's restroom. She locked the door behind her, pulled off her top, and dropped it on the filthy floor. Standing on her bloodied shirt, she removed her shoes and stepped out of her blood-soaked jeans. Wetting several paper towels, she wiped the blood from her body. She was careful to toss each paper towel she used into the toilet—leaving DNA evidence in a trashcan would not be a sound move. Kathy was pleased to see the clotting had stopped the bleeding, and was careful not to undo what her body's natural defenses had done for her.

The cut was four inches in length. Satisfied she'd cleaned enough blood from the area, she blotted the water off her skin with a dry paper towel. Kathy opened the package of Krazy Glue and carefully covered the cut. It was not deep enough to require stitches; the Krazy Glue technique she learned in Section Nine training would be enough.

After several applications, she blew the glue dry. Satisfied with her work, she reached in her bag and pulled out shorts and a T-shirt and put on clean clothes. Placing the bloody clothes in her bag, she took the cleaning supplies from the corner of the bathroom, pouring cleaning solution on the floor. She let the solution sit without mopping it up, ensuring she covered the place where her bloody clothes had been. She wiped down everything she might have touched, exited the bathroom, paid for her glue and a Coke, and left the isolated convenience store.

39

JASON FIDGETED in his billeting room, wearing khaki shorts and a short-sleeved button-down that needed ironing. Kathy should have arrived at Edwards shortly after lunch, but it was almost six in the evening and he had not heard from her. He left her name at the front gate for the guard to let her in when she arrived. It frustrated him she did not have a cell phone. He had no way of getting in touch with her. Memories of her disappearing years ago flooded his consciousness, and he wondered whether Caldwell's suspicions about her were correct. Would she show up? Why would she put him through this again? Why? That was the key question. Caldwell was right—he had never talked with Kathy about what happened, where she disappeared to, and why she returned now. They had a whirlwind reunion based solely on physical contact. There was no substance to their relationship. Other than eating, drinking, and sex, they had not done much else in their two-and-a-half-day reunion.

Jason tried to relax by turning on FOX News, but it was background noise at this point. He couldn't get his mind off Kathy. Shortly after dark, someone knocked on the door. He momentarily hesitated, realizing Jennifer could be making another attempt to get him into bed. Grabbing the handle, he opened the door and saw Kathy standing there in cutoff jean shorts and a T-shirt. She dropped her purse and the bags she held as the two hugged and kissed. A strange feeling came over Jason. Something was wrong. He could feel it. The enthusiasm and energy she'd shown in Enid last week were missing.

"Is everything okay?" he asked.

Kathy pulled back. "Yes," she said. "Why?"

"You seem a little distant."

She pulled back farther, breaking contact with him, and bent down to pick up her purse and bag. "Well, hell, Conrad, I just flew into LAX, rented a car, got lost, and drove around the Sierra Mountains. It's been a long day. Sure," she said sarcastically, "everything's okay."

This was new. He'd never seen a reaction like this before, even six years ago. He cursed himself silently, aware of his selfishness.

"I'm sorry, I didn't realize you'd had such a rough time. Do you have any other bags?"

"No, this is it," she said, handing him her carry-on.

Jason carried the bag into the billeting room. "Well, this is home for now. Not much to it. It has a small kitchenette, bedroom, and bathroom."

"How long are you staying here?"

"I'm moving into a house on Saturday—I mean, *we* are moving into a house on Saturday. It's a furnished rental owned by one of the pilots in the squadron. I'd like to find out more about this assignment before I commit to anything."

Kathy's head jerked up sharply. "What's that supposed to mean?"

"It means I don't want to get a lease on a house or an apartment, or buy a house, until I find out more about my job."

"What are you doing here, again?"

Jason chose not to mention his true role. "I'm going to be a T-38 pilot. I guess I'll fly the chase plane when the space shuttle lands here, and I'll fly the chase plane for different test missions. First flight is Monday."

"Oh."

The two stood in awkward silence for a moment, then Jason spoke up.

"Did you bring a dress?"

She looked at him curiously. "What?"

Jason grinned. "There's a reception Friday night. It's formal. I'll be in my mess dress."

"Oh, that's just great, Jason, thanks for the heads-up. I show up and the first thing you tell me is I have a formal function to go to Friday night? Hell, no, I don't have a dress! You see this bag? Does it look like there's a dress in there?"

Jason was stunned. He started to say something, but the words wouldn't come out. He quickly realized how out of practice he was with relationships. Women didn't appreciate surprises like this, especially at the last minute.

"Look, I didn't know about this until today. And I wasn't sure I was supposed to go until this afternoon," he said, leaning against the wall, shoulders slumped, glancing at the floor. "I'm sorry. We don't have to go."

Kathy said nothing as she grabbed her bag, tossed it on the bed, and started to unpack. She found the empty drawers in the dresser and placed her clothes in the top drawer. Jason watched her unpack without saying a word. She finally turned to him after she emptied the suitcase.

"I'll get a dress tomorrow after we return the rental car."

Jason, studied her carefully. "Okay." It was all he dared utter.

"I'm going to take a shower. I feel filthy."

Jason grinned. He knew this part. "Would you like me to join you?"

Kathy turned to him without expression. "No thanks, Conrad. I've got this. You sit tight." She stepped into the bathroom and shut the door.

Jason, dejected, sat back in the recliner in the corner. His instincts were correct. The fantasy of his relationship was better than the relationship itself. He wanted Kathy to be the sweet, caring woman he met six years ago. But things were different. Physically, it was fantastic. The sex was amazing. Maybe it was too good. But one thing he was sure of— Kathy didn't capture his heart like he expected. This was not the Kathy Delgato who was in Enid six years ago. This wasn't even the Kathy Delgato who showed up in Enid last week.

THE TWO C-5 GALAXIES from Palmdale landed at Edwards AFB several hours after dark and plodded toward their final destination. A variety of vehicles waited on the ground outside the hangar while the two massive transport aircraft trudged along the parallel taxiway for the F-2000. It was an older building, but TRENCOR Industries had refurbished it to make it appear brand new.

The first C-5 pulled onto the ramp, turning so the rear faced the hangar doors. The ramp opened and a swarm of men piled in and started working. In a matter of minutes, the first pallet slid aft and down the ramp. The first pallet contained the two engines for the prototype. These slid down the ramp slowly to the K-loader, an oversized forklift, waiting at the bottom of the ramp. The K-loader moved the engine pallet into the hangar while the men returned to the interior of the jet.

Several minutes later, they pushed a second pallet to the rear of the first C-5 and down the ramp. This pallet contained several items, most of them in boxes and covered with a heavy-duty cargo net, tightened securely in place. The K-loader returned by the time the men had the pallet on the ramp extended from the back of the jet.

The second C-5 pulled next to his partner and the process started over there. The K-loader returned to the second jet and unloaded pallets covered in similar cargo netting.

Five minutes later, ten men rolled the final pallet to the rear of the jet. This one, a specialized pallet containing the fuselage of the F-2000, was covered in a protective cloth, which also had a covering of heavy-duty bubble wrap. The specialized pallet rolled slowly along the rails to the rear of the C-5. Carefully, the team of workers maneuvered the special pallet down the ramp to the ground. Once on the ground, workers ascended up the pallet on each corner and in the middle on the sides. Operating hydraulic pumps attached to the pallet, wheels from the bottom of the pallet slowly pushed the pallet away from the ground. Once all six positions had their wheels extended and locked in place, a small tow truck pulled the pallet with its tow bar secured. With a firm tug, the truck pulled the specialized pallet into the hangar as the first jet closed up and all the workers moved to the second jet.

Unloading both C-5s took less than one hour. When the contents of the second jet were unloaded, the team of workers filed into the hangar as the two C-5s taxied to the runway and departed for home. Base operations turned off the lights of the ramp by the hangar. When the massive doors closed, darkness once again surrounded the flight line. No one could tell the most expensive aircraft in history was being pieced together inside.

40

I T WAS A QUICK DRIVE back to the base for Jason and Kathy. They returned her vehicle to the rental car agency in Rosamond, stopping by a woman's clothing store so Kathy could buy a dress and matching shoes. When they finished, they drove to the clothing sales on the base. Jason needed to pick up a mess dress, the "Air Force tuxedo." It pissed him off he had to buy a new uniform since his remained boxed up with the rest of his possessions on the way from Oklahoma. But he didn't want to miss the reception. After all, the staff had been kind enough to invite him, even if he was a FAIP. The opportunity to network with personnel in the program would be invaluable, and being seen with Kathy might get Jennifer off his back.

Jason and Kathy entered the billeting room, where Kathy hung up her dress and placed her shoes in the closet. Jason snuck behind her, wrapping his arms around her waist. Kathy jumped when he did this, and Jason recoiled in frustration.

"What did I do wrong this time?" he asked.

"Nothing," she replied. "What do you mean, *this time?*"

Jason stood in front of her, arms crossed in front of his chest, and looked her in the eye. "What's going on, Kathy? You've been acting strange since you arrived here."

"What the hell do you mean by 'strange,' Conrad?"

"The cursing, for one. I don't recall you ever cursing. And you act totally different. In Enid, you couldn't keep your hands off me. For two-and-a-half days, we were all over each other, and now you won't touch me. What's going on? Have I done something wrong?"

Kathy sat in the lone recliner, leaning forward, her elbows on her knees with her head in her hands. They both sat silent for a minute.

"I'm sorry," she said. "So much has happened so fast."

"Well, let's process it together. We haven't really talked about anything."

"What do you mean?"

Jason sat on the bed in front of her. "What have you been doing the last five years? Where did you go? Why did you leave?" He gazed at her longingly, desperately searching for answers. Kathy looked into his eyes with a longing he had wanted to see since she arrived. A look saying she wanted him and always would.

"Jason, I'm sorry. I never wanted to hurt you. After the San Antonio incident, I didn't want the press or the pressure of any of this on my parents."

"The police couldn't find your parents. Your home was deserted when they came looking for you."

She nodded her head. "I know. We left. We put most of our things in storage and lived like nomads for a while. Staying with different relatives around Texas, then in various other states. We were afraid."

"But I don't understand why."

"I shot someone, Conrad. I could go to jail."

Jason searched deep in her eyes. Kathy had saved Jason's life by shooting the assassin as he was about to slice Jason's throat. She never would have gone to jail—too many people knew what happened—but he understood her fear.

She placed her finger to his lips, leaned over, and kissed him. The two lay back on the bed, embraced in the passionate kiss Jason had longed for. The embrace was strong, and Kathy ran her fingers through his hair. Jason started to move his hand toward her waist, and Kathy grabbed it.

"What?" Jason said, more concerned this time than frustrated.

Kathy sat up on the bed. "I need to show you something." She stood by the bed and lifted her shirt, showing Jason the wound above her waist.

"Oh, my God! What happened?"

"It's not as bad as it looks. I cut myself on barbed wire at a friend's farm before I flew out here."

"You've got to go to the hospital and get stitches."

Kathy laughed, "Didn't you go to survival school, Conrad? This scratch isn't deep enough for stitches."

Jason edged closer to inspect her wound. "It's an awfully clean cut for barbed wire."

"I don't explain 'em, I just fix 'em," she said. "I cleaned it off, slapped some Krazy Glue on it, and jumped on the plane."

"Is this why you've been acting strange?"

"I'd prefer you to stop using the word 'strange' when describing my behavior, but yes, my thoughts have been preoccupied with my medical condition."

"Medical condition, my ass." He laughed. "Okay, enough said. I'm wrong for not putting you first."

"Apology accepted," she said, offering her hand to pull him to his feet. "Now, let's go for a stroll. I haven't worked out in days, and I need to stretch my legs."

Jason nodded in agreement. It had been over a week since he'd worked out, and going for a walk with Kathy might be just the thing to perk him up.

THE THUNDERSTORM BEAT on the building as if it were trying to drag its occupants outside. Sheets of rain pounded the glass and lightning bolts lit up the afternoon sky. Dane sat at his desk in the newsroom, his head tilted to the side, gazing at the storm outside. He could not get the image of the army of windmills in western Oklahoma out of his head. So many in such a small area. It was unusual. The story behind it was a mystery—a mystery he was going to solve. He dove into it with the enthusiasm of an undergraduate journalism major, and he realized that for the first time in years, he wasn't focused on Jason Conrad.

His research uncovered several facts. Purchased by a variety of companies, hundreds of windmills were popping up throughout Oklahoma, Texas, Kansas, and Nebraska. There was also a huge number of land purchases, some by the same companies purchasing windmills. It was a mess to try to sort out. Dane worked for days, but it wasn't until an old friend of his in the real estate business "accidentally" found a pattern in some of the contracts that he started to make headway. The pattern was the individual signing all of the contracts for the land by a single attorney named Amanda Johnson Rieffelming.

THE SURVEILLANCE ROOM on the second floor of the office

at Langley sat dark. Artificial air freshener permeated the room, as the tightly enclosed space tended to quickly collect the odors of the occupants. A myriad of computer systems vibrated a low hum throughout the room. Recessed lighting on its lowest possible setting assisted the computer screens and audio panel in supplying the room's ambient light.

Carl Smith drummed the table with his fingertips, watching the computer screen intently. He was ecstatic when the computer bypassed all the bogus stations Nikolai's cell phone had been routed through. They still had the ability to track the phone even though the call was made over twenty-four hours ago. The point of origin had been tracked to a shoddy neighborhood in East Los Angeles. Someone had moved the phone from the original location to an intersection of I-210 and I-5 in the northern part of Los Angeles.

Sitting dormant for twenty-three hours, the phone was found on the side of the interstate as if someone tossed it of the car. The CIA had one of their personnel in the L.A. unit retrieve the phone. The agency sent a team to the location where the call had initiated, but when they arrived, the LAPD had it roped off. "Crime scene," they said. Three gangbangers were wasted in broad daylight. Not uncommon for that part of town, though what was uncommon was that witnesses said a white woman did the killing. Was this the Ann they were looking for?

Unbuttoning the top button on his shirt and loosening his tie, Carl ran his fingers through his hair as he awaited the phone call from Los Angeles. Exhausted from twenty-four hours of detailed research, he swung over to another computer screen and began writing a report on the situation. He'd give the L.A. team another thirty minutes, then e-mail Aaron Caldwell the information he had already collected. His head hurt as he waited on details from the L.A. team, but he had the big picture. Whoever called Nikolai Gregarin had called from Los Angeles.

SHERRI TURNED AND SCRUTINIZED herself in the three-paneled mirror in the women's section of the department store.

"I'm not sure this is going to work," Brent said, pushing his glasses up the bridge of his nose. "You're way too attractive to go somewhere with me."

"That's nice of you to say, but why don't you think an attractive woman would date you?"

"Are you kidding? Look at me. I'm overweight, losing my hair, and I wear comic book T-shirts. I'm an engineer, for crying out loud. If anyone talks to me, they'll see our personalities don't match."

"Relax, you'll be fine. You're a very nice guy. I don't know you well, but the fact that you are so concerned about your friend's death shows what a good person you are."

"Uh, I . . . uh . . ."

"Relax. If it makes you feel better, you can tell them I'm your cousin, or an in-law, or a paid escort. I don't care, but whatever story you choose, don't tell them I'm a reporter. Now relax, this will work and we'll have a good time. TRENCOR is footing the bill."

"Okay." He was nervous. He wasn't sure if what he planned was illegal, but he was sure it was disingenuous. And he still wasn't convinced showing up with a gorgeous redhead on his arm wouldn't arouse suspicion. His mind wandered as he stood in the ladies department near the dressing room.

"Brent. Brent! Are you okay?"

He shook his head as if waking from a dream, his mind drifting. "Sorry, I got distracted."

"Is this going to be a problem?"

Brent faced her when she asked the question. Her beauty was going to be a problem. The breathtaking dress she wore was going to be a problem. Sherri looked like a supermodel, or at least as close to one as he'd ever get. She didn't have to worry about him telling anyone she was a reporter. He'd be lucky if he didn't spend the entire night speechless.

"No," he said. "It's not a problem. I'm running different scenarios through my head about what can happen to me if we're found out. Fines, prison, death, more prison—you know, the usual. Security is going to be tight tomorrow. Spouses and dates will have to wait for us at Club Muroc while we go to unveiling of the F2K—"

He stopped short and watched her as she stopped examining herself in the three-panel mirror and turned to him.

"What's the F2K?" She paused. "Never mind. I know you can't say anything."

Brent cursed himself as he realized this was the second time he'd mentioned classified information around her. It wouldn't be an issue, unless she wasn't who she said . . . then he began to worry.

CARL SMITH LEFT the surveillance room and returned to his office. The thirty-minute time limit he'd set was almost up, and he was exhausted. Gathering his belongings, he prepared to leave for the weekend when the phone rang. He set his briefcase on the desk and picked up the phone on the third ring.

"Smith," he said.

"Agent Smith, this is Agent Robert Collins in Los Angeles."

"Go ahead."

There was a pause on the other end of the line. "Is Caldwell around?"

"No, he's not here. I can pass the message though."

"Fair enough. We found the phone you guys were tracking exactly where you thought it would be. It was within five meters of the point where we started our search. That's good triangulation."

"Thank you."

"No problem. Later that day, we went to the location where the phone call was initiated. It was roped off as a crime scene."

"Yes, we know all that."

"Well, we did some digging and here's what we found. There were three 'victims' at the crime scene. Although, given their rap sheets, we could hardly consider them victims. Gangbangers who picked the wrong person to roll is what it looks like. Anyway, we got hold of the lead investigator, who was more than willing to close the case, satisfied three more troublemakers are off the streets."

"And?"

"And he tells us, those witnesses to the homicides say the assailant was female. A 'hot' brunette, as described by one witness."

"A woman did that? Took out all three of these guys?"

"Yeah, that's what they said. And they had weapons. One had a gun, and the other two had a baseball bat and a crowbar."

"Anything else?"

"Here's the interesting part. One of the witnesses gave a description of the car and a license plate to the cops. The license plate turned out to be stolen from another car parked in the airport parking lot at LAX. The car, however, did turn out to match a rental car rented from LA that same day. It was a one-way rental, dropped off at a rental car dealer in Rosamond."

"Let me guess—it's north of Los Angeles," he said, placing the location of the phone on the side of the interstate.

"Yup. It was rented to someone named Ann Ramirez. She dropped it off earlier today. Drove it in from LAX. I'd say there's a strong probability this is the same car used in the East L.A. killings."

"Anything else?"

"Nah, that's about all we could decipher. But it sounds like your target has a source in Southern California. It's possible the woman simply picked up another vehicle somewhere and moved on. She could be back in LA, or could have gone to the airport in Mojave and flown somewhere else."

"Is there any way you can find out?"

Agent Collins laughed on the other end of the phone. "Yeah, if I had about twenty other guys assigned to me. The easy part is over. It's gonna take a lot of serious leg work to find out what happened to our mystery lady."

"I understand," Carl said. "Thanks for the call. I'll inform Caldwell. Keep us posted on any new developments."

"Will do. Out here."

Carl hung up his phone, settled back at his desk, and finished his report. He attached it to his e-mail, hit "Send," and set off to search for Caldwell.

41

IT HAD BEEN A SHORT WORKDAY for the F-2000 team. Jason spent most of the morning roaming around the squadron. He talked to several pilots after he received his new flight gear. They reviewed local procedures, and Jason signed off his Flight Crew Information File (FCIF) card. He returned to the VOQ by noon, but Kathy was gone. She returned three hours later, hot and sweaty, saying she had been 'exploring' the base.

Kathy told Jason to shower first because once she started the process, she would commandeer the entire bathroom. Her makeup covered every inch of level space in the bathroom. He took his shower quickly, relinquishing control of the small bathroom.

Kathy finished her shower, put on her makeup and fixed her hair. When she finished getting dressed, Jason was breathless. He'd seen the dress yesterday—a black, short, stretch satin dress with lace trimming along the shoulder straps, neck, and back. But with her makeup on and her hair done, she took the dress to the next level. The form-fitting dress accentuated her athletic figure, and the four-inch peep toe pumps highlighted her elegant legs.

"You're beautiful."

Kathy smiled. "Thanks, Conrad, now get ready," she said, putting on her earrings. "It's hot outside. I want to be able to cool down before I have to put on my show-pony act for the old codgers tonight."

The mess dress uniform had remained unchanged for years. Not as impressive as the other branches of the service, but when you put on the silver wings and added some medals, it worked fine. When Jason finished, they posed in front of the mirror, then laughed out loud. This was not their personalities at all. They were downhome, outdoorsy types, more comfortable in shorts and T-shirts. Kathy turned to him, kissed him softly, and ran her fingers over the small metal wings pinned to his coat.

"I remember when you weren't sure you'd ever get these," she said.

Jason grinned. "It was a struggle."

"And now here you are, at Edwards Air Force Base. I'm proud of you, Jason. You've worked so hard and overcome so much. I know you have a bright future ahead of you."

"Thanks," he said, pressing his forehead to hers, looking into her eyes. "My life hasn't seemed complete until you came back."

Kathy's eyes welled up as a small tear ran down her cheek. Jason wiped the tear away with his thumb and kissed her again.

"Come on, let's get going," he said.

As they made their way to the door, Kathy stopped. "I need my camera," she said.

"You're not going on the bus."

"I know, but there will be important people at the reception, and I'd like to have a picture with them," she said, rushing back inside their room. "It's called networking."

Jason paused. "Really? That doesn't seem like you."

"Conrad, let's face it. We haven't been around each other much lately. There's a lot about me you don't know."

AT 1645, EVERYONE PILED into Club Muroc at Edwards AFB. In all, two hundred people were there: one hundred twenty-five TRENCOR/Air Force personnel and seventy-five spouses or dates. The one couple turning heads was Brent O'Malley, the aeronautical engineer Jason met earlier in the week, and his date. She appeared to be a stunning redhead from a distance. Jason never saw that coming. Good on you, Brent.

At 1655, the team moved outside toward the posh air-conditioned buses. While the F-2000 team boarded the buses, the spouses and dates moved to the reception room at the club.

After a quick drive to the hangar, everyone exited the buses. The sixty-foot-tall hangar doors opened ten feet as each guest funneled through one at a time. Civilian security personnel, with the Air Force Security Police, checked names off a list again as the guests came through the doorway. They entered the hangar and sat in white fold-out chairs placed in the hangar in front of a large blue curtain hiding the fantastic jet. Music blared while a video played on a huge screen in front of the blue curtain. The video displayed the evolution of fighter jets through history and the impressive combat capabilities of the US Air Force. TRENCOR spared no expense for the event. It was a professional job worthy of Hollywood as the bombs dropped to the beat of the music. An impressive piece of work to keep the guests occupied while they took their seats.

The floor of the hangar was spotless, a huge effort considering the jet had been assembled yesterday. Jason was surprised the F-2000 could be assembled this fast—then someone told him this was for display purposes only. TRENCOR Industries needed to do something to show they were making progress. After tonight's reception, the aircraft prototype would be disassembled and put back together in working order.

As soon as everyone took their seats, the video stopped and the screen retracted upwards. The test wing commander, Brigadier General Mark Oglesby, said a few brief words, then introduced Jeremiah Wellington. Wellington spoke for five minutes, and while never actually confessing TRENCOR was behind schedule, he alluded to some of the issues placing them in this position. "None of it matters now," he said, "as the future of combat air operations is about to become a reality."

When the curtain drew back, there was the expected gasp among the audience, followed by whoops and cheers. The F-2000 stood against a black background, a beautiful, seamless aircraft, sixty-two feet long with a forty-five-foot-wide wingspan. The cockpit was long to accommodate the second seat. This was unique for the prototype, installed for the software engineer. While the streamlined fuselage was thin and cylindrical, it neatly housed the large cockpit. Triangular wings stuck out on each side, while the vertical stabilizer was a twin-tail design angled inward sixty degrees on each side. The landing gear retracted into the fuselage, and the pilot's seat sat forward of the nose gear. A smooth radar-absorbing material, similar to the B-2, covered the entire jet. After a moment, everyone left their seats and crowded the rope line surrounding the historic jet. Painted in the standard "combat gray," the jet was impressive, and everyone strained to get a better glimpse of this technological wonder. I'm going to get to fly this jet, Jason thought, grinning ear to ear. He could not take his eyes off it. He had never seen anything like it.

The F-2000 was roped off to keep the guests from touching the aircraft, but they were close enough. The guards spaced out every ten feet eyed the crowd, ensuring no one had snuck a camera into the event. It would be devastating if the project leaked to the press.

Jason saw Major Samson move away from the jet's rope line, meandering back toward the buses. Brigadier General Oglesby approached Samson. The general pointed at the buses, and Samson walked over and boarded the first bus. A very pissed-off general walked away.

Gradually, the crowd thinned and drifted in the direction of the buses. A horn sounded, indicating it was time for everyone to get back on the buses. Jason had that uneasy feeling, the kind that makes the hairs on the back of your neck stand up. Turning to his left, he saw Jeremiah Wellington scowling at him, a disgusted look on his face. The look puzzled Jason. Wellington shook his head as he wandered to the buses. Jason glanced around, to see who Wellington might be looking at, but no one else was near him. Brent walked over to Jason.

"Don't worry," Brent said. "He's an asshole toward other pilots."

Jason nodded. "Thanks, I think I figured that out," he said, and they walked to the bus Samson had entered minutes earlier. He saw Samson sitting in the back row, alone, staring out the window toward the hangar.

He started moving to the back and Brent grabbed his arm.

"I wouldn't go back there."

Jason looked at him unsure why he would say that and continued to the back of the bus. When he approached, Samson gave him a look that told him to get lost.

"Major," he said, "is everything alright?"

Samson's face contorted in a state of drunken disbelief. "Fug off, new guy," Samson mumbled and returned his gaze out the window. Jason back peddled and sat behind Brent who watched the brief exchange.

"Told you not to go back there."

"Yeah," Jason said. "You might want to keep an eye on him tonight."

42

May 11, 2001

THE RECEPTION AT CLUB MUROC was nothing fancy at first glance—the impressiveness was in the details. It took Jason a minute to realize TRENCOR had an open bar, and the hors d'oeuvres were brought in from an outside restaurant. The servers, while numerous, were discreet yet timely. The first one he noticed popped out of nowhere, offering Kathy a crab-cake-type substance on a cracker. She declined, but Jason took one, despite not being able to pronounce the name. The drinks started flowing as the crowd came alive. A rock band from L.A. took the stage at 1830, really loosening up the crowd. Jason and Kathy hit the dance floor for several songs. When the band played the standard *Stairway to Heaven* slow dance, Kathy grabbed him around the waist. The two star-crossed lovers stared at each other longingly as Jason pulled her closer. Kathy closed her eyes, resting her head against Jason's chest. But Jason's eyes remained open, watching her. He had longed for such a moment for years. Internally, he struggled with his emotions. He was happy, wasn't he? The woman he'd waited years for was finally in his arms, but she wasn't the woman he remembered.

When the song ended, Kathy stood on her tiptoes, kissing Jason softly on the lips. They left the dance floor and worked their way to the bar. Kathy hung on his arm lovingly as they mingled in the club, making small talk. They finally had a moment to themselves when Brent strutted over with his date.

"Jason, this is Sherri," he said.

Up close, Jason recognized her immediately as the woman from the Texas Cattle Company who called him an asshole. It was obvious when it registered with Sherri. Her eyes widened, and her face flushed. Jason had to admit she was gorgeous, despite her rudeness when he first met her.

Jason, expressionless, stuck out his hand. Sherri smiled as she shook it. "Hello, Sherri, it's nice to meet you. I'd like you both to meet Kathy. Kathy, this is Brent and Sherri. Brent is one of our aeronautical engineers."

As Kathy shook both their hands, Jason could see her sizing up Brent's date. "What is it you do, Sherri?" Kathy asked.

"I'm an actress," Sherri said. "Or trying to be."

"Oh." Kathy beamed. "That's exciting! TV or movies?"

"Well, uh, I don't know," Sherri said. "Anything, really. I just came out here from New York."

"Have you been in anything we might have seen?" Kathy said.

"Not unless you've been to dinner theater in Sheepshead Bay." They smiled at her joke, but had to admit they hadn't. "Let's just say I haven't been a successful actress."

"That's too bad. Maybe it will work out for you. What brings you to the base?"

"I'm visiting a friend, and thought I'd check out the scene—didn't pan out. I was on my way out of town when I met ol' Brent here. He asked me to this little function you folks are putting on, and here we are."

"You don't sound like you're from New York," Kathy said suspiciously.

"Well, I'm not. I'm from Missouri, I just work, er . . . ah, live in New York. I was hoping for Broadway." She smiled and poked her elbow at Jason. "But I can muster a Bronx accent when I need one."

They all chuckled, the polite, awkward chuckle people do when no one knows what to say. Sherri broke the awkward silence. "It was nice to meet you both. Brent, let's go to the bar and get that drink."

"Okay," Brent said. "Kathy, it was nice to meet you."

"It was nice to meet both of you," she said.

Jason pulled Kathy close, kissing her on the cheek as Brent and Sherri walked to the bar. He could tell something was bothering her as her eyes narrowed and her lips tightened. Jason felt her body tense.

"Something wrong?"

Kathy's mouth fell open and her eyes grew wide. Then she snickered and shook her head.

"What?" he said as he rubbed her back.

"She likes you," she said, moving her head in the direction of the bar where Sherri now stood.

"Huh?"

"She likes you . . . a lot."

Jason moved in front of her and looked deep into her eyes. "What are you talking about?"

"A charming, beautiful redhead is checking out my man, and you don't think I notice?"

"Charm is deceptive and beauty is fleeting, the good book says."

"Conrad, trust me. Women know these things. You men don't get it. Your egos think it's all about you. Women don't dress up for you. Women dress up for other women. We size each other up. Verify who the competition is and isn't. That redhead is the competition."

Jason was perplexed. Sherri was attractive, okay, very attractive, but he didn't think he gave any outward signs. He didn't indicate he'd met her earlier in the week, but the idea of her being interested in him, after their last meeting, was ludicrous.

"How are you arriving at this conclusion?"

Kathy jabbed her elbow in his side and said in a mimicked voice, "I can muster a Bronx accent when I need one."

They both laughed and Jason said, "I've had my fair share of actresses in my life, and I'm not interested in another one. Come on, let's get a drink."

"See?" Kathy giggled. "You want to go to the bar because that's where the redhead went."

Jason grinned. "You caught me. But let's get a drink anyway."

KATHY AND JASON moved through the crowd toward the bar. Every time they stopped to speak to a general or someone important, she made sure she and Jason were photographed with them. "It's for your career," she told Jason. "It's always good to schmooze with the power structure." Jason was holding his own very well. He stood naturally, with his shoulders back and his chin held high, and the gleam in his eyes drew people to him.

When they reached the bar, Kathy saw a female officer in her mess dress uniform wearing the gold oak leaves of a major. She had the pilot wings with a little star above, indicating she was a senior pilot. She was talking to a handsome, older gentlemen. The major stopped paying attention to what he was saying when she and Jason approached the bar.

The female major's eyes followed them as they approached. Kathy watched her unbutton her jacket, which opened as her breasts pushed through. Figures. Boob job. This wench needs to work for Nikolai. What a tramp. Kathy noticed the tailored shirt accentuated her breasts, which she had no problem showing everyone. The bra she wore was transparent, leaving nothing to the imagination in the thin white blouse beneath her jacket.

The older gentleman watched the major's every move. It was obvious he was jealous when he stormed away with a pissed-off look on his face. The major had no idea he'd left.

"Friend of yours?" Kathy said softly as they approached.

"Hush," he said.

"Jason," the major said. She moved quickly toward him and he reached out a hand to shake, but she dodged it, maneuvering next to him and hugging him. "It's sooo good to see you."

"Uh, hi," Jason said awkwardly.

The major pushed herself away from Jason and looked at Kathy with a blank expression. "You must be her," she said, taking a sip from her wine glass.

Kathy forced a faint smile. "Yes, I am."

"Thank God you're here. He won't shut up about you."

"Well, that's nice to say," Kathy said.

"Well, it's tough to hang in a crowd like this when you're just a waitress," the female major said. "I'm sure Jason will take good care of you." She stood back and re-buttoned her coat. Kathy knew exactly what she was doing, trying to point out to Jason she had been a waitress while the major was a pilot. Such amateurish psychological games. Kathy glared at the major until her training took over. Section Nine had prepared her for situations like this many times.

"Yes. Yes, it is," Kathy said flatly as she ignored the insult. She'd like to put a bullet in this bimbo's head, but that wouldn't be very professional.

Jason grabbed Kathy by the hand, slipping to another section of the bar, dragging her with him.

"That bitch didn't introduce herself," Kathy said.

"That 'bitch' is Major Jennifer Walton. She's the number-two pilot assigned to my project."

"'Number Two' is a good title for her. Who was the older guy hanging with her before she blew him off?"

"That was retired Brigadier General Jeremiah Wellington. He's the site manager for this project."

"They're sleeping together."

Jason stopped at the bar and turned to her. "That's the rumor."

As she started to respond, he handed her a glass of Chardonnay.

"Drink this. It'll make you feel better."

"Don't change the subject, Conrad. She likes you, too."

"Yeah, well, she likes everybody," Jason said as the two laughed out loud.

SAMSON SAT AT THE BAR, drinking Crown Royal on the rocks. Weed was not served at this function. He had lost count, but surely he was nearing, or already in, the double digits. It didn't matter. He hated functions like this, especially being alone. He made a decision years ago when his wife gave him a choice: his marriage or his jet. You can always get another wife, but you can't always get another Eagle assignment. Or test assignment. He'd buried himself in his work ever since.

He slammed three Crown Royals before they left on the bus to the F-2000, and when they returned, drank several more. As he scanned the crowd, he saw David Ming and his wife standing next to his giant guard dog Li Zhong. Samson decided to tell Ming he knew what was ailing the F-2000. He wasn't sure why. Alcohol was bad.

Samson pushed his way through the crowd toward Ming and his companions. Ming turned to him and said, "Ah, Major Samson. I hope you are enjoying our festivities. This is my—"

"I g-got something to say to you . . . Ming," his words slurring.

He took a deep breath and poked his finger in Ming's chest. "I know what's wrong with your simulator, and why it doesn't work."

43

BRENT WATCHED THE SCENE from a distance while Sherri talked to Brigadier General Oglesby and his wife. Brent couldn't hear Samson about to send his career up in flames, but he could sense it. After a couple minutes, the test wing commander and his wife moved on to socialize with others.

"What's going on, Brent? You kind of left me hanging."

"I'm sorry. Something's not right," he said, staring at Samson talking to Ming.

"Who are those people?"

"The officer is my lead pilot on this project, Curt Samson. The tall Chinese man is named Li Zhong. He works for TRENCOR. The shorter guy is the man you're looking for, David Ming."

"The woman?"

"That's Ming's wife."

"Let's go over and say hi," she said, starting to move in their direction.

Brent reached out, grabbing her arm. "Not yet. Something is going on; I can tell by the way Samson's talking to Ming. He's been working on this project for years, but there are plenty of problems. Maybe he's talking to him about it. All I know is, Samson's put more hours into this project than anyone else. There's no way of knowing what they're talking about."

"Unless we go over there," Sherri said, cutting through his rambling.

"Well, yeah. Unless we go over there."

"Looks to me like he's drunk."

"Ah . . . yeah, he's drunk all right," Brent said, as Samson staggered, almost falling. "I'd better go get him."

MING STOOD WITH HIS ARMS CROSSED. His wife, who was standing next to him, began to fade into the background, and Li Zhong stood close to Ming, observing everything.

"What exactly is the problem with my simulator, Major Samson?" Ming asked.

"Thought about it a long time . . . Checked and rechecked our procedures." Samson struggled to focus. Ming could tell he was drunk. "I troubleshot the wiring diagrams. Then I said, I got it. Or *it's* got it. There's a bug in the software."

"Excuse me?"

"You heard me, Ming. There's a bug in the software. It . . . it self-corrupts."

"Interesting," Ming said, "go on."

"Go on? We can't go on because the software stops us every time we get started."

"Really?"

"It's a piece of crap! It's designed to f-fail. Question is, why? Why would you choose to spend all that money on a system that don't work?"

"This is an interesting theory, Major Samson. Who else have you spoken to about this?"

Samson glared at him, tilted his head sideways, his eyes bulging out. "Spoken to? Are you friggin' kidding me? I can't believe this shit myself. I didn't tell nobody."

Ming gave a sideways glance to Li Zhong.

"What do you propose to do, Major Samson?"

Samson struggled to stand straight, pointing his finger in Ming's chest again. "I'm gonna tell somebody to fix this piece of crap!" He was getting loud now, and several guests stared in his direction.

"Thank you for your insight, Major Samson. I'll have my people look into it," Ming said.

"You do that because we can't do nothin'," Samson blurted out.

An overweight member of the Air Force team approached Samson from behind, grabbing him from the shoulders. Ming recognized him—the aeronautical engineer, Brent O'Malley.

"I'm sorry, Mr. Ming, my friend has had too many drinks," Brent said. "I hope he isn't a bother."

Ming nodded as Brent steered Samson to the other side of the club. Ming and Li Zhong's eyes followed them the entire way until the two sat across the room.

Ming turned to his wife. "Does he know what he's talking about?"

"From what I know of Major Samson, I would say he's done his homework. He is a detail-oriented man. I haven't seen him form a hypothesis based on a hunch yet. The other gentleman is Brent O'Malley. He's no dummy either. Wouldn't be surprised if they're working together on this."

The three of them displayed blank expressions, their arms crossed in front of their chests, speaking without looking at one another.

"My darling, I need you to contact General Jingguo. Let him know we need his team at the facility in the morning."

"Yes, dear," she said and walked out of the club.

"Li Zhong, Major Samson has proven himself worthy of our attention."

"Yes, Mr. Ming. Do you want me to take care of him?"

"Not tonight, but I have an idea to further our cause."

KATHY STOOD IN FRONT OF THE MIRROR, touching up her lipstick. She grew tired of the "grip and grin" part of the reception and found her refuge from it all. It surprised her Jason's father wasn't at the event. After nosing around the last couple of days and questioning Jason in the evening, she'd determined Jonathan Bowman was somehow tied to this project. But she'd heard no one utter the word "Lima." At one point, she mentioned the phrase "Lima Project" to one of the TRENCOR technicians she was speaking to, who gave her a strange look. Kathy brushed it off as something similar to the "Greenlight Project" started that year in Hollywood. Of course, the technician had heard of *that* project. Jason and his father had a much closer relationship these days, but Jason didn't talk much about what he did professionally. Kathy realized it might take longer than Nikolai expected to get the information.

She finished with the lipstick and placed it in her purse. When she turned around, Major Jennifer Walton was standing five feet behind her, hands on her hips. Crap. Who has time for this?

"What do you have in mind with Jason?" Jennifer asked. There was a slight slur to her voice.

"Why do you care?"

"Look, being the queen of Enid, Oklahoma is one thing. But Jason is at Edwards Air Force Base now. He's part of something special," Jennifer continued, "and the types of relationships he maintains are very important."

"I'm not sure my relationships are any of your business, Lieutenant."

"I'm a major, you dimwit. If you're going to be around this base, you need to learn the rank structure," Jennifer said.

Kathy had to keep herself from smiling. Obviously, she hit a sore spot. "I've always been told name-calling is a last resort of someone who is ignorant or has already lost the argument."

"We're not arguing about anything."

"Exactly. You've proved my point," Kathy said, smiling, turning back to the mirror. She pulled out her lipstick again, making a quick application. "Oh, and I'm a civilian," she said, watching Jennifer in the mirror. "I don't need to learn anything about your rank structure." In the mirror she saw Jennifer's face turn red behind her as she moved closer, her fingers flexing open and closed.

"Look, a waitress from Enid is a little out of her league in this crowd."

"Just like a woman with a boob job is out of Jason's league," Kathy said with a sneer.

"You bi—" Jennifer lunged at Kathy, who deftly sidestepped her assault and instinctively threw her forearm into her solar plexus. The tiny pilot doubled over in pain, falling to the tiled floor.

Kathy started to worry whether this would impact Jason's job. She regretted her actions, but it was too late to change anything.

She knelt down, helping the major to her feet.

"I'm sorry," Kathy said. "I thought you were going to hit me, and I over-reacted."

The major, breathing heavily, said nothing as her eyes burned with anger. Kathy turned and marched out of the ladies' room.

Jason was waiting ten feet from the door by the small potted palm, sipping on a beer. "Everything okay in there?"

"Yes, why do you ask?"

"Uh, you took a while. Didn't know if there was a problem."

"Conrad, you do have a fertile imagination," Kathy said.

Jason grinned, but it faded instantly. "What the—"

Kathy turned in time to see Jennifer rush from the bathroom door and try to strike her from behind. Training and instinct took over again as she thrust her left forearm up in a defensive posture, deflecting the blow and delivering a quick punch to Jennifer's right cheek. The punch was high enough not to break any teeth and low enough not to do any damage to her eye.

"Jenn— . . . Kathy . . . what the hell are you two doing?" Jason said.

Jennifer screamed, lunging at Kathy again. Kathy grabbed Jennifer's arm and twisted it behind her back, pushing her to the floor. Jennifer hit the carpet with a dull thud and a loud grunt. A small crowd gathered around the two women. Kathy moved away from Jennifer and Jason grabbed her by the arm. "Kathy—stop! What's going on?"

Kathy grabbed his hand, broke his grip, and pushed his wrist back toward his forearm, pressing a vital nerve. Jason yelped as he went to his knees.

"Don't ever grab me again," she said, gritting her teeth.

Kathy turned her attention back to her assailant, and no one in the small crowd moved to stop her. Jennifer rushed Kathy again, wildly swinging at her head. Kathy dodged her fist and threw a crushing blow to her jaw, which stopped any further assault. Grabbing Jennifer's arm, she twisted it, flipping Jennifer on her back. Jennifer lay there, defeated. Brent's date and some of the females rushed to Jennifer's aid.

Kathy slid over to Jason, who stood shaking his wrist. "I'm ready to go," she said.

Jason said nothing as he gestured to the front door, and the two scurried out of Club Muroc.

MING LINGERED IN THE BACKGROUND, watching the catfight, but not with the interest of Li Zhong. Ming diverted his attention from the two sexy young females fighting to his bodyguard, curious about his obsession with the incident. The pretty one was victorious. Wasn't that the way it always worked?

Li Zhong glanced at him. "She looks familiar."

Ming raised his eyebrows slightly. "Someone special?"

"No," Li Zhong said. "I've seen those moves. She's a fighter. I've seen her fight somewhere. The move she used to stop her date? I've seen a girl use the exact move, with the same result. She's a pro, and I don't think her date knows it."

Ming raised his eyebrows more as the brunette left the club with

Jason Conrad. Ming turned to leave. "Come, Li Zhong. We must be going."

Li Zhong didn't move. He watched the woman as she moved toward the front door. "I know her from somewhere."

SHERRI KNELT ON THE FLOOR with the female pilot's head resting on her thighs. Another woman got a wet towel and wiped the woman's face. She had taken a hell of a beating. That girl is a fighter, Sherri thought. Bet that Conrad guy has no idea where she learned that.

Glancing up, she saw Ming and his associate start to leave the scene. Damn. She tried to move Jennifer's head to the floor. "Excuse me, I need—"

"Don't move, she may be in shock!" the overweight woman with the wet towel said.

"She's not in shock. She's conscious and moving. If she were in shock, we'd be making it worse by raising her head."

"Are you a nurse?"

"No, I'm a—", she hesitated for several seconds. "I'm a friend."

Sherri sighed and slouched as Ming and his associate slipped out the front entrance. Jennifer's head turned slightly as she moaned. Glancing at her, Sherri returned her gaze to the two men as the front door shut behind them. Her heart shrank as she recognized her opportunity was gone.

44

May 12, 2001

SHERRI WOKE UP Saturday morning, and after pulling off her nightgown, took a quick shower. She threw on a pair of white cutoff shorts and a pink T-shirt—perhaps a little too small. No worries, it was just a quick run for coffee.

As she strolled to the lobby of the Best Western, she retraced last night's events in her head. The fight between Jason Conrad's date and the female pilot had been awkward, although entertaining. She feared she might have lost her best opportunity to meet the mysterious David Ming.

Entering the lobby, she headed for the coffee machine. She poured four packets of sugar in an empty cup, then three small containers of French vanilla creamer on top of that. She stirred the coffee as she poured it in. It was a technique she developed years ago to speed up the coffee line.

"Oh, my God," she heard behind her. "This can't be possible. Is it you?"

Sherri paused, focusing on the wall in front of her. The voice sounded familiar, but she couldn't put a finger on it. She felt that tingly sensation in the back of her neck. Turning slowly, she saw a middle-aged man in a wrinkled suit standing behind her. He was slightly overweight with an expression on his face like an eight-year-old on Christmas morning.

"Sherri? Sherri Davis? It's me! Don't you remember? The correspondents' dinner in '96? It's me, Dane Robinson, TV news reporter!"

Sherri remained expressionless. How in the world did this jerk end up here?

"Uh . . . hi," was all she could muster.

"Don't tell me you don't remember me," he said as he maneuvered closer to her.

How could she forget him? He was at the dinner, bragging about some story he'd uncovered, desperately trying to get her into bed. Sherri had been young and impressionable, and had had a little too much to drink at the time. Fortunately for her, a female reporter from CBS recognized what was happening and saved her.

"Oh, yeah," she murmured. "Dane Robinson, TV news reporter."

"See," he beamed, "you *DO* remember. Let me get a cup of coffee. We can sit down and catch up."

"Dane, I really need—"

"Oh, don't worry about me, I just checked in." Dane poured a cup of coffee, black, grabbed her hand, and dragged her to the couch. "Wow . . . you look absolutely fantastic. What have you been doing the last five years?" he asked as they sat on the couch facing each other.

"I'm an investigative journalist for *The New York Times*."

"Still? That's great, but you should be in TV. What are you doing in California?"

"I'm . . . visiting friends," she said, aware of Dane's proclivity for stealing other reporters' stories.

"Well," he said as his gaze drifted from her eyes to her chest, "they must be really good friends for you to come out here to this hellhole."

Sherri took a sip of coffee as she drew up her legs, propping her elbows on her knees. She wished now she had picked a different shirt . . . and worn a bra.

"They are. What are you doing here?"

He adjusted his posture, like an old housewife spreading the latest neighborhood gossip. "I stumbled onto a huge story. Listen to this— someone is buying up a huge amount of land in the American Midwest and building windmills."

"Okay, people build windmills all the time. All you have to do is drive twenty minutes west toward the mountains. You'll see hundreds of windmills."

"Oh, my dear, they aren't that kind of windmill, and it isn't that kind of farm. They aren't producing energy, they're producing—"

"Water."

"Yes, water. There are huge storage tanks scattered amongst

them. Anyway, kind of strange, so we started doing some research. We, okay, *I* found out the majority of the land these windmills occupied had been purchased recently. Now keep in mind, when I say recently, I mean within three years. All through the Midwest: Texas, Oklahoma, Kansas, and Nebraska. It's a huge undertaking!"

"Well, aren't those types of windmills built in those states all the time?" Sherri said.

Dane hesitated, his eyes desperately trying to find a way around her arms to her chest. What a pig. After an uncomfortable amount of time, he said, "They are, but not this many, and not this many contracted at one time. I'm talking hundreds of windmills within a three-year period."

"So maybe a bunch of different companies get the same idea at the same time and made the same investments. It happens all the time in business."

"That's exactly what I thought when I was first assigned this story. Then I went to one of the locations in western Oklahoma and saw for myself. It's much, much bigger than that. After extensive research, I uncovered a critical piece of evidence. The attorney, whose name keeps showing up on the paperwork on behalf of an unnamed client—in every case, it's the same person."

Sherri leaned forward, her reporter instincts taking over, recognizing a real story. "Okay, I'd say you're onto something. So why are you *here*?"

Dane leaned back in the couch, a smug look on his face. "The attorney for the list of unnamed clients is Amanda Johnston Rieffelming. I had to do a ton of research, but I tracked her down. She's the corporate attorney for TRENCOR Industries."

"WHY DO I HAVE TO EXPLAIN MYSELF?" Kathy screamed.

It had been a rough morning. Kathy and Jason hadn't spoken much since they'd woken up, showered, dressed, and packed. Jason quickly loaded the truck, and they drove to Rosamond to the house they would stay in until Jason found something more permanent. It was a quaint two-story house, sitting a mile south of Rosamond Boulevard, west of town. The inside was designed circa 1960 and the washer and dryer didn't work, but it was off base, and it was furnished.

The argument started shortly after he unpacked the truck.

"You don't have to explain yourself. I'm asking what happened."

"You saw what happened. Your other girlfriend tried to blindside me, so I kicked her ass."

"She's not my girlfriend."

"Well, you'd better tell her that, because she thinks you two are an item."

Jason stared at the floor, shaking his head. "I don't understand how this started."

Kathy glared at him as if she had told him several times.

"Okay, Jason," she said. Jason's head snapped up. She never called him Jason; it was always Conrad. "I'm in the bathroom. She comes up behind me and starts giving me lip about how I don't fit in here. She's a smart jet pilot, I'm an uneducated waitress, and I need to stay away from you." A tear started to roll down her cheek as she lowered her head.

Jason moved closer, but she stepped back.

"Then she tried to attack me from behind."

"Just like that? Out of the blue? She tried to attack you from behind?"

Kathy looked up and snickered. "Well, I might have said one or two things to her first."

Jason grinned. Jennifer Walton did have a reputation for being a hothead, but this was the first he ever heard about her attacking someone.

"I gave her an elbow to the stomach. That should have finished it. She's got spunk, I'll give her that. The rest I guess you saw."

"Oh, yeah, I saw it, all right. Hell, I lived it. Where did you learn to fight like that?"

She glowered. "I'm a single female. I took a women's self-defense class, all right?"

"It looked like you taught the women's self-defense class."

Kathy smiled. "My instructor said I caught on quickly."

"Yeah, well, he's a hell of an instructor."

"She."

"Okay, she's a hell of an instructor," Jason said. "Look, I'm responsible for you when you're on the base—"

"I'm responsible for my own actions, Conrad. Not you. Me."

"Kathy, relax. Don't read too much into this. I know there's going to be a lot of questions Monday morning about this . . . and I need to have some answers."

Her smile turned to a frown. "Oh, so this is about how Jason Conrad can cover his ass and not how I had to protect myself!"

Realizing how it had come out, Jason attempted to move toward Kathy, and again, she moved away before he grabbed her and pulled her to him.

"It's not like that at all," he said, searching her eyes for a sign of understanding. "Look, I'm the new guy here. Nobody knows me except the person you beat up. Other than that, no one. I'm going to have to tell your side of the story to someone. Unless they send the police after you—then you'll get to tell your side."

For the first time in the conversation, she glanced at Jason with concern. Kathy had been acting strange since she showed up at Edwards, but he was starting to think she might be higher maintenance than he previously thought.

She pulled back slightly. "Do you think she'll call the police?"

THE TRENCOR BUILDING was not as quiet as a normal Saturday morning. Ming had come into the office out of necessity. He had called in several of his engineers and technicians, all of whom arrived with General Jingguo. They were there to work on Operation Dragonfly. This, too, was part of Beijing's "Greater China" policy. One of Ming's front companies worked closely with the son of a state legislator and purchased a hundred thousand acres of Nevada desert for the secret experiment. The F-2000 was the ideal platform to secretly disperse the chemicals. If the experiment was successful, Ming had another one hundred thousand acres of new farmland. If unsuccessful, it was a failure no one would know about.

The F-2000 was key in the implementation of the cloud-seeding program. Beijing needed a stealthy jet capable of flying undetected. The F-2000 had been fitted with the spraying device. It was a waste of effort, but Ming gave up arguing the issue and followed his orders. While the F-2000 would never achieve its goals as a fighter jet, it could easily accomplish the tasks needed for General Jingguo's mission.

General Jingguo and his team needed to finish creating the chemical compound and installing the components on the jet. Operation Dragonfly needed to move ahead of schedule if the technology was going to be validated for use in China.

Ming listened to the engineers discuss the implementation of Operation Dragonfly. When they finished, he described the new project he needed done within the next thirty-six hours. When the team left Ming's office, Li Zhong approached and sat in one of the chairs in front of the desk. "Are you sure this is something you want to do?"

Ming's immediate concern was that Samson had discovered the malware installed in the software of the F-2000. He glanced at Li Zhong and grunted as he continued to sift through a stack of papers on his desk.

"Are you sure Samson figured it out?" Li Zhong said. "Maybe someone told him."

Ming looked up again at Li Zhong. "I'm convinced he knows. Samson is intelligent enough to figure this out; he was too sure of himself. He gave too much detail on the technical specs of the software. Whether he's informed anyone about the self-corrupting software is another issue."

"And you think if he has, this will convince anyone else who might know to remain silent?"

"Precisely."

Li Zhong nodded in silent agreement.

"I need you to ensure the item is installed by tomorrow evening," Ming said. "The timing of this is important in case anyone else knows."

"I'll take care of it," Li Zhong said. "The engineers say it has a digital control system which will make the conversion simple. I do need to speak with you on another issue, one of perhaps more importance."

Ming stopped reviewing the papers. It was rare Li Zhong made such a statement. This was serious.

"Go on."

Li Zhong sat up in his seat. "I remember where I know the brown-haired girl from the fight last night. Only she had blond hair and lived in the Philippines. She was married to an American missionary."

David Ming's face reflected the horror coursing through his mind.

"She is Irena Vodianova, a Russian agent from Section Nine of the GRU."

45

May 14, 2001

JASON HAD A BUSY MORNING. He flew his T-38 local area orientation ride with one of the test pilots. He saw all the landmarks of the local area and how to enter and exit the Military Operating Areas (MOA). Jason marveled at the details available to pilots from above the airfield. The test pilot pointed out how the different runways cut into the dry lake and the use of each. He particularly liked the massive compass rose you could see from the air in the north portion of the airfield. Etched into the dry lake next to NASA's Dryden Flight Research Center, it was at least a half mile in diameter.

The flight took less than an hour, and they were back by eight-thirty in the Life Support building. He left his helmet with the tech behind the desk and hung his parachute on the rack. Unzipping his g-suit, he smiled at how good it felt to be in the jet again. Something about being in the sky, even when working, was exhilarating. His neck hurt slightly again as he made the high-G turns, but not enough to risk seeing a doctor. The last thing he wanted was to be grounded. Jason headed back to the vault in the test squadron to meet Major Samson, who was waiting for him.

"How'd the flight go?" Samson said.

"Fine. It was good to get back in the jet."

The two moved to the desk and sat across from each other. Samson pulled out a stack of papers, handing half to Jason.

"Okay, Captain Conrad, you're our monkey in the capsule."

"That's twice you've said that to me, sir. I don't mind metaphors, but what are you referring to?"

"Don't think so hard," Samson said. "It's from the movie *The Right*

Stuff, when the Mercury Seven Astronauts were told a chimpanzee was going into space before one of them."

Jason nodded. Now he remembered. He loved that movie. He also remembered Jennifer referred to Samson as being 'uptight.' Perhaps *he* was the one who was uptight.

"Your objective today—study what we call 'the flow.' Don't read the checklist to accomplish the items. Go ahead and do everything, then reference the checklist afterward to ensure you didn't miss anything. We'll start you off with the basic checklist in front of the paper Indian."

"Paper Indian?"

"Yeah, it's just a paper cutout of the instrument panel. Same concept as what you used in Tweets." The T-37 Tweet was the former primary jet trainer used by the Air Force. Vance AFB was the last base to replace the Tweet with the T-6, and they were almost complete when Jason left.

Samson gathered a stack of publications for Jason, and brought them back to him.

"Here you go," Samson said. "This page is the proposed syllabus. Study these items this morning. Mostly checklists. You'll hop into the sim this afternoon and get plugged in there."

"Plugged in?"

"Yeah, the F-2000 has a wide variety of sensors attached to your body. The seat kind of molds to your body and the controls adapt to your hands and feet. It remembers your settings and automatically adjusts the seat placement when you power up the jet. The helmet has integrated sensors and a helmet-mounted HUD as well.

"You'll need to get a mold done of your head so the device can see where your eyes are looking. It also has a night-vision setting. It's really cool. It will take a couple of days for them to get you linked into the system, so get that stuff done as soon as you can. We'll use this opportunity to begin your ground training."

"Kind of quick, isn't it?"

"Speed is what this program is all about. The Air Force is striving to save money by reducing training time. You know the motto, *Do more with less.*"

"Yeah, I understand. This just seems awfully quick."

"Sorry, Captain," Samson said as he stood. "I've got a proficiency ride in the Eagle in an hour. We'll head over to the simulator after lunch."

Jason nodded as Samson left the vault. This program moved very fast for a student, even a simulated student like him. It would be written up in his critique. That didn't bother him—he knew he'd get through the course. What bothered him was that, although he'd seen *The Right Stuff*, he couldn't remember what happened to the original "monkey in a capsule."

THE ROOM SAT IN TOTAL DARKNESS with the exception of the glow of the computer monitors. The technicians were quiet, and the only sound was the low hum of the electronics in the room. Li Zhong entered the modified control room located next to the lab at TRENCOR Industries. General Jingguo's team had worked around the clock since midnight Friday, ensuring the modifications were made to the jet. The RPA package developed by Century Aero-Bot wasn't difficult to install, but the command and control station took time, and their modifications to the jet were . . . unique. How well the system would work was the burning question.

With the control system in place, General Jingguo's "pilot" took his seat. He had a joystick and several display screens showing aircraft instruments and maps. It was rudimentary, but sufficient for their objective today. The signal from the jet was strong, indicating there would be no problem with satellite communications connectivity. Li Zhong sat in a chair in the back of the room. His presence made some of the technicians nervous. He liked that.

One of the technicians wearing a headset turned to Li Zhong. "It will be less than an hour from now," he said.

Li Zhong nodded. The morning might prove to be most interesting.

THE LIFE SUPPORT ROOM was not crowded, and Samson swiftly donned his g-suit and harness. Grabbing his helmet, he checked his oxygen mask. Stepping out the door, he walked toward the F-15C Eagle a hundred yards away. The twin-tailed fighter sat alone on the ramp, prepped and ready. Samson loved flying the Eagle. The F-15C had been the world's air superiority champion for decades, and quite frankly, was tons of fun to fly.

The crew chief handed him the orange-covered 781, and Samson handed him his helmet bag. Climbing up the ladder, the crew chief hung the helmet on the glare shield, rolled up the helmet bag, and placed it next to the ejection seat. Samson reviewed the maintenance history and handed it back to the crew chief on the ladder, who stored it in the jet.

Completing the walk-around, he climbed into the cockpit, strapped in, and put on his helmet. The crew chief climbed the ladder and ensured he was good to go. Removing the ladder, the crew chief took his position out front for the engine start. Samson accomplished his pre-start flows and made a pulling motion with his right hand, signaling the crew chief he was initiating the Jet Fuel Starter. The JFS is similar to the auxiliary power unit in other aircraft, providing pneumatic power, or air, to start the engine.

When the JFS powered up, Samson raised his right hand again. Extending his forefinger and pinky, he twisted the raised hand left and right, signaling the crew chief he was starting engine number two. He lifted the right throttle to start the turbine spinning. The low-pitch whine told him the shaft had engaged the JFS to mechanically turn the engine. He pushed the throttle over the hump and the fuel/air mixture in the powerful jet engine ignited. The big Pratt & Whitney F-100 engine spun up rapidly. When the number-two engine provided enough hydraulic pressure, he pushed the canopy lever forward, allowing the canopy to close. Once the canopy rested on the rails, he pushed the lever forward with his right hand, locking the canopy into position. This allowed the cool air from his Environmental Control System to flow into the cockpit.

While he was accomplishing this, the crew chief scurried underneath the large fighter jet and retrieved the three gear pins that locked each of the landing gear in place. Once the crew chief displayed them to him, he signaled to start the number-one engine. Samson continued his flows and called ground control for clearance to taxi the aircraft to the runway. The F-15C taxied straight to the runway and was immediately cleared for takeoff.

After verifying stable engines at eighty percent power, he released the brakes and pushed the throttles over the hump past one-hundred-percent military power to full afterburner. He pushed the throttles into afterburner and the nozzles in the rear of the jet flexed, adjusting for the extra fuel dumped into the engines. Confirming the fuel flow increase on the engine gauges, he felt each acceleration boost as all five stages of the afterburner lit. The jet leaped forward, rapidly accelerating down the runway. The F-15 became airborne and he raised the landing gear. He lowered the nose to level the jet fifty feet off the ground; it quickly accelerated, and he raised the flaps. As he pulled the throttles out of afterburner, the F-15 accelerated to 350 knots, and he smoothly raised the nose forty degrees high as the jet continued to increase its airspeed. Reaching .9 Mach, he continued to raise the nose to hold that speed. It takes the F-15 about sixty seconds to climb to 30,000 feet due to the powerful thrust of the dual F-100 engines. In the test configuration, without any external weapons or fuel tanks, the combined thrust of the two engines is greater than the weight of the jet. This gave his F-15 the ability to accelerate in the climb.

Samson continued his vertical climb up to 30,000 feet, pulled the jet onto its back, and rolled upright. He pulled the throttles back to maintain .9 Mach, accomplished his level-off checks, and flew the jet north to its working area at 30,000 feet.

THE RAIN FELL STEADILY for the past hour. Caldwell sat alone in his office at Langley, staring out the window. He couldn't find any information regarding Kathy Delgato prior to 1994. She was a ghost. Literally. The Social Security number she used belonged to a woman who died in 1990. He was shocked at the information Carl delivered five minutes ago.

Caldwell wanted to bounce the information off his superiors before talking to Jason. It tied in too neatly. Carl contacted him with information about a woman in East L.A. who called Nikolai. Then a woman fitting Kathy Delgato's description killed three gangbangers at the same approximate location and time the phone call was made. Finally, the car the woman who killed the gangbangers was driving was dropped off near the base where Jason works, on the day after Kathy arrived.

It was her. Caldwell was disturbed that the woman his friend loved was a Russian mole from Section Nine. He pulled the file from the San Antonio incident, reviewing everything they had on Kathy while she'd been in Enid. It made sense. He maneuvered through the crowded halls at Langley, into the director of operations' office, and approached the secretary who worked for his old boss.

"Is he in?"

SAMSON RELISHED HIS TIME in the jet. Once established in the area, he practiced a series of basic fighter maneuvers, including break turns and double ditches. He always appreciated the control afforded by the Eagle's twin vertical stabilizers. Even in low-speed loaded conditions without the hindrance of fly-by-wire controls, he could maneuver the jet with precision, while other computer-controlled fighters limited the pilot's inputs. This was an issue he argued about regarding the F-2000. The computer controlled everything. In his opinion, the computer was there to enhance the pilot's abilities, not replace them. The Air Force grew more interested in having the ability to override the pilot. Taking the pilot out of the fight and turning it over to a guy in a box thousands of miles away didn't make sense, but it was the direction the Air Force was moving.

When he completed his maneuvers, he began his flows to return to the base for an instrument approach. Samson coupled up the two-toggle-switch autopilot and pulled out his approach plate. He switched the radio to the ATIS frequency for the altimeter setting back at Edwards. A crackling sound, then a loud pop came over his headset, and the Multi-Purpose Color Display (MPCD) blinked off momentarily, then flashed on again.

Samson wondered what happened as his jet began a thirty-degree right turn. He attempted to roll the jet straight and level, but the stick wouldn't budge. Slowly, the nose of the jet descended through the horizon. When he applied back pressure on the stick to raise the nose, the stick still didn't move. Samson toggled the paddle switch below the nose gear steering button several times to verify the autopilot was disengaged. He attempted to disengage the autopilot several times, but the jet continued to fly itself. He pulled the throttles back to idle to reduce the airspeed as the jet gradually accelerated as it descended in the right-hand turn.

It was several moments before he realized the radios were silent. He dialed up ATIS, which should be an automatic continuous broadcast of the weather back at Edwards, but the radio was silent. He changed the frequency, keyed the mic, and attempted to call Approach Control with both the main and auxiliary radio. No response. Samson moved the transponder switch to the emergency position and dialed in 243.0, the emergency UHF frequency.

Nothing.

46

May 14, 2001

JASON SPENT THE PAST ninety minutes reviewing the operations limits of the F-2000 and reading through the checklist items. It frustrated him that he couldn't take any notes because of the classified nature of the jet. He had trouble wrapping his head around some of the items on the checklist. His eyes grew tired and his mind wandered. He had been lonely for so long and suddenly, out of nowhere, Kathy returned. Why? And why was she different than the old Kathy?

Closing his book, he advised the airman monitoring the classified vault he would be back in a few minutes. Coffee was imperative.

Exiting the vault, he shuffled down the hallway to the break room. He found Brent sitting there, eating a bowl of brightly colored cereal.

"Jason, hi," Brent said. "Have a seat."

"I'm sorry, Brent. I'm in a hurry. Need a cup of coffee. Studying the pubs is killing me."

"I understand." Brent spooned another mouthful of Froot Loops. The two were alone in the small room consisting of a sink area and small tables with chairs. Jason headed straight for the coffee machine. Brent swallowed and said, "Hey, I wanted to ask you . . . what was up with your date on Friday?"

Jason paused as he poured his coffee. "What do you mean?"

"Really? Don't you think it's kind of obvious? She kicked Jennifer's butt." Brent was animated with his hand gestures, waving his spoon as if it were a club. "I mean, I'm not complaining, but it is unusual to have one of our pilot's dates kick the crap out of another pilot."

Jason finished pouring his coffee. Turning to face Brent, he shook his head. "This is not how I wanted to make an impression here."

"I think you're okay. The water cooler talk is mostly in praise of your date. Most folks around here can't stand Jennifer. Especially the wives. Jennifer is on the top of their gossip list."

For the first time, Jason felt relieved. "That's good to know . . . about Kathy, I mean. I know how Jen—I mean, Major Walton, is, or is rumored to be. I'm sorry she has to live with that following her."

Brent stared at Jason with a blank expression on his face.

"What?" Jason said.

Brent shook his head. "Either you're one hell of a bullshitter, or you're the last of the Jedi Knights."

"Well . . ." Jason paused. He wasn't sure where this conversation was going and had never been referred to as a Jedi Knight. He assumed it was a compliment. "Seriously. Life's too short. It's not my style." Jason leaned against the doorjamb, frustrated. "I want to put this behind me. I spent my first hour this morning apologizing to Major Walton."

"Fair enough. So, where did she learn to fight like that? It was kind of awesome."

"She took a women's self-defense class."

"She must have been a good student."

"That's what I said," Jason said. It was time to change the subject. "So, who were you with?"

Brent beamed. "You mean the gorgeous redhead?"

"Yeah." Jason said. He chose not to mention their run-in at the Texas Cattle Company. "You two been dating long?"

Brent's smile faded and his shoulders slumped. "We aren't dating."

Jason's head tilted to the side.

Brent's eyes darted to the left, then right as he edged closer to Jason. "Can you keep a secret?"

"I think so. I'm the 'monkey in a capsule'."

"Okay, that should have been obvious. Her name is Sherri Davis," he said just above a whisper. "She's a reporter for *The New York Times*."

"A reporter? What's she doing here?" Jason's brow furrowed.

"She's investigating Georgiana's murder," Brent said. "She stumbled on the sheriff's department when they found her body in the desert. I met her at the sheriff's office the next day."

"How did *The New York Times* get a reporter here that fast to cover the story?"

Brent set his spoon in his cereal bowl, staring blankly at Jason.

"Haven't you thought about this?" Jason said.

"Thought about what?"

"Doesn't it strike you as a little unusual that a gorgeous redhead who happens to work for *The New York Times* shows up at a murder scene in the middle of a desert?"

THE F-15C LEVELED OFF at 20,000 feet and punched its way through the empty, clear blue sky, uninhibited by any control inputs by the pilot. Samson, for the first time in his flying career, was stumped as the aircraft pushed the lateral boundaries of his working airspace.

As he reached the border, the jet banked forty-five degrees to the right, changing direction; Samson adjusted the throttles to maintain his energy through the turn. Samson's initial instinct was to force the controls in an attempt to fly out of the maneuver, but it didn't take long to realize he was still along for the ride. His training told him he should eject because he could no longer control the aircraft, but the test pilot in him wanted to know what was happening. He still had plenty of altitude to eject if needed.

Being a modified test aircraft, Samson's F-15 contained the same digital Control Augmentation System (CAS) as the F-15E Strike Eagle. The digital CAS made control inputs much more responsive than the older analog systems in the standard F-15C. Perhaps something in the flight computer corrupted the CAS, making the flight controls unresponsive. It made sense. After all, he still had control of his throttles; only the flight controls were affected.

The jet continued its bank to ninety degrees, and Samson moved the throttles forward as additional back pressure on the stick increased the G-loading on the jet. The g-suit inflated as normal. Samson tensed his body for the high-G maneuver, following the aircraft's progress through the maneuver. He relaxed and reduced the power as the jet returned to straight and level flight. How the hell—?

Samson checked the INS panel, but he knew he hadn't input anything for this short profile. It was impossible for the jet to have a corrupted flight plan integrating itself with the autopilot—it wasn't that type of system. From a programming standpoint, this was not possible, but he was out of ideas. He turned the MPCD off hoping it might have an impact. Again, nothing.

The aircraft continued to drone around the area for a minute at

20,000 feet. Suddenly, the jet rolled inverted and pulled its nose forty-five degrees nose low. Samson again fought with the controls to no avail. He reduced the power to idle, but the F-15 rapidly accelerated to six hundred knots as he raced toward the ground inverted.

JASON AND BRENT sat alone in the break room. Brent's gaze drifted to the few remaining Froot Loops floating in his milk, as he contemplated Sherri and who she might be. "I hadn't considered that. She told me she was here working on another story."

"What other story?"

"I-I don't know. Do you think she lied to me? Do you think she is searching for information on the F2K?"

"Hell, Brent, I don't know . . . I just met her. She's your date," Jason said. "The issue is, you need to find out why she is here. You need to tread with caution. I learned a long time ago you never really know who your friends are."

"Yeah, clearly. I'm betting you didn't know your girlfriend was a kung-fu ninja."

Now the tables turned. He's right. Who knew suspected Kathy could win a fight like she did.

"No," was all Jason could mutter.

"Sherri didn't know TRENCOR was involved in aviation research and development. She was familiar with some of the corporate interests, but was surprised when I told her about the complex they had built in California City. She is far more interested in David Ming and his activities than she is about the F-2000."

SAMSON STRUGGLED AGAINST the stick as the F-15 pushed its way through 10,000 feet. As he reached for the ejection handle, the aircraft up-righted itself and reduced its descent rate. Cross-checking his airspeed he was over 800 knots, 1.2 on the Mach meter. His heartbeat slowed, grateful he didn't have to eject at such a high airspeed. If it didn't kill him, it would have severely crippled him. The aircraft leveled off at 2,000 feet as he flew over the dry lake heading south back toward the base. Samson moved the throttles to the fifty percent position as the aircraft started to decelerate.

Taking advantage of the lull in the action, he turned off everything he could in the cockpit. His displays went dark, but had no impact on the jets maneuvering. He reached over to his oxygen panel and moved the switch to the one-hundred-percent position. Breathing in the pure oxygen, he tried to clear his mind. Sweat poured down his face, the tight seal of his oxygen mask causing the sweat to collect and drip along his cheeks. The Nomex and leather flight gloves loosened as his hands perspired. Samson ignored this as he methodically covered every aspect of the jet.

The F-2000 had an RPA module that was the overall system-management control for the Sensory Integration Package and the Integrated Thought Control System. But the RPA portion would give someone, somewhere the ability to fly the F-2000 when the pilot was unconscious. The digital CAS would make it plausible that—

Time finally slowed enough for him to think. Samson subconsciously still made an effort to fly the jet when the realization overcame him and he cursed out loud.

"I'm the monkey in the capsule."

Someone outside was flying the jet.

47

May 14, 2001

THE DIRECTOR OF THE Operations Division at the Central Intelligence Agency didn't have much interest in seeing Agent Caldwell. Director Philip Hastings had more politically expedient issues to deal with tonight, such as picking up his wife for dinner with a group of senators in Georgetown.

"What do you want Agent Caldwell?" Hastings said.

"Sir, it's about Nikolai Gregarin."

Director Hastings rolled his eyes. "It's always about Gregarin, isn't it, Caldwell?"

Caldwell put both hands on his hips. Hastings realized he had made the agent's issue seem as irrelevant as he thought it was. *Not good form in front of the troops. Need to pay better attention to what I'm saying.*

"Nikolai received a phone call in Eastern Europe," Caldwell said. "We tracked the call to East L.A."

"L.A. as in Los Angeles?"

"Yes."

Hastings put the folder he had been reading on his desk and leaned back in his chair, motioning Caldwell to sit. "No thank you, sir, I'd rather stand."

"Go on," Hastings said. Yup, he'd pissed off Caldwell. No bother. He's young; he'll get over it.

"The phone call came from a woman named Ann, likely codenamed Ann Rodriguez, the same woman we believe killed three gangbangers in the middle of the street around the same time as the phone call. The phone was ditched at an intersection north of Los Angeles."

"How do we know it was a woman?"

"Voice on the phone and witnesses to the killings."

"Where is she now?"

"A vehicle matching the description of the one at the murder scene was turned in to a Rosamond Dollar Rent-A-Car. A woman matching the description of the woman who shot the gangbangers dropped it off. The license plate from the East L.A. shooting is different from the rental vehicle."

"What's the connection?"

"They matched a set stolen from a car at LAX. We believe the woman Gregarin was talking to, arrived at LAX two hours before the shooting."

"That's enough for me," Hastings said. "Let's contact the boys at the Bureau and have her picked up."

"There's more, sir. I believe this woman is the missing woman from the attempt on Senator Jonathan Bowman's life in San Antonio six years ago."

"The mystery woman? No shit?" Director Hastings leaned forward, resting his arms on his desk. "Bowman's kid wouldn't say anything about her."

"Jason Conrad."

"Right . . . Conrad. The OSI guy wouldn't rat her out either"

"The girl, Kathy Delgato, came back to Enid before Jason moved two weeks ago. I saw her."

"Is it her? Nikolai's contact?"

"Fits the physical description, but more importantly, Jason Conrad is now stationed at Edwards. Rosamond sits west of Edwards. And Kathy Delgato arrived the same day this phone call was made, to move in with Jason Conrad."

Director Hastings spun his chair around, opening a filing cabinet behind him. He dug through until he found the old file from 1996. Pulling it out, he set it on the desk and opened it. He pulled out pictures of Jason, Kathy, and Nikolai.

"Do you think this Conrad kid is in on it? One of Nikolai's spies?" Hastings said. "He had a classmate who was one."

"No, I don't think Jason is one of Nikolai's spies, but she is. I'm sure of it."

"Standard checks?"

"Done. She fails. All of them."

Director Hastings sat back in his chair, staring through Caldwell as if he wasn't there. The implications were devastating. He rubbed his chin, his mind racing. "What's next?"

"I need to contact Jason Conrad."

"SHERRI AND I STARTED talking outside the Sheriff's office," Brent said, pushing his glasses up the bridge of his nose. "When I mentioned TRENCOR, she got excited. That's all she could talk about."

"TRENCOR?"

"Yeah, wouldn't stop talking about it. Do you think Sherri is some kind of spy?"

Jason shook his head. "I'm sure it's nothing. Is she aware of TRENCOR's F-2000 program?"

"That's not the issue," Brent said, swirling the remaining cereal with his spoon, "She doesn't seem interested in the airplane or the base either. But she is sure interested in the simulator complex. She drives by there every day."

"Soooo . . . she does know about the F-2000."

Brent's head jerked toward Jason with a look of despair as he wiped off some milk that spilled on his beard. "Well, uh, I, um . . . I may have let something slip out. But she only heard the name."

"Could it be she knows TRENCOR's facility is the central training hub for the F-2000?"

"That's just it. She didn't know anything about the jet before coming to California. She found out about TRENCOR being her when she stumbled across Georgiana's death. One of TRENCOR'S companies manufactured a combine that her father was killed in years ago. She blames the company. She blames David Ming. She doesn't like that guy."

"I can see why," Jason said. "I tried to speak to him at the reception, and he wasn't interested in me at all. He literally walked off."

"He's a billionaire, and you're just a peasant jet pilot. It happens."

"Yeah, I guess. But why is Sherri so interested in David Ming?" He knew revenge was a good motivator, but it only took you so far. She must know something.

STREAKING ACROSS THE DRY LAKE, Samson pulled back the F-15C's throttles as the jet began a gradual descent out of 2,000 feet. Samson watched the Attitude Direction Indicator (ADI), the round dial indicating whether the jet was in level flight, a climb or descent, a left or right turn. It showed two degrees below the horizon. Looking far in front of the jet, Samson could see the base. The jet continued its track toward the ground. The vertical velocity indicator showed it was descending at five hundred feet per minute. His jet had slowed to three hundred knots. The TACAN showed he was nineteen nautical miles from the field. At this rate, he calculated he would impact the ground just south of the base.

The jet continued its descent through 1,000 feet as Samson felt the nose dump a few more degrees, increasing the jet's descent. Watching the rushing terrain outside, Samson decided he'd waited long enough. He reached for the ejection handle and pulled.

Nothing.

He pulled the handle again, much harder this time, and the handle came off in his hand.

Samson screamed every curse word he knew as the jet leveled at 100 feet above the terrain. He beat his fist against the canopy as his frustration overcame him.

Five miles from the field, the jet rolled into an eighty degree bank turn, heading north again.

Samson noticed a T-38, the smaller two-seat trainer, taking off from the runway. As he approached the field, he turned to see where the jet was now.

The T-38 headed toward him. Samson breathed a sigh of relief knowing the base was aware something was going on in his jet. He searched for a piece of paper to write a note. The F-15's airspeed was three hundred knots; at this airspeed, the T-38 should catch him.

The jet climb to four hundred feet and Samson pulled the throttles back to help the T-38 catch him. The airspeed decreased through two-hundred-seventy knots when the nose pitched up violently and the airspeed rolled back dramatically. Samson pushed the power up to avoid a stall, and the nose came back down. The jet accelerated back to two-hundred-eighty knots as Samson again pulled the power back. Once again, the jet pitched up dramatically. He shoved the throttles forward, and the nose of the jet gradually returned to the horizon.

Whoever controlled his jet was letting him know not to slow down. He turned and watched the T-38 a thousand feet higher accelerate, gradually closing the distance between the two aircraft. Normally, when two dissimilar aircraft accomplish a rejoin, one aircraft would start a turn. This gave the trailing aircraft the ability to use lead pursuit to gain closure despite any power differential between the two aircraft. A straight-ahead rejoin took significantly longer. He tried the stick yet again in an attempt to turn the jet toward the T-38.

No such luck today, as his jet took him straight ahead. He now focused less and less on his jet and more on the closing T-38. They were a half a mile back now and Samson saw them dump the nose to increase their jet's airspeed to close the gap.

Samson was relieved as the jet pulled two aircraft lengths to his left side. He held up a note saying "NO CONTROL" against the canopy.

The pilot in the front seat of the T-38 shook his head, then put his hand over his eyes. Samson realized that the sun must be reflecting off the canopy in just the wrong spot. He started to give the visual signal for an electrical malfunction and the F-15C banked up and toward the T-38. The abrupt action caused the smaller white jet to break out from the formation as it banked sharply to the left, pulling away hard. The T-38 was at least a half mile away again.

Samson noticed the nose climbing again, forcing him to add more power. By the time he managed to get his jet stabilized, the airspeed indicator read four hundred twenty knots. There was no chance the T-38 would catch him at this speed. The jet began a gradual descent and the jet's speed noticeably increased.

For the first time, Samson released the flight controls of the jet. He tilted his head upward, cursing, beating the canopy with both fists. He didn't need to guess what was going on. Someone was trying to scare the crap out of him or have him killed.

He was spent. Physically, mentally, emotionally. The jet flew three hundred feet off the ground and accelerated to five hundred knots indicated airspeed, heading straight for a mountain. Samson stared at it for a moment, motionless. Instinct overcame despair as he closed in on the mountain. He tugged on the stick with both hands as the climbing landscape filled the windscreen.

48

May 14, 2001

LI ZHONG LEFT the isolated room in the vast complex at TRENCOR Industries feeling good about the operation. He watched the entire scenario play out on the video screen. The RPA system performed as advertised. General Jingguo's team did a perfect job installing the RPA system and integrating their control center. Since the United States military had shifted much of its maintenance force to civilian contractors, the installation had been easily accomplished over the weekend. No one paid attention to the work General Jingguo's men did on the F-15.

The jet impacted the mountain with the force of a small earthquake. It had been Ming's idea to deactivate the ejection seat. Li Zhong had the technician sever the handle so when Samson pulled a second or third time, it would come off in his hand. Li Zhong had a flair for the dramatic. TRENCOR's team, pre-positioned off the highway to the north, waited for the impact. The recovery team had the precise GPS coordinates of the scheduled impact and knew exactly what they needed to recover, eliminating any evidence of the RPA.

The team blocked off the highway for five miles in either direction. That gave them time to retrieve the parts from the wreckage. Their hired-gun deputy who'd escorted General Jingguo and his team to TRENCOR would block the roads. He ran interference as much as possible. The deputy's acquisition had been one of Li Zhong's major coups, the perfect blend of ignorance and greed.

Li Zhong's cell phone rang as the team moved toward the wreckage. He told them to call him when they secured the package and departed the area. The phone flipped closed as he left the room and hurried toward the lobby.

The white Mercedes sat in front of the building. Li Zhong climbed in and drove through the gates of TRENCOR Industries. His cell phone rang again.

"She's on the move," the voice said. "She just left the VOQ. Heading for the front gate."

"Is the team in position?"

"Yes, we're ready."

"Okay, you know what to do," Li Zhong said, hanging up. He made a U-turn in the middle of the street and headed south toward Edwards.

KATHY LEFT BILLETING AFTER doing her laundry. Her feelings for Jason grew stronger than ever. Section Nine trained her to push her emotions out of her head during operations, but it never accounted for feelings this strong. She loved Jason Conrad. Section Nine had assigned her the mission of finding out about the "Lima Project" his father was working on, and when she did, kill him. She knew she couldn't kill his father and have a normal relationship. Thoughts of coming clean with Jason and defecting constantly twirled through her head, but she knew even if he were willing to accept her situation, he would never go into hiding with her.

She worried this op was going bad. She wasn't sure if it was her being sloppy or the op being a bad idea from the beginning. The reunion with Jason in Enid changed everything. It had been fantastic, and was something she desperately needed. That didn't mean Jason would give in to her seductive charms in favor of mother Russia. He would definitely turn her in. Kathy had made a huge effort in the last few days to gather as much intelligence as possible while at Edwards. Recognizing her days here were numbered and Jason's father was nowhere around, she knew this mission had to be aborted. She needed to contact Nikolai.

Driving out the gate in Jason's truck, she headed toward Rosamond. Something seemed unusual when she passed through the gate, but she wasn't sure what. Her training kicked in and within seconds she noticed a dark sedan two cars behind her. The car struggled to maintain a constant distance. Kathy decided to test her observation. She slowed her vehicle, and the sedan slowed, as well. Then she took a quick right turn and checked her rearview mirror. The sedan stayed two car lengths behind her. Damn. Who was this? Could it be the CIA? FBI?

Hell, the local police? She had gotten sloppy. She cursed herself for her actions over the past week. Kathy made a left turn onto Sierra Highway and stared in the rearview mirror. In a matter of seconds, the dark sedan continued straight through the intersection. Next, a right turn into a residential area. After another right, she pulled to the side of the road with the engine running. She reached into her purse, pulled out the Glock, and chambered a round. Checking the mirrors on the truck, she confirmed the empty streets. No traffic flowed on this back street.

Situational awareness kept her alive in the Philippines; she needed the same skillset here.

She pulled the truck away from the side of the road and turned to rejoin the main road into Rosamond. The house Jason rented sat on the southwest side of town in an isolated area off the main street. She needed to get back—the appliance repairman was scheduled to show up and fix the washer and dryer.

She continued along Rosamond Boulevard, turned south on 60th Street West, and drove for nearly a mile. The small two-story house was quaint, but adequate. The monthly payment was what interested Jason. The owner, a pilot in his squadron, let him stay there for the cost of utilities plus two hundred dollars until he could find a more permanent place. Not a bad deal.

When Kathy reached the house, she noticed the repair van out front, but no repairmen. Could Jason or the owner have let them inside? Turning into the driveway, she pulled the truck to the left, forward of the van. The magnetic sign attached to the van said "Dave's Handyman Repair," with a small cartoon of a repairman on the side.

Approaching the back of the house, she saw two repairmen sitting on the steps, smoking cigarettes. Only they didn't *look* like repairmen. Oh, they were dressed for it, but something about them wasn't quite right.

"How long have you guys been here?" Kathy said. The delay in response troubled her as she reached for the pistol in her purse.

"Don't try that, miss," one of the men said. "We've got four guns trained on you right now."

As she turned to check behind her, two men brandishing AK-47s appeared on her right. When she turned back, the two "repairmen" pointed pistols at her.

Damn.

THE SQUADRON WAS CHAOTIC. People raced back and forth, carrying stacks of papers, gathering around the operations desk. Jason had been in the isolated vault studying when he stepped out to use the bathroom and been exposed to the chaos. He wandered down the hall and noticed a "DO NOT ENTER" sign placed on Major Samson's office door. Jennifer wasn't at her desk, but as he walked toward the ops desk, he saw her. She'd been crying, and even now fought back tears.

"Major Walton, what's going on?"

"Oh Jason, it's horrible. Curt Samson crashed his F-15 about twenty minutes ago."

Jason couldn't believe it. "What? How? Did he get out?"

Jennifer shook her head. "We don't have any details yet, but I heard the jet impacted a mountain to the north. It's kind of confusing because the first report to emergency services was a call about a jet crashing a hundred miles south of here."

"Could two jets have crashed?"

"It's possible, but not likely. Edwards had two jets airborne. Range Control alerted the Control Tower, and they moved all traffic south of the field. They launched a T-38 to see what was going on with Samson, but his F-15 outran them. The tower says it can see smoke in the mountains to the north, and they saw Samson's F-15 flying very low to the north. They weren't sure why. The T-38 crew called him on guard, as did Approach Control. He never answered. It's all so strange."

"What did the T-38 crew say?"

"They're not back yet. The wing commander and safety officer met them at the jet and drove to headquarters. The SOF isn't relaying what was said on the radio to anyone. Word is they saw Samson impact the side of a mountain, but that hasn't been verified."

Jason stood in the hallway wondering what to do next. The SOF was the supervisor of flying and had been ordered to keep quiet.

"I was supposed to meet with him this afternoon and start my simulator orientation," Jason said. He was more thinking out loud than seeking guidance.

"Oh, General Wellington called five minutes ago. That training is still a go. He wants you there at 1300 sharp."

"What?" How could they have solved this problem already?

Normally all training goes on stand-down following an accident.

"Everything can't stop because we had a crash, Jason."

Jason was astonished. The quick emotional transition puzzled him. For someone so distraught over Samson's death, she was eager for him to get to the simulator. He was aware everything didn't stop because of a crash, but training should have stopped. All that aside, what alarmed him most was that Wellington knew about it so fast.

ONE OF THE MEN, the one with crossed eyes, grabbed Kathy's pistol from her purse and tucked it in his waistband. He grinned, exposing his crooked, yellow teeth, and raising his AK at her. Her eyes darted back and forth, desperately searching for a way out.

She studied the two men with AK-47s. It's pretty bold to be running around the streets of the good ol' USA brandishing an AK-47. They'll make a hell of a noise when fired. That's right, they will make noise. Lots of it. With closer observation, she noticed the safety on both rifles in the "safe" position. The rifle wouldn't fire even if a round was chambered.

Both "repairmen" had pistols with suppressors on them. The heavier one tucked his pistol in his pants and moved toward Kathy to tie her hands. He tried to put her hands behind her back, but she struggled, writhing her hands so he couldn't tie them together. The AKs moved closer to her head, but they had no effect; she knew they weren't going to use them.

"Hurry up and tie her damn hands!" the tall one said, lowering his pistol.

"I'm trying," the stout man said. "Hold still, dammit!"

Kathy strained vigorously as he tried to tie her hands. Finally one of the men, who had a flat-top haircut, slung his rifle around his back and moved over to assist.

"C'mon Kenny, she's not that big," he said, laughing at his partner's struggle. Flat-top grabbed her from the front, pinner her arms behind her.

Sensing her opportunity, she shrieked and let her body relax. The stout man behind her, seeing she no longer struggled, moved in to tie her hands.

"I kinda like this, don't you," Flat-top said to her, ogling in her face as he squeezed her into his chest.

Kathy spied the man five feet away with the pistol pointed at the three of them. She knew the second AK-47 with the crossed eyes and crooked yellow teeth was somewhere behind her with the safety on. Feeling the stout one moving closer behind her to get leverage to tie her hands, she moved. Thrusting her left heel back and up, she found the stout man's groin with a second effort. He doubled over in pain, releasing her arms as he fell.

Swinging her right arm forward, she grabbed Flat-top's groin and squeezed as hard as she could. Flat-top screamed as she used her body weight to push him toward the tall one still holding the pistol. She gained better footing and accelerated toward the man as he pointed the pistol at them. The tall one stepped backward, unsure of what happened until he backed into the side of the house. Seeing his movement halted, Kathy pushed harder on Flat-top and slammed him into the tall man with the pistol. Flat-top's head slammed into the tall repairman's head with a loud smack.

The tall one's grip on the pistol loosen, and it fell to the ground to her left. Time stood still, but it had been five seconds since she first struck the stout man behind her. Her eyes locked on the pistol as it fell to the ground. Instinct once again took over as she released her grip on Flat-top and dove for the pistol.

49

May 14, 2001

KATHY LUNGED FOR THE PISTOL as Flat-top fell to the ground. As her hands moved within inches of the pistol, a dirty boot from behind stepped on it.

Kathy's hand landed on the boot covering the pistol. On her hands and knees, she turned her head to the left, following the leg up toward the man's face. When she looked up, the butt of an AK-47 stock came crashing into her forehead. Kathy fell to the ground, conscious but in a haze. Her body tried to react, but her brain didn't function. A warm trickle of blood slid down the side of her face, the sweat from her brow dripping into her eyes, stinging them.

Groggy, she struggled for awareness. Everything that happened from here on was important. Focus and detail were key if she was going to get out of this. She still didn't know who these guys were—CIA? FBI? Hell, they could be GRU.

Through her hazy vision she saw three men hop out of the side door of the repair van. Two of them lifted her to her feet, and the third handcuffed her behind her back. Pain shot through her skull as a man's hands bounced off her head as he threw a black hood over her face. Kathy hated the hood over her head, as her ever-shrinking world shrank faster. She was in no position to struggle as they frisked her—professionally, she noticed, not like the gangbanger she had killed days before.

"All of this for little old me?" she quipped.

Someone hit her across the jaw as the two men released her, and she fell back to the ground. The blow was not hard enough to knock her out, but hard enough to let her know they meant business.

Two of the men lifted her to her feet and marched her to the van. Her shins hit the edge of the van sharply; she grimaced in pain as she heard the men laugh. They thrust her into the van and she fell forward.

She hit the floor of the van with a grunt. Several sets of hands were on her, sitting her upright. There were at least three other people in the back of the van with her. She struggled to pay attention to everything. She heard several vehicles start outside.

The van started, backed out to the driveway, and headed left. North. She started counting the seconds in an effort to figure out where she would be held captive. Her hands searched the floor behind her for anything that might help her when a needle punctured her neck and warm fluid pushed into her bloodstream. The warmth spread throughout her body and in seconds, her heartbeat pulsed in her eardrums, then faded, until she was unconscious.

JENNIFER DROPPED JASON off at TRENCOR that afternoon for his training with Wellington. He tried to call Kathy throughout the day and had not been able to reach her. She had been at billeting to do laundry and was supposed to return to the house to meet the repairman. He hoped he would hear from her soon. Jennifer had been more than happy to drop him off at TRENCOR and insisted she come back after work to give him a ride home. Well aware of the trouble it would cause, he wanted to decline, but if he was unable to reach Kathy, Jennifer might be his only choice.

When he arrived, Jeremiah Wellington was there waiting for him.

"About time you showed up, Captain Conrad. We start in five minutes."

Jason didn't appreciate the condescending attitude. "My apologies, sir. I had to catch a ride since I loaned my truck to a friend." He didn't bother to tell him Jennifer gave him the ride. Not after his reaction at the reception.

"Hhmpf," Wellington grunted. "Get over here and get started." Wellington handed Jason a checklist. "We designed this jet so well that even a FAIP could fly it. We figure if a FAIP can fly it, a fighter guy out of UPT will have no problem."

Jason let the insults roll off his shoulders. Brent told him the charming Jeremiah Wellington didn't like other pilots, but he seemed to get extra grief from the retired general. It didn't matter; Jason wasn't the least bit intimidated by Wellington. He just wanted to do a good job.

"Sir, did you hear about Major Samson?" Jason said, attempting to break the ice.

"Of course I heard about Major Samson, numb nuts, that's why I'm here instructing your sorry ass. If he weren't such a crappy pilot, he'd be here doing this. I guess we don't make pilots like we used to."

Jason stood dumbfounded. Did Wellington actually say that? He didn't mind the insults, but the comments about Samson were extremely inappropriate—even for a prick like Wellington.

"Okay, Captain, we're going to forego the Sensory Integration Package today. Can you tell me what that is?"

Jason scowled at him. This asshole was treating him like he was a second lieutenant at UPT.

"Yes sir," he replied. "The Sensory Integration Package consists of the hardware, the software, and the parts connecting the two. The main component is the Integrated Thought Control System, or ITCS, which is built into the specially designed helmet I'm getting fitted for tomorrow."

Wellington frowned. "Don't get smug with me, Captain. All right, climb in and let's get started."

Damn, Jason thought, climbing into the simulator, this is going to be a long day.

Jason worked through the ground checklists: before engines start, starting engines, after engines start, taxi, and before takeoff. He had difficulty with the before-starting-engines checklist. Never having used the Flight Management System (FMS) for inputting a flight plan made it difficult. With time and repetition, he could turn it on and work through the pages. Jason wished someone would give him some training on the system before getting in the simulator.

The jet itself proved easy to operate, at least at this stage. User-friendly, intuitive, and uncomplicated, as well as ergonomically engineered. The all-glass system displays with organic light-emitting diode (OLED) touch-sensitive screens worked very well, even with the pilot wearing gloves. The F-2000's mission computers were lightning fast, far more advanced than anything he'd ever seen. Jason found himself enjoying the training, despite the death of Major Samson earlier and the prick overseeing his training.

Jason picked up quick on the fact that every time he started to make progress, Wellington asked him an obscure question in an effort to shatter his confidence. He admitted to himself it's getting close to that point, but he pushed through. They worked through the afternoon into the early evening and Jason wondered why Wellington was unfazed that his lead test pilot had died in a jet crash hours earlier.

When Jason finished in the simulator, he walked to the lobby to call Kathy. After several unsuccessful attempts, he called Jennifer. She was more than willing to pick him up, she said. She would wait for him out front.

Other than Wellington letting Jason know how badly he was doing his first time in the static simulator, the training session was uneventful. They went to Wellington's office to debrief the training. Jason wasn't expecting good grades in his grade folder, and he wasn't wrong. Wellington made him feel like he was supposed to know this material already, which was a joke for the first day. He talked to Jason like he was someone who'd never flown an airplane, and Jason tuned him out. Wellington spoke as he wrote grades in the folder, never looking at Jason or asking him questions.

Jason scanned Wellington's bookshelf and noticed that he had a gold model of the F-2000 like Jennifer. Wellington was mumbling to himself as he wrote in the grade folder; Jason ignored him completely. He stood up and stepped to the bookshelf to get a closer look at the model. When he reached out to pick it up, Wellington barked, "Don't touch that!"

Jason, unfazed by Wellingtons voice, stopped, and said, "Why? What's so special about this?" He wanted to see if Wellington's and Jennifer's stories matched.

"That statue is almost solid gold, Captain," Wellington said in a terse tone.

"This thing? Solid gold? How can you tell?" That was a hell of a different story from the one Jennifer gave him.

"I can tell because I had them made. There were only ten of these produced, and each one is twenty ounces of gold."

"Twenty ounces? Gold is going for what these days—three hundred bucks an ounce?"

"That's about right. They cost seven thousand dollars each."

"Sounds awesome. Where can I get one?" Jason said. He was badgering Wellington now. He knew there was no way in hell he could get one, and he certainly couldn't afford it if one was for sale. The question was, how did Jennifer get one? Well, he didn't have to ask.

He knew. Those two had been an item for years.

"You can't get one. No lowlife Air Force pilot gets one. Second, you couldn't afford it, and third, there's none to be had. Everyone that's supposed to get one, got one."

Okay, that's a lie. Jennifer has one. Why would he not tell Jennifer it's real gold?

"You must make a great salary if you bought ten people solid gold statues."

"I didn't say I bought them, smart ass. I said I had them made."

"Oh. Guess I'm out of luck."

Jason studied Wellington's response. Something was up, but he couldn't put his finger on it. Maybe it was because Jennifer didn't know the models were solid gold. Maybe it was because he wanted to know who had the other eight.

50

DANE SAT IN THE LOBBY of the Best Western in California City thumbing through a three-day-old issue of USA TODAY. Sherri proved to be rather elusive, as he had tried to find her all weekend. He enjoyed the thrill of the hunt. Once she knew what his story entailed and the international coverage he would garner, she would be all over him.

It must have been his lucky day because Sherri traipsed around the corner resembling a vision from heaven. Dane thought she was more attractive now than when he first met her back in '96. She wore beige capri pants and a black sleeveless shirt with high-heeled sandals.

"Sherri, hi," he said.

She stared blankly at him.

"It's me, Dane."

"Yes, I know. Hello, Dane."

"Sherri, I thought we might have dinner and I could, uh . . . I could bounce my story off you. I think you'd find it truly compelling. If we team up, this could be a Pulitzer Prize winner for you."

She glanced at her watch. "Dane, I'm sorry. I'm not hungry."

"Oh," he said. "I thought because you dressed up, you might be going out to eat."

She paused. "I'm going to meet a friend."

"A friend, or a contact?"

Sherri crossed her arms, shifting her weight to one side. "It's none of your damn business who I'm going to see."

Aware he'd crossed a line, Dane blurted, "Sorry. I guess that didn't come out right."

"Damn right it didn't," Sherri replied.

"Look, I figured we grab a bite to eat, I tell you about my story, and we drive by TRENCOR Industries a little later. You know, follow up on my lead."

Sherri tilted her head. "Do you have a contact there?"

For the first time, he had her attention. He had information she wanted. Should he tell her now or hold out for dinner?

"Dane?"

"Yes," he lied. "I thought maybe after dinner, we could ride by there."

"TRENCOR Industries?" she said. "After dinner, no one will be there."

"Uh . . ." Damn, she had him.

"Forget dinner," she said, turning toward the door. "We'll go by there now to meet your contact. I'll drive."

Dane froze. The doors slid open as she reached the hotel entrance. She turned back to face him.

"Come on," she said.

Dane snapped out of his stupor and with a big smile on his face, raced to the door.

SHERRI PULLED OUT of the parking lot, heading to TRENCOR Industries. She didn't enjoy bringing Dane anywhere, but she was curious how his story involved TRENCOR. These bastards were turning up everywhere these days. Dane tried to carry on small talk, and Sherri decided it had better remain strictly business.

"I don't understand how you tied TRENCOR into your land-grab and windmill story," she said.

"It wasn't easy," Dane replied. "When I first received this story, I knew it was a wild-goose chase. Hell, my options were the windmill story out west or a cloud-seeding conspiracy at Tinker Air Force Base in Oklahoma City. If I didn't know any better, I'd say my producer was trying to keep me out of the spotlight."

Sherri glanced at him with a look that let him know he was right.

"Anyhow, my cameraman and I drove from Tulsa across the state to western Oklahoma to investigate a bunch of windmills. When we arrived, well, what we saw was surprising."

"How so?"

"My dear Sherri, windmills covered the horizon . . . everywhere you could see. Windmills! We knew then and there we were on to something."

"And?"

"I traced the land purchases back to a variety of front corporations. The one factor in common is the lawyer."

Sherri nodded; surprised Dane actually did something like a journalist. He simply didn't go far enough to get the details.

"Dane, I've been busy since you told me about this on Saturday. The Internet is amazing. Saturday morning, you said the lawyer's name was Amanda Johnston Rieffelming."

"Yeah, that's her," Dane said.

"Actually, her name is Rieffel-Ming, with a hyphen. She's the wife of David Ming, CEO of TRENCOR Industries."

That news impressed Dane. "Looks like we make a good team."

Sherri shook her head. She had to admit Dane had actually done some real reporting, although he didn't follow through. That didn't change her mind about him, though. He was still a pig.

They pulled into the parking lot as the setting sun nestled above the small peaks far to the west. As they drove through the unfinished entryway, they saw three vehicles at the facility. A white van was backed into a service entrance on the side when they pulled in the massive parking lot, but there was no activity around the facility.

Sherri pulled into the far side of the parking lot, a good distance away from the three vehicles out front, and parked her car. She had been running this information through her head. Did it make any sense? Why would David Ming's wife be involved in these land buys?

"How did you discover she is married to Ming?" Dane said.

"Google," Sherri said. "It's wonderful."

"The new search engine?"

"Yes," she said, surprised he was aware of it. "I found an article about her when she was a young law student about to marry Ming. It was from her hometown, of course. I also found an article out of her law review newspaper. Actually, it was more of an editorial about the sloppiness of the administration of the law school on the diplomas. One year they had the wrong date. One year they misspelled names. In Amanda's case, they left out the hyphen between her maiden name and her married name, thus creating Amanda Rieffelming."

Dane nodded.

"So, what's the plan for your TRENCOR contact?" Sherri said.

"Plan? Oh, I don't have any kind of plan. I just wanted to find out where it was. I'm going to come here tomorrow and find Amanda Rieffelming."

There was the Dane Robinson she knew from before. Sherri slammed her hands on top of the steering wheel. "Dane, are you kidding? You said you had a contact. You lied to me," Sherri said loudly.

"Sorry. I didn't think you'd come."

"You're damn right I wouldn't," she said, gritting her teeth. She lowered her head toward her lap with her hands on the steering wheel. She should throw him out of the car and make him walk back. "I can't believe you, Dane. Are you telling me you've put no other thought into this story?"

"Hell yes, I did. Do you know how hard I worked to get my station to send me out here? This cost a lot of money. I put a lot of work into this story."

A grain of brilliance on a beach of stupidity—that was how she remembered Dane Robinson.

They stared at the entrance to the building, when the front doors swung open and a pilot walked out. Dane sat up, leaning forward in his seat. Sherri recognized the pilot leaving the building. In fact, his date—

"Holy shit," Dane blurted. "I'll be damned . . . It's Jason Conrad."

Sherri blinked. How does he know Jason Conrad?

Before she could say anything, Dane opened the passenger door and jumped out.

51

May 14, 2001

DANE STOOD BY THE PASSENGER door as if afraid to go farther.

"Jason Conrad," he yelled.

Sherri saw Jason stop and look their way. She wanted to shrink in her seat, but there was nowhere to hide. As Jason stepped toward her car, Sherri wondered what he was doing at TRENCOR.

"What the hell are you doing in California?" Jason said.

"Following a story," Dane replied. "That's what reporters do, Captain Conrad. What are you doing in this fine facility?"

Jason stopped ten feet away and started to answer, when he recognized her sitting in the driver's seat. His eyebrows raised as his mouth turned down at the corners. "Actress, huh? You're pretty good. Maybe you should consider it," he said as he turned around and trudged toward the Jeep sitting in the parking lot. From this distance, the driver appeared to be the female pilot who'd been knocked out at the reception Friday night.

Dane rushed to climb in the car and shut the door. "He's getting away," Dane blurted as he buckled into his seat. "Follow him."

"No," she said, staring straight ahead.

"What do you mean, no?"

"No means no. I made that clear a long time ago. And this 'no' means I'm not following him. He's not part of the story." Dane embarrassed her, although she wasn't sure why. No, she knew why. She was attracted to Jason Conrad, but she didn't know how to recover from something like this. "How do you know him? Why the obsession?"

"Sherri, do you remember when we first went out, back at the correspondents' dinner in DC?"

"We didn't go out, Dane. You tried to get me drunk."

"Okay, you remember," he continued, as Jason rode off with the woman in the Jeep. "My story was *that* guy, his father, and their relationship to a bunch of Russian spies. His father is Senator Jonathan Bowman. You remember the San Antonio incident back in '95, don't you? Apparently, Russian spies attempted to assassinate Bowman, but Conrad stopped them. That was the public story. Back in Enid, Oklahoma, where Jason Conrad was based, there were lots of crazy things going on."

"Like what?"

"Like students stealing tests, jets crashing, CIA agents being killed, people turning up missing . . ."

"All of that happened in Enid, Oklahoma?"

"Yes. All of it. Jason Conrad is associated with every last one of those events. You didn't forget my award-winning report, did you?"

"How can I forget, Dane? You never stop talking about it." Sherri didn't realize the man she met Friday night at the reception was the guy from Dane's story years ago. Jason Conrad certainly didn't act like he was the son of a senator who had been a presidential contender. He seemed much nicer than Dane portrayed him in his stories. "So, what's he doing here?"

"That's what we need to find out. Last month, he was involved in another jet crash back in Oklahoma. My broadcast was picked up internationally. You didn't see it?"

Sherri shook her head. "Sorry, no."

"Anyway, he moved to another assignment, but I didn't realize it was here. My producer put me on this windmill story, and I kind of got sidetracked."

"Maybe you should focus on the windmill story and not Jason Conrad."

"Yeah, maybe so," Dane said, "but now Jason Conrad is on the radar, and I'm going to find out why."

ONCE HE ACKNOWLEDGED the fact that Dane Robinson was now in California, Jason worried how it would impact his job. This guy wouldn't go away. He was glad Jennifer picked him up, but now he had to worry about a potential round two when he arrived home.

Jennifer said earlier in the day she wasn't upset with him, but his girlfriend better stay out of her way. Jason wasn't sure what she meant, but was glad their fight didn't go any further. A police blotter girlfriend was the last thing he needed.

They made idle chitchat on the ride to Rosamond. The open-air Jeep helped. Couldn't talk, couldn't hear the radio, just the wind blowing in his eardrums. Perfect. Perhaps the scuffle with Kathy made Jennifer realize she needed to focus on other men. Regardless, it was easier on Jason when Jennifer wasn't trying to get him in bed.

Jennifer dropped him off on the road in front of his rental house, and Jason walked to the driveway. He noticed Jennifer turned the Jeep around in the street rather than the driveway. Whatever it takes to keep the peace.

He was happy to see his truck in the driveway, but wondered, if the truck is here, why isn't Kathy answering the phone? Picking up his pace, he darted to the back door and grabbed the handle. Locked. Pulling out his key, he deftly stuck it in the lock and opened the door.

The house was eerily quiet.

Jason shuffled through the kitchen. There was no sign Kathy had been there today. No purse, no keys.

"Kathy?" he called out as he meandered through the house. Jason made a complete circuit through the house; she was gone, though her clothes and the small amount she brought with her, were still here. The washer and dryer didn't look like they'd been worked on. Maybe she hadn't made it back in time for the appointment. Jason trudged to the refrigerator, pulled out a Coors Light, and sat at the kitchen table. He unzipped his flight suit to his waist, leaned back in his chair, and took a long swig of beer.

None of this made sense. He rummaged around the kitchen. After ten frustrating minutes, he found the number to Dave's Handyman Repair, and called to see what time the guy came to fix the washer and dryer. When he was told the appointment had been cancelled earlier that morning, he began to worry.

52

May 15, 2001

YESTERDAY HAD BEEN a long, chaotic day, and this morning was proving to be just as hectic. Teams were still on the mountainside recovering what they could of Samson's F-15, and in Approach Control, they were gathering evidence for the SIB and AIB.

Jennifer stepped out of the squadron commander's office in a state of both unparalleled joy and serious self-doubt. She had just been notified that due to Samson's death, she was now the lead test pilot for the F-2000. It answered the question she had been asking herself since yesterday morning. The significance of the role didn't escape her; it was an incredible honor. The sixth-generation fighter, once it became publicly known, would be the center of attention in the Air Force and the aviation world. She giggled at the prospects of her being the first female lead test pilot on the newest, most-advanced fighter in history. Book deals, lectures, talk shows. Heck, she could be a general herself if she chose to stick around long enough.

But to get there, she had a lot of hard work to do, and she questioned her capability. Jennifer had never considered herself brilliant, but she wasn't stupid. She knew her limitations and was concerned she might be pushing the outside of that envelope. She was a good pilot, but she was aware her breast augmentation often received credit for her successes.

Climbing in her Jeep, she drove to TRENCOR Industries. When she arrived, she hurried straight into Wellington's office, shut the door, and locked it.

"I'm the lead test pilot now," she said, half smiling.

"I know," Wellington responded expressionlessly from behind the desk. He looked up from his stack of papers spread across the top of the mahogany desk. She expected him to be happy to see her.

"I'm not sure I'm capable of completing this project," she said, reaching for the zipper of her flight suit.

"You'll do fine. I'll guide you along the way," he said, returning to his papers.

"But, General, I—"

"That's all, Major, thank you. I'm busy right now," Wellington said, still reviewing his papers.

Confused, Jennifer released her zipper, turned, and left his office. *What's going on here? Did that just happen?* Wellington was distant. More importantly, he paid no attention to the shutting and locking of his office door. That was their unspoken communication that they were going to have sex—and he ignored it.

Jennifer shuffled along the unlit hallway toward the simulator bay. Jason had another sim training session this afternoon, and she wanted to get a quick sortie in before his training started. When she entered the sim bay, it surprised her to see Jason sitting in the simulator. His simulator time didn't start for another five hours.

"Jason, what are you doing here?"

Jason hung his head over the side and hollered back, "Oh, hello, Major."

Jennifer climbed the stairs and crossed the bridge to the simulator cockpit.

"You're not scheduled until this afternoon," she said.

"Wellington wasn't too happy with my progress yesterday, so I'm trying to familiarize myself with everything. The Flight Management System is kicking my butt. I need to practice more."

"There's an emulator on the desktop in the vault at the squadron."

"I did not know that," he said, his face showing his disappointment.

"Samson . . . I guess I should have shown you last week. I didn't realize we would be running as fast as we are. Especially after Samson's crash."

"I kind of wondered about that myself. Everything stopped when Mrs. Anderson was killed, but we're charging right along after the lead test pilot was killed in a jet crash. Something is strange about that."

Jennifer tilted her head to the side, contemplating Jason's comment. He was right. It was strange. Wellington's reaction to her was strange, too.

"Would you mind if I jumped in here for about an hour, Jason? I've got a lot of rust to knock off."

"Sure, let me get my gear."

Jason gathered the various papers and checklists he had spread out in the cockpit as he climbed out of the simulator. Jennifer watched Jason closely as he climbed out. Something was different about him.

"Are you okay?" she said.

He paused. "Personal issues."

"Anything I can help with?"

There was a longer pause. Hopefully, he was having problems with that bitch he brought to Club Muroc. If she never showed up again, that would be okay with her.

"No. No. I've just got some things I need to work out."

Jennifer tried to look concerned but she didn't know how successful she was. When in doubt, deflect.

"I've been made lead test pilot for the F-2000," Jennifer said.

Jason grinned. "Congratulations. This is a good thing for you, right?"

"Yes," she said, staring at the instrument panel, biting her lower lip. "I hope I'm not in over my head."

CALDWELL LANDED at Kern County Airport at ten-thirty in the morning. The unmarked Airbus 330 was efficient. It surprised him the agency had access to one. He appreciated them giving him a ride across the country. It had been short notice, and he left early in the morning. Fortunately, the crew was scheduled for a proficiency sortie and had no problem changing their plans to fly to California. They would eat lunch in town while the jet refueled and Caldwell met with Jason.

He had forgone the team from Los Angeles meeting him at the airport. This was something he needed to do alone. It would be traumatic enough after what Jason had been through—to have the lost love of his life return, only to find out she was a Russian mole. He made sure he had all the information with him before he left. It hadn't occurred to him until now that this was how he and Jason met—Caldwell coming in from out of town to tell Jason Conrad a friend of his was a Russian mole. The thought made him feel worse. Caldwell pulled out his cell phone and dialed Jason's number.

Jason answered on the second ring. "Hello?"

"Jason, it's—"

"Caldwell, what the hell are you up to?"

"I'm in town for business. Are you free for lunch?"

"Sure, where are you?"

"I'm over in Mojave," Caldwell said.

"At the airport?"

"Yes."

"Why don't I meet you there? There's a pretty good restaurant there, I'm told. I'm in Cal City. I can be there in twenty minutes."

Caldwell felt grim, but he hoped it didn't sound that way over the phone.

"Sounds great, Jason. I'll meet you here."

DANE WAITED MORE THAN forty-five minutes for the television crew to arrive from Los Angeles. He was grateful his television station still had some faith in him. Dane had been told he no longer would be allowed to broadcast live. All of his reports would be taped and vetted before being aired.

Dane reviewed his script while sitting in his car near the front entrance of Edwards AFB. He read through it a hundred times over the last twenty hours. As soon as he saw Jason Conrad outside TRENCOR Industries, he knew he had a story. When he found out about the F-15 crash that morning, he surmised it was no coincidence that, once again, Jason Conrad was near a fatal jet crash.

The television crew pulled up in a shiny new van with various satellite dishes mounted on top. Thankful his producer in Tulsa had done the coordination, Dane bustled with nervous excitement. A large, burly man stepped out of the passenger's side and retrieved his camera equipment from the back of the van. Accompanying him was the driver, a smaller, effeminate man, who had a stack of papers for Dane to sign.

The paperwork complete, Dane took a position that would prominently display the name of the base behind him as he taped his report. The smaller man took charge and started barking orders like a Hollywood director. Dane found himself listening to what he had to say, realizing he must be a field director. He started to get a little nervous as the smaller one got a little "touchy-feely," but Dane gutted through it. These guys were pros from the big city, and he was going to take the opportunity to learn from them.

Once the smaller man had it set the way he wanted, he pinched Dane on the rear. "Okay, handsome, do your stuff," he said as he sauntered back behind the cameraman.

"Rolling," the cameraman said.

The director put up three fingers, counting down to one, then pointed at Dane.

"This is Dane Robinson, TV News Reporter for WTSR, the Taaaser from Tulsa. I'm at Edwards Air Force Base in California, home of the United States Air Force's historic aircraft testing program. It was here in 1947 that Chuck Yeager broke the sound barrier for the first time, and now we have another first. It was several weeks ago that this reporter launched a story about Russian spies in our military, destroying our force from within the Department of Defense. Unfortunately for America, this travesty continues. Yesterday morning, an F-15 fighter jet was destroyed when it struck the side of a mountain north of Edwards Air Force Base, its pilot killed.

"How are these two issues related? One man, Captain Jason Conrad, the son of former presidential candidate Jonathan Bowman. Captain Conrad has been involved in numerous incidents outside the scope of an officer of his rank in the Air Force. Links to Russian spies, missing persons, and now, a *third* jet crash tied to Jason Conrad. Could he be single-handedly destroying our military from within? Only an in-depth investigation will tell. In the meantime, your watchdog will stay on top of this story. This is Dane Robinson, TV News Reporter for WTSR, the Taaaser from Tulsa."

The director clapped, jumping up and down, "Oh that was fantastic! What a pro! And on the first take!" The skinny man rushed over and gave him a big hug, kissed him on both cheeks, and pinched his rear again.

Dane, blushing, said, "Well, thank you. It's not every day someone like me gets to work with a great director like you."

The skinny man giggled as he and the burly cameraman looked at each other, then started laughing uncontrollably.

"What's so funny?"

The cameraman placed his camera equipment back in the news van.

"He's no director," the cameraman replied. "He's just an intern. Sweeps the floor in the studio and drives our vans sometimes." The two continued laughing as they climbed in the van and cranked the motor.

Dane's stomach gurgled as he suddenly wanted to vomit.

CALDWELL AND JASON sat in the restaurant at the Kern County Airport. The waitress took their order as the two sipped their glasses of water.

"What brings you out here, Caldwell?"

Caldwell shifted uncomfortably in his seat, glancing outside at a taxiing VariEze aircraft. He'd seen pictures of the futuristic-looking aircraft with the forward canards, but had never seen one in person. He welcomed any distraction from what he was going to say.

"I've found out where Kathy has been the last six years. Actually, I've found out everything about her."

"Yeah? Do you know where she is right now?"

"Wait, she's missing?"

"She didn't come home last night. I don't know where she is. I'm deciding whether I should file a missing person report. I mean, she's disappeared before, but…"

"Do it, Jason. We're looking for her, too."

"What do you mean? Why is the CIA looking for her?"

Caldwell took a deep breath and pushed forward with the bad news. He reached into his briefcase, pulled out a manila envelope, and slid it across the table.

"Kathy is a Russian mole," Caldwell said. "I know it's hard to believe, but it's all right here. Everything."

Jason sat there expressionlessly for several seconds. He grabbed the envelope, pulling out the contents. He read through the items, his face blank. After ten minutes, the waitress brought their lunch, but Jason ignored both her and the food. After another five minutes, he set the papers on the table and glared at Caldwell.

"Well, shit. I knew it was too good to be true."

"Jason, I'm so—"

"Don't," Jason said, putting up his hands. "Why are these things happening around me? I thought I was past all this. I guess it makes sense now."

"We don't believe you were the original target in Enid six years ago. You were a target of opportunity. The association with your father was unknown to everyone at the time. She was there to find a pilot to marry and infiltrate the DOD. The first guy dumped her, as you know. You were going to be the next target until Section Nine's assassin went rogue. Then her mission changed."

"So why did she come back?"

"We don't know. We think the broadcast of your crash in Oklahoma sparked a renewed interest in you, especially now that the Russians know you're Jonathan Bowman's son."

Jason nodded his head, deep in thought.

"The timing is right," he said, "but what did I have to offer? At that time at least? As far as they knew, I was a T-38 instructor in Enid, Oklahoma. Kind of boring from an international espionage point of view."

"Maybe they knew you were coming out here."

"No," Jason said. "I was picked for this assignment three days after the crash. Unless my name was tossed around before the crash, that's not it."

Jason leafed through the packet again, as if to double-check what he was being told. He didn't need to—he knew it was true.

"Are the feds going to swarm Edwards searching for her?" Jason said.

Caldwell shook his head no. "We're going to delay contacting the wing commander right now. He'll be read in on this later. We want Kathy in custody first, then we'll approach the Air Force."

"You sticking around?"

"No, I've got to go back to Langley today. Our field office in L.A. will conduct the search with the FBI. Just don't be surprised when they contact you."

53

May 15, 2001

SHERRI SAT ON HER BED in the small, modest hotel room, sipping a bottle of water. She was shocked by what she saw on the news: Dane Robinson reporting on yesterday's F-15 crash. To make matters worse, he blamed Jason Conrad and claimed he was a Russian agent. Could it be?

She had her doubts about the accuracy of Dane's report, and in no time, he would be persona non grata at Edwards. It had been a mistake to get sucked into Dane's world thinking he had information she needed. But now she was associated with him, at least as far as Jason Conrad was concerned. She needed to separate herself from Dane.

Picking up her cell phone, she dialed Steven's number back in New York.

"Hello, Sherri darling, where are you?"

"Hello, Steven. I'm still in California."

"When are you coming home?"

"Soon, I think. Sooner than I expected."

"Problems?"

"Yes. And no. I've reached a stalemate here. There are external factors I need to disassociate myself from."

The phone was silent for a moment.

"Oh, dear," Steven said. "You're not involved with the crash I'm watching on television right now, are you?"

"No, not the crash. The reporter."

"Oh, God, Sherri, what happened? Too much alcohol?"

"No, Steven. Not that kind of involved. We were working on a story, and he went on a tangent when this Conrad character walked out of the building."

"Well, darling, get back to New York. The Saudis you followed out there are still popping up in various places."

Sherri paused.

"How are you finding out this information, Steven?"

"Oh, I have sources in various alphabet agencies, as well as a certain building across the Potomac with five walls."

"Okay, enough said. Can you contact travel and make my reservations? I'm coming back tonight."

"Splendid, I'll call you back with the information."

"Make it the red-eye. It will take me about four hours to get ready and drive to the airport."

Sherri hung up her phone and glanced at the clock. It showed quarter after five. She had to get moving.

THE ACTIVITY IN THE 445th Flight Test Squadron remained hectic throughout the day, but gradually began to settle. Despite two deaths and some reporter putting Edwards AFB all over the news, the leadership's main concern was the secrecy of the F-2000. Everyone in the news—Georgiana Anderson, Curt Samson, and Jason Conrad-- was attached to the project.

Brent wobbled past Samson's office and stared at the door. The safety officer had come by and sealed Samson's office. It would stay this way until they sorted through everything in his possession, searching for any contributing factor to the accident. It remained untouched as the yellow police tape across the door ensured no one would enter. No doubt they were still working at the crash site and hadn't made it back yet to sift through his office.

A door closed at the end of the hallway with a loud bang. Brent saw Jason leaving the vault. Strange—he's putting in a lot of extra time, he thought.

"Jason," he said, "what are you doing here so late?"

"Hi, Brent," Jason said. "Just trying to wrap my head around this airplane."

Brent nodded. "Have you seen the news?"

"How could I have missed it? That asshole reporter has been a thorn in my side for years. I'm to blame for everything going wrong in the Air Force because I'm supposed to be a Russian spy."

Brent marveled at Jason's cavalier attitude. Was it sarcasm or a confession?

"How are you able to stay—?"

"In the Air Force? At work? It's tough, but I've got friends in high places. What hurts me is the wing commanders. When they get tired of the attention, they do everything they can to get rid of me. Hasn't helped my Officer Performance Reports any."

Brent nodded. "I guess there are pros and cons to being a senator's son."

"Yep."

"I don't know if you've heard, but the scuttlebutt is they're calling Major Samson's death a suicide."

"Suicide? How the hell are they coming to that conclusion?"

Brent looked up and down the empty hallway, ensuring they were alone.

"Samson was an alcoholic. Totally. He was lonely out here, but he loved his job too much to find a lady friend."

"I can relate," Jason said. He recalled his own issues with his now ex-wife seven years ago before he went to pilot training. Being a bachelor in Enid was a lonely experience. Hence, he'd evolved into the coast-to-coast playboy he was today.

"But I don't know how the hell the Safety Investigation Board came up with that information," Brent said. "As far as I know, I'm the only person he talked to about that."

"Well, I'm the new guy, and I could tell at the reception something was up," Jason said. "He was totally blitzed."

"Yeah, I guess."

"By the way," Jason said. "I saw your girlfriend yesterday."

"Girlfriend? Oh, you mean Sherri Davis. Uh, we're not really . . . where did you see her?"

"Outside TRENCOR, yesterday afternoon."

"Really? What was she doing there?"

Jason shook his head. "Don't know. She was driving around that asshole reporter from TV."

Brent's chest tightened. He'd seen the broadcast earlier. Was she working with the reporter? Could she be using him to expose the F-2000? Was he wrong about her?

"Well, I don't know what to say. I guess you never know about people."

"Yeah," Jason said, "you can say that again. Why are you still here?"

"I, uh, well, I'm supposed to clean up Georgiana's office. Her husband came by earlier and picked up her personal things after QA pulled out all of her work-related items. I'm the cleanup crew to make sure nothing important was left behind, throw away the trash, you know."

The two walked to Georgiana's office. Brent turned to enter the doorway.

"Do you need some help?" Jason said.

"Sure, that would be great. But don't you have a cute brunette to get home to?"

Jason grimaced as he shook his head. "Not so much, hence my 'you never know about people' comment."

"Want to talk about it?"

"Absolutely not."

Brent nodded. "Okay, fair enough. Well, if you can grab those magazines on the credenza, I'll get the garbage picked up."

The two worked diligently for the next five minutes. Brent filled the garbage can with trash, and Jason had all the magazines and a few notebooks stacked in a box. Brent opened the mini-fridge sitting on the floor behind her desk. A few items remained. Yogurt, spoiled vegetables, V-8 juice, and a can of Coke—which was out of place with her normal diet—along with a few containers of Tupperware.

"Jason, this garbage can is full. Can you go get me another one?"

"Sure," Jason said and left the office.

Brent reached in the fridge, pulling everything out and stacking it on the desk. When he grabbed the can of Coke, he noticed the can felt empty yet appeared unopened. He turned it upside down to see if there was a hole anywhere, and the can rattled.

Something was inside.

This wasn't a can of Coke, it was a mini-safe. An inconspicuous container you could buy to store valuables. Brent's curiosity got the best of him. Why would she store jewelry at work?

Brent opened the can, pouring the contents into his palm. It was one of the new external USB ThumbDrives. Brent stared at it for a moment, wondering what could be on it. Hearing Jason walk back to the office, he screwed the top back on the "Coke can" and stuck the ThumbDrive in his pocket.

LIGHT GLIMMERED IN THE DOORWAY of the small room, giving her a glimpse of the interior. She had trouble focusing her eyes and keeping her thoughts organized. She wasn't sure how long she had been here or what day it was. Mental focus proved challenging, and she realized she had been drugged.

After several moments, she attempted to move. Her body hurt. Someone had beaten her. She lay on her back on some kind of cot. When she tried to roll over, she realized she was chained, her hands firmly secured next to her hips, her feet bound to the end of the bed.

Kathy Delgato/Irena Vodianova struggled against her restraints. She tried to scream, but her mouth was gagged. After what seemed to her clouded mind like several minutes, she stopped wrestling with her bindings and lay still on the cot. Perspiration gathered on her forehead, dripping along the sides of her head to the pillow. *How did I get here? Where is 'here?'* Her thoughts were a mishmash of Russian and English, with a bit of Spanish, which only confused her more.

It was a struggle to focus. She remembered her Russian name first, then her English alias. She realized she spoke several languages, but she could not remember who had done this to her or why she was chained to the cot.

Several minutes later, the door opened and the lights illuminated. She closed her eyes until someone approached her cot. A large lamp illuminated her face. She jerked her head to the side, trying to shield her eyes, but the effort was in vain. When she opened her eyes, a short oriental man stood next to her.

"Irena Vodianova, agent of the GRU, welcome to our home," the man said. "Or maybe I should call you Kathy Delgato, your American name."

It was starting to come back to her now. She was an agent of the GRU, Section Nine to be exact. The corps of assassins. And when she got off this cot, she would kill this son of a bitch.

"Your drugs should be wearing off soon, but not to worry, we have a new batch for you. Then we will talk. We will talk a great deal about why you are trying to infiltrate TRENCOR Industries and what interest the Russian government has in us."

54

May 16, 2001

IT COULDN'T BE. Brent's first thought when he downloaded the files from Georgiana's ThumbDrive was to delete them. All of them. But he didn't.

Brent sat in his apartment, deeply disturbed by the information. Had Georgiana known about this? Could this be why she was murdered? Her case, for all practical purposes, had dropped off of the radar. The sheriff's office hadn't been around in over a week to investigate her death.

The ThumbDrive's data mostly related to the F-2000 and TRENCOR Industries. There were thousands of documents, covering a number of subjects. Sorting out the relevant items would take time.

Brent picked up his phone and dialed the number he had contemplated calling for the last hour.

"Hello," the voice said.

"Sherri, hi, it's Brent O'Malley."

"Oh, hi, Brent. What's going on?"

Brent paused as if someone close by might actually hear him. It was possible his phone was bugged. Or Sherri's. He didn't know who to trust anymore.

"I was hoping I could see you again."

"Brent, I don't think that's possible."

"Oh. I was hoping you could come over for... coffee maybe. It's important."

There was a pause on the other end of the phone.

"Brent, I'm sorry. I'm back in New York."

"New Yo—When did this happen?"

"Yesterday. I, uh, came back suddenly. It was very short notice."

"Okay. Are, umm, are you coming back to California?"

"I don't think so. Not any time soon, anyway. I'm working on the story that brought me to California in the first place. My leads aren't there anymore."

"Oh, okay. Well, I'm sorry to bother you. I'll call if I find anything important. If I'm ever in New York, I'll look you up."

"Brent, I—"

"Bye," Brent said, hanging up the phone. He wasn't angry; his mind was just moving forward, trying to decipher what avenue to take next. Sherri hadn't worked out. Brent focused on his monitor and the files onscreen.

LI ZHONG STRUTTED through the lobby of TRENCOR Industries. The receptionist smiled at him, but he ignored her. Entering the hallway for the corporate offices, he marched to Ming's office. The secretary bowed her head as he entered and shut the door behind him.

"Li Zhong, thank you for coming," Ming said.

Li Zhong bowed from the waist. "Is something wrong?"

Ming stood up from behind his desk and walked over to the shelf on the far side of the wall and poured a glass of Glenlivet.

"I've talked to Beijing. We're done here. Operation Dragonfly is directed to shut down immediately. TRENCOR is to ship its assets and various holdings back to China, and we will withdraw from the United States."

"Because of the Russian?"

Ming nodded.

"The Russian agent is too close to our operation. The depth of her relationship with the new pilot, Conrad, has not been determined. He is too close to the F-2000. The premier does not believe this is a coincidence."

"She isn't talking yet," Li Zhong said.

"If she is who you say she is, she won't."

"True. But everyone has a breaking point."

Ming put his hand up. "We cannot get distracted. We have a job to do. It will take coordination to get the team here early."

"How long do we have?" Li Zhong said.

"Two, maybe three weeks. My wife is working on shipping our tangible assets and records. Do you have any questions on what you need to do?"

"The Russian?"

"She's disposable. I see no long-term value in her. We've had no contact from their side or the Americans. They don't know we have her. Short-term, she may be valuable, but that is more your line of work. I'm a businessman."

Li Zhong nodded. He knew what to do.

55

OVER A WEEK had passed since Jason first climbed into the simulator, and his learning increased exponentially. But he had his issues. He slammed his hands on the dashboard of the simulator. For the third time in as many days, he overstressed the jet during his simulator training. The screen turned red with the word "CRASH" on the screen, freezing the simulator. The technicians would take the simulator off motion and reload the mission computers. Another flaw in this simulator. They shouldn't have to reload the mission computers after a "crash." During the last three days, he had discovered plenty of flaws in both the simulator and the training system.

He spoke to Brent about this two days ago. The F-2000 software should not allow it to over-G. The last fighter the Air Force bought that could over-G was the A-10, and with the money they spent on this jet, it shouldn't happen. Brent thought it was the software, another of its many flaws.

As the simulator settled to its static position, Jason opened the canopy and the walkway lowered into position. Jeremiah Wellington strutted from his position at the simulator operator's desk and up the stairs to the cockpit.

"Don't unstrap, Captain. Since you've screwed up again, we'll try this once more."

Jason looked at Wellington in disbelief.

"This is the third day in a row you over-G'd the jet as you approached cornering velocity." The cornering velocity is the minimum speed you can fly the maximum G-rating. It also translates into a tighter turn radius.

"Look, every time I approach cornering velocity, the jet becomes unstable and doesn't respond to the controls."

"Or maybe the pilot becomes unstable and rips the wings off the jet for the third day in a row."

"It's not me," Jason said tersely.

"Captain Conrad, I'm beginning to think you are the wrong person for this program."

"Why is that?"

"I'll be blunt, you're not that good a pilot. We brought you here as a favor to your dad, but this aircraft is obviously a little too much for you to grasp."

"I'm grasping it just fine. I don't know what kind of training program you're running here, but from an instructional standpoint, it sucks."

Wellington appeared shocked to hear those words coming out of the young captain, but Jason was undeterred.

"There are no training materials, and the syllabus looks like it was written on the back of a napkin in a bar somewhere. Everything I've learned, I've done on my own. Major Walton has been some help, but she's been spending time either in the simulator or on the flight line."

"Well, Captain, this is a gentleman's course. Obviously, you can't handle it. I'm sure you're not that good in the jet either."

"I'm just fine in the jet, thank you."

Wellington leaned into Jason's face, his eyes squinting. "Look, you little snot-nosed twit," he said in a low growl, "I was waxing Ivan's ass when your momma was still changing your diapers. I think I'm a little better judge of who is 'just fine in the jet'."

Jason didn't back down. "I've seen your records and read your FEF, Jeremiah. I've got a hell of a lot more experience training pilots than you do."

"You can call me General Wellington."

"I can, but I won't. You're not in the chain of command. Anywhere. You are a civilian contracted by the Air Force."

Wellington leaned away from the cockpit as Jason felt a small victory inside. He was sure no one had ever talked to Wellington like this. The shock quickly faded, and the scowl returned.

"Captain Conrad, bringing in a damn FAIP to this program was a bad idea from the start. You'd better watch your six. Your days here are numbered."

THE ROOM WAS DARK, but several electronic devices
generated enough ambient light to see her environment. There were
no windows, which indicated she was either in the middle of a building
somewhere or below ground. Kathy eyed the IV needle in her right
arm, the bag hanging slightly behind her.

Kathy struggled to move, aware she was strapped to a bed. It was
different from the cot she remembered earlier—an older-model
hospital bed that rolled as she struggled against her straps. They had
secured her well. She had straps across her chest, her stomach and
arms, each wrist, her thighs, her shins, and each ankle.

Giving up on the struggle, she heard echoes outside the door. Kathy
strained to listen as the echoes turned into footsteps. The door handle
turned, and light from outside spilled in. A tall figure entered the room,
but the sudden addition of light was too much for her eyes. The man
stood taller than the one she met earlier.

"Good afternoon, Major Irena Vodianova, or should I say, Kathy
Delgato?"

She squinted at the tall man as he moved closer, but could only
make out the outline of his figure.

"I-I don't know what you're talking about. I'm Kathy Delgato from
San Antonio, Texas."

There was a pause, and the man spoke again.

"Major, we will not be playing this game for long, will we? You see,
I've seen you before. I've seen you fight, I've seen you kill . . . and I've
seen you love."

"What are you talking about?" Kathy said.

"Your name is Irena Vodianova. You are a major in the GRU. You
are a part of Section Nine, a group of moles trained to be assassins.
Not quite two years ago, you were in Manila posing as a missionary's
wife. Why you were there, we are not sure, but surely you remember
eliminating a team of Chinese "bandits" who raided your church?"

Kathy was shocked. How could they know all this? Section Nine's
counterintelligence told them their existence was still unknown to the
world's intelligence agencies. Clearly, under Nikolai's supervision, the
organization had deteriorated.

"Your silence tells me I'm right. Of course, I don't expect you to
talk right now, which is why I've brought Doctor Mai. He is very

persuasive with his techniques."

Kathy saw the outline of the second figure, one much smaller than the one talking. The small figure moved toward the bed, reached for the IV with a syringe, and injected it into the IV tube. In a moment, the cool fluid entered her bloodstream as her heart pumped the chemical throughout her body.

"Who are you?" she asked groggily as the chemical took effect.

The tall man leaned forward. "My name is Li Zhong. I work for the Ministry of State Security for the People's Republic of China. I'm a big fan of your work, Major Vodianova."

Kathy noticed his expression never changed. Her body was giving in to whatever they injected in her.

"I re-recognize you . . . you . . . you were . . . TRENCOR . . . at base . . ." her voice trailed off as she began an internal struggle in her mind. Slowly she moved her head from side to side as her body began to relax.

Li Zhong loomed over her. "I think it's time. Major Vodianova, who are you and what is your mission here?"

FLYING THE F-2000 in the simulator was fun once he got the hang of it. Jason really taught himself. He received no instruction from Wellington, only criticism. He was frustrated that once again someone judged him based on his father, not his performance. He spent another hour in the simulator, repeating the full profile. The difference this time was that he would not put the G-loading on the jet required by the profile at that airspeed. His concern was simple. Was this an error in the simulator software, or was the simulator emulating exactly what the jet would do?

By the time he unstrapped himself and climbed out of the sim, Wellington was gone. He grabbed his gear and descended to the floor of the sim bay. Jason walked to the mission manager's desk and found his training folder filled out. Wellington had graded him UNSAT for the sortie.

Jason read the poorly written write-up. Wellington recommended that he be placed in a Commander's Awareness Program, or CAP. On two separate occasions in his write-up, Wellington mentioned that Jason should be sent to a Flight Evaluation Board. Jason wasn't worried about that. He wasn't in a formal training unit, and this wasn't his primary aircraft, so by regulation, he couldn't go to a Flight

Evaluation Board. He had asked that question of his new squadron commander when briefed on what he would be doing here. But Wellington could make it painful for him at Edwards—there was no doubt about that.

He stuffed the training folder in his helmet bag as he left the sim bay. When he entered the long hallway leading to the lobby, he felt something was different. Glancing around, he couldn't put his finger on it, but as he walked down the hallway, it hit him like a bomb.

Jason stopped and moved closer to the wall, focusing on the large picture of a P-38 Lightning. It was a nice World War Two air-to-air combat print, double matted and under glass. The problem was, it hadn't been there earlier. This hallway had been lined with original oil paintings of airplanes from across the decades of aviation.

He slid to the next picture and it was changed also. As he moved along the hallway, he realized all the oil paintings had been replaced with matted prints. The wall lamps had been turned off or disconnected.

Jason approached the receptionist, an older Chinese woman, who sat alone in the lobby.

"What's happened to the oil paintings in the hallway?" he said.

The receptionist gawked at him.

"That hallway?" the receptionist said, pointing toward the hallway.

"Yes, that hallway."

"Nothing. The paintings should still be there."

"Well, they're not."

The receptionist stood up from her seat and walked around her desk to the hallway entrance. She counted the pictures; then turned to face him.

"They're all there," she said.

"I know there are pictures there, but three hours ago they were oil paintings. Beautiful oil paintings that gave this building grace, elegance, and class. Where did the oil paintings go?"

"They're still hanging on the wall."

"No, those are crappy prints. Well, they're not crappy, but they are prints. The oil paintings have been here ever since I've been coming here."

"Captain, if you don't like the pictures, I can contact our designer to find new ones."

Jason shook his head defeated. "Ma'am, I'm not complaining. I noticed the pictures were changed while I was in the simulator, and now I'm asking why. There's not a problem. Forget it."

"Yes, sir. Thank you," she said as she slid back behind her desk and returned her gaze to her computer monitor.

Jason shook his head as he turned to leave. Approaching the door, he glanced to the side and stopped in his tracks. He examined the furniture in the lobby. It was different, as well. The nicer plush chairs and couches had been removed. The artwork and decorations in the lobby were different, too. Hell, everything was different.

56

May 23, 2001

DARKNESS ENVELOPED THE RAMP as the large hangar doors crept open. The yellow glow of the warning light rotated on the side of the building. Several black SUVs sat on the ramp in silent darkness.

Wellington sat in the vehicle closest to the hangar with a handheld UHF radio in his lap, monitoring communications. He was glad he was done with Jason Conrad for the day. *The kid's days are numbered. Jennifer was adamant about getting Jason into the program. When he saw the two of them enter her apartment that night, he knew why. But after Conrad's girlfriend showed up, and after the catfight at the reception, he wondered if his suspicions were correct.*

A lone crew chief stood on the ramp three hundred feet in front of the hangar with lighted wands in his hands. When the hangar doors opened, a small tug vehicle emerged. Attached to it was the F-2000. The tug taxied the jet to a position fifty feet in front of the crew chief, who stopped them by forming an X with his wands.

Two men jumped out of the tug and ran to the nose gear of the jet to disconnect the tow bar, climbed back into the tug, and drove to the side of the ramp.

"Engine start," Jennifer said over the radio.

"Cleared," came the reply from Wellington's man in the tower.

Wellington had coordinated with the control tower and had one of his people up there to ensure they had no hiccups. Jennifer strapped in the jet tonight for the F-2000's first high-speed taxi test. Her job: take the jet below takeoff speed, then abort the takeoff. The test was run at night to ensure as much secrecy as possible.

Kirby sat in the seat behind her, monitoring the various systems and flight computer. The engineers recognized early on that there was enough empty space behind the seat to rig a second ACES II ejection seat into the jet, though it was a tight fit despite not having any flight controls. If the pilot ejected, once the canopy departed, the engineer could eject, as well.

Wellington watched from his SUV with great joy. The first engine started; the large flame from the boost of fuel ignited, shooting out the back of the engine. Shortly afterward, the second engine started. For the next two minutes, the crew chief conducted various hand signals with Major Walton.

There was a longer-than-expected pause. The crew chief stood with his hands on his hips. Not knowing what caused the delay irritated Wellington. He started to key the mic on his radio, but stopped himself.

After two minutes, Jennifer made the next programmed radio call. "Taxi."

"Cleared."

The crew chief waved his lighted wands, saluted smartly, and pointed the jet to the main taxiway. Wellington smiled. For the first time since this dream project of his started, the most advanced fighter jet in the world took the active runway.

MAJOR JENNIFER WALTON sat in the most expensive jet in history. After the crew chief cleared the chocks underneath her main tires, she followed the marshaller's directions. She taxied to and held short of the active runway, looking for a green light from the tower. When she saw it, she taxied onto the runway for the test. They were scheduled to accomplish three separate engine run-ups, the last one a rolling test using afterburner, before the actual high-speed taxi test. If they decided they needed more data, they would taxi back and accomplish another high-speed taxi test. Two was the maximum. They didn't want the F-2000 exposed too long, even at night.

"How's the ride back there, Kirby?"

"It's fine. The jet is much quieter than I expected."

"The jet is insulated very well." Jennifer replied. "The modified, impact-resistance canopy cuts out the noise, and the titanium lining has a similar effect."

"True."

Jennifer liked Daniel Kirby. They became good friends throughout the course of this project. Ironically, they became friends because his wife accused him of having sex with her. They'd been in the same meeting after five in the evening. That, apparently, was enough to convince Kirby's wife. She confronted Jennifer, who had no idea what she was talking about. Up to that point, they'd never actually associated with each other. Kirby's wife moved home to mother for a few weeks before coming back to California. Jen apologized to him, which of course, he said she did nothing wrong and apologized to her for his wife hurting her reputation. The two bonded over the accusation and have been friends ever since.

"How's your computer running?"

"Functioning at one hundred percent."

"Super. We'll be at the hammerhead shortly. Just let me know when you're ready to start the test cards."

"Will do, Major."

Jennifer accomplished all of her before-takeoff checklists, and in another four minutes, she reached the hammerhead.

"You all set, Kirby?"

"I'm ready back here."

She sat at the hold short line, watching the control tower. In another two minutes, the tower flashed a green light. Jennifer pushed the throttles forward, and the F-2000 took the active runway for the first time in history.

The jet taxied to the center of the runway, and she stepped on the brakes. She accomplished all of her line-up checklists out of habit pattern and pulled out her test cards. Since Kirby was on board, she would not fill any out, but she wanted them for reference and backing up Kirby.

"Ready for the first engine run?"

"Run 'em up," Kirby replied.

She pressed the brakes harder with her toes and slowly pushed the throttles forward to forty percent power. Her eyes locked on the engine instruments.

"Fuel flow . . . EGT . . . rising. Oil temp, oil pressure—steady."

"Checks," Kirby said. "Keep the power there, I've got a couple more checks to run through the computer back here."

"Roger."

Jennifer held the power at forty percent for another five minutes.

Her ankles grew weary from holding the brakes. Sweat started to roll down her face, her back ached, and her legs shook.

"How much longer do you need, Kirby?"

"We're good. You can bring it back to idle."

Kirby took fifteen seconds to recalibrate his computer, then said, "Okay, I'm ready to go again."

"Okay, here we go."

Jennifer pushed the throttles up again, pausing at forty percent as Kirby checked the power with the last run-up.

"Okay, looks like everything is working as advertised. Run it up to sixty percent."

"Coming right up," she said.

Jennifer pushed the throttles up at the same steady rate to sixty percent. They called out the instrument readings, verifying everything was within limits. When Kirby was satisfied, he called for the reduction of power, and Jennifer pulled the throttles back again.

The third power run-up pushed through forty percent, then sixty percent. When Jennifer released the brakes, the jet leaped forward as she pushed the throttles to one hundred percent and added the afterburner in MAX power. Again, everything worked as advertised. She brought the throttles back to idle, and the aircraft decelerated as she applied brakes. She exited the runway at the first intersection and taxied back to the end of the runway. Getting a green light from the tower, Jennifer taxied onto the runway once again.

"Okay, Kirby, are we ready for our high-speed taxi?"

"Ready in the back," he said.

Jennifer flashed her taxi lights off and on, watching the tower. Two green flashes let her know she was cleared to perform her high-speed taxi. Jennifer pushed the power slowly forward to forty percent, calling out all the engine instrument readings to Kirby as they stabilized.

"Takeoff speed is one hundred forty knots. I'll abort the high-speed maneuver approaching one hundred twenty knots."

"Roger," Kirby said, confirming the speeds briefed earlier in the hangar.

"Releasing brakes, here we go," Jennifer said as she pushed the throttles over the hump. The afterburner lit up the dark night once again as excess fuel dumped into the engine, mixed with air and a spark and exploded out the engine exhaust. The jet lunged forward and she pressed back into her seat.

"Engines look good in burner," she said.

"Check."

The F-2000 bolted down the runway. Jennifer kept her cross-check between the runway and the airspeed indicator. The rudders became effective at sixty-five KIAS, and she disengaged the nose wheel steering. The acceleration rate increased, and in no time they were at one hundred KIAS. She was amazed how easily the aircraft handled. The airspeed started to approach one hundred twenty KIAS. Before she could bring the power back to idle, there was that familiar seat-of-the-pants feeling.

"Oh, shit!"

"Not part of the test, not part of the test, Major!"

"I know, dammit," she yelled.

She quickly transitioned to her instruments as the aircraft leaped away from the ground and into the air.

57

May 24, 2001

SHERRI SAT IN HER APARTMENT on Staten Island gazing across New York Harbor. The small apartment's view of the New York skyline lived up to the building's name, The View. She had mixed a Jack and Coke, slipped into her sweat shirt, and moved to the small patio outside her sliding glass window. It was well past two in the morning, but she couldn't sleep. She took a soothing sip as she gazed across the water at the view of the Twin Towers and downtown Manhattan. Her recent trip to southern California made her question her priorities. Sherri appreciated the simplicity of the high desert and—

RING! RING! RING!

The shattered silence startled Sherri and she nearly spilled her drink. Fearing it might be important, she leaped up and ran into the living room. She grabbed the cell phone from the coffee table.

"Hello," she said, without checking the number.

"Sherri, it's Brent O'Malley in California."

"Do you know it's past two in the morning in New York?"

Brent paused on the other end. "I'm sorry. Normally, I'm aware of those things. At the office, I keep my clocks based on Greenwich Mean Time. That keeps everything normal. I'm on the same time zone as the rest of the planet. But I'm at home, and everything is Pacific Time. Thanks for reminding me. I'm a little confused. I should be . . . I should be somewhere else right now. But I've been in my apartment going over a lot of paperwork."

Sherri pulled her phone away from her ear, glaring at Brent as if rambling about Greenwich Mean Time was meaningless.

Sherri heard sounds in the background.

"What's that noise?"

"I'm calling from a payphone."

"Why? Brent, what the hell is going on?"

"Sherri, I need to talk to you. Can you come back to California?"

"Brent, you called me. I'm here on the phone, right now, talking to you. I picked up as soon as I saw it was you." She hoped the lie would convince him to open up. Sherri sensed something was wrong. Brent was an engineer and not given to emotion, but she didn't know him to be this scatterbrained.

"Right. Yeah, okay. It's just... things are worse than we . . . I thought."

"What do you mean?"

"I mean, I found out some things validating everything we were thinking... or feeling."

Sherri paused. Her mind fought its way through her Jack and Coke, recalling what they'd discussed about TRENCOR. "Give me what you got," she said, reaching for the pencil and pad of paper on the coffee table.

"I can't talk about this over the phone."

"Brent, I can't simply hop out to California on a whim."

"I haven't had a chance to review all the . . ."

Sherri waited silently for him to finish his thought.

"I think Georgiana was murdered by someone at TRENCOR Industries," he said.

"Wait, you think . . . how did you come to that conclusion?"

"I don't know, it's just a hunch. But everything points to it."

"What's pointing to it? What are we right about? Brent, I know I'm drinking here, but you're the one not making any sense."

"Remember I told you a couple of weeks ago . . . I asked you to write a story about Georgiana?"

Brent never mentioned her writing a story writing a story about Georgiana. Their discussions were strictly about TRENCOR Industries.

"Yes," she said. "You said you'd call if you found out more information."

"Well, this is that call. The company is composed of bad men. Real bad men."

"I know, Brent. That's why I was checking them out."

"I know it sounds . . . wimpy, but I'm terrified. I think I'm in danger."

"Why?"

"I can't talk about this over the phone. They-they're going to kill me. I-I'll talk to you in person but I can't say this over the phone."

Sherri considered Brent's statement. It was all related, but she couldn't put her finger on how. Regardless, this was enough information for her to return to California tomorrow afternoon. She'll have to tread lightly here. Steven would be furious, but given the magnitude of this, he'd bend. They had invested so much time and money on the Saudi story, yet it never had the legs to make an impact. Steven had more leads, but they were thin.

"What else do you have?" she said.

"I'm not sure. There's a bunch of encrypted files on here I'm trying to crack. There's some chemical formulas . . . I think I know what they are. I've got a friend who teaches biochemistry. I'm going to see if he can confirm these formulas."

"All of this is interesting, but what makes you think Georgiana was murdered by someone at the company?"

Again there was silence on the phone for a moment.

"It looks like this stuff came from David Ming's computer."

WELLINGTON WAS BOTH amazed and appalled watching the F-2000 lift off into the blackness. Amazed in the sense he watched a technological marvel make history and appalled by the fact the pilot flying it had taken off unintentionally. He checked the squelch on his handheld radio and placed it up to his ear.

"Oscar Kilo Five-Four, this is Tango Base," he said.

There was a slight pause, then Jennifer's voice came over the radio.

"Tango Base, this is Oscar Kilo Five-Four. Kind of got my hands full right now."

"I can see that. What can we do to help?"

"Stand by," she said.

The time had come to stop screwing around with these simulator tests and get the jet in the air for testing. Jennifer proved it airworthy tonight. It was time to prove it could fly when it was supposed to fly. No one need know what happened today. He would schedule the "first official flight" for next week when they had the standard documentation for such a momentous event. Video, interviews, photographers, all of them Air Force personnel who would sit on the pictures until the aircraft was made public. But first she had to get the jet back on the ground.

Jennifer was a good pilot, and she had plenty of time in the F-2000 simulator, but Wellington could not remember how much of it was actually landing the aircraft. This night had the potential to become even more interesting. And if she survived, he figured the adrenaline-fueled sex they would have would be amazing.

He realized he let his jealousy of Jason Conrad get the best of him. He'd been distant from her, and she needed his help. Almost as much as he needed her. Tonight, he'd let Jennifer know his feelings and tell her he was going to divorce his wife.

Wellington moved his truck to the hammerhead at the departure end of the runway she took off from. If she was thinking, she would land in the opposite direction avoiding populated areas. He grabbed the NVG monocular out of his bag and turned it on. Searching the skies to the north, she was nowhere in sight.

Ten minutes later, the F-2000 appeared in the distance, still blacked out. It came in at about a thousand feet above the ground. Initially, he expected her to fly the overhead pattern but based on the pitch of the jet, its speed, and descent, he realized she was flying a straight-in. It pleased Wellington to see Jennifer minimize exposure of the jet over public areas. His pleasant thought vaporized at about two hundred feet above the ground. The exhaust nozzles suddenly shifted downward and the nose of the jet pitched down and the jet climbed from its normal glide path as Jennifer added power to compensate for the abnormal thrust vectoring.

The sound of the jet engines could be heard spooling up and Wellington saw the nozzles shift back to the normal position. There was a significant wobbling of the wings as the jet struggled to find its optimum airspeed. Jennifer was able to stabilize the approach and other than landing two thousand feet further down the runway than anticipated, she landed the jet without much difficulty and taxied straight to the hangar. One hundred feet from the hangar entrance, she shut down the engines. The tug hooked up to the nose wheel and towed the jet into the green-lit hangar.

Wellington drove to the dark building holding the jet inside and parked. He grabbed his paperwork and walked through the entry door on the runway side of the hangar. Jennifer and Kirby climbed out of the jet. He knew what was going on in her mind. Despite the fact that she had taken the jet airborne for the first time in history, she had a bigger problem. The damn jet was never supposed to get off the ground tonight in the first place.

Wellington stepped over to her, his face grim.

"General, I—"

Wellington put up his hand to stop her from saying anything else. "Major Walton, do you know what the hell you did tonight?"

Jennifer lowered her head toward the ground sheepishly, mumbling something incoherent.

"You moved our program forward several weeks," he said with a toothy smile. Placing his hand under her chin, he gently lifted her head up to look at him. "The first 'official' flight of the F-2000 will take place next week. You're going to be famous."

58

May 25, 2001

JASON SPENT A LOT of off-duty time in the simulator, and his skill in the new jet increased exponentially. If Wellington was going to kick him out of this program, Jason was going to make it harder than hell for him. For the first time in years, he had something to work toward. When he graduated pilot training, he slipped into an insidious state of personal depression. The F-2000 breathed new life into him, and he had something to prove. Although he'd fought it, the move out here had been good for him. It was an incredible opportunity to boost his career.

His struggle with Wellington awakened a dormant spirit inside Jason. He was a fighter who never quit. Pete had been right that morning in the VOQ—Jason hadn't become complacent, he'd became content, and that made him stagnant. He didn't respect himself, which led to him not respecting quite a few women over the years.

He knew he was brought here to convince his father to provide the ITCS for the F-2000. It bothered him initially, but he'd reached a point where he decided it didn't matter. Many people in the Air Force had someone who helped them along in their career. Why shouldn't he?

Jason, however, was as perplexed as everyone else by the various simulator malfunctions. He'd put together the fact that two Air Force personnel directly associated with the program had died within the last couple of weeks. He worried he'd been hanging around Caldwell too much, developing his conspiracy-theory mindset. But Jason had learned over the years that Caldwell's conspiracy theories usually turned into "conspiracy fact."

Then there was Kathy.

Another conspiracy theory or conspiracy fact?

He'd wanted her to fill the void in his life, and for several days, she had. He wanted a good woman to settle down and raise a family with. Jason realized he needed to change himself first before he could ever have a good relationship with any woman. Of course, who knew he would fall in love with a Russian mole?

Jason shook his head and chuckled. It all made sense when he laid it out. Kathy, the situations at Vance AFB when he was a student, the assassination attempt on his father, her mysterious disappearance. He was more shocked by the fact that he wasn't broken up by the news Kathy was a Russian mole.

"What are you doing up there?"

"Huh, what?" Jason said. Jennifer stood on the floor of the sim bay. "I'm just getting extra practice."

"Well, climb out. I've got work to do," Jennifer said. Jason had noticed a change in Jennifer over the last few weeks. After the fight with Kathy, she'd seemed to . . . mature. Being named lead test pilot changed her. She actually acted like a field grade officer. At least she wasn't hitting on him.

Jason gathered his gear and climbed out of the cockpit. Jennifer stood on the platform next to him when he exited.

"What's going on?" Jason said. "The sim wasn't scheduled for the rest of the day."

"There's been a change of plans," she said, climbing into the cockpit. "The high-speed taxi test was successful. The decision was made to eliminate the rest of the test cards and begin the flight phase."

"Really? That's odd, isn't it?"

"Jason, you're new to this. You're not a test pilot. Do you really think you know what is and isn't normal around here?"

Shocked by her response, Jason backed off. "No, I'm just trying to learn. Can I help?"

"No. I need to practice the profile for the flight. It takes place Tuesday."

"That's fast. Why the big move?"

"That's classified."

"Don't I have clearance?"

"No."

"What about my training?"

"Your training is on hold. You can still access the simulator as far as I'm concerned, but you are the last priority. The engineers still need to do a lot of work on the image generator."

"Okay. What am I supposed to do?"

Jennifer stopped strapping into the sim and looked at him. "General Wellington is contemplating your status·now."

JASON DROVE FROM TRENCOR back to the 445th Test Squadron, dejected. Finally, he was confident he performed at the level he needed to be in the airplane, and now his training was put on hold. He wasn't sure if it was because of the flight test phase or Wellington trying to get rid of him. Either way, he wasn't happy and was determined to stay in the program.

Parking his truck, he turned off the ignition and entered the building. As he walked to the vault, his home away from home, he heard Brent's voice. When Jason stuck his head in the doorway, Brent spoke excitedly on the phone. "Okay, fine. I appreciate the help. When you find out, please let me know . . . yes . . . okay, goodbye."

Brent hung up the phone and waved for Jason to come in the office. "Sorry, that was a friend of mine at UCLA. I sent him some formulas to decipher for me."

"Formulas? What kind of formulas? Aeronautical formulas?" Jason said.

"No, chemical formulas. I, uh, found them, and I'm trying to figure out what they mean."

"Where did you find them?"

"It's not important."

"If it's not important, why is your friend at UCLA deciphering them for you?"

Brent leaned back in his chair. His eyes were bloodshot and sunken; his hair uncombed. "You sure do ask a lot of questions."

"Habit pattern. I find it keeps me out of trouble."

"Hmm, interesting."

"Are you okay? You look like you had a rough night."

"Huh? Yeah. No, I'm fine," Brent said, his hands shaking over the computer keyboard. "I haven't gotten much sleep lately."

Jason saw his opportunity. Tired men were always more agreeable. "Are you aware they canceled my training?"

"What? When did this happen?"

"Today. I heard they moved up the flight test."

"I didn't hear about . . . Oh, the taxi test was last night. I . . .uh . . . was doing something else."

Jason sensed something was wrong. Brent was one of the few people here who had their act together, and he was crumbling. He looked as if he had not showered or slept in days, his clothes were disheveled, and he was talking in circles.

"Brent, you look like crap. You sure everything is okay?"

"Uh, girl trouble."

"Girl trouble? You mean," he lowered his voice to a whisper. "You mean Sherri?" Jason chuckled to himself. *He has no concept of girl trouble. Try "my ex-girlfriend is a Russian agent". That's girl trouble.*

"Yes," Brent said softly. "I mean no. I mean . . . I don't know what I'm trying to say.

"Dude, what the hell is going on?"

Brent motioned for Jason to come in. "Come here. I want to show you something."

Jason stepped into the office and sat in the empty chair. Brent shut the door and returned to his desk, pulling out two sets of schematics.

"Have you seen these before?"

"No," Jason said. "But they look like external schematics of the F-2000."

"They are. See any differences between them?"

Jason studied the documents for a moment, checking everything from the dates and titles to the physical attributes of the jet. He shook his head. "No, looks like the same document."

Brent nodded, "That's what I thought, too," he said, holding up the paper in his left hand. "But look closer. There's something different in the top and aft views."

Jason studied the schematics again and this time he saw it. "Is this what you're talking about?" he said, pointing at a small port on the left side of the rear of the jet.

"Yes," Brent nodded excitedly.

"Is it a RAM dump port?"

"Either that or an exhaust of some kind," he said, pulling out another set of schematics. He pointed to the object on the internal set of schematics. "See where this is?"

"Yes. What is it?"

"I'm not sure. I know it shouldn't be there. But it lines up with the port on the external schematic."

"Are these schematics legitimate?"

"Yes," Brent said.

"Maybe they're old."

"Maybe."

"Why is it there?"

Brent sat back in his chair and raised his hands. "Precisely."

59

May 25, 2001

LI ZHONG ENTERED the laboratory in TRENCOR's massive facility. General Jingguo and his team diligently sealed a half-dozen wooden crates. The lab had been stripped down over the past week, with equipment shipped out each night.

"Good evening, General," Li Zhong said with a bow.

"Good evening, Li Zhong. What can I do for you?"

"No, General, what can I do for you? The breakdown of the facility continues. We are moving slowly but steadily."

"Beijing has ordered us to return the jet to the mainland."

"Before or after the operation?"

"Our part is over," General Jingguo said. "Operation Dragonfly is cancelled."

Li Zhong lowered his head, shaking it slowly. "Do they not know how close we are?"

"They do, but the Russian changed things. Ming has been ordered to dismantle his operation. His assets have already been shipped back to Hong Kong."

"What about our Saudi connections?" Li Zhong said.

"They will be informed soon enough. China cannot be associated with this. We will move ahead for withdrawal. Has Ming found out anything about Operation Dragonfly?"

"No. He still believes Operation Dragonfly is cloud seeding. The cloud-seeding concept fell neatly into our strategy. He never investigated any deeper."

"And he was never the wiser?" General Jingguo said.

"Ming has gotten lazy. He only focuses on money, and where to hide it. He is very much like the capitalist pig from whom he is stealing."

"True, but his role was critical," General Jingguo said. "In the event of China's role being discovered, we needed an American to take the fall. He was Beijing's chosen one."

"I suppose. His life here has been an embarrassment to the party."

"Yes," General Jingguo said, "but a necessary evil. Sun Tsu said, 'Know your enemy and know yourself, and you will win a thousand battles.' David Ming served his purpose. The party will reward him upon his return."

Looking at the large canister in the Pelican case, Li Zhong eyed it suspiciously and wondered to himself what could have been . . . or what could still be.

THE BEST WESTERN hadn't changed while he was in Los Angeles. Dane had returned from his vacation/work trip to follow up on Jason Conrad. He received significant backlash from his network for the California broadcast. That faded quickly when Dane was contacted by a producer from the History Channel about his stories on Jason Conrad.

Two days after the Edwards AFB broadcast, Dane visited Los Angeles for several days, meeting with the producer and different writers of *48 Hours*. When it was all said and done, it wasn't what they were looking for in a story. They needed something with a bit more pizzazz, more concrete data. Dane had spent a couple more days in L.A. playing tourist and eating at famous restaurants before returning to California City and Jason Conrad.

He entered his hotel room and unpacked. While in Los Angeles, he acquired some unique equipment for his investigations—a night-vision monocular and a parabolic microphone, allowing him to listen to conversations from a distance of one hundred feet. Dane figured this would help him uncover more information about the elusive Jason Conrad.

Crawling into bed, he turned on the TV. Over the years, television reporting had changed, and Dane felt cheated he wasn't a network anchor. Dane was unimpressed with the anchor on the national news channel, envisioning himself sitting in the seat. It would take something big to propel him there. He grabbed the folder on Jason. Conrad, opened it, and stared at the black-and-white photograph of the young pilot.

When the news broadcast ended, Dane left his room for the lobby to get a cup of coffee. As he poured the sugar into the steamy cup, the doors to the hotel swept open. He couldn't believe his eyes. His dream girl walked into his life once again.

"Sherri? Hey!"

She scowled at him momentarily, then turned to the check-in desk. Keeping her excitement in check, he figured.

"So, did you miss me?" he said, waddling over to her.

"I have work to do," she said.

"We're still a team, right?"

"We were never a team."

"But we staked out the TRENCOR building. We exposed Jason Conrad."

Sherri turned to face him. "I'm going to check into my room. I've got work to do. Leave me alone. I've traveled too far on too little sleep to listen to your bullshit."

"That's not a no."

"Yes, it is," she said as she turned to speak with the desk clerk.

Deep down, he was disappointed she avoided him. No matter—her loss. But she's back here for a reason, and he was going to find out why.

SHERRI ENTERED HER ROOM, locking the door behind her. The quaint room held an inviting aura, simple yet homey. She tossed her suitcase on the bed. Too tired to be pissed off, she cursed herself at her bad luck running into Dane Robinson, her personal nightmare. He refused to go away. It would be difficult avoiding him, but she remained curious how his story of land purchases and water wells tied in to TRENCOR Industries. What was that company up to?

Tonight, she and Brent were supposed to meet, but she hadn't been able to reach him since yesterday. She called his number when she landed in L.A., and again on the drive into Cal City. Opening her suitcase to unpack, she dialed Brent's number again.

"Hello?"

"Brent, it's Sherri. I'm here . . . in California City. What time did you want to meet?"

"Oh, crap. I'm on my way to Los Angeles. I'm meeting a friend who can decipher . . . that stuff I told you about. He's—he's as nervous as I am."

"Brent, are you kidding me? I flew all this way to speak with you about TRENCOR."

"I know, I'm sorry. But this is related. Look, I've got a ThumbDrive full of documents for you to review."

"How long are you going to be there?"

"Sherri, I'm sorry. We'll have to meet tomorrow. Same restaurant as the first time we talked. Two o'clock."

"Brent, damn it! I'm busy! I'm not doing this for accolades. I'm—"

"Sherri, this is much bigger than we thought. Well beyond corporate espionage and theft."

"What the hell is going on?"

There was a pause on the line.

"I think they're planning on killing a hell of a lot of people."

60

May 26, 2001

THE SUN BEAT DOWN on the ramp at the airport in Mojave, and Jeremiah Wellington completed his preflight of the company F-16A. The jet was his pride and joy. He had convinced David Ming to buy the jet three years ago. There were other ways to meet this need, of course. The Air Force could always supply a chase plane, but Wellington wouldn't get to fly their jet. Now he had his own personal F-16, courtesy of TRENCOR Industries and the US Air Force.

Wellington signed the receipt for the fuel and climbed in the jet. He proceeded with his checklists and started the engine. Once the canopy lowered, he sped along with the rest of his checklists. Taking the jet out for a quick spin, he wanted to ensure there were no issues with the F-16 before the test flight of the F-2000 in three days.

The TRENCOR F-16 taxied to the active runway, towering above the smaller home-built aircraft peppering the ramp. Wellington had nothing but disdain for the civilian pilots prepping their aircraft. They had their tiny prop-jobs for a toy. He had an F-16 Fighting Falcon.

Cleared for takeoff, Wellington taxied onto the active runway, pushing the throttle into afterburner. The exhaust nozzle expanded and contracted, adjusting for the sudden dumping of JP-8 into the combustion chamber as the flame shot fifteen feet behind the aircraft.

The jet leaped forward, racing 6,000 feet down the runway until it lifted off the ground. Wellington raised the gear and flaps, let the jet accelerate, then climbed to 15,000 feet. The TRENCOR F-16 performed flawlessly for the next thirty minutes. Wellington took the jet through a series of maneuvers before returning to the traffic pattern for several visual patterns to low approaches before accomplishing a full-stop landing.

Wellington parked the jet, grinning ear to ear as he opened the canopy and the company crew chief of TRENCOR's F-16 placed the ladder on the side of the jet.

"How'd she fly today, Mr. Wellington?"

"Great, Ted. She's a beauty. You guys have done great work once again," Wellington said. His greatest perk working for TRENCOR— having his personal F-16. That, coupled with the incredible salary and bonuses he received each year, ensured he would never quit this job, regardless of Ming's condescending attitude.

"Super. We'll have her ready for the flight Tuesday night."

"Great, Ted, that's great. Any problem getting the Vulcan installed?" he said, referring to the 20 mm cannon installed on military-configured F-16s.

Ted hesitated before answering. "No. We used some of the armament guys from across the ramp and did it. I'm not so sure about the legality of installing a gun on a civilian aircraft."

Wellington acted surprised. "Well, hell, Ted, it's not legal, but it's necessary. You've been at TRENCOR since you retired. You know what it's like with these projects. What if the test pilot of the most advanced jet in history decides to make a run for it?"

"I hear you, but I'm not sure—"

"Did I pay you?"

"Yes, sir," Ted said.

"Is it installed correctly?"

"Yes, sir."

"Okay, I want the full drum of 20 millimeter loaded today. I'll be back Monday to check on your progress. Don't screw this up, Ted. It's national security."

"Mr. Wellington, first the ejection seat, which isn't legal, then the radar, and now the gun? I'm worried—"

"Ted, you've made plenty of money from this. It supplements your Air Force retirement well, doesn't it?"

"Yes, but—"

"Then don't stand in the way of progress. Or national security. I have a multibillion-dollar jet to protect."

Wellington strutted back to TRENCOR's operation shack on the ramp and dropped off his gear. Chuckling to himself, he shook his head. National security—that's funny. He wasn't worried about Jennifer stealing the F-2000. He was more interested in playing with his multimillion-dollar toy. A case of Johnny Walker helped him coordinate with the range officer at the Nevada Test and Training Range. He would call him to slip into the airspace to "test" the civilian F-16.

With the jet pre-loaded with ammunition, it saved him the aggravation of trying to coordinate everything on a moment's notice. Wellington did not know exactly how many federal laws he broke. Until TRENCOR could work out the legalities of parking their F-16 on Edwards AFB's ramp, they'd have to stay here. If he parked the jet at Edwards, he wouldn't get to load his ammo or have the 20 mm Vulcan cannon installed, and that just wouldn't do.

HIS DRIVE FROM L.A. to the Mojave airport took longer than expected, and Brent arrived twenty minutes late, but now the two of them sat at a table by the window in the restaurant. He wore his sunglasses inside to block the sunlight. He looked as if he hadn't slept in days. His clothes were wrinkled, and his hands shook. She sat with her laptop open, waiting for Brent to speak. The waitress brought them both coffee, and Brent leaned forward when the waitress left.

"I don't have all the details yet, but the jet they're designing doesn't work. At least not the way it's supposed to work. It's like they've created a money pit, and the Air Force keeps throwing money in."

"Can you give me some specifics?"

"The jet is designed to fail."

"Say again?"

"The jet is designed to fail. The software is what we call self-corrupting. It creates random mistakes. One of the documents mentions it. It's intentional. The Air Force has invested too much money into the project not to get results. That's why Ming hired Wellington. Everybody loves the guy. He's in so tight with Congress and the Pentagon he gets whatever he asks for."

Sherri shifted in her seat.

"To make matters worse," Brent continued, "I'm not sure the jet will fly. At least, not like a fighter jet."

"Interesting," Sherri said.

"No, not interesting. Intentional. Curt Samson discovered the flaw in the software. Now, he's dead, too."

"Why did you go to L.A.?"

Brent shifted his weight in his seat and scanned the room again.

"I found a formula in the documents. I thought I knew what it was, but it was slightly different. I had to be sure, so I went to get a second opinion. From an expert."

"And?"

"It's sarin gas," he said in a hushed tone.

"Wait—what?"

"The formula—my friend at UCLA confirmed it. He wouldn't talk to me over the phone. He's scared to death now too."

"Why?"

"It's sarin gas, but a highly concentrated form. Much more potency per cubic inch which would compensate for being sprayed from an aircraft. He's never seen anything like it."

Sherri squinted her eyes and leaned in slightly. "Help me out here. I'm pretty sure that's bad, but what is it exactly?"

"Sarin is an organophosphorus compound, a liquid with no color or smell and—"

"Wait," Sherri said, "an organo-what? Speak layman's terms here. I'm a reporter, not a scientist."

"Sorry, I'm still going on no sleep. This is blowing me away," he said, taking a sip of coffee.

"That's fine," she said, patting his forearm with her hand. "Take your time."

Brent set his coffee back on the table. "Organophosphorous compounds are degradable organic compounds containing . . . uh, okay, sorry. Think of bug spray. The same type of effect bug spray has on insects, sarin has on humans."

"That's bad."

"Yeah, tell me about it. Anyway, sarin can induce death in a human one minute after exposure."

"How does that happen?" Sherri said.

"You suffocate. You can't breathe. The lung muscles become paralyzed. It's possible to receive minor doses that won't kill you, but you might have permanent neurological damage. It's a nerve gas."

Her eyes fixed on her screen momentarily as her fingers danced across the keyboard.

"You don't have to take notes. I made you a copy of Georgiana's Thumbdrive. All the information is right here for you," he said, handing her the ThumbDrive.

"Thanks," she said, taking the ThumbDrive from Brent. She looked at it blankly, as if she didn't know what she had in her possession. She placed it in her jeans pocket and continued typing. "These are just thoughts. So, what is David Ming doing with sarin gas?"

"That's just it . . . I'm not sure he knows it's sarin gas. The documents suggest he thinks it's cloud-seeding chemicals to induce rain over the desert."

"What? Why would they do that?"

"The documents say the Chinese need water. They have over a billion people living there, and they are in a global effort to find resources to send back home."

Sherri recalled Dane's story in Oklahoma. Windmills popping up everywhere across the plains states. Those states all sit on top of the Ogallala Aquifer, the largest aquifer in the United States. Sometimes people talked about it back home in Missouri. More water acquisition tied to TRENCOR. A cloud-seeding program that was really sarin gas? What was TRENCOR up to? She continued writing for a minute, then glanced back at Brent.

"Okay, Brent. Put a pretty bow on this package; tie it all together for me. I want to take TRENCOR Industries down for good," she said. She wanted to do it for her father.

Brent sighed. "TRENCOR Industries is this massive multinational conglomerate. They've got their fingers in everything from agriculture to aviation, genetic research to arena football. It's crazy the different things they're involved in."

"I know all that."

"The project we're working on—"

"The F-2000," Sherri said.

"Yes, the F-2000. It's a sixth-generation fighter. The most advanced fighter jet in the world. Ever. TRENCOR was awarded the bid for the project six years ago after hiring retired Brigadier General Jeremiah Wellington. Wellington managed to pull the right strings at the Pentagon to get this through. The cost overruns have been astronomical. The DOD has never seen anything on this scale. They've spent more on this than on the F-117 and the B-2 combined. Anyway, the DOD is getting ripped off. This jet can't do what it's advertised to do. And we're not seeing where the money is going. We've got one simulator and one jet. The first flight is scheduled to take place on

Tuesday, May 29th, between midnight and 3:00 am."

Sherri put up her hand as she took notes on her laptop. Brent had gone past the point of no return on the classified aspect of this project. "Wait, is it the *morning* of the 29th or the 30th?"

"The 29th," Brent said. "This jet has been a money pit from its conception. No one is admitting the figure publicly, but the estimate is in the range of two hundred fifty billion dollars."

"Billion? With a 'B'?" Sherri said, her eyebrows up.

"Yes. It's been frustrating these past six years. Three years ago, they started construction of their facility in California City. There were a lot of issues with putting it there due to the high crime rate. I guess they bought the land cheap. Meanwhile, they were developing the simulator and software for the jet."

"How are they able to spend so much money without congressional oversight?"

"Oh, there is oversight, with more and more cash thrown at it every time an issue comes up. That's why TRENCOR hired Wellington. He's a charmer. They *love* him on Capitol Hill *and* in the Pentagon. I suspect there are payoffs along the way," Brent said, unwrapping a pack of crackers from the table. "Trust me, this is one issue that will never see the light of day. Too many big and powerful people will be exposed if it did."

"Well, we'll see about that," Sherri said

"No, no, it's not just people in the government. It's bigger than that. That's what happened to Georgiana Anderson. She was on to something. She was always suspicious of TRENCOR. Couldn't ever figure out why we were only allowed in certain areas of the building despite the fact the US government paid for the damn place."

"You've got to have more than that for a murder."

"I do, I do," he said. "It's all on the ThumbDrive. Everything I talked about. The data on the F-2000, the sarin gas. It also contai—" Brent stopped speaking as he focused beyond her toward the entrance of the restaurant. Sherri turned her head to see what he was looking at.

Staring back at them was Jeremiah Wellington.

61

May 26, 2001

HIS ORDER WAS READY when he entered the restaurant. He had called ahead after landing, charging it to the company account. Wellington was not one to pass up a good deal. The food at the airport was good, and the company covered the cost.

The manager brought his order to him, as he usually did, and Jeremiah tipped him generously on the receipt. His eyes scanned the restaurant and stopped on the two people sitting by the window: Brent O'Malley and his gorgeous reception date. Brent stared at him as he approached the table. The guy looked like shit. Scraggly beard, hair uncombed, bloodshot and baggy eyes. Must not have slept for days. She, on the other hand, looked perfect. How does this happen?

"Hello, Brent," Wellington said.

"Mr. Well-Wellington, how are you?"

"I'm great. I just took my twenty-five-million-dollar jet for a little joy ride, and I'm feeling fantastic."

"Congratulations?" Brent stammered.

"And you are?" Wellington said, ogling the pretty redhead.

"Mr. Wellington, this is Sherri Davis."

"Yes," he said, reaching out to shake her hand. "You were at the reception at Club Muroc. You're an actress, I'm told."

Sherri shook his hand. "Yes," she responded with a weak smile. "But not a very good one, apparently. I keep getting rejected for all my auditions."

"I'm sure a woman of your beauty will find something soon." Wellington stood back, analyzing her. "Yes, if I were casting a film, you'd be my star."

"Thank you," Sherri said.

"What are you two doing here?" he said to her without acknowledging Brent.

"Just catching up on old times," she said.

What was wrong with this picture? Brent looked like crap on a good day. Why was a smoking hot redhead hanging out with this guy? He eyed her suspiciously for a moment, then turned to Brent. "I'll see you at work on Monday, Brent."

"O-Okay," Brent said.

"Nice finally meeting you, Ms. Davis, I look forward to your first motion picture."

"Me, too," Sherri said.

Wellington turned toward the door. He'd run a check on Sherri Davis when he returned to his office. He didn't know who she was, but he knew she was no damned actress.

"WHAT WAS THAT all about?" Sherri asked.

"I-I'm not sure," Brent said, taking another sip of coffee.

"He certainly looked at us strangely."

"Y-yeah. The fact that he walked over to talk to us was stranger. He's normally a self-centered asshole—unless he wants something. He must have wanted to meet you."

"Say again?"

"Wellington has a reputation of sorts. He's married, but his wife rarely comes around. He's been screwing Major Walton for the last two years."

"The pilot who took a beating at the party?"

"Yes. They've had something going on since he was the wing commander at Vance. He even got her into test pilot school. Wellington's been her sponsor before she showed up on base."

"Interesting."

"It gets better. The pilot who crashed the F-15 a couple of weeks back, Major Curt Samson, used to be the lead test pilot on the F-2000 project. Curt couldn't stand Jennifer. He considered her an average pilot, at best, and a worse test pilot. Of course, now she gets to fly the F-2000 on its first flight while Curt is six feet under."

Sherri typed away on her keyboard. "Isn't he the one who argued with Ming after a little too much to drink?"

"Yeah. And the following Monday, his jet crashed."

"That's convenient."

"Yeah. Samson told Ming he discovered the self-corrupting software."

Sherri tilted her head to the side. "Okay, now you have my attention."

"Oh, yeah, he let Ming know," Brent leaned forward enthusiastically. "And three days later, boom! He's dead. He doesn't eject. The Air Force says it was pilot error, maybe even suicide."

"Suicide?"

"Yeah, somehow they knew Samson was depressed because he was a lonely alcoholic. The information they gathered in such a short amount of time is astounding. And suspicious. They determined he was distraught and crashed his jet to end it all."

"Is this true?"

"The loneliness is true. The suicide isn't. He loved his job. Told me that all the time. He was one hundred percent pilot. His jets came first. That's what cost him his wife and a few other women. Hell, I'm alone, but that doesn't mean I'm suicidal. Know why? Because I love my job!"

Sherri reviewed her notes, but as always, she found the best way to new information was another question. "What are you trying to say here?"

"I'm saying TRENCOR Industries killed Curt Samson."

"And Georgiana Anderson?"

"Yes."

"And they are stockpiling sarin gas?"

"Well . . . I'm not sure if they're stockpiling it. We haven't seen it. But they have a formula for it, and a plan to use. And it all came from David Ming's computer." Brent finished his cup of coffee, signaling the waitress for a refill. "Hell, I need to contact the police, the FBI . . . somebody."

"Where would they store it?"

"Store what?" Brent said.

"The gas. If they made it, where would they store it?"

Brent stared out the window for a few moments, falling silent as the waitress filled his cup again. Once she was gone, he refocused on Sherri. "It's not a matter of where they *would* store, but a matter of where they *could* store it. They've got a facility with over 400,000 square feet, most of which none of us has seen."

Sherri grimaced. The corruption of the company responsible for her father's death was far bigger than she ever imagined. "Brent," Sherri said, gathering her laptop and purse, "we need to get inside that building."

62

May 27, 2001

MING SAT IN THE LIVING ROOM of his Sierra Mountain mansion west of Edwards Air Force Base. The sparse room seemed larger than normal with most of the ornate furniture and decorations removed. At thirty minutes past midnight, he was still wide awake. Amanda kept the workers feverishly packing all day long, and Ming had been on a teleconference with Beijing until about an hour ago.

It surprised Ming when Wellington called him earlier. He was more surprised when Wellington wanted to meet him after midnight. Ming sat in the vast living room with a fire burning in the fireplace, yearning for the days when he worked in his Chicago office. The fast-paced boardroom meetings, the high-rise buildings, the power lunches. When the operation acquired the aerospace branch, the majority of the corporate work moved to California. Regardless, his life's work was about to come to a close. He would miss this home surrounded by the beautiful mountains, but he wouldn't miss his office. The TRENCOR facility was a thorn in his side; a massive eyesore in the miserable desert. Amanda worked hard with the interior decorations to spruce up the place with original aviation art and modern sculptures, but even in its prime, it never resembled anything more than a quiet, poorly attended museum. Now, it didn't even look that good. When Beijing made the decision to collapse his operation, Amanda prepared to ship the original art back to China.

Ming watched the fire burn in the fireplace as he sipped on his scotch, his newspaper open but unread.

"He's here," Amanda called out from the kitchen. She walked into the living room, set her Chardonnay on the table next to the couch, and moved to the front door. She nodded politely to Wellington as she welcomed him into their home. Amanda then escorted him to her husband, picked up her wine, and left the two men alone.

"Please, sit," Ming said, motioning toward the couch opposite him. "Now, what can I do for you, Jeremiah?"

"Mr. Ming, I appreciate you seeing me tonight. I know it's inconvenient," he said, sitting on the leather couch. He scanned the vast yet empty living room. "What's going on here?"

Ming's forehead wrinkled as his jaw tightened. "Termites. We spray later in the week."

"Hmph," Wellington replied. "Sir, the reason I came by . . . I was flying the Falcon this afternoon. When I finished, I went into the restaurant for lunch, and I saw Brent O'Malley sitting in there."

"My memory escapes me, but the name is familiar," Ming said. He knew exactly who Brent O'Malley was, but wanted Wellington to think he was not aware of what was going on with the operation.

"Brent O'Malley is one of the Air Force's aeronautical engineers on the F-2000."

Ming nodded his head. "I remember, yes."

"Well, he's sitting with this redhead," Wellington said. "The same one he brought to the reception. Supposed to be an actress."

"Ahh, yes. Very beautiful, if I remember."

"Yes, very beautiful indeed. Problem is, she's no actress."

Ming's left eyebrow raised as he leaned forward intently.

"I did a little research when I went home, made some calls." He produced a printout from the internet with Sherri Davis' picture on it. "She's a reporter. For *The New York Times*. And the question is . . . why the hell is she hanging out with an aeronautical engineer from a top-secret project on the world's most advanced jet?"

Ming looked at his feet, shaking his head. "This is problematic, Jeremiah. What do you propose we do?" Ming stood and moved behind the couch where Wellington sat.

"We bring him in for questioning," Wellington said. He turned his head as he talked, watching Ming as he moved. "He's an Air Force asset, so they will have to be informed. I can talk to—"

"No, I'll handle it. I have a meeting with the wing commander on Friday. We'll discuss it then."

"Isn't that waiting too long?"

"Jeremiah, what do we have to hide? The plane has its first official flight in two days. If *The Times* gets a scoop, we get more publicity out of it, and get to hang a disloyal Air Force engineer at the same time. It can wait," he said, putting a reassuring hand on Wellington's shoulder. Ming had plenty to hide, but he only needed to hide it for three more days.

"I guess you're right."

"Of course I am. I appreciate you coming by to inform me of this situation, but I'm sure it's nothing. I'll address it Friday."

"Yes, sir."

"Very good," Ming said. "Thank you for coming by this evening, Jeremiah."

"I was sorry to bother you, but this information couldn't wait until morning," Wellington said as the two men shook hands. "I always like to cover my six."

"Excuse me?" Ming said. He liked to toy with Wellington when he used his little pilot phrases in his presence.

"Never mind, sir," Wellington said. "I'll show myself out."

"Good night, Jeremiah," Ming said as he watched the retired general exit the front door.

When the door closed, Ming pulled his cell phone out of his pocket, hitting the speed dial.

Li Zhong answered on the first ring.

"Meet me here at nine in the morning," he said, and hung up.

DANE STRUGGLED TO GET out of bed late the next morning. He spent most of the night arguing with his producer in Tulsa about why he stayed in California. It was a losing argument as Dane struggled to understand why he was here himself. Dane came out to land an interview with Amanda Rieffelming, only to put her on the back burner when he ran into Jason Conrad.

Once again, the Conrad angle had died on the vine. The initial report was good, but the interest in the follow-up wasn't there—again. He couldn't understand it; the guy was at most a spy and at least a traitor, but nobody cared. The producer told him he had an overactive imagination, and that he needed to drop Conrad for good.

Frustrated, he dressed, grabbed his laptop, and slogged to the lobby for a cup of coffee. When he entered the lobby, he spotted Sherri working on her laptop at one of the tables. Dane's excitement was well hidden. He waved and wandered to the coffee pot. With his coffee in hand, he walked to her table.

"Good morning," he said. "Mind if I join you?"

"Good morning," she replied, pounding away on her computer keyboard, never looking up.

"What are you working on?" he said as he sat opposite her, opened up his laptop, and hit the power button.

"Work."

"What kind of work?"

"News work, Dane."

"That's nice. Any interesting stories?"

"All stories are interesting. It's the reporter's job to find the interest."

"Hmm, good point." He took a sip of coffee and glanced around the lobby. "Why are you working out here?"

Sherri looked up for the first time. "The maid is cleaning my room, and I have a lot of work to do. Do you mind?"

Dane looked at her, confused. "No," was all he could muster.

After several moments of silence, Dane stopped working on his computer. "Look, I want to apologize."

He wasn't sure why he blurted out the words. Sherri stopped typing, her head moving up slowly from her laptop.

"For?" she replied, eyebrows raised.

Dane shifted uncomfortably in his chair. "Everything, I guess. I know I come on too strong . . . but I can't help it. Do you really know how beautiful you are?" He saw Sherri blush. That was an unexpected response.

"That's sweet, Dane."

"No, no. There's more. I'm sorry I come across as an obnoxious ass. I'm chauvinistic and self-absorbed. I don't know why. Look at me. I'm forty-two years old, single, and overweight. I'm sorry I tried to get you drunk in DC five years ago. I'm sorry I lied to you to get you to go to TRENCOR. That was wrong, but I just wanted us to work together. And Jason Conrad . . . maybe it's time I find a story that resonates with the public." The words were flowing now. He thought he meant them; they felt sincere. He studied Sherri's face, which held a faint smile, and he realized they came across as sincere.

The two worked in silence for a couple of minutes before Sherri's cell phone rang.

"Hello," she said. Sherri listened for a few moments, then said, "Hang on one second." She put her hand over the phone and turned to Dane. "Would you mind watching my computer? I need to take this call."

Dane smiled. "No problem. Take your time."

Sherri closed her laptop, stood, and wandered out the front door of the lobby. Dane stared at her shapely figure as she walked out the door. She was perfect. He fantasized about her once again. His confession and apology surely killed any chance he ever had with her, but maybe it brought them closer together personally, if not sexually.

He eyed her computer, then looked at her through the door. He stared at the ThumbDrive sticking out of the USB port. It was wrong, but it was brilliant. Dane snatched the ThumbDrive from her laptop and stuck it in his. There were tons of files, and he had no time to review them. Selecting all of them, he dragged and dropped them into his laptop.

The documents started copying onto his computer as Dane glanced back at the door to check on Sherri. If she caught him, he would never get in her pants.

He continued watching Sherri outside. At one point she peeked back in to see if he was still there, the phone still stuck to her ear. Dane waved with a big, desperate smile, and Sherri popped back outside.

Dane checked the progress; it was ninety percent complete. His eyes darted back and forth from the computer screen to the door. His heart pounded in his chest as the percentage slowly clicked its way toward one hundred percent. After four minutes, the upload completed. Dane removed the ThumbDrive, sticking it back in her USB port. Satisfied he'd copied everything, he closed the lid on his laptop and drained his coffee.

Standing, he shuffled to the coffee pot for a refill. As he poured, Sherri walked back in the lobby.

"Good phone call?" he said, returning to their table.

"Business," she said, sitting and opening her computer.

"Well, that's nice," he said. "When are we going to dinner? We have so much to catch up on."

"Dane," she said, taking a deep breath, "that's not going to happen. Trust me when I tell you there is nothing, personally or professionally, we will ever do together."

"I can see you still need time to think about it," Dane said with his usual snake oil salesman wink. "I'm going to let you work. I'll see you later."

"Goodbye, Dane."

Dane picked up his laptop. He left Sherri at the table and hurried back to his room. His day just got busy, as he gripped his laptop like a kid on Christmas morning. He had a lot of reading to do.

AFTER HANGING UP with Sherri, Brent treated his pervasive headache. He'd had little to no sleep for the last four days, living on caffeine and high-sugar junk food. The cap to the bottle of aspirin opened after a brief struggle, as Brent took two aspirin with a pint of O'Shea's Traditional Irish Pale Ale. Not the optimum means of delivery, but it was wet. His inability to cope with his situation and the events surrounding him overshadowed the relief of having Sherri back in town. She provided him stability, at least regarding TRENCOR. There was significant information he had not yet told her, but he realized at some point he'd have to provide full disclosure. At this point, his security clearance was the last thing he worried about.

They planned to meet at 10:00 pm tonight outside of TRENCOR's perimeter and drive to the facility. Together, they would explore the vast complex, searching for the sarin gas. He knew he needed to notify the authorities, but he couldn't make such accusations without some form of proof. If events went like he expected, by this time tomorrow, TRENCOR would be swarming with feds.

Brent's stomach growled. He grabbed his phone and wallet and headed toward the door.

He moved briskly to his car and jumped in his car. Feeling lightheaded from the O'Shea's, he wondered whether he was too drunk to drive. Or too tired. His stomach growled again, and he turned the ignition. The motor roared to life, much like his stomach. He backed out of his parking spot as he headed to Lancaster. Brent headed south on Sierra Highway in an effort to avoid potential law enforcement since he'd already had a beer. He drove with the windows rolled down and the radio blaring, enjoying the beautiful day. With some food in his stomach and another beer or two in his system, he might be able to come back home and get some sleep.

Approaching West Avenue E, Brent noticed a black van racing above the brush line bordering the two roads. This guy is hauling ass. Is he going to stop in time? The van slowed as Brent approached the intersection. Zipping past the four-way-intersection, Brent noticed the blacked-out windows on the dust-covered van.

Scary-looking, he thought, a second before the van whipped onto Sierra Highway, accelerating toward him. Brent continued to watch the black van in his rearview mirror. It moved closer, and Brent figured the van would pass him any minute now. He focused forward—no one was in the oncoming lane. Brent checked the mirror again and noticed the van sliding back. Peering over his shoulder, he could tell the van was indeed moving away from him. What the hell was this guy doing?

As Brent focused again on the road in front of him, his eyes grew wide. He screamed as he squeezed the steering wheel, slamming on the brakes. Time stood still; his heart pounded in his chest.

His car came to a halt twenty-five feet from the black helicopter hovering in the middle of the road in front of him.

63

A S THE HELICOPTER FLOATED over the road, Brent imagined the world of *Star Wars*: floating vehicles, imperial soldiers, and lone renegade rebels. Brent shook his head to force the hallucination out of his mind, returning to reality. While the helicopter in front didn't move, a black van pulled up behind him. Four black-clad men with guns leaped out of the van and approached his car, two on each side. Stormtroopers? No, they wore white. They took position on each side of the car as the one closest to him grabbed the handle and opened the door.

"Get out of the vehicle," the man yelled.

Brent turned his head, aware his situation was not good. He waved his hand from left to right in front of the man speaking to him.

"These are not the droids you are looking for," he said with a grin, attempting to hide his fear. It was one of his favorite scenes from the original *Star Wars* film. Obi-wan Kenobi and Luke Skywalker were in a land rover on the desert planet of Tatooine being questioned by Imperial Stormtroopers searching for Luke's droids, C-3PO and R2-D2. Everything fell into place in Brent's world, life imitating art.

The second man on the driver's side stepped up to the car, thrusting the butt of his rifle against Brent's head, knocking his glasses to the floorboard. His vision was hazy, from both the impact and the loss of his glasses. One of the two reached in, unbuckled his seat belt, and dragged him out of the car, throwing him onto the pavement.

Brent struggled to talk, but words weren't coming out. He couldn't gather his thoughts through the painful haziness in his brain. More dark figures gathered around as two men bound Brent's arms behind him. Brent felt a sharp prick to his neck, and a warmth oozed to his heart, moving throughout his body. He tried to lift his head but could no longer hold his eyes open.

LI ZHONG DROVE back to TRENCOR Industries before dark. The nosy aeronautical engineer was subdued in the back of the black van. When they arrived at TRENCOR, Li Zhong parked at the loading dock. His men brought O'Malley inside the facility strapped to a gurney. He ordered him taken to the executive offices. Li Zhong didn't have a plan on what to do with him, but finding out what Brent knew should be done without Ming's knowledge. Ming was concerned that Brent knew about the flaws in the jet. General Jingguo's men had monitored Brent's phone calls the last thirty-six hours. He knew something. If he knew about the sarin gas, Li Zhong would know soon enough.

Li Zhong walked inside and met General Jingguo in the laboratory.

"How is your progress going, General?"

"We are almost done. The various chemicals have been isolated and stored appropriately. There is only one package we must be destroy, but I don't have the means to do it."

"Don't worry," Li Zhong said, "I do."

General Jingguo nodded. "Good. We will finish with our work here within the hour. We'll drive to Los Angeles tonight and leave for San Francisco in the morning. When do you see Ming again?"

"I'm on my way there as soon as the helicopter arrives."

"Good. Feel out Ming. See if he suspects anything regarding our chemical warfare program."

Li Zhong bowed and left the room, heading for the helipad. He stood outside for five minutes before the helicopter broke the horizon. Dust swirled in all directions as Li Zhong shielded his eyes. Climbing inside, he silently strapped in as the helicopter lifted off. The sun fell beneath the small mountain range as the sky gradually faded from an orange/red to a blue/black.

Twenty minutes later, the helicopter landed at Ming's mountain home, shutting off its engine. Li Zhong went inside and headed directly to the secure room where Kathy was held prisoner.

Li Zhong grew tired of dealing with the Russian agent. They'd interrogated her for days, but she had not yielded any information beneficial to them. Ming's mansion would be empty soon, and she had to be moved. Li Zhong suggested they move her to TRENCOR. Ming was indifferent as he focused on the finances of the company.

As he entered the room, two of his men unstrapped her from her bed to board the helicopter. Deeply sedated, she couldn't stand, so they placed her in a wheelchair and pushed her to the helicopter.

The spinning blades blew sand in their faces as the three men wheeled her outside, shielding their eyes as they approached. The two men lifted Kathy from the wheelchair into a seat on the helicopter, secured her seatbelt, and took seats on either side of her. Li Zhong collapsed the wheelchair, placing it behind the seat. He climbed in the front, shutting the door as the helicopter lifted off into the black sky.

THE DARK ROAD WAS DESERTED. Sherri felt nervous sitting in the desert alone at night. Brent should have arrived thirty minutes ago. She pulled her cell phone out of her purse, dialing his number once again. Nothing.

She hadn't talked to him since earlier in the day, and she began to worry. The scenario Brent painted was a deadly one—they were rapidly getting thrust into the middle of a deadly conspiracy. When they were in the restaurant, he mentioned the first scheduled test flight tomorrow night. That was another thing she wanted to talk about with Brent. Tapping her fingers on the top of the steering wheel, she glanced around in all directions, hoping to see the headlights of Brent's car speeding toward her. Nothing. Perspiration formed on her forehead and she huffed as she thought about Brent's tardiness. He was the reason he flew back to California.

Sherri stepped out of her car, pacing, trying to figure out what to do next. In the distance, the lights on the exterior of the TRENCOR building split the darkness, but the lights in the parking lot were not illuminated. Much different from the first time she saw the building weeks ago.

Without warning, a blacked-out helicopter flew over her head at about one hundred feet. Dust swirled around her, flying into her hair and mouth. Sherri shielded her eyes with her left forearm as she braced herself against her car with her right.

Spitting the dust out of her mouth, she rubbed her eyes, searching for the helicopter. It was heading straight for TRENCOR Industries.

64

THE F-2000 RESIDED inside a discreet, secure hangar sitting exposed in the California desert sun. The recent upgrades TRENCOR made to the hangar, in addition to the NVG-compatible lighting, included insulation and air conditioning. Neither of those additions were needed until the summer, but the air conditioning provided circulation, as the hangar doors were always closed.

Jason approached the building and several armed guards appeared from different directions. He glanced around; numerous cameras and motion detectors were in the vicinity. His first chance to inspect the F-2000's unidentified port, and he already had guns pointed at him.

He raised his hands with his line badge and security credentials held in his left hand. "Take it easy, fellas," Jason said, "I'm just here to check out the aircraft."

"We'll see," one of the guards said. He took Jason's credentials and scanned them on his handheld scanner.

"Who do you guys work for?" Jason said, noticing the M-4s slung around their necks and the non-standard Smith and Wesson 645 sidearm the guards carried. SP's carried the Beretta 92F.

"We're SPs," the guard said.

"No, you're not," Jason said. Why not call a spade a spade? "You guys work for TRENCOR?"

The guard handed Jason his credentials with an arrogant smirk on his face. "You're okay. You checked good."

Jason, surprised it had been this easy to get in, entered the hangar. Several offices on both sides of the hallway bustled with activity.

The hangar bay appeared as clean and organized as it had during the reception. The difference this time was various workers moved around the jet, and their tools sat close by in their containers. Special mats lay on surface of the aircraft so the workers could climb on top to work without damaging the special radar-absorbing skin of the jet.

Jason marveled at the wondrous piece of technology. He had a burning desire to fly it. Of course, he worried he might never get that opportunity. Wellington had placed his training on hold. Despite this, he continued to study and grab as much simulator time as possible. He had come a long way in the past week.

Workers scurried around him as he approached the jet. He was one of only three pilots who had clearance to be in here.

"Captain, can I help you?" one of the workers said as Jason stared at the jet.

"Hi, I'm Jason Conrad," he said, extending his hand.

The worker shook his hand. "Bill Hastings, foreman. You the one flying this thing tonight?"

"No," Jason responded. He didn't know the test flight was scheduled for tonight. "I'm attached to the program, but I'm not one of the test pilots. You guys work for TRENCOR?"

Hastings shook his head. "Subcontractors. It was a bitch getting security clearances for this project. I regret the whole thing."

Jason tilted his head. "Really? Why?"

"It's been an ass-pain from the beginning. Clearances for everyone, work schedules, deadlines, 'need-to-know' BS. The only thing that made it worth it was the amount of money they paid us. Or were supposed to pay us."

"You mean you guys aren't getting paid?"

The man scratched the back of his head, glanced at the jet for a moment, then back at Jason.

"We're getting small drippings of what's owed us. The way the contract is written, we received thirty percent up front and thirty-five percent when our portion is completed. The final thirty-five percent we get when the Air Force accepts the jet."

"Is that standard?"

"No, but the money was so good up front, our bosses thought we couldn't lose. That was before these guys got two years behind schedule. We're losing money like crazy. Had to lay off other folks in the company just to curb costs."

"What are you guys working on?"

"It's a new form of titanium plating. Super-thin, lightweight. Designed to deflect shrapnel and rounds up to 20 mm."

"You're not installing it, are you?"

"No, we're inspecting the fittings. Since it was put together, taken apart, and put together again, we check to ensure it's still secure and nothing came loose to breach the aircraft."

"I read about this," Jason nodded. "Do you mind if I look around the jet? I've been flying the simulator for weeks, but this is the first time I've had a chance to touch the thing."

"Sure, just don't break nothing," the contractor said with a grin.

"I won't. Thanks."

Jason approached the jet, placing his hand on the smooth surface. It looked and felt smooth, not porous like he remembered from the reception. Walking from the right side of the cockpit to the left, he climbed the stairs standing next to the jet.

The interior looked exactly like the simulator. Letting out a deep breath, his brain worked fast, confirming each panel, light, and switch. Behind the pilot's seat a second ACES II ejection seat was installed for the software engineer. While cramped, it seemed like it would work. He studied the interior for several minutes, going over the checklist procedures from start to finish.

Remembering his mission for Brent, he climbed down the portable staircase. At the rear of the jet near the twin-engine exhaust, Jason found the port exactly where Brent showed him it would be.

The port was about an inch and a half in diameter. Jason placed his finger around the edges, inspecting what he could see. A secondary RAM dump valve, perhaps? Who knew? It was exactly where the older schematics showed it to be.

"What are you looking at?" Jason heard from behind him.

"Huh, wha—" Jason, startled, couldn't finish his sentence. A short contractor stood behind him, watching him.

"You one of the pilots?"

"Yes. I've seen the jet before, but I never noticed this port. Do you know what it's for?"

The short contractor shook his head. "No, but if you want, I can drop the panel and we can look. We're still piecing this thing together."

Jason smiled. "Really? That would be great."

"You're timing is perfect. If you came in tomorrow, you couldn't touch this thing. Hang on one second." The contractor walked over to a table, grabbed a screwdriver, and came back.

"We've got these special composite screwdrivers to match the composite screws on the aircraft," he said with a smile, bending over, moving under the rear of the jet. The bottom of the jet sat five feet off the ground, and both men hunched over while the contractor removed the screws holding up the panel. The panel, like most of the ones on the jet, was held in place by about forty screws. The contractor removed the last screw as the panel came free.

"Well, I'll be damned," he said, turning to Jason.

Jason leaned forward and checked out the space. Empty. He saw a nozzle leading from the external port that would attach to something, but that something wasn't in the aircraft.

"I don't get it," Jason said. "This area is sealed off. What's the purpose of this port? You can see the nozzle, but where does it go? The walls in here are solid."

The contractor moved in closer and pointed at the top of the nozzle. "If you look closely, you can see an electrical connection and a pneumatic connection coming from the jet into the top portion of the nozzle."

"Yeah, I see them."

"What probably happens is . . . from somewhere inside the cockpit, an electrical valve opens and pneumatic air is pushed into whatever container sits back here, pushing its contents out."

"Strange," Jason said, analyzing the empty space.

"Most likely a design mod that they either forgot or ignored. Maybe it's a smoke generator for airshows. This damn jet has had so many changes, it would make your head hurt. I know because it made *my* head hurt. Seen enough?"

"Yeah."

The short contractor held the panel back in position and began replacing the screws.

"Thanks for helping me out," Jason said, waving as he walked away.

"No problem," the short contractor said, screwing the panel back to the jet.

Jason left the hangar and walked to his truck. He pulled his cell phone out of his flight suit pocket, dialing Brent's number. The phone rang four times, then went to voicemail. Jason left a quick message without details as he climbed in his truck and put on his sunglasses.

Cranking the engine, he drove off base to TRENCOR Industries.

SHERRI STOOD BY HER CAR on the same deserted road she had been on a little over twelve hours ago, staring at the TRENCOR facility. The building sat about a mile away, but the way her skin crawled, she felt it might be too close. Last night, the blacked-out helicopter came from somewhere in the west and flew directly to the facility. Her reporter's instinct went into overdrive; something bad was going on at TRENCOR Industries. Perhaps something worse than losing contact with Brent, and that had its own sinister implications.

On the horizon to the east, the dust of a vehicle heading in her direction billowed along the ground. Could it be Brent?

As she waited, she quickly realized it was not Brent's car. The truck rolled to a stop, the dust-covered window on the driver's side rolled down. Jason Conrad stared at her with a smug look on his face.

"Well, well, well," he said. "What do we have here?"

"Uh . . . hi," she said, ambling over to his truck. Her last encounter with Jason didn't go that well. Not as well as she'd hoped.

"Car broke down?"

"Uh . . . no."

Jason nodded his head. "Sightseeing?"

"No, I'm waiting for someone." Sherri felt embarrassed, although she wasn't sure why.

"Dane Robinson? If you stick around, I'm sure he'll be here any minute. He follows me everywhere I go."

That's why. Clearly, subtlety wasn't one of Jason Conrad's attributes.

"No, I'm waiting for Brent. I haven't been able to reach him. I was hoping he'd show up here." Sherri placed her hands on her hips as she glanced behind her toward TRENCOR's facility. She caught herself and looked back at Jason. "Not here, I mean, TRENCOR. I hoped he might be coming from, or going to, TRENCOR."

Jason removed his sunglasses, glaring at her suspiciously. It made her feel uncomfortable. "Brent is a busy man. What makes you think he would drive by here?"

Sherri wanted to tell Jason, but she didn't know if she could trust him. "I had lunch with him on Saturday. We talked yesterday morning and were supposed to meet last night, but he never showed. I haven't seen or heard from him since."

"Does Dane get jealous when you have lunch with other men?"

Sherri's eyes shot daggers at Jason. She felt disgusted. Disgust at him for making such a comment, but mostly disgust at herself for associating with Dane. She chose not to say anything. It was well-deserved.

"Let me guess—you're not really an actress."

"No, I'm not. I'm . . ." Sherri paused, though she wasn't sure if it was hesitation or for dramatic effect. ". . . a reporter for *The New York Times.*"

"I know, Brent told me. At least you have some sense of integrity. Honesty and attractiveness can get a person a long way."

She fought back a smile as her heart warmed, but she still hung on his comment earlier. *Okay, somebody needs to broker the peace here.* "Look, I'm sorry," she said. "I don't work with Dane. We know each other, but it's not what you think."

"Sure looked that way a week ago."

"I know, and I'm sorry. I don't know you or your background, but his creepy obsession with you is very annoying."

Jason chuckled. "Yeah." He put his sunglasses back on and placed his truck back in gear. "When you find Brent, tell him to call me. I have some information for him."

"How about we look for him together?" she blurted.

He paused as her eyebrows raised. "That might be something I'd consider," he said. "How can I get in touch with you?"

Sherri handed him her card, which he glanced at, then tucked in his left chest flight suit pocket.

"I've got work to do, but I'll be in touch," he said, the corners of his mouth turning upwards. "Good luck finding Brent until then."

The silence was shattered by the sound of a helicopter zooming overhead. Sherri figured it was the same helicopter that flew overhead last night. A black helicopter pulled up, turned to fly back toward them. Sherri noticed the left side door of the helicopter was open, where a man stood on the skid, strapped to the inside of the helicopter.

"Sherri, get in the truck," Jason said.

"What are they do—"

"Get in the truck!" Jason yelled as the man on the side of the helicopter opened fire.

65

May 28, 2001

SHERRI THREW HERSELF over the side and into the bed of Jason's truck, pounding on the window to let him know she was on board. Jason floored it and the truck surged forward.

Dirt and gravel flew upward as bullets struck the ground a few feet behind the pickup. The truck fishtailed as it raced along the ground until the rear tires gripped the road. The truck straightened out and accelerated. Sherri bounced around as she struggled to keep the helicopter in sight. She crawled close to the cab as the helicopter maneuvered into position for another attack run. Grabbing the section of the bed next to the cab, Sherri realized she was exposed as the helicopter zoomed in, the blast from the machine gun muffled only by the helicopter and the roar of truck. Bullets danced across the bed, and Sherri screamed.

She desperately looked at Jason through the glass as he jerked the truck to the left and entered a paved road that dumped out into the TRENCOR compound. He raced through the front gate, streaking by two sets of barbed-wire fence.

The black helicopter made another pass at Jason's truck as he headed straight for the three-story building. The machine gun now fired in front of the truck in an effort to stop them. Jason accelerated, zipping through the bullets' impact zone. The helicopter banked away and headed to the northeast and the isolated desert to disappear over the horizon.

Jason pulled up to the front door of TRENCOR, hiding the truck underneath the front entrance's overhang. Turning off the ignition, he jumped out and rushed to the truck bed. Sherri sat curled against the cab, gripping the side of the truck, unable to uncurl her fingers. Jason smiled when he saw her and reached out his hand.

Breathing heavily, she reached out and grabbed it. She stood up, and Jason lifted her by the waist to help her out of the truck. Instinctively, Sherri wrapped her arms around him. She felt him hesitate, but then he put his arms around her. Sherri let go, using her hands to gently push herself away from Jason, even though she didn't want to.

"I'm sorry," she said. "I was scared."

"Don't be," Jason replied. "I was scared, too."

She wanted to leap back into his arms, but realized that might not be the best thing. Wandering to the rear of the truck, she examined the bullet holes in the bed.

"Who were those guys?" Jason said.

"I don't know. Last night I watched a helicopter fly overhead to TRENCOR, but I don't know if that's the same helicopter."

Jason stepped to the back of the truck and stood by Sherri as he examined the bullet holes. Sherri pulled out her cell phone and started to dial.

"Wait," Jason said. "What are you doing?"

Sherri was perplexed. "I'm calling the sheriff's office. We've just been shot at by a helicopter. That kind of thing doesn't happen every day. We need to report it."

"Please . . . don't."

"What?" Sherri replied, as she lowered her phone and hit the off button.

Jason looked at the ground as he shifted his weight from one foot to the other. "I—I just don't think that's something we want to do at this point."

"Are you crazy?"

"No," he said. "My life . . . my life is kind of complicated. I just arrived here, and I'm in kind of an important position. Of course, you know about my father."

"Yes," she said, looking at him curiously.

"I would prefer to be left out of this. If you feel like it's something you need to report, go ahead. But leave me out of it."

Sherri pondered Jason's request for a moment. "Why did they attack us?"

"It was a warning."

"Against what?"

Jason shook his head. "I don't know. We were exposed, out in the open. We were an easy target. If they wanted us dead, we'd be dead."

It reminded Sherri of her incident in Pensacola. She leaned against the truck, her thumbnail in her teeth.

"The question is," Jason continued, "who's the real target?"

66

May 29, 2001

A MOONLESS NIGHT settled over the Mojave Desert like a blanket on a cold winter night, and the stars stayed hidden as if they were intertwined with the cycle of the moon. It would be another four hours before the moon peeked above the horizon. The black night sky was the perfect setting for this secret yet historic event. The Public Affairs office at Edwards had released a statement regarding night flying for the base pilots' semi-annual night currency requirement for the next two nights. The majority of the lights on the base near the flight line were turned off, while in the housing areas, lights were turned on. The residents were told to turn on all exterior lights to "aid" the pilots in finding their way back to Edwards. The purpose was to wash out the vision of people on the ground, limiting what they might see in the distance. Several of the pilots from the base were directed to take off in a variety of different aircraft. The goal was to fly around the local area, creating a pattern of jets flying at night. The F-2000 would slip into the middle of the chaos. It was all uniquely timed and choreographed to appear mundane. They would hide in plain sight.

Major Jennifer Walton stood in front of the mirror, examining herself from every angle. Her hair: perfect. Her makeup: more than regulations allowed. Her favorite flight suit, with the exception of a few areas, seemed airbrushed onto her body. In future test flights, she wouldn't be able to wear this flight suit because of the electrodes positioned everywhere on her body for the ITCS, but today was all about her, the first female to make an initial test flight of the Air Force's newest jet fighter.

One photographer and one videographer were there to document the occasion, so Jennifer wanted to look her best. One of the Edwards AFB historians interviewed her; he had the proper security clearance and was read in on the project. This interview, along with the pictures, would be released to the Associated Press at a future date yet to be determined. It disappointed her the notoriety wouldn't come until the F-2000 was made public, but she could wait.

Right now, her life was perfect. Wellington told her earlier he was going to divorce his wife so they could be together. Finally, she was getting some normalcy in her life. It was a good day for her—she secured her man and was about to make history. She wished he could be here, but he was in Mojave prepping his jet. He would take off in the TRENCOR F-16 twenty minutes before she took off, orbit the field, then follow her on her takeoff roll, through liftoff, and back to the ground.

They would celebrate later.

Her helmet bag sat on a chair in the corner. Jennifer pulled her checklist out of the bag, reviewing each step. She had accomplished these hundreds of times in the simulator, but she didn't want anything to go wrong today. This needed to go perfectly.

She checked and rechecked everything. Satisfied she was ready to go, she gathered her gear and moved to the door.

Wellington timed everything out for her. The clock read 2344. At 2345, she would step outside, pose for pictures, and do a quick video interview. At 0000 local time, midnight, she would climb into the jet and begin her checklists. Wellington would take off at 0030, when Jennifer started her engines. Jennifer's takeoff time was 0045.

She had pouted to Wellington about only Air Force photographers and reporters at the hangar. Wellington assured her as soon as the program was declassified, the pictures would be released. With the public release, television and magazine articles would quickly follow.

The digital clock hit forty-five. Jennifer took a deep breath, exhaled, and opened the door, her smile as radiant as an actress on the red carpet. Light bulbs flashed as a group of twenty to thirty people—photographers, TRENCOR employees, and Air Force maintenance personnel—stood outside her door clapping. She smiled, waved, and posed for the camera. It was as if she were a movie star making her big debut. It might not have been professional to pose as she did, but today was her big day.

SHERRI SPENT THE afternoon at the sheriff's office, filling out a report about the helicopter. They looked at her like she was crazy, but quite frankly, she was tired of people shooting at her. Jason refused to go, telling her he would deny any knowledge of the event. She knew that wouldn't cut it legally, and the bullet holes in his truck bed would refute his stance, but she chose to honor his wishes. Without Jason as a witness and his truck as evidence, Sherri came off as a kook. She swapped out rental vehicles and changed hotels in case she was the intended target.

After taking a hot shower, she fell asleep for three hours, waking to the sound of her alarm. She dressed quickly and drove to Edwards. The sun had set over five hours ago, and darkness hung over the high desert of California. Less than two percent moon illumination was present, with no stars visible. She was fortunate Brent had sent her the schedule of the test flight. The fact she still had not been able to reach Brent troubled her. It had been three days since they last talked, and the comments he made could have put them both in danger.

Sherri Davis sat in her parking spot outside the front gate of Rosamond Boulevard for the last hour. The runway was located to the northeast, over a mile away. When the jet took off, she would be able to see it with the binoculars she brought with her. A jet took off every fifteen minutes. There was a constant presence of jet aircraft in the air. Most likely to lull any observers into complacency. Glancing at her watch, she saw it was eleven-thirty pm. The information Brent gave her said the F-2000 would take off at forty-five minutes after midnight.

Pulling out her phone, she dialed Brent's number. Still no answer. Sherri had a bad feeling about Brent and about this flight. Brent had explained some of the problems they had with this aircraft. For the first time, Sherri wondered if the jet would be able to fly.

THE WASHOUT HE FOLLOWED led away from the road, up to the fence south of the main runway. Occasionally, the security police drove by, shining their spotlights on the fence, but he could see them coming and hid until they passed. Dust caked his body as he perspired incessantly, his constant rolling around in the sand causing the fine granules to stick to his clothes.

Dane trudged back to his car, removing the camera and tripod. He wasn't sure when this mystery aircraft would show up, but he needed to record it. He would have to hold the night-vision monocular he brought with him up to the camera lens to get the mystery jet on film.

Spending the last thirty-six hours devouring the information he had stolen from Sherri's laptop was strenuous work. He felt like a jerk for stealing the data, but such was life in the journalism world. That which one isn't given, one must steal. Or make up. It didn't matter to Dane. He did struggle internally with the lack of success in his life. He was sincere about what he'd told Sherri before he stole the data from her. He really was sorry for the things he'd done and the way he had treated her, but this world was about survival. Dane knew he was on his way out if he didn't come up with something big. Fortunately, he discovered this secret test flight listed in Sherri's notes. He praised himself for sorting the documents by date. Her set of notes, while incoherent and scrambled, focused on this event. The secret test flight information was the newest document on the ThumbDrive. He would know soon if it was accurate.

More interesting was why Sherri came to California in the first place; Saudi Arabians running around all over the country. What was that about? And why did she stop pursuing that story? Dane determined first thing tomorrow, he would start reading those files earnestly.

The tripod was stable on the rock-hard sand surface by the fence. With the small video camera and tripod set up, he pointed it toward the runway. Dane decided to tape the event, then do a quick storyline in front of the camera, describing what he saw. His producer coordinated with the local affiliate to come over that night and use their editing equipment for an early morning broadcast. A college intern named Debbie would let him in the building to use their equipment. His producer in Tulsa stood by, waiting for the product to push it nationally if Dane's claims were true. All he could do now was wait.

67

May 29, 2001

THE F-2000 SAT INSIDE the hangar attached to a tow vehicle pointed toward the door. Jennifer approached the jet and saw Daniel Kirby strapped in the seat behind hers, wearing his helmet with his oxygen mask hanging to the side. When she climbed into the jet, the lighting switched from fluorescent white to NVG green. It cost a small fortune to rig these lights, but TRENCOR— really Wellington—convinced the Air Force it was necessary.

Jennifer adjusted herself into her seat as the crew chief climbed up the ladder to snap her harness into the ACES II ejection seat. He reached across to her right side to strap her in but paused. Jennifer smiled brightly at him.

"Ma'am, you'll need to buckle that," he said.

"I'll get to it in a minute . . . unless you'd like to take care of it for me."

"Uh, okay," he said. The young staff sergeant reached across the cockpit, connecting her harness.

"Tighter," she said, grinning at him.

The crew chief tightened her strap.

"Thank you," she said.

The crew chief grinned like a schoolboy and climbed back down the ladder. Jennifer put on her helmet, plugged in her oxygen and comm cord, then proceeded with her checks.

"Welcome aboard, Major Walton. Please don't tease any more enlisted personnel. It degrades the status of the officer corps," Kirby said from the back.

"Screw you, Kirby," she said.

"We tried that once already."

"Oh, I guess we did. Sorry, I must have forgot." She enjoyed joking with Kirby, but he was right. Flirting with the enlisted troops was something she needed to stop. She was a field grade officer. And when Wellington divorced his wife, she would be the wife of a retired general.

Jennifer finished her checks, nodding at the crew chief. The tow vehicle cranked its motor, and the NVG lighting dimmed further. Massive doors to the hangar strained to slide open, and the F-2000 was towed onto the ramp. Two crew chiefs unlatched the tow bar from the nose gear of the F-2000 and ensured the vehicle was well clear of the jet before giving Jennifer the thumbs up.

Jennifer began the "Before Starting Engines" checklist, meticulously accomplishing each step of the flow. Moving on to the "Starting Engines" checklist, she quickly accomplished the first five steps, then signaled the crew chief she would start the JFS. It spun up, and she signaled "two" with her fingers. She hoped the crew chief could see her through the faint green glow exuding from the cockpit. The crew chief pointed at the engine on the right side of the jet with His left hand and bent his right arm ninety degrees, pointing up and making a twirling motion.

The throttle easily slid into position, and she pushed the start button. RPM on the powerful engine spun as the fuel flow came to life. Ignition was instantaneous as the exhaust gas temperature (EGT) rose to the green. The engine hummed at a steady beat as she reviewed the last two checklist items for the engine. When she finished, she signaled the crew chief for the number one engine on the left side, and the process repeated.

After engine start, Jennifer accomplished the pre-taxi checklist items. It required numerous built-in-tests (BIT) for the computer system, checking the accuracy of the FMS. Operational readiness tests (ORT) for each of the various navigation and sensor systems were completed. Kirby worked feverishly in the back, monitoring Jennifer's checks and re-running them on a separate network, to both record the inputs and to verify the accuracy.

"Ready to go in back?" she asked when she finished her checks.

"Affirmative."

Jennifer keyed the mic, requesting her taxi clearance. She motioned for the crew chief to remove the chocks he placed under the right main landing gear. Once clear, he waved the jet to move forward. Jennifer pushed the power up, and the F-2000 taxied to the active runway.

The crew chief saluted crisply, and she returned the salute. The F-2000 left the ramp and taxied onto the parallel taxiway into the darkness.

THE SOUND OF A DIFFERENT set of engines alerted him. It was a . . . softer sound, if you can say that about jet engines. Dane scrambled to turn on the video camera and peered through the viewfinder, attempting to see the jet. He pulled the NVG monocular out of his pocket, placing it in front of the camera's lens. After a brief search, he found the jet on the taxiway and pressed "RECORD."

From this distance, he had difficulty making out specific attributes of the jet. Dane continuously adjusted the zoom and focus, trying to get the best picture possible. After several minutes, the picture became clearer. He shifted his weight as the outline of the jet grew sharp and clear through the green image on his video screen. The jet didn't resemble anything he had ever seen.

He kept the night vision monocular in place until the jet made a ninety-degree turn onto the runway. The heat from the exhaust washed out the monocular, making the small screen turn white. When the jet turned and the fuselage blocked more of the exhaust, the jet came into better focus. The jet settled on the runway and advanced its throttles, washing the image out in the viewfinder again. Dane removed the monocular and refocused the video camera to take the raw video. The picture was not as good as the night vision footage, but the contrast of the two pictures would make for a great broadcast. Dane smiled as the jet lit the afterburners and raced down the runway.

SHERRI SAT OUTSIDE the main gate by the Century Series static displays. She pulled out her cell phone to call Brent. Again, no answer. Quickly, she dialed Steven.

A gruff, sleepy voice answered after four rings. "Sherri, do you know what time it is?"

"Hello, Steven," she said. "It's almost one in the morning."

"No, it's almost 4:00 am, that's what time it is. What's going on?"

"I'm sorry, I'm desperate. I'm outside Edwards Air Force Base. A top-secret jet is about to take off and I have reason to believe the jet may crash. Intentionally, of course."

There was silence from the other side of the phone.

"Is someone else monitoring this phone call?"

"Probably. Hell, I hope so. Steven, don't you have any contacts that can stop this flight?"

Again there was another pause.

"Sherri, if I did know someone who could do that, how am I going to explain that I know about a top-secret test taking place across the country as we speak?"

"Are you saying you won't help me?"

"No, not at all. I'm saying I *can't* help you. I don't know who to call . . . and if I did, I wouldn't know what to say. What exactly are you expecting to see tonight?"

"I'm not sure. I—"

"Well, call me tomorrow and let me know what happens. If the jet crashes, I can help you with the story," Steven said as he hung up the phone.

He wasn't going to be any help. Not at this time of night anyway. She wished she'd gotten Jason's contact information. He would be a good person to talk to about this—if he was willing. He seemed like a strong-willed individual, but he might not appreciate her knowing about this project.

After thirty minutes of waiting, she heard a different type of engine start in the distance. Through her binoculars, she saw a jet taxi to the runway. This had to be the jet. The time matched her documents. She noticed that she hadn't seen a jet take off or land in the last fifteen minutes as she monitored the taxiing jet.

The sound was deafening as a jet flew overhead at about two hundred feet. It headed straight for the runway and made a wide 360-degree turn. At first Sherri was confused; for a moment, she thought someone was attacking the classified test jet.

Halfway through its turn, the jet on the runway pushed its throttles into afterburner and the massive flames shot out the back of the jet. The F-2000 began its takeoff roll, accelerating every second as the second plane turned back to follow the F-2000 through the takeoff. From where she sat, it seemed to be a very well-choreographed ballet.

Sherri wasn't sure what she expected to see tonight. Based on what she read in Ming's files, the jet might not work. But in the back of her mind, something told her it might be more sinister than simply a malfunction. It might be sabotage.

68

JENNIFER BREATHED A SIGH of relief as the F-2000 lifted off the ground. *Not* getting airborne had been her biggest fear after the last test when the F-2000 accidentally took off. Passing fifty feet above the ground, she raised the landing gear, which imbedded themselves into the body of the jet. Once the light in the landing gear handle went out, she raised the flaps and lowered the nose to accelerate to climb-out speed.

Off her right wing, Wellington hung out in route position, five hundred feet away and slightly aft. His role was to stay at a distance and monitor. His jet had a video camera mounted on the dash next to his HUD. When they reached 10,000 feet and started the test cards, he would videotape the F-2000 in flight using a specially adapted camera with a night-vision lens.

When the airspeed reached 300 knots, she raised the nose to climb at 2,000 feet per minute to the 10,000-foot operational altitude for the first portion of the test cards. Accomplishing the test cards would take about fifteen minutes. The next set of test cards would take place at 20,000 feet, with a third set at 30,000 feet, if she had enough fuel.

Jennifer worked her way through each set of test cards. The jet performed flawlessly at each of the three different altitudes. Kirby monitored his equipment during each maneuver, tracking the results on the test cards. They wrapped up the final test, and she began accomplishing her descent checklist when the cockpit went dark.

"What happened up there?" Kirby said.

"Not sure. I'm checking."

"Is it an electrical failure?"

"No. Stand by."

"How do you know? Everything back here shut off."

"We have power, stand by," she said, pulling out her in-flight guide which contained non-standard checklist procedures for different malfunctions. Jennifer could sense the nervousness in his voice, but she had bigger problems to deal with at the moment.

"How can we have power? Nothing back here works," Kirby said.

"Can you hear me?"

"Yes, dammit, I can hear you."

"Then we have electrical power. Now shut up and let me work this."

Jennifer pushed the end of the small finger light secured to her right index finger. A green beam shot out and she searched around the cockpit for any sign of malfunction. The circuit breakers were in place. She reset the main AC power circuit breaker out of habit, but nothing happened. She recycled the power to everything that had a switch in the aircraft. Nothing. A quick scan of the in-flight guide provided no helpful information.

"I guess we're done here, Kirby. The damn jet isn't working."

"Are we going to bail out?"

"Not yet. I'm taking the jet back to the field to land."

"Oh."

Jennifer pulled out a flashlight, shining it at Wellington in the TRENCOR F-16. He shined a light back, indicating he tried to contact them via radio and received no answer. She knew he would now coordinate her return with ATC and the tower. She accomplished her checks and signaled Wellington again. The F-16 slid out front as Jennifer moved the F-2000 behind him to follow him back to the field.

SHERRI LEANED AGAINST her car, sipping on a Coke. She wasn't sure what she was waiting for—a fireball, a missile launch, or heck, anything. She simply waited. After hanging up with Steven an hour ago, she sat frustrated and bored. It wasn't until after he hung up that she remembered to tell him about the helicopter shooting at her and Jason. It was probably better she hadn't, as Steven had a tendency to be overprotective. Pulling out her cell phone, she stared at the number in the display. Hitting the green button, she tried Brent's number once again with the same result.

Her time frame was an hour to an hour and a half. She knew most fighters didn't carry much more fuel, and a test flight might even be shorter. Approaching the one-hour mark, the darkness rattled as the sound of the two jets screamed overhead. The F-2000 and its chase aircraft flew toward the field. It was too dark to make out the design of the F-2000, but she knew that was it. The jets flew several hundred feet above the ground, slower than when the jet had previously flown overhead.

One aircraft landed as the second jet pushed its power up, making a climbing turn to the west. Sherri breathed a sigh of relief that the flight had been uneventful. Based on what Brent said and what she had been able to read from the ThumbDrive, she expected something to happen. Perhaps this was all just a waste of time.

69

May 29, 2001

JASON SIPPED HIS COFFEE on the couch watching television when when the story broke. The early morning broadcast had national coverage, and the fact that FOX News had picked the story up from the network proved how big it had become.

"This is Dane Robinson, TV News Reporter for WTSR, the Taaaser from Tulsa. I'm in Southern California on special assignment. We've tracked the alleged Russian agent, Jason Conrad, to the Air Force's top-secret test base, Edwards Air Force Base, located in the Mojave Desert northeast of Los Angeles.

"Tonight, we witnessed the latest bit of technology being tested by the Air Force. It's called the F-2000. It's a sixth-generation fighter jet possessing capabilities far beyond any jet in the world. What is Jason Conrad's role in this program? That remains to be seen. Conrad was seen by this reporter leaving the building of the main contractor, TRENCOR Industries, just days ago . . ."

Jason's mind wandered as he leaned back on the couch. How did that SOB find out about the F-2000? How did he know about the flight last night and get in position to videotape the jet? Jason knew it wouldn't be long before the commander called him to his office to explain himself.

He rose, plodded into the bathroom, and turned on the shower. When he closed the door to the bathroom, he noticed Kathy's lingerie still hanging on the hook inside. She hadn't left his thoughts since she disappeared once again, but these weren't the same thoughts he'd had over the past six years. He wondered where she was now—halfway back to Moscow, no doubt. At least Dane didn't mention her in the broadcast. He was heartbroken about Kathy's true identity. *Always trust your instincts*, his father told him. Ever since Kathy showed up again, he'd known something was different. He didn't have the feelings he should have, and now he knew why.

Jason stepped under the shower, the warm water relaxing his sore muscles. He'd spoken to no one about the helicopter shooting at his truck. Since this broadcast was aired, he doubted he would ever bring up the helicopter.

After a quick shower, Jason checked his phone. He had four missed messages: the wing commander, his squadron commander, Major Walton, and Jeremiah Wellington. He figured he would start at the top and work his way down the list.

SHERRI GLARED AT THE TELEVISION and her heart sank. Who is Dane's source? How could this moron still have a job? Why the hell was he exposing national secrets on nationwide TV? And how was he not getting sued by Conrad? She was fortunate Dane didn't name her as a partner, which was possible as much as he stretched the truth.

Turning off the television, she walked to the lobby to get a cup of coffee. When she arrived, she couldn't believe what she saw. Dane Robinson stood in the lobby in front of a group of guests and employees, telling his tale of last night's investigation. The ass was even signing autographs. What looked like a young college girl was coordinating the activities in the lobby. She shook her head. No wonder everyone was starting to distrust journalists.

Sherri walked to the coffee pot, picking up a cup.

"Sherri, my dear," Dane said from across the lobby. "Come celebrate our discovery! Everyone, this is my partner, Sherri Davis." Dane put his arm around the young girl as they meandered toward Sherri. "Sherri, this is the intern from our local affiliate, Debbie. She has been enormously helpful with my big story."

The intern stuck her hand out to shake, but Sherri ignored it. She was angry. She took a deep breath and turned to Dane.

"You idiot. First of all, I'm not your partner. There is no way in hell

I'd ever associate with someone like you, personally or professionally. Second, you're probably going to prison after that report. Third, how the hell did you find out about the test? It was wired pretty tight, yet you knew exactly when and where to go."

The previously exuberant crowd around Dane lost their enthusiasm for their pseudo-celebrity, looking back and forth between the two journalists. Dane picked up on the change in mood. He surveyed his surroundings, eyeing the silent fans standing in the lobby, slowly turning his gaze back to Sherri.

The bellman entered the sliding glass doors. "Your car is right out front, Mr. Robinson," he said, handing Dane his car keys.

Sliding closer to her, he whispered in her ear, "I found out from you. You shouldn't leave your laptop unattended in a public place." Sherri's right hand came above her chest, her fingers spread out beneath her collar bones, her mouth partially open as the realization of what he said sunk in. She felt betrayed, robbed . . . violated. Her eyes narrowed and her fists clenched as Dane grabbed the intern by the hand and hurried out to his car.

THE TWO MEN STOOD silently as the workers gathered the bags in the sparse living room. There were twelve large suitcases and eight smaller ones. One by one, the bags were carried outside to the awaiting vehicles. Amanda sauntered down the curved staircase into the large, empty foyer. Her husband stood in the living room with Li Zhong, watching the last of the luggage being packed away. The workers scurried back and forth gathering the bags as Amanda entered the living room and stood next to her husband.

"I'm going to miss this house," Amanda said, rubbing her hand against the small of Ming's back.

"Fear not, my dear, everything will be rebuilt however you would like when we return home," Ming said.

"I was starting to feel like this was home."

"Home is where the heart is, my dear. My heart is in China."

"And my heart is with you," she said, smiling at him. "I received a phone call from Caleb Nelson's attorney today."

Ming raised both eyebrows as his head turned slowly toward his wife.

"He wanted to know if I'd spoken to his client since he left for the Bahamas. I told him I had not. Nelson apparently bought a couple of new cars before he signed the deal with us and never made a payment. The car dealership went to his attorney to collect, and after some investigation, discovered Caleb Nelson had disappeared and all of his money had been removed from his account. I told him we haven't spoken since he left the porch on his prior home," she said with a subdued smile.

"Thank you, my dear. That is most excellent work. Mr. Nelson proved to be most problematic. Now, not so much," Ming said. He turned to Li Zhong. "What of Operation Dragonfly?"

"The lab is neutralized. After tonight, there will be no issues."

"It's a shame," Ming pondered. "Cloud seeding was an interesting plan to address China's water shortage. Perhaps we can accomplish it back home. What about the reporter?"

"We've tracked him to his hotel," Li Zhong said with an expressionless glance at Amanda. "He is staying at the Best Western in California City."

"Eliminate him," Ming said. "The Department of Defense will be interested in this man. You need to take care of him before they get any information."

"I understand, Mr. Ming."

"What about our Middle Eastern friends?"

"Everything will be ready to go. The team will arrive this evening to set up. We should have no complications."

"Good, make sure of it. What of General Jingguo?"

He paused. "General Jingguo and his team left for Los Angeles early this morning. Most of their work has been incinerated; the rest will be destroyed tonight."

"And the Russian?" Amanda said.

"She is in place at TRENCOR. After tonight, she will be identified as the culprit. Unfortunately for her, she will be unable to escape and succumbed to her own devices."

"Very good," Ming said. "We will see you this afternoon at the airport."

Li Zhong nodded as he left the sparse living room. Ming turned to his wife, "Amanda, contact Mr. Wellington. Have him meet us at the airport this evening. It's time for total withdrawal. We'll leave for Los Angeles, then Hong Kong."

"Is he going with us?" Amanda said as she rose from the couch.

"Absolutely not," Ming chuckled. "We have a great deal invested in this aircraft. Beijing requests we salvage the jet by moving it to Mexico. We'll fly it from Mexico to Venezuela and put it on a ship back to China."

"Do you expect Wellington to fly the jet?" she said.

"Either him or his tramp test pilot. I suspect they'll both run. They'll realize they face a lifetime in jail when I explain what they've been involved in over the last several years. No one will believe they were ignorant."

JASON LEFT THE wing commander's office with his rear end intact. His was a case of guilty until proven innocent. Although he had nothing to do with the broadcast earlier this morning, he was the primary suspect. He was the only member of the DOD mentioned, and the reporter identified him at TRENCOR. Why didn't he report the run-in with the reporter, the general asked? Hell, he didn't know he should report everyone he met. Jason knew he had some obstacles to overcome with this issue, but these type of problems were nothing new to him. What the wing commander really needed to worry about was how a reporter got close enough to his runway to videotape a top-secret jet.

Something caught Jason's eye during the meeting, though—the wing commander had a gold model aircraft of the F-2000, exactly like the ones in Wellington's office and Jennifer's apartment. That was a lot of money sitting on the wing commander's shelf. Jason wondered if he actually knew what he had, or if it had been given to him to blackmail him in the future.

Climbing in his truck, he left the base, heading north to TRENCOR Industries. No doubt there would be a large group of reporters at the facility, all with questions about the F-2000.

When he reached TRENCOR, news vans from every network and cable news outlet were parked outside. For the first time he could remember, security guards kept people off the grounds of the facility. Jason showed his credentials to the guard working the entrance, who waved him through. Hopefully, the reporters would be gone by the time he finished training later this evening.

DANE ROLLED OVER IN BED and glanced at the clock. It was ten minutes until six in the evening. He woke up hungry. He heard the intern in the bathroom, and a smile formed on his face when he saw her clothes on the floor. His initial feeling of guilt about taking advantage of the young girl disappeared quickly, but hey, that was the broadcast business. He heard the toilet flush, and the girl stepped out of the bathroom. Dane leaned over to the nightstand and hit "PLAY" on his portable CD player. For the twentieth time today, he played Britney Spears's *Oops! . . . I Did it Again.* The teenage pop sensation's song echoed in the small room. Dane was surprised how excited the intern became when he told her she resembled Britney Spears. After that, it was only a matter of time before Dane talked her into bed. Like Bo Derek's use of Ravel's *Bolero* in the film *10*, Britney's song was their tantric tune.

The intern bounced across the room, hopping back on top of Dane.

"How about I give you some money, and you get us Chinese food?" Dane said.

The intern climbed off of Dane as quickly as she climbed on.

"Okay," she said, smiling as she put on her clothes.

Dane reached for his wallet and gave her two twenties.

The young intern took the money and grabbed the keys. She bent over, kissed Dane on the forehead, and bounced for the door. She wasn't the sexiest girl in town, but he had needs. She kind of looked like Britney. Until he could get Sherri to get over her attitude, the intern would have to do.

Swinging his legs off the bed, Dane stood, stretching his back. He opened the curtains to see the sun nestled in the mountains. His window from the second floor had a pleasant view of the sunset, and he could see his rental car in the parking lot. Despite the desert plains, beauty could be found here just like in the flatlands of Oklahoma.

Glancing at his idle cell phone on the nightstand, he waited to hear from his producers about his next move. Exposing the jet was big, and he needed direction from the top from here on out. The lawyers were already working overtime in defense of the station's stance with Dane.

After a minute, the young intern popped into view, skipping to the car. Dane waved, but she didn't see him. She climbed in the car and shut the door; Dane shifted his view back to the mountains.

The flash got his attention first, followed quickly by the noise, and the concussion. Dane watched in horror as his rental car exploded in flames.

70

May 29, 2001

THE SUN WAS SETTING in the mountains—a kaleidoscope of red and orange, gradually transitioning into a deep blue beautiful sky to the east. Sherri Davis parked along the northern portion of the compound, plodding at least a half mile before finding a weak spot in the bottom of the fence. An occasional car passed her, but she had no trouble hiding as they approached. The journalists who showed up at TRENCOR earlier in the day had found it to be a non-story, at least for now. They saw the same thing as everyone else—a huge, yet basically empty, complex, which made Dane's story seem less than accurate.

Sherri knelt by the weak spot in the bottom of the fence, tugging fiercely. She determined she would have enough room to wiggle through the gap. Laying on her back, she slowly maneuvered herself under the fence. She did the same at the second fence. Pulling a ribbon from her pocket, she tied it on the fence so she could find her spot when she returned.

In the distance, the outline of the simulator building stood majestically on the horizon. She had hiked toward the building for five minutes when she heard the familiar sound of a helicopter flying in her direction. Instinctively, she dropped to the ground as the helicopter passed by her right side about a half a mile away, about three hundred feet above the ground. She prayed she wasn't seen; she had nowhere to go if the helicopter started shooting at her.

She determined she was unseen as the helicopter flew to the TRENCOR facility, settling on the helipad. Sherri stood up, straining for a better view, but it was too far away and too dark for her to see who exited the helicopters. The helicopter shut off its engine. Whoever had shown up planned on staying a while.

DANE SAT ON HIS BED, his heart beating excessively fast. He never thought he would have a heart attack; perhaps this was what it was like knowing you were about to die. Someone had planted a bomb in his car, killing the young intern. Only Dane realized the bomb wasn't meant for her—it was meant for him. Someone wants him dead.

It had to be related to his broadcast. But how? It didn't take him long to decide it really didn't matter. It was time to leave this hellhole. Dane called a cab as he gathered his clothes. A small crowd had gathered around the burning vehicle, increasing in size by the minute. Three minutes after the explosion, the first police car showed up. Within two minutes, five more showed up, just before the first fire truck. When the second fire truck arrived, Dane was out front, climbing into the cab.

"Where to?" the cabbie asked.

Dane considered his options. He should go to the nearest police station and report what happened but after his report last night and what just happened to the intern in his car, he had no idea who to trust. Better to beg forgiveness than to ask permission. Even if it's from jail.

"The airport," Dane replied.

"Mojave?"

"No," Dane said, "Los Angeles."

THE QUIET AND DESOLATE perimeter around the TRENCOR building reminded Sherri of a graveyard. She approached the building from the rear without being detected. Reaching the loading dock, she climbed onto the platform, testing each of the doors. All of them were locked.

Working her way around the west side of the building, she eventually found an unlocked side exit. Sherri slipped into the building and found herself in a stairwell. She climbed up the stairs to the second floor. The door at the top was also unlocked. She cracked the door, peering inside.

Nothing. No lights, no furniture, no walls, no nothing. She opened the door further as she entered the vast, empty space.

What the hell? Where was everything? Was this what Brent referred to when they spoke? Was this what Georgiana discovered, causing someone to murder her? This was a shell of a company, there was nothing here.

THE GULFSTREAM SAT OUTSIDE the hangar, engines running, the crew waiting for their passengers. David and Amanda Ming waited for Wellington to arrive. Ming didn't normally wait for people, but for his final day in Southern California, he deemed it necessary.

After a fifteen-minute wait, Li Zhong escorted both Wellington and Jennifer toward Ming. Wellington wore a business suit, but Jennifer wore her signature spandex miniskirt, cut-off top, and high heels.

"Mr. Ming," Wellington said, reaching out his hand, "I'm sorry we're late. We were . . . working."

"I'm sure," Ming replied. "I'll be blunt, Jeremiah. There's a conspiracy involving TRENCOR Industries."

Wellington paused, tilting his head to the side.

"Conspiracy? What the hell are you talking about?"

"The F-2000 is a phantom program. The jet will never meet the specs it is advertised to meet. It—"

"Hold on one second, Mr. Ming," Wellington said, putting up both hands as if to stop Ming's train of thought. "We've just had our first successful test flight. We can—"

Ming held up his hand, and Wellington stopped talking.

"The F-2000 is the result of over a decade of planning. The concept was to create a jet so perfect, the United States Air Force would beg for the jet to be built. And we built it. Only, the jet is designed to fail. The US government has spent a quarter of a trillion dollars on this project. What do they have to show for it? Nothing. One simulator that doesn't work and an unproven jet that will ultimately disintegrate in flight."

Wellington's body slumped as his brain tried to process what Ming told him. Jennifer's face contorted as the realization sank in. "Are you saying . . . are you saying this has all—I mean the malfunctions have all been intentional?" Wellington said.

"Yes."

"Who . . . what . . . who's responsible for this?"

"You are, Jeremiah," Ming said.

Wellington's head snapped up. "Me?"

"Yes, you. You are the Air Force liaison working for a front company for the Chinese government for the last six years. Your compensation has been far above the industry standard for someone in your position. You are the one who testified before the Senate Armed Services Committee to get approval for the no-bid contract. You are the one who testified before the House Appropriations Committee, several times, requesting more funding. You are the one who earned a $250,000 bonus every time Congress approved your request. You are the one who worked the backdoor negotiation with Century Aero-Bot to acquire their Integrated Sensory Package. A one-of-a-kind system used to kill your lead test pilot in order for your mistress to take his place."

Wellington began to tremble. He looked back at Jennifer as she sobbed in deep gasps.

"You, Jeremiah, are the one who recruited Captain Jason Conrad, who arrived with his girlfriend, who, as it turns out, is a Russian agent. And you, Jeremiah, have the contacts who will be seen destroying our simulator facility this evening with the Russian agent."

"You son of a bitch!" he screamed. Wellington's body shook as he started to move toward Ming. Li Zhong moved to the side, where Wellington could see him point a 9 mm at his head. Amanda had pulled a snub-nosed revolver out of her purse, as well, pointing it at his chest.

"There's no need for violence, Mr. Wellington," Ming said. "There is a way out for you."

Wellington stopped. He had worked for David Ming long enough to know there was always an out. Ming always had an angle. "Go on."

"This time tomorrow, both of you will be considered traitors who will no doubt go to jail for a very long time. We've put a great deal of effort into the jet your country paid for, but our government has the capability to repair the 'flaws' induced into our little jet. We want to take it home."

"Home? To China?"

"Yes."

"It can't fly that far. Anyway, who's going to fly it? Dipshit here?" he said, pointing to Li Zhong.

Ming ignored the insult to Li Zhong, who still showed no expression. "No, you are. My country is willing to offer you political asylum. We've already emptied your bank account and placed your money in an account in Hong Kong. We know you will have no Problem leaving your wife. And you can bring your tramp with you," he said, pointing to Jennifer.

"What do we need to do?" Wellington said.

Ming handed a slip of paper to Wellington. "Tonight, you steal the F-2000."

CAUTIOUSLY, SHERRI WALKED through the empty second floor of the TRENCOR building. It started to make sense. These guys were not what they claimed to be. She wasn't sure who they were or what their goal was, but it wasn't building the next-generation fighter jet. She needed to find proof of chemical weapons in this building, but clearly it wasn't on this floor. When she arrived at the reception area for the second floor, she felt as if she were on a movie set. It stood in stark contrast to the desolate space she had just passed through.

Sherri elected to take the stairwell to the first floor. She pulled a small flashlight out of her coat pocket, piercing the darkness. Empty. Carefully, she worked her way to the first floor and opened the door. A darkened empty hallway lay before her. To the right, offices and the reception area; to the left, more offices and the entrance to the simulator bay. It was a set of double doors with a swipe-card lock and a large sign overhead that said "Classified in Progress."

Sherri crept along the hallway toward the reception area. A sign on one of the doors read "Executive Suite." She continued past it toward the empty lobby.

Relaxing for the first time, Sherri concluded she was alone in the vast building.

A flash of light outside, however, got her attention, and Sherri noticed three vehicles driving toward the front of the facility.

Damn.

Turning around, she hustled down the hallway. She tried the handle of the door labeled "Executive Suite." The door opened smoothly, and Sherri slid inside. Reaching for the light switch, she stopped herself because she realized the light would show underneath the door. The last thing she wanted was for the men in the vehicles to come in here. She grabbed the deadbolt lever and turned it, locking the door.

She stood in Ming's reception area and pulled out her flashlight again. A series of offices lined another hallway; at the end, another large area with a secretary's desk. Next to the desk, a door with intricate carvings highlighting the trim. The plaque on the door said it all: "David Ming, CEO".

71

May 29, 2001

HE HAD BEEN ALONE for well over two hours. Jason climbed back into the simulator for his third iteration of drills. His practice of coming in during off-hours to use the simulator was paying off. The procedures were becoming second nature. He had memorized "the flow", the sequential process of preparing the jet for engine start. Not only could he do it without his checklist, he could do it quickly.

The last TRENCOR employees left for the day after his first round. The third would be like the second, with no motion. That was fine with him—Jason was at a point where he needed repetition, not realism. Three times should be good. He learned long ago that a pilot doesn't practice until he gets it perfect—he keeps practicing until he starts making mistakes. Then it's time to stop.

Closing the canopy to the simulator, the darkness enveloped him as began his routine for the third time that night.

WELLINGTON AND JENNIFER stood in the hangar, watching the Gulfstream taxi to the runway for takeoff. Neither one said a word. Li Zhong stood to the side of the hangar, waiting for their decision.

Jennifer scooted closer to Wellington and asked, "What just happened?"

Wellington glanced at her before looking back at the Gulfstream climbing in the distance.

"I believe we were identified as fools," he said.

"We've got to tell someone."

"No," he said, turning as he grabbed her arm. "Ming is right. We will go down for this. We'll go to prison for a very long time."

"What are we supposed to do?" She cried as mascara streaked her cheeks.

Wellington pondered her comment. If they emptied his bank account . . . that was over three million dollars they moved to an account in Hong Kong. He could make a call and have a contact meet him in Mexico . . .

"Jennifer, darling," he said. For the first time, her stress wavered; a subtle smile showed on her face. "We can start over. We can leave all of this," he said, gesturing with his arms out.

"But I'm supposed to be famous," she said, the slight smile disappearing as fast as it showed, her eyes welling up and tears flowing. "I'm the face of the new Air Force. I'm going to be on TV and in magazines."

"Sweetheart, if we stay, you're going to be on TV and in magazines, but not in the way you want." He let go of her arm as he paced back and forth across the hangar floor. "Damn it, I'm not going to jail! Our trial will be the biggest story in years. It will dwarf the 'blue dress' scandal and O.J.'s murder trial, and we *will* lose. We will get no top cover from anyone in this administration. No doubt they'll accelerate the process to get us in jail quicker."

"I don't want to go to jail," she wailed. Her mascara streaked down her face, painting a gruesome portrait of a distressed woman.

Wellington hated women crying; it annoyed him. He wanted to backhand her, but the plan he formulated needed her. *He* needed her.

"Jennifer, darling, this is our chance to be together. Forever."

"Oh, yeah. *Now* you're willing to leave your wife? That's great."

"Look, we have a very small window of opportunity. I'm coming up with a plan. You can be a part of it, or go to jail. I refuse to go to jail. I'm no traitor, but I don't plan on spending the rest of my life trying to prove it from behind bars."

Jennifer paused. "What do you think we should do?"

"Ming has moved all of my money from my account to a Hong Kong account. That's over three million dollars and—"

"Three million dollars?"

"Yes. Now—"

"Where the hell did you get three million dollars?" she said, confused.

"I earned it. And saved it. Now, here's my plan. I'll fly the F-16, follow you to Mexico—"

"Follow me? You expect me to steal the F-2000?"

"No, darling, *we* are stealing the F-2000, but you are the one who is going to fly it. It makes sense. No one will suspect anything. If I were to try this, all kinds of alerts would go off. I'll think of something . . . a legitimate reason why we've got to move the jet tonight."

She hung her head as she considered it. "But I don't want to go to Hong Kong."

"Do you want to go to jail?"

"No."

"Look, I need to make a phone call to set this up. I can follow you to Mexico in the F-16. When we get there, I'll have my contact meet us there, and he'll find a buyer for the Falcon. We can make an easy eight million on that sale alone after we pay my middleman."

"Are you serious?"

"Hell yes, I'm serious."

"Eight million?"

"Yes, darling." He knew he laid the "sweetheart/darling" crap on kind of thick, but she needed to be persuaded. It appeared to be working. "Plus the other three. That's eleven million dollars for us to start a new life together. Or, we can go to jail."

"That's . . . appealing. I need to think about it. I—"

"Sweetheart, you can think about it as we walk to the car. If you're not on board, I'll have to go to the base myself, and you'll have to get *him* to drive you home," he said, gesturing over to Li Zhong. He knew she understood the implication.

Jennifer glimpsed over at Li Zhong briefly, then back to the ground, her hands clasped behind her back. Twisting slightly back and forth, she released her hands, bent her knees, and buried her face in her hands.

"AAAUGH! Okay, okay. I'll do it. Let's get this over with before I change my mind. I'll need to grab some things from home."

"Perfect," Wellington said, his toothy smile seemingly forced onto his face. He hugged her, lifting her off the ground.

She simpered, wiping the running mascara from her face as they walked hand in hand toward Li Zhong. Wellington gave him a thumbs up as a smile came across Li Zhong's face. Wellington realized he had never seen him smile before.

THE DARKNESS SWALLOWED her as she closed the door to
Ming's office. Sherri wasn't sure she would find proof of sarin gas in
here, but it was as good a place as any to search. The darkness made it
difficult to see, but a trace of moonlight slithered between a break in
the curtains. Sherri turned on her flashlight to navigate through the
room.

The smell hit her as she shut the door. A pungent, filthy odor, one
she was familiar with yet couldn't identify. No air conditioning or
circulation ran in the office, making the air thick and rancid. As she
scanned the dark room with her flashlight, she saw the room was
empty except for the furniture. No pictures, no vases, no paperwork.
Strange setup for an office, if it still was an office.

The smell became worse as she moved along the left wall to Ming's
desk. Could it be the gas? No, she'd be dead by now. Plus, she'd
smelled this odor before. A slight buzzing sound distracted her as she
reached the other end of the room. She could see the window partially
open between the curtains. Perhaps it explained the temperature in the
room.

Approaching the desk, she noticed the chair faced the window. She
approached the chair slowly, placed her hand on the headrest, and
shook it softly. She spun the chair around slowly and focused her
flashlight on the chair.

The top of a head rested on the back of the chair, and an arm with
the hand rested on the knee. Sherri wanted to scream, but she couldn't
make a sound. It was if her body had seized up and she no longer had
any control. She stood frozen in place for a moment until the tears
burst from her eyes; her body convulsed as she threw up next to the
desk. The buzzing were flies that had come in from outside; the smell
she recognized from Sarajevo. It was the smell of death.

Brent O'Malley sat in the chair in a pool of dried blood, his throat
sliced from ear to ear.

72

THE SIX MIDDLE EASTERN men climbed out of their cars in front of the building, entering swiftly. Each carried an olive-drab duffel bag, and three of the six had AK-47s slung around their backs. They moved in teams of two, splitting off in three different directions. Each man had a predetermined purpose. The hallway to the left contained their primary objectives: the simulator, but more importantly, the sarin gas in the lab. The almost four foot long container tube to be eliminated weighed almost eighty pounds. It would take two men to move it safely. Ensuring the gas would be fully destroyed was the main priority.

Hassan had been directed on the right type and amount of explosive to destroy the gas. His task would take the longest to set up. The container would be placed in the steel tub in the lab. He would place foaming thermite on top of the tube, which would eventually ignite the JP-8 jet fuel surrounding the container in the steel tub. The temperature of the foaming thermite would reach 2700° C at its peak. That would be enough to destroy most, if not all, of the chemical weapon. This would occur five minutes before the rest of the bombs exploded throughout the building. Theoretically, the ensuing fire would destroy any sarin gas not broken down from the foaming thermite. If any sarin gas remained after the explosions, there was no telling where it would go.

It bothered Hassan that all of the effort for this plan had been put together for years. They were so close. Now with the first sign of trouble, their liaisons were destroying everything and running back to China. Hassan didn't understand these godless men. Allah would surely punish them. After tonight, he would be done with them. They would head to Los Angeles and then south, through San Diego into Mexico. He pulled out his map of the building and followed the directions to the sim bay.

SHERRI SLID OUT OF Ming's empty office and leaned against the wall, tears running down her cheeks. Now she knew why she hadn't heard from Brent for a couple of days. She sat on the floor with her head between her knees, taking deep breaths.

After several minutes, she had herself under control. She scanned her surroundings as the flashlight cut a solid chunk out of the darkness. Sherri pushed herself back up the wall, and her flashlight beam bounced around as it moved along. For the first time she realized how much she shook. She was terrified. After finding Brent, she was clearly aware she was in danger as long as she remained in the building. Now, someone else had entered TRENCOR Industries. Whoever arrived in the cars could be heading here any minute.

Her light moved around the room, desperately searching for another way out. Then she saw it between a set of bookcases, an obscure door made of the same expensive wood as the paneling and bookcases. Sherri approached it and tried the handle. It opened smoothly. Her flashlight cut inside the pitch-black doorway, revealing a very different environment. The space was a hallway, with large tiles lining the floor and the walls consisting of a heavy, opaque Plexiglas from three feet off the floor to the ceiling. This might be the place to search for the sarin gas. Going out the way she entered the hallway wasn't an option, so she pressed forward.

Slipping through the doorway, she tiptoed at a steady pace. The hallway led her straight to a laboratory. The door here was unlocked like many of the others, and Sherri wondered why a military contractor housing a top-secret aircraft would have such lax security in general, and no security at all tonight. She pushed thoughts of her own safety from her mind as she entered the room.

The lab contained work stations with Bunsen burners, sinks, and microscopes. The sterile room was filled with various beakers and test tubes, chemicals stacked on the shelves, and most importantly, biohazard signs posted everywhere. Why was there a biochemical lab in an aerospace contractor's simulator building? Brent was right. This was totally out of the ordinary. It appeared everyone had moved out of TRENCOR except the scientists. As far as Sherri could tell, it looked like a functioning laboratory.

Sweeping her light across the room, she found a hard plastic container sitting in the middle of the room. She approached it slowly, as if not to disturb it. Holding the flashlight between her teeth, she released the clasps on each side of the plastic box and lifted the lid. Inside was a long metal tube, ten inches in diameter and about four feet long, with a nozzle on one end and a connector at the other. It sat nestled in its foam cutout within the container. Her hand moved forward touch it, but an unseen force made her hesitate—that feeling one gets when the hairs on the back of your neck stand up.

Examining the tube more closely without touching it, she found a small placard mounted by the nozzle. Sarin gas. Sherri recoiled in fear as if she'd seen a rattlesnake, her worst fears confirmed. What if it was contaminated? Could she be exposed right now? Sherri had the information she had been searching for; now she had to develop an exit plan.

Carefully, she closed the top of the container and secured the latches. Suddenly, light from the hallway illuminated the room. She heard voices in the hallway as she desperately searched for a way out.

HASSAN AND ALI WORKED quickly and quietly. Together, they planted explosives at the base of the F-2000 simulator and on the computer bank operating the simulator. They had specific instructions on what must be destroyed and where to place the explosives. Leaving the sim bay, Ali noticed several of the computers at a work station still running. Picking up a chair, he smashed the terminal, sending sparks flying. Ali hammered the chair into any machine with a light on.

"Ali, enough," Hassan said. "Let's go."

"My apologies, Hassan. I've always wanted to do something like that."

Hassan shook his head at his less stable partner as the two men left the sim bay and headed toward the lab. Ali had always been more militant, wanting to directly attack the Western way of life. Hassan had to spend many nights calming his young partner, explaining what it would take to reach their goal.

The lights in the hallway were a pleasant change; they hadn't been able to find the light switch in the sim bay, and setting the explosives in the dark using flashlights made them nervous.

Hassan and Ali found the lab exactly where their maps said it would be, and the case with the sarin gas exactly where they were told. Together, they opened the container's lid, revealing the four foot tube inside. Hassan had considered stealing the tube for use at a later time, but the thought was quickly discarded. He deemed it too big and heavy to smuggle back in to Mexico and he had no means to release or transfer the gas to a different type of container.

He shook the thoughts away. What the Chinese had in mind was irrelevant. The tube would be destroyed.

Ali slid a giant steel container from against the wall toward the table where they were working.

"That is good," Hassan said. "We can work from here."

Ali nodded, stopped sliding the steel behemoth, and opened the lid. The interior was empty, just as the instructions said it would be. Ali and Hassan worked together to lift the heavy tube from the Pelican case into the metal tub.

Ali removed ten plastic containers from his duffle bag, each about a half-gallon size, which contained a special mixture of jet fuel and slow burning plastic—a poor man's napalm. These were placed strategically around the container of sarin gas. Coupled with the foaming thermite, the fire should reach an intensity high enough to break down the gas until it was no longer dangerous.

Hassan worked on the foaming thermite when, out of the corner of his eye, he saw movement under a table across the room. Slowly, he set the small time bomb to the side and reached for the AK-47 hanging behind his back.

Ali started to speak. Hassan put a finger to his lips, grabbing the forward stock of the AK-47 with his left hand as his right index finger slid above the trigger.

The weapon hung waist-high as he crept forward. Hiding behind a table was a woman with deep red hair.

JASON SAT FOR SEVERAL MINUTES in the dark simulator attempting to reestablish power. All of his instrumentation and lighting had stopped a couple of minutes ago. His flashlight pointed straight up, its beam bouncing against the rounded top of the canopy and spreading across the small cockpit. Jason decided he'd had enough problems for the day. It was late and he wanted a beer.

Finally convinced the power outage had nothing to do with the simulator, Jason gathered his gear and stowed it in his helmet bag. He cracked the canopy and pushed it open, the effectiveness of his small flashlight dwarfed by the expansiveness of the dark, empty simulator bay. That's different. Jason checked his watch. It was ten-thirty in the evening. Late, but not unreasonably so. He looked across the sim bay toward the computer room. It looked as if the power had gone out in not just the sim bay, but the whole building.

SHERRI'S HEARTBEAT PULSED in her ears as two Middle Eastern men shouted at her in what she determined to be undistinguishable Arabic. What the hell were these guys doing here? Were they with the men she'd been tracking for months? She put up her hands as she maneuvered her way from underneath the table. The first man's bloodshot eyes bulged as he frantically moved back and forth, yelling at her and the other man.

Then Sherri focused on the second man, and she gasped. His eyes were crossed, his yellowing teeth jutting out of his mouth when he grinned. He was one of the men from the coffee shop in New York when her informant was shot. Sherri noticed he wasn't looking at her face, but her body.

More importantly, their guns were pointed at her. Her presence made them unhappy and extremely nervous. She was familiar enough with their culture to know she was not in a pleasant position.

"Who are you?" the taller one with the AK-47 asked.

"I'm, uh, Sherri," she replied.

"Why are you here?"

"I, uh . . . who are you guys?"

"Shut up," he yelled. "You not ask questions. Who sent you here? This office is closed, but you are here late at night."

Sherri searched desperately for a way out of this situation. She could tell the smaller man was not as committed as his partner by the leer in his eyes. He had a gun pointed at her, but his eyes wandered like most men, only worse.

"Why are you here?" the taller one asked again.

"I'm a secretary," she blurted out. "I had to get some notes for my boss." It was the best lie she could invent with a gun pointed at her.

"Liar," he said, backhanding her across the face. "Why are you in the lab?"

Sherri fell and caught herself on the edge of the table. She placed her hand against her cheek, but the pain remained. "I . . . I got scared when I heard men enter the building. No one is supposed to be here this late."

"How many men?" he said as he raised the rifle to his shoulder, leveling the barrel at her head.

"I don't know! I didn't see any! I hid in here right away."

Staring in the black abyss of the rifle barrel, her body tensed. She knew what was going to happen. Her eardrums resonated with the sound of her pounding heart as she watched him wrap his finger around the trigger.

73

J ASON WORKED HIS WAY along the metal staircase to the floor
of the sim bay. The lights he left on in the computer room were
out. Either someone came in and turned them off, or there was a
power failure in the building. His flashlight beam tracked around the
sim bay out of habit when something out of the corner of his eye
caught his attention.

Wires ran from one leg at the base of the simulator to another one.
He moved closer and saw the wire was attached to all the legs of the
sim. It wasn't there when he climbed in a couple of hours ago.

Inching closer, he discovered the wire attached to a small brick of
clay at the base. He knew enough to recognize a bomb when he saw
one. C-4. Explosives. Jason hastily moved around the base of the
simulator, realizing that each leg had a clay brick attached. The last one
had a timer, its red illuminated numbers counting down, with twelve
minutes remaining.

HASSAN'S FINGER TWITCHED as it pressed against the
trigger. This woman was irrelevant to his mission; he was losing time.
He glanced at Ali, whose pistol now pointed at the floor. His head
tilted to the side, a slight grin across his face. Hassan had seen that look
before, but he didn't care. They didn't have time for this. His finger
tightened as he pulled the trigger rearward on the AK-47.

Ka-blam.

"Damn!" Hassan said as the woman shrieked. Ali had shoved the
barrel up away from her head and the round impacted the ceiling. Rage
burned in his eyes as he swung the rifle back to his shoulder and

pointed it at her.

Ali leaped in front of the woman. "Hassan, no. I will take her. She will be mine for now."

"Ali, get out of my way!" His eyes burned with rage. "We don't have time for this. The woman must die!"

"My work is complete. You, however, must finish. I will guard the woman while you finish."

Hassan didn't have time for this argument. The timers were counting down throughout the building. Swinging the rifle behind his back, Hassan turned back to see Ali dragging the woman by her hair across the room.

"Keep her out of my way. We are running out of time," Hassan ordered.

"I will," Ali said. He grabbed the female by the upper left arm, dragging her to the wall by the door.

Hassan went back to work. He saw Ali had placed his containers exactly where his instructions directed. Cautiously, Hassan finished placing the foaming thermite over each of the containers of sarin gas. Each explosive package contained a timer set to activate two minutes before the rest of the timers. With the steel container sealed, it should destroy the virus.

When each of the timers was finally set, Hassan placed the lid on the steel container and secured the clasp. He watched Ali tie the woman's hands in front of her with an electrical cord he found.

"Let's go," he said to Ali as he moved swiftly by them, opening the door to the hallway.

Hassan noticed the woman give him an evil stare as he passed. It didn't bother him. When Ali was finished with her, she would wish he had blown her brains out.

JASON BACKED AWAY FROM the simulator. He considered pulling the wires out of the plastic explosives, but convinced himself he didn't have any idea what he was doing. He tried to use his cell phone to call the police or the command post at the base, but he couldn't get reception inside the sim bay.

Scurrying into the computer room, he went straight to the simulator operator's station to use the phone. The area was pitch black when it should be lit up like a Christmas tree.

When his flashlight beam reached the desk, he stopped. It was destroyed. The monitors broken, various knobs and switches on the desk, and numerous wires ripped out and left hanging. Several other work stations were in the same condition. He picked up a phone at one of the desks; no dial tone. He tried every phone in the room with the same result.

Jason realized it was time to get the hell out of here. Someone was trying to destroy the F-2000 simulator, and if he didn't leave soon, he'd go up with it. Once outside, he could contact someone. Jason picked his helmet bag off the floor as he moved to the door.

Then he heard the gunshot.

74

THE FAINT LIGHT from the hallway peeked underneath the door, assuring Jason there was no power outage. It was sabotage. He peered into the semi-dark hallway as a woman screamed. Not twenty feet away, two men struggled to force a woman back to her feet. Within seconds, there was enough light from the lobby to determine it wasn't just any woman, it was Sherri Davis, the reporter friend of Brent's. And that asshole Dane Robinson.

It didn't matter. Two men wrestling one woman was enough for him to step in. What did matter was that the two men carried guns.

The taller one had an AK-47 slung across his back; his hands carried two duffel bags. The shorter one carried a semi-automatic pistol in one hand, dragging Sherri with the other. Setting his helmet bag on the floor ever so softly, Jason crept along the wall, swiftly closing the gap as quietly as possible. The taller one lagged behind the other, most likely to keep an eye on Sherri.

Closing the gap within ten feet, Jason charged. Hitting the taller one from behind, he knocked him to the floor, the impact echoing in the empty hallway. Jason felt a twinge in his neck, a familiar feeling that would have troubled him had he not chosen to ignore it. He continued his forward progress, sliding to the right of the smaller man.

As Jason was almost upon him, the smaller one turned to his left, looking over his shoulder, slightly behind Sherri.

"Hassan?" Jason heard the man say. Jason slid to the man's right side, grabbing the gun in his hand. The man let go of Sherri with his left hand, swinging wildly at Jason. The ineffective blow hit him in the right shoulder.

Sherri braced herself against the wall, away from the two men fighting.

"Jason Conrad?" Sherri said. He didn't answer as he struggled for control of the pistol. "Look out!" Sherri yelled.

Glancing over his shoulder, Jason saw the taller one rising to his feet and reaching for his AK-47. Jason swung the arms of the man still holding the pistol at his taller partner, pointing the pistol at Hassan. Forcing his finger inside the trigger guard on top of the smaller man's finger, Jason squeezed several times.

The hallway roared with sound of the semiautomatic pistol as the taller man doubled over, his shirt turning scarlet as his weapon clanged on the floor.

Jason put pressure on the right wrist of the man and pried the pistol from his grip. The man slid back behind him and grabbed him around the neck. Jason thrust his elbow into the man's gut, forcing him to release his grip. Jason then spun around, throwing a right cross against the man's jaw, sending him to the floor. The impact of the punch vibrated through his hand and up his arm. Shaking his arm, Jason picked up the pistol from the floor. The man lay still on the floor. Confident his opponent was incapacitated, Jason turned to Sherri.

"Are you all right?" he said.

"Yeah," she replied, "thanks to you."

"What are you doing here?" Jason asked as he retrieved the AK-47 from the other man. Jason inspected the wounds in the man's chest and stomach. If he wasn't dead, he would be soon. He picked up two extra magazines the man had been carrying. A quick glance showed they were full, and Jason stuffed them in the left ankle pocket of his flight suit.

"I'll explain later. We've got to get out of here." She was sobbing, but no tears flowed.

"Yes, we do. Let's go," he said, moving toward the front door.

"No, not that way. They've got friends."

He stopped. "How many?"

"I-I don't know. Three cars pulled up, but I didn't see how many came inside."

"How did you get in here?"

The one he'd wrestled with for the pistol start to rise.

Sherri focused on Jason, her breathing coming in large gasps.

"They-they-they've killed—"

Jason turned toward the rising man when he heard voices in the lobby followed by several shots. A half-dozen rounds ripped through the smaller man he had fought, sending him back to the floor in a pool of blood.

"GET DOWN!" Jason said, pushing Sherri to the floor. He dropped, rolled to his left, and raised the AK-47 at the reception area. Another man fired in their direction, the indiscriminate fire hitting all around the hallway. They were fortunate the hallway behind them was dark, giving them cover.

Jason, placing the first one in his sights, squeezed the trigger. A short burst hit the wall above the assailant's head. Jason lowered his barrel and squeezed off another short burst. The man dropped his AK as he slid to the floor.

The second man in the lobby sprinted across the opening, sporadically shooting a volley of cover fire with a pistol as he moved from one side to the other. The sounds of gunfire echoed loudly as the man repositioned himself, inserted another magazine in his pistol, and started firing again. Jason observed he wasn't aiming his weapon. He blindly pointed the pistol, firing from his cover position.

Jason crawled into a doorway to conceal himself. He had a little cover, but for the most part, he and Sherri lay exposed in the dark hallway. Scanning his immediate area, Jason searched for ideas. His frustration clouded his mind until he saw two more men take position in the lobby. Then he got scared.

KATHY STRUGGLED AGAINST her restraints in the dark room. The gun battle somewhere in the building had her worried. Either way, she was in trouble. She would either be killed by the Chinese or imprisoned by the Americans. She had only one option. Escape.

The leather belts securing her wrists to the table cut into her flesh. They were secured with chains to the metal rod attached to the rail on her bed.

The Chinese operatives left her here to die. Thankfully, they didn't put her back on an IV, a mistake that allowed her to slowly recover to a semblance of consciousness, although she had no sense of time or how long she had been here. She had seen the blocks of C-4 they carried into the room. This room was set to blow, she was sure.

Confident no one would return for her, she feverishly worked on her restraints with her left hand, sliding its chain up and down the metal post restraining her. Her hand gradually became numb as she continuously forced it upwards, slamming against the upper rail. Maybe it was just in her mind, but she believed the upper rail was loosening.

WELLINGTON SPENT THE EVENING in silence, calculating his plan in Jennifer's apartment. Jennifer was a basket case. He had to get her to calm down or this would never work. Gathering the few items he needed from her apartment, included the gold F-2000 from her mantle, he placed them in a backpack. Jennifer was frantically placing her things in a gym bag. Wellington pulled out his cell phone and dialed.

"Mark, good evening. Jeremiah Wellington here."

"Wellington, why the hell are you calling me at this time of night?"

"Mark, I'm sorry. I've got . . . no, *we've* got a problem, and as wing commander, you need to be aware of it."

"What kind of problem?"

"There's a serious operational security failure. Actually it's an intelligence failure, but it's impacting all of us."

"What the hell are you talking about?"

"Mark, there's a Russian spy running around the base."

"What?"

"It's partially our fault. Well, not really our fault, but she's here because of us."

"Jeremiah, what the hell are you talking about?"

"The new pilot we brought in for the F-2000, Jason Conrad. We just found out his girlfriend is a Russian spy."

"Where the hell did you get this information?"

"Mark, you know I've got better connections at the Pentagon than you—"

"Well, I'm the damn wing commander. I should be the first one told about this shit."

"I agree. That's why when I found out, you were the first one I called. Look, we've tried to find Conrad, and he's nowhere around. I know it's not my place, but I recommend a BOLO for Conrad. I'm not sure if he's aware of this girl's background, but either way, he belongs to you and he needs to be brought in for questioning."

The wing commander agreed a "be on the lookout" for Conrad was appropriate, sending a warning to all security personnel, and eventually everyone on the base. The phone was silent for several moments. Wellington smiled—he understood exactly what the wing commander was thinking.

"Thanks for the call, Jeremiah. I've got to get dressed and head to the command post."

"I'll contact you when I get back to the base," he said. It was a lie. He would be heading to the airport in Mojave. "We're going to move the F-2000 back to Palmdale."

"Why?" the general replied.

"Mark, there's a Russian spy running around the base. The secrecy and security of that jet is our number one priority. If Captain Conrad's girlfriend is a spy, then she damn sure knows what the F-2000 is and where it's located. We want to move it until this thing dies down and those two are captured."

"You don't need to move the damn jet. My base is secure."

"Well, it doesn't look that way right now, does it?" Wellington said.

There was a brief pause. The silence spoke volumes to Wellington.

"Okay," the general said. "I'll have my exec notify the tower that your team is scheduling a takeoff later tonight."

"Thanks, Mark. I appreciate it. I've contacted Major Walton, who will be flying the jet to Palmdale. She'll be in shortly to move the jet. We'll have the TRENCOR helicopter waiting in Palmdale to pick her up after she's secured the jet in the hangar." Wellington grinned. His lie was getting better and better.

"Fair enough. I've got to run. Thanks for the heads up," the wing commander said as he hung up the phone.

Wellington grinned at Jennifer, who zipped up her flight suit.

"Well," he said, "it looks like we've got our patsy."

JASON RETURNED FIRE. He didn't have much ammo and didn't know how long this firefight would last. The initially intense firefight subsided. Most of the shots were directed at his side of the hallway. Sherri remained motionless on the floor. Jason could see her eyes open, looking anxiously at him.

"Are you hit?" he said in a loud whisper.

"No," she said.

"Don't move."

Jason lost track of how much time had passed since this fight started. Well aware of the bombs' countdown, he desperately searched for a way out.

The three men continued shooting at Jason in the dark hallway. When he returned fire, the three men unloaded everything they had. Jason rolled as close to the wall as he could, minimizing his target profile, when he heard her scream.

"I think I've been hit," she said in a loud whisper. Jason picked up on the pain in her voice.

Just as quickly as the surge of gunfire started, it ceased. Jason peered down the hallway to see the other two men skirt across the lobby to join the lone gunmen, and the three dropped out of sight.

Recognizing the pause in action, Jason leaped to his feet, sprinted across the hallway, and picked up Sherri.

"Are you okay?" he said.

"Yes," she replied, "I think it grazed my thigh. It stings. A lot."

"We'll check it out once we're outside. We need to go."

"Do you think you can get me out of this?" she said, holding up her hands.

Jason noticed, for the first time, that her hands were bound with an electrical cord. He leaned the AK-47 against the wall and started to untie her hands. As he finished freeing her, he looked at her and said, "We've got to get out of the building now."

"It's going to blow up," they said in unison.

75

May 29, 2001

KATHY MANAGED TO BREAK the top rail on her left side, freeing her left hand. She unbuckled the right hand and struggled to sit up to release her feet. She desperately worked at the leather restraints around her ankles and freed her legs. She rolled herself off the table and when her feet found the floor, her knees buckled. Kathy struggled to keep her balance. Her head spun in circles as her vision narrowed into near-blackness.

Staggering, she worked her way toward the only door in the room. None of this seemed familiar as she had trouble focusing. She had no idea where she was or what lay on the other side of the wall. As she reached the door, she realized for the first time that the gunfire she heard earlier had stopped. Unsure of the direction or location of the gunfire, she wasn't in any condition to care. She needed to get out. Her vision narrowing, she focused on one door after the other, not knowing where any of them led. Eventually, she pushed through a heavy door with a loud grunt, falling into a large hallway.

"WE NEED TO GO now," Jason said.

"We can't go that way. They've got us blocked in," Sherri said, pointing toward the lobby.

"You have any suggestions?"

"Follow me." She turned, sprinting with a slight limp back down the hall to the stairwell.

Jason followed her, stepping backward, his weapon pointed toward the lobby. For the first time, he realized how bad his ears hurt, pulsating from the gunfire in the enclosed space. Sherri reached the stairwell first, flinging open the door, and racing up the stairs. When Jason reached the stairwell, he heard a crash and saw a woman fall into the hallway halfway between him and the lobby. He stopped. Gradually he moved toward the woman, who he realized was not just any woman.

Pushing herself to her knees, the woman turned toward him. The light from the lobby highlighted the familiar silhouette. Tattered, soiled clothes, a dirty face, and unkempt hair didn't hide her identity. Jason recognized her at once.

It was Kathy. What was she doing here? She looks like she's been a prisoner since she disappeared. Was she involved in this . . . this mess somehow?

SHERRI REACHED THE TOP of the stairs, darted through the reception area, and was well into a painful sprint across the barren second floor. Ignoring the agony building by the second, she moved faster. Steven had told her not to get shot. She hoped to live long enough for him to gloat about his warning.

The stairwell to the outside was in sight when she sensed she was alone. Sherri glanced over her shoulder.

"Jason?" she said. What the hell happened to him? She stopped for a moment, her breath coming in large gasps. The split-second decision was not a difficult one. Jason Conrad had just saved her life; she couldn't leave him here.

THEIR EYES LOCKED as Jason moved toward her. It was the first time he'd seen her since Caldwell told him she was a Russian mole. He blinked his eyes and shook his head. Was it her? It had to be. His heart pounded in his chest. It was her. He tried to speak, but the words never came out. Kathy lay forty feet away when his legs stopped. He wanted to move to her, but his feet wouldn't cooperate.

"Kathy," he said, "I—"

The explosion ripped through the side of the hallway, knocking Jason off his feet. The blast blew debris into the hallway between the two. A second later, portions of the ceiling fell onto the floor. Dust and smoke filled the now dark hallway as Jason struggled to his feet to find Kathy.

THE EXPLOSION ECHOED through the building and at the top of the stairs, Sherri feared the worst. She struggled down the dark stairwell, holding the handrail the entire time. She reached the bottom, fearful of what she might find on the other side of the door.

Taking a deep breath, she pushed the door open. The hallway was illuminated by the intermittent sparks from several severed electrical wires. Jason braced himself against the wall, dust swirling around, as he stared into the pile of debris.

Well aware of the sarin gas, Sherri rushed to him. She grabbed him by the arm, pulling him toward the stairwell. "Jason, we can use these stairs to reach the second floor," she said. "We can get out through another stairwell that leads outside."

He shook himself free, and their eyes locked. "Wait," Jason said, holding up a finger as he moved toward the pile of debris covering the hallway.

"Jason, there's sarin gas in here," Sherri screamed. Jason continued toward the pile, moving sheetrock, cinder blocks, and pieces of furniture.

KATHY SHOOK HER HEAD. The flashing bright sparks interrupted the soothing blackness, the damaged electrical wires illuminating the hallway. Pinned beneath something, she moved slowly, increasingly aware she could escape the debris pile.

A warm, salty taste hit her lips. It wasn't sweat—it was blood. Her blood. Placing her hand on her forehead, it burned as she realized she had a gash above her left eyebrow. She confirmed it with the small pool of blood on the dusty floor beneath her.

Her head ached as she struggled to get out of this trap. The debris moved as she pushed at the pile on top of her. Kathy looked to her right, squinting her eyes. She thought she saw Conrad digging through debris to get to her.

She was confused. Where the hell was she? Did the Chinese hand her over to the Americans? She knew she had to escape, but would it be with or without the help of Jason Conrad?

JASON STRUGGLED THROUGH the debris, but his arms seemed to lack strength and his neck was still sore. He wasn't sure what he was doing. He loved her at one point; maybe he still did. There was never any closure, never any face-to-face resolution. He'd be damned if he could love a Russian mole, but here he was digging her out.

Sherri yelled behind him, but it didn't matter. Not right now. He needed to reach Kathy. He moved a large piece of sheet rock and there, ten feet away, lay Kathy lay under a small pile of sheet rock and splintered two-by-fours. She turned her head in his direction and—in the midst of sparks, dust, and debris flying around them—she smiled at him.

"Conrad," she said softly. "No matter what you hear . . . or what happens . . . know that I've always loved you."

His heart struggled to take control of his actions, but his head took over. Kathy was a Russian mole. Possibly an assassin. Who was her target? Should he bring her in? Should he let her go? Jason started to force a smile on his face when a second explosion erupted behind him.

76

May 29, 2001

THE CONCUSSION OF THE BLAST propelled her sideways. Sherri tripped over some cinder blocks, slamming against the wall, then to the floor, unhurt by the blast. It was the steel beam falling toward her that got her attention. Unable to get out of the way, she fell flat on the floor as the beam impacted with a loud crash. Sherri screamed as the beam landed on a pile of blown-out cinder blocks that had once been part of the walls. Pinned between the wall, the cinder blocks, and the beam, she struggled to move.

JASON HEARD SHERRI SCREAM following the explosion, and he turned to see the beam falling toward her. He wasn't sure what happened when the beam fell, but it hit with a sickening echo. Dust flew everywhere in the darkness, stinging his eyes, making it more difficult to see or breathe. Jason dropped the sheetrock he'd been moving and raced back to Sherri.

Debris prevented her from sliding out from the beam resting on the cinder blocks in front of her.

"Are you hurt?" he said, coughing through the dust. Jason didn't realize he was yelling, his ears still ringing from the blasts.

"No," she replied, just as loud. "Can you get me out of here?" He could see the concern on her face in the glow of the sparks overhead.

He started moving the cinder blocks behind her to pull her out. In a matter of seconds, he slid her out of her cocoon, the heavy I-beam propped against the cinder block wall. He helped her stand as he looked into her eyes. He didn't see fear—he saw confidence.

"Jason, we've got to get out of here now!"

Analyzing his options and the debris where Kathy lay, he knew he had to make a choice. His heart ached as he realized the Russian would not be it.

"Let's go," Jason said.

He slung the rifle over his head, following her as she raced up the stairs. In a few moments they reached the landing, threw open the door, and ran into the second floor reception area.

KATHY PULLED HERSELF FREE following the second explosion. Leaning against the wall, she strained to see through the debris. Dust floated through the area and her eyes burned. She lifted the collar of her shirt up to cover her mouth and nose so she could breathe. The wall to her prison now covered the floor of the hallway and the ceiling fell in on top of the room she had occupied. Sparks from the severed electrical wiring gave her some light as she struggled to see what happened to Conrad.

The woman's scream following the blast got her attention. What the hell was going on here? Chinese, TRENCOR, Conrad, and now— her eyes caught a glimpse of a pretty redhead from . . . where? She'd seen her before. At the reception. Yet here she was, standing in the dark with Conrad.

She imagined Conrad looking in her direction as he and the redhead turned to run through another door. Clearly, he had a choice to make, and he made it. She didn't blame him, though. She loved Conrad, but she probably would have made the same choice.

Kathy turned and staggered along the hallway toward the lobby. She found a body in the lobby with an AK-47 near it. Instinctively, she reached for the rifle and chambered a round. Gradually, she staggered out the front door to find a car running with its lights on. A Middle Eastern man jumped out of the car, hollering in Arabic.

Kathy had no idea what he said as she swung the rifle up and fired a quick burst into the man's chest. He fell straight back, hitting the pavement with a flat thud. Stepping over the dead body, she climbed into the car. In the mirror, she studied the gash across her left eye and down her cheek. Kathy found a towel in the passenger's seat and patted the moist blood, now caked with dust, from her face. She put the car in drive and peeled away from the building.

She didn't know where she was going, but she was sure of one thing: if she survived this, she would kill those Chinese bastards, and then she would find Jason Conrad.

THE TWO REACHED THE SECOND floor and entered the reception area. Sherri made a hard left and started running across the empty floor. Jason rounded the corner and abruptly came to a halt.

"What the hell happened up here?" he said.

Sherri stopped and turned. "Nothing. That's part of the problem. I'll explain later. We need to get far away from here, fast."

"We'll be good once we're outside the building."

"Not good enough," Sherri said. "There's sarin gas in a lab downstairs. I think they're trying to destroy it, but I don't trust anyone right now." She turned and ran, Jason following close behind.

They reached the far stairwell and opened the door when the first major blast occurred. The two looked back at the empty floor space as debris flew around and the second floor collapsed in several locations.

"Let's go!" Sherri yelled, running down the staircase.

Jason turned and followed as the third floor collapsed onto where the second floor once stood. He followed Sherri down the dark stairwell, catching up with her by the time she reached the first floor. Grabbing her around the waist, he pushed firmly against the door as they both stumbled outside.

The ink-black sky radiated with the reflection of TRENCOR Industries exploding. Jason glanced to the right as they raced across the parking lot toward the desert. Each door on the loading dock exploded from the force within. He could feel the heat from this distance, suspecting these guys didn't set all of this tonight. They just triggered what was already there.

Sherri and Jason ran for another two hundred yards in the soft sand before collapsing to their knees. Jason turned to see if Sherri was all right. She lunged toward him, wrapping her arms around his neck, sobbing.

Jason wrapped his arms around her waist as they turned back to watch the building's destruction. They both flinched as the secondary explosion from the center of the building erupted. The miniature mushroom cloud climbed tumbled skyward, a mixture of red, black, orange, and yellow fading into a grayish cloud that rose to the sky.

He turned to face Sherri, her arms still wrapped around his neck, their faces inches apart.

"Sherri, do you mind telling me what the hell is going on?"

77

JASON INSPECTED HER THIGH. They stood a safe distance from the still-exploding building, the fire providing adequate light. It was a nick, two inches long and about an eighth of an inch deep. He was sure it was painful.

The two began hiking to the outer perimeter fence she had crawled under earlier in the evening. Sherri struggled to keep up, and he reached back to grab her hand.

"Who the hell are those guys? Mexican cartel?" he said.

"No, they were Middle Eastern. My bet is Saudi," she said as she picked up her pace.

"What do they want with you?"

"I think I was just a target of opportunity. They were here to blow up the building."

"Sabotage? Industrial espionage?"

"I'm afraid it's deeper than that." She breathed heavier now as the sand grew softer near the fence surrounding TRENCOR.

"They've murdered Brent," she said.

"What?" His face was a mixture of exhaustion, sadness, and confusion. "Are you sure?"

"I snuck into Ming's office," Sherri said, nodding. "Brent's body was in Ming's desk chair, his throat sliced. He's been dead a couple of days."

"My God."

"Have you noticed that facility was empty? I went into the executive suite, and there nothing in the office. I mean there's furniture, but nothing to indicate anyone occupied the office space."

"You know," he said, "I've noticed over the past week the interior of the building changed."

"How so?"

"There was some incredible artwork in the lobby and hallways. Original artwork. Expensive artwork. But it all disappeared over the last week or so."

"They have been systematically removing everything they want to keep. This was planned."

"Planned?"

"Yes. Didn't you notice there was no security tonight?" she said. "These guys knew exactly where to go and what to do. They were hired to destroy the building and everything in it."

Jason shifted the AK-47 to his left hand and rested it on his shoulder as they trudged in the soft sand. He wiggled the fingers on his right hand as a tingling sensation returned, recalling his father's advice regarding his ejection from the jet last month. It must have been the fight or the blast that aggravated his neck injury.

"But why?"

"This jet you're flying . . . it's a cover."

"What do you mean?"

"I'm not sure. I mean, this goes back to Georgiana Anderson's murder. She suspected something nefarious about TRENCOR. Apparently, she did her own investigating and pissed off someone who had her killed."

"What did she discover that would get her killed?"

"From what I gathered, Georgiana discovered the facility was a shell, and according to Brent's notes, it's always been empty. There was never anything there. Anyway, there was a pilot who discovered a bunch of problems with your new jet—"

"Let me guess—Major Curt Samson, who died in the F-15 crash a couple weeks back."

"Yeah. Brent believed Samson was murdered because he knew the software on your jet was designed to fail. And now Brent's been murdered, too."

"I can't believe these bastards," Jason murmured as he absorbed the information. Jason wondered how deep this rabbit hole went. "Perhaps that's why we were shot at yesterday. Maybe they linked you two together."

"Wellington saw us in the restaurant at the airport. Brent got really nervous."

"That's it," he said. "Wellington's a part of this. It makes too much sense."

"I was supposed to meet Brent on Sunday. I hadn't seen or heard from him since Saturday."

"Neither had I," Jason said. "He sent me on a scavenger hunt that seemed peculiar at the time. There is a nozzle shown on a set of older schematics he had, but it didn't show up on the 'official' schematics of the jet."

Sherri stopped. Jason turned back to her as she lifted up her head.

"Is there a nozzle on the jet?" she said.

"Yes. It—"

"Was there a place to hook up a bottle about ten inches in diameter and four feet long?" she said, holding up her hands depicting the size of the object she described.

Jason paused a moment, then said, "Yeah."

"The nozzle. Was the port a screw-in about an inch wide?"

"I think so. Why? What's up?"

Sherri's shoulders slumped and her knees buckled slightly. Jason moved closer with a concerned look on his face. "Are you okay?"

Slowly, she raised her head. "I think I know what their plan is, or was. They were going to use the F-2000 to spray sarin gas."

78

L I ZHONG STOOD in the distance, watching the developing inferno. He let a subtle grin show with every secondary explosion. Although he only saw one vehicle leave the complex, he wasn't worried—the remaining two vehicles were untraceable, and their bodies could never be tied to TRENCOR.

Satisfied the job was well underway, Li Zhong returned to his car. He would go back to the apartment and pick up Wellington and Major Walton, then drive them to their respective aircraft. Once they were in motion, he would drive to Las Vegas and catch a plane to Mexico City. He'd grown tired of America and was glad to finally be heading home.

THE TRENCOR FACILITY resembled a massive bonfire by this point, and the fence line was in sight. Jason and Sherri plodded through the soft sand as Sherri continued filling Jason in on the details.

"I think is the Chinese government is using TRENCOR to deplete the US government of their assets," Sherri said.

"How so?" Jason replied, slinging the AK-47 over his head and shoulder.

"The data shows this thing is a money pit. Hundreds of billions of dollars have been spent on this jet with nothing to show for it. Nada, zip, zero. And your pal Dane Robinson has input that may tie up some loose ends."

Jason gaped at her. "I have a hard time seeing him doing anything constructive."

"Dane tracked the purchase of a great deal of land, windmills, and water storage systems back to TRENCOR. David Ming's wife is the attorney who closed all of the deals."

"I don't see the relationship."

"I'm reaching," Sherri admitted, "but I think the Chinese government is using the money the US is paying TRENCOR to buy up land and other valuable natural resources. According to Dane, there are several front companies making these purchases throughout the Midwest, all the way down into Texas. All of it sits over the Ogallala Aquifer, the largest underground source of water in the United States."

"That's crazy. What about the sarin gas? If they're making so much money off Uncle Sam, why kill their cash cow?"

She shook her head. "I don't know. I'm struggling with all of this as well."

Jason noticed the flashing red lights of a firetruck a hundred yards away racing in front of him toward TRENCOR Industries. "Looks like the secret is out," he said, referencing the truck speeding by with its lights rotating. He pulled out his cell phone.

"What are you doing?"

"I'm calling the sheriff's office. We can't let them fight this fire with a chemical weapon inside. Those firefighters could be exposed."

Sherri nodded. "That's a good idea."

"Were we exposed?"

"No."

"How do you know?"

"Because we'd be dead by now."

"Oh, right."

"I think those guys were sent there to destroy the gas," she said. "It may have been destroyed before the early explosions, or it may still be in there. We have no way of knowing."

He started to dial 911, but paused.

"What's wrong?"

"I'm not sure I want to be associated with this," he said, pointing back to the burning building.

"What can we do? The firetruck is almost to the building."

He dialed another number. It picked up instantly.

"Jason, I was going to call you in the morning. How are you adjusting to the news about Kathy?"

"Great, but I've got a bigger problem."

"Bigger than a Russian mole?"

"Yes. I need you to contact emergency vehicles responding to a fire at TRENCOR Industries in California City and advise them there is sarin gas inside the facility."

"Sarin gas? At TRENCOR? Isn't that where your—"

"Yes. Hurry, man. We don't want these guys exposed if the gas is there."

"Understood. I'll call you back."

Click.

Jason closed his phone and stuck it back in his flight suit pocket. "That's a friend of mine. If anyone can stop them, he can."

"What is he? FBI?"

"No. CIA."

"Really? I was being facetious. Here," she said, pointing to the fence in front of them, "I crawled under right here."

"Where's your car?"

"About a quarter mile down the road."

Sher lay on her back and started to shimmy under the fence. Once she passed through, he slid the AK-47 to her and shimmied himself through. When they reached the outer fence twenty feet away, they crawled under it, as well. Jason stood, dusting himself off. Sherri knocked the dirt off his back and they began walking to Sherri's car. By the time they saw it, Caldwell called. It had been about fifteen minutes since he hung up with Jason.

"Okay, I made the call. Now what's going on?"

Jason told Caldwell everything, starting with Georgiana Anderson up to the gunfight he just experienced. TRENCOR Industries was fully ablaze now and the emergency vehicles retreated to the outskirts of the parking lot, when another, larger explosion went off.

"What was that?" Caldwell said.

"Secondary explosion."

"From TRENCOR Industries?"

"Yeah. About a mile away."

"Wow. So what's your plan?" Caldwell said.

"What do you mean, 'my plan'?"

"Your next step. I can confirm David Ming has been on our watch list for years, but he's kept his nose clean, other than a few associates of his."

"Can you guys bring him in?"

"No, I just ran a check on him," Caldwell said. "He boarded an Air China 747 in Los Angeles three hours ago, final destination—Peking.

We won't see him again in the United States."

"So what should I do?"

"Standby . . ."

Jason glanced at Sherri. She was fixated on TRENCOR burning in the distance. How did she get herself involved in this mess? For that matter, how did he get himself involved? He'd experienced things outside the "norm", but tonight he reached another level. He shot someone tonight, for Christ's sake. And he noticed he wasn't bothered by that.

"What about the jet?" Jason said after a few moments of silence.

"What do you mean, 'What about the jet?' Is there a jet? Where is it?"

"Yes, there's a jet. It's in a hangar at Edwards," Jason said.

There was a brief pause.

"Can you guard it?" Caldwell said.

"What the hell kind of question is that?"

"Look, TRENCOR is destroying everything on this project. I'm sure that includes the jet."

"I can go there, but TRENCOR's guys guarding the hangar are not the standard eighteen-year-old security officer," Jason said. "They are experienced door-kickers, heavily armed. I don't think the security police at Edwards have the capability to fight their way into the hangar."

"If TRENCOR has control of the hangar now, I promise you they'll try to destroy the jet tonight."

There was another brief pause over the phone.

"Can you fly it?" Caldwell said.

"Yeah, I'm sure I could. I mean, I never have, but I've flown the crap out of the simulator."

There was another pause, longer this time.

"Go to the hangar and get your eyes on the situation there. Call me back with what you see."

"What are you thinking?"

There was a delay of several seconds.

"Jason, I'm in direct contact with the National Security Council," Caldwell said. "Because you and I know each other, I'm acting as a liaison on the president's behalf. Your orders are to steal the jet."

79

May 30, 2001

IT WAS THIRTY MINUTES past midnight as Li Zhong drove to the East Kern Airport District in Mojave to drop off Wellington. No one spoke along the way. They sat in the back seat of the white Mercedes, each wearing an olive green flight suit, Jennifer squeezing his hand the entire trip. Wellington didn't mind. It comforted him knowing she felt she needed him. Both of their lives were about to change dramatically. The truth was, their lives changed a long time ago.

He exited the SUV and grabbed his bags. Jennifer stepped out the other side and gave him a big hug. There were tears in her eyes. He knew they weren't tears because they were leaving. She was terrified. He reminded her what they were trying to accomplish. Nothing he said comforted her. They would both be labeled traitors. Everybody has a price; theirs was eleven million dollars.

His situation didn't escape him as he hugged her tightly. He was a fifty-five-year-old pilot about to run off with his thirty-five-year-old mistress. Everything he'd worked for his entire life would be left behind. Jennifer and his money would be all he had—and he'd have to work at keeping her around.

They reviewed the plan and timeline, then Li Zhong escorted her back to the SUV. Wellington watched them drive out of sight. Biting his lower lip, he slowly picked his bags off the ground and shuffled to the ramp and the TRENCOR F-16.

"THEY WANT ME TO STEAL this jet. I can't, it's impossible," Jason said as he drove back to Edwards.

"He's right," Sherri said. "You're the only person who can keep this from getting out of hand. It's the right thing to do."

"Do you realize the trouble I've gotten into for doing the 'right thing'?"

Sherri snickered; Jason did a double take, glaring at her.

"What?" he said.

"You're kind of impressive, Jason Conrad. It's a shame you're a pilot."

"Very funny."

"No, I'm serious. I believe you'll figure something out. You have the experience to fly the jet. In fact, you're the only one on our side capable of flying that jet."

"Maybe I could call the wing commander. One phone call from him, and the base is locked down," Jason said.

"Possibly. Or it's possible the wing commander arrests you and puts you in a small, dark room for a year or so while they figure out what to do with you. Wait and see what Caldwell has to say."

Jason shook his head. He knew how this would end; he wouldn't come out of this smelling good, no matter what. It was time to seek guidance higher up the chain of command, outside the Air Force. He called his father.

Jonathan Bowman wasn't surprised at what was taking place. It was quite a tale, he told Jason, but knowing the players involved, it sounded legitimate. Jason's father had connections to the White House. Hell, he *knew* the president. He promised to make some phone calls and get back to him.

He was aware of his father's connection to the F-2000. His position at Century Aero-Bot placed him in direct contact with Jeremiah Wellington. His father was part of the reason Wellington didn't like him. The other part was Wellington was an asshole. He didn't buy the "charm assault" Wellington used on everyone but pilots.

They drove in silence most of the way to the base. Jason contemplated what it would take to fly the jet. The ITCS developed by Century Aero-Bot was the heart and soul of the F-2000, but Jason hadn't been "fitted" for the F-2000 yet. He wasn't sure stealing the jet was something he should do, let alone *could* do. Regardless of his pilot skills, it seemed everyone in the F-2000 chain of command was involved. Jason's biggest fear was if the Air Force was notified, it might set off a firefight between them and the TRENCOR guards.

By the time they reached the gate, there were three cars in front of them waiting to enter. The guard was slow passing cars through the gate. The fire at the TRENCOR facility lit up the sky and everyone focused on the unusual occurrence on the northwest horizon.

SENIOR AIRMAN CHRISTOPHER BREAUX was distracted. The fire was huge and the explosions abnormal. The young airman had never seen such a sight in Southern California. He was very slow checking everyone's ID at the gate. The chitchat was also extra thick as everyone wondered what was going on in California City.

Distracted by the fire, he never heard the telephone in the guard shack ring, indicating a fax was coming through the machine.

The paper pushed its way out of the fax machine, onto the floor, rolling up, hiding its prominent photograph and headline:

BOLO—CAPTAIN JASON CONRAD ARMED AND EXTREMELY DANGEROUS

THE GUARD SHIFTED his focus from Jason's ID card to the fire on the horizon and back again. Jason grinned as the guard waved him through, positive he wouldn't be as lucky next time. His cell phone beeped as he drove through the gate. He recognized the number.

"Hey, Dad. Find anything out?"

"Nothing I can tell you right now, other than it's recommended you follow Agent Caldwell's plan."

"That's easy to say. What kind of problems will I encounter?"

"Unknown, but you're on your own. Things are happening too fast. The agents within range aren't going to be effective with these guys. The situation is unfolding exponentially. Only moving the jet will slow things down."

"Any idea on how I'm supposed to do that?"

"You're creative. Figure something out."

"Gee, thanks for the vote of confidence. Why don't we contact the wing commander and have him lock everything down?"

"There is suspicion the wing commander may be compromised. There are rumors of bribes taking place."

Jason remembered the gold airplane in the wing commander's office. Was he part of this? Had he been bought off?

"Okay, so who do I trust? Am I going to get any kind of top cover?"

"You'll get the top cover you need. We need to keep you alive to recover the jet."

"All right," Jason said, his confidence in the "plan" less than strong. And he wasn't thrilled with the "We need to keep you alive" comment coming from his father. That verified how dangerous this plan was.

"The NSC has approved this plan. As of right now, you're working for the president. Caldwell should be calling you with details on where to fly the jet," Bowman said.

"How do you—never mind. All right, let me get off the phone. My battery is dying. See you later, Dad."

"Good luck, son."

Jason looked at Sherri as he hung up the phone. "I can assure you *The New York Times* will back you up," she said.

"I believe they will. I just want to be alive to read it."

Jason drove another two minutes before pulling into a parking lot across from the hangar.

"Are you going in?"

"Not yet," Jason said. "I've got to come up with a plan. This place has an obscene amount of security. I'm trying to figure out why I would be wandering around the airplane this late at night, because that's what they're going to be thinking."

Sherri retrieved a first-aid kit from her backpack in the backseat of the car. Without saying a word to Jason, she slipped her jeans down to her knees, using all the alcohol swabs to clean the wound. She grimaced in pain, but Jason was impressed with her courage. Maybe he'd been wrong about her. After placing Neosporin on the wound, she placed a large Band-Aid on top. It wasn't optimum, but it was the best she could do under the circumstances.

Sherri pulled her jeans back up and stuck the first-aid kit in her backpack. In the dark, the blood on her jeans wasn't too obvious, and the bullet hole looked like another fashion statement. She grabbed two bottles of water from her cooler, handed one to Jason, and the two sipped slowly, gradually starting to relax. Sherri pulled out a pack of Wet-Naps and wiped off her face and hands. She then pulled out another pack and handed it to Jason, who did the same.

As the events of the evening caught up with them, Jason mulled over the fact he'd killed a couple of men, been in the TRENCOR facility when it blew sky high, and was now attempting to steal the most expensive, most classified jet in the world. Dane Robinson will have a field day. Jason considered cancelling the whole crazy plan until a familiar white Mercedes pulled up next to the hangar. He saw Jennifer in her olive green flight suit and black boots hop out and grab a duffel bag from the back seat. Li Zhong then exited the Mercedes and slinked over to Jennifer.

80

THE SCENE UNFOLDING before him raised more questions as he watched.

"Look at this," Jason said. "What the hell is Jennifer Walton doing hanging with David Ming's hired muscle?"

Li Zhong handed Jennifer a slip of paper, which she tucked into her thigh pocket on the right leg of her flight suit. Pointing a finger at her, he turned, strutted back to his car, and drove toward the front gate. Jennifer watched him drive away, then walked into the hangar, carrying the large duffel bag. She approached the hangar, where security personnel surrounded her.

"See how the external perimeter is supported?" Jason said, pointing at the guards. "We can expect a greeting party just like hers."

"We?"

"Uh, yeah. I was planning on you coming with me. Don't worry, it has two seats."

"Oh, no. No. You're not going to get me in that thing. It's a test plane. We don't even know if it works."

"It works. It's flown twice already. Besides, it'll be a lot worse if you stay here. You'll be on a military base with no ID moments after a top-secret jet has been stolen and its training facility destroyed. You're better off in the air."

"I'm scared of flying," Sherri blurted as she leaned back against the passenger-side door.

He wanted to reach out and touch her, to let her know it would be okay. Then the pilot mindset kicked in. "You travel all around the world in jet airliners. How the hell can you be afraid of flying?"

"I travel with my friend Jack Daniels," she grimaced. "He helps me get started."

Jason nodded. "I understand. If you want to stay here and hope things work out, you can. But if you want to live through the night, I recommend you get over your fear, come with me, and catch up with Jack Daniels later."

He could see her thinking.

"You're right," she said. "What do we do?"

"I'm coming up with a plan," he said as his phone rang. He clicked the "ON" button and held the phone to his ear.

"Jason, it's Caldwell."

"What's the word?"

"I have someone on the line who wants to talk to you," Caldwell said.

"Okay."

"Go ahead, sir," Caldwell said.

Jason heard a beep over the phone.

"Captain Conrad? Can you hear me okay?"

"Yes, sir," Jason said.

"This is the president." Jason swallowed hard as he glanced at Sherri. Suddenly, this had been elevated to another level.

"Yes, sir, I recognize your voice." Sherri leaned closer in an effort to hear.

"Captain, I know you're in a tight spot. We are concerned with the destruction of TRENCOR's simulator facility and believe the jet may be targeted next. Now, we need to recover that jet. Agent Caldwell tells me you can fly that thing, is that correct?"

Jason swallowed hard again. "I think—yes. Yes, sir, I can."

"I heard Agent Caldwell use the term 'steal' earlier. Well, we've been writing the checks for that jet, and I believe it's ours. Do you think you can *move* it for me?"

Jason nodded his head. "Yes, sir, I'll do my best."

"That's all I can ask, Captain. I know it's dangerous, given the circumstances. You have my authorization to move the F-2000 to another field. I'm going to turn you back over to Agent Caldwell, who will give you the coordinates. Good luck."

"Thank you, sir," Jason said.

The phone beeped again and Caldwell came back on. "Do you have something to write with?"

Jason retrieved a small notebook and pen from a pocket on the sleeve of his flight suit.

"Ready to copy."

Caldwell read Jason the latitude and longitude of his destination. Jason copied the coordinates, reading them back to Caldwell.

"Where is this?" Jason said.

"About three hundred fifty miles northeast of where you are right now. My guys tell me if you have a full tank of gas, the average fighter will make it, no problem."

Jason did some quick calculations himself. This wasn't the average fighter, but the distance should be easily covered.

"Okay, sounds good. There will be two of us in the jet."

"Two? Who are you bringing?"

"She's an innocent bystander."

"She? Is it Kathy?"

"No, it's not Kathy. She's long gone. Her name is Sherri Davis. She's a reporter for *The New York Times*."

"Roger, I know who she is. I remind you, Jason, this is a classified operation. If she knows about this, you need to bring her. We'll work it out when you get there. Good luck."

"Thanks, Caldwell. Hopefully, we'll talk in a few hours."

Jason hung up, sliding the phone back into his pocket. He knew Caldwell would run a deep background check on Sherri as soon as they hung up the phone.

Jason turned to Sherri and looked her in the eye. "The president has given me authorization to move the jet."

"I kind of thought that. Let me guess. He hasn't told anyone else about it," she said.

"Correct."

"Therefore, as far as whoever has the jet now is concerned, you won't really be 'moving' it, you'll be stealing it."

"Correct," Jason said, climbing out of the car.

"Is Kathy your girlfriend from the reception?" Sherri asked as they climbed out of the car.

"Yes, kind of . . . I mean, no, I mean, she was my girlfriend, but not anymore." He was *not* going to tell her Kathy was at TRENCOR tonight and that was who he went back for in the hallway.

"Having a little problem with your social life?" She chuckled from across the roof of the car.

"A little. Turns out she's a Russian agent," Jason said as he stuffed the AK-47 into a large gym bag from Sherri's car. "She's disappeared, of course. Story of my life."

She stared blankly at him. "Okay, I'll be honest. That was not the answer I expected."

Jason grinned. "Stick around, sweetheart, nothing will turn out like you expect. Let's go."

Sherri followed him as they crossed the street and headed toward the hangar.

JENNIFER SAT IN HER makeshift locker room in the hangar, flipping through her address book. Who could she call to tell she was leaving? There was no one who wouldn't keep her on the phone. It would take too long to explain what was going on. It would take even longer to talk around the subject of stealing the F-2000 and running to China. Glancing at the clock on the wall, she knew she didn't have time to contact anyone. She had to make decisions on her own.

She had worked hard all her life to get where she was today. Now, in a matter of hours, it crumbled around her. Somehow, she and Wellington had been blackmailed and set up for crimes they didn't commit. Or did they? Wellington explained it to her, but she cried constantly and couldn't pay attention. She went along with it because she knew Ming's attack dog, Li Zhong, would have killed her on the spot if she said no. There was always another option. She could fly the jet to Nellis AFB in Las Vegas and turn it over to the wing commander there. Then she would only face charges of unauthorized use of military aircraft. Maybe.

Did she love Wellington? She thought so. He captivated her when he spoke, and for a guy in his mid-fifties, he was a tiger in the sack. But was he worth being labeled a traitor for the rest of eternity? She didn't know. But then there was the eleven million dollars.

The clock on the wall said she had another hour before takeoff. It would take her about twenty minutes to climb in the jet, accomplish her checklists, taxi to the runway and take off. She would have to make a decision soon. Within the next thirty minutes, she'd be strapped in the seat.

JASON AND SHERRI stood outside the hangar while the civilian security guard checked his credentials. Sherri used her backpack from the car to cover her blood stained jeans. The guard crosschecked his entry list. He was on the list, but she wasn't. He had to think quickly.

"She's a reporter with *The New York Times*," Jason said.

Sherri's eyes narrowed to a squint as her head turned toward him.

"A reporter?" the guard said. "Who authorized this?"

"David Ming. Oh, and the wing commander. Has he been over here to speak with you guys?"

"Do you have any credentials, ma'am?" the guard asked Sherri.

She handed him her press pass, unsure of how Jason was going to pull this off.

"Seems the power structure is concerned with the two flights we've already had," Jason said. "Apparently, some civilian photographed the aircraft during those flights, and you saw that guy with the video footage. They don't want the story breaking in some small market. They want a big paper to carry the story and get the press they want, you know? So they've invited *The Times* for this 'unscheduled' event as a sign of good faith for the public rollout next month."

"Why isn't Mr. Ming here to escort her?" the guard asked, handing Sherri her credentials.

"I guess she's so hot they want a good-looking pilot to show her around," he said with a wink and a smile. He glanced at Sherri, who blushed.

The guard shook his head. "Okay, hotshot, we'll contact Mr. Ming to see if she needs to be on the list permanently. Nice meeting you, Miss Davis."

"Thank you," she replied. "Nice meeting you, too."

Jason shook hands with the guard, leaning toward him as he did so, and spoke softly. "Listen, if you don't see me for about an hour in there, don't come looking for me . . . if you know what I mean."

"I hear you," the grinning guard said.

"Do me a favor? Can you hold off on that phone call to Ming until I come back out? His tongue has been hanging out every time she's around." He placed his hand on the guard's shoulder and gave him a quick wink. "I've been working this all night. I think I'm about to make it happen."

The guard paused. "Sure. Good luck," he said. "Oh, and I'd make it quick. They're getting ready to move the jet to Palmdale, so it's gonna get busy around here fast."

"Thanks, buddy."

Jason grabbed her by the hand and walked briskly into the hangar.

"What was that all about?" she said.

"I had to convince him we were going in there to have sex to buy us some time."

Sherri looked at Jason as if analyzing him. "I've heard stranger things in my time, but I guess it worked."

They entered the interior of the hangar to find the NVG-compatible lights were already on, casting an eerie green glow throughout the large structure. The hangar doors facing the flight line were open, and the crew chiefs had fastened the F-2000 to the tug and were towing it out to the ramp.

"Is that it?" Sherri said.

"Yes, they're getting it ready to fly." He was sure Jennifer was going to fly the jet somewhere other than Palmdale. Even if she wasn't, he had his orders—from the president.

"What are we going to do?"

"First, we've got to get some flight gear."

"Where do we get that?"

"Right in here," he said, opening the door to the makeshift locker room.

81

JONATHAN BOWMAN LEFT Caesar's Palace in a hurry. The evening had gone well for the former senator and presidential candidate. He had chosen an elegant dinner in his penthouse suite with the lovely former model who accompanied him this weekend. It was a nice vacation following all the hard work he'd done the last few years for Century Aero-Bot.

They were in bed asleep when his son had called. Bowman expected something like this to happen eventually. He knew TRENCOR was an unstable company and was surprised they'd developed the jet as far along as they did. He had his suspicions as to what was going on this evening and would discuss it further with Jason when he arrived.

It had been a quick ride to the airport; the private jet was ready with the engines running. Once airborne, his pilot told him they would be there in twenty minutes. Bowman hoped that would be soon enough.

JASON AND SHERRI stepped through the doorway of the makeshift locker room in the back of the hangar. Jennifer sat alone in the middle of the room, crying. Jason and Sherri gave each other a curious look as Jennifer's focus shifted back and forth between the two of them.

"What the hell are you doing here?" Jennifer said, looking at them.

"I was about to ask you the same thing," he said.

"Who's the bimbo?" Jennifer said, tears still flowing.

Jason could see Sherri's face tense.

"The 'bimbo' is the woman who helped you out when you had your ass clocked at the reception a couple of weeks ago," Sherri said.

"You sure are making the rounds," Jennifer replied.

Jason slung the gym bag off his shoulder. "Jennifer, I need you to get undressed," he said as he reached in the bag.

She glared at him with a look of disappointment and annoyance at the same time.

"Well, that's great," Jennifer said. "Your timing is fricking perfect, Jason. Of all the times to finally come around, you choose now. Well, I've got bigger shit to wo—"

Jennifer stopped talking when he pulled the AK-47 out of the bag, pointing it at her head.

"Jennifer, get undressed. Now," he said. "No talking, just get undressed."

Her eyes wide, she unzipped her flight suit. She loosened the laces on her flight boots, kicked them off, and then dropped the flight suit onto the floor. Jason motioned for Sherri to pick it up, never taking the gun off Jennifer.

Sherri grabbed the flight suit and held it in her hands for a moment, unsure. He nodded at her, letting her know it would be okay.

"What the hell are you doing, Jason?" Jennifer asked.

He grabbed Jennifer by the arm, dragging her to a support pole in the middle of the room. He set the old metal chair against the back of the pole and grabbed the 550 cord sitting on the table. He cut a length from the spool, tying Jennifer's hands behind her back.

"See if you can find some duct tape," he said.

Sherri opened every drawer, locker, and cabinet she came across until she found an olive-green roll of speed tape. Jason nodded as she brought it over.

Placing Jennifer in the chair, he proceeded to tape her hands behind her back over the 550 cord. Tears streamed down her cheeks.

"What is happening to me?" Jennifer wailed. "Everything is so—"

Jason placed a strip of duct tape over her mouth.

"I'm really sorry about this," he said. "I'll explain it later . . . if I'm not dead."

He continued to secure her to the chair, then the chair to the pole. Occasionally, he checked on Sherri's progress. She was two inches taller than Jennifer with a slightly larger body frame, but she would pass for Jennifer. The flight boots didn't fit, so she'd have to wear her hiking boots. Hopefully, no one would notice.

"What do you think?" Sherri said once she was dressed.

"It'll work," he said, handing her a parachute harness. "Here," he said softly, "let's get you in this. Here's the plan . . ."

WELLINGTON FINISHED HIS PREFLIGHT walk-around. He smiled as he thought about the 20 mm ammunition on the jet. It would increase the price of the Falcon significantly.

He was doing something that could put him in jail for a long time. Wellington wasn't willing to go to jail for his relationship with TRENCOR, but if he stuck around, he surely would be the scapegoat. He knew the rules of the game, and he cursed himself for being careless.

He couldn't focus on that right now; he had to focus on their mission. Checking his watch, he saw it would be another forty-five minutes before Jennifer took off in the F-2000.

Climbing into the jet, Wellington strapped in, building his nest, placing his pubs and equipment everywhere he needed them. Pulling out his cell phone, he sent a quick text message to his contact in Mexico. The price was going up because the F-16 was loaded with 20mm ammo.

JASON AND SHERRI STEPPED OUT of the locker room into the eerily illuminated hangar. They walked through the hangar, their pace brisk. Both wore their helmets since leaving the locker room, hiding their faces and the NVG lighting made them less identifiable. Once in the darkness outside the hangar, Jason set a helmet bag outside the hangar door.

The F-2000 sat two hundred yards from the hangar on the blacked-out ramp. They both walked around the jet, Jason instructing her along the way to point at certain things, as if she were telling him what to do. The crew chief looked at them strangely, just as Jason had suspected he would. No one accomplishes a preflight with their helmet on, and Jason was sure Daniel Kirby had never done a walk-around.

They finished at the ladders, and the crew chief approached them cautiously, handing Sherri the Form 781s in the orange folder. Sherri took the forms and leaned over to talk to the crew chief.

"Can you be a sweetheart and get my bag for me? I left it by the hangar door," she said. When the crew chief nodded, Sherri reached around, grabbing the senior airman on the butt cheek. He smiled like. a kid on Christmas morning and ran back to the hangar two hundred yards away.

"Don't run," she hollered at him. "It's dark out. Safety first."

The senior airman glanced back at her and nodded, as he walked toward the hangar.

"Safety first? Nice touch," Jason said.

"Thanks," Sherri said with a smile.

"Okay, climb in," he said and followed her up the ladder. Jason strapped her into the seat and hooked up her oxygen. Once she was set, he climbed back down the ladder and pulled it off the F-2000, setting it on the ground away from the jet. He climbed into the front seat. He couldn't believe how fast he was able to get ready. The time he'd invested in the simulator was paying off.

Jason accomplished everything he needed before the crew chief returned with the helmet bag. He approached the front ladder of the jet because that is where Major Walton would sit. By the time he started to climb up the ladder with the bag, Jason waved him off, letting him know he didn't need it. He pointed at the ladder. The crew chief nodded, removed the ladder, and placed it off to the side with the other ladder. Jason breathed a sigh of relief, knowing the crew chief couldn't tell it wasn't Jennifer up front.

He lowered the canopy as the crew chief moved twenty feet to the front of the jet. Jason started the JFS, followed by both engines. In a matter of minutes, he had completed all of his engine start checks.

"Well, that was easier than I anticipated."

"Yeah, I've got to give you credit, you knew exactly what to do," Sherri said. "I just want to say before we go . . . I'm scared to death."

"I understand. Just do me a favor—don't touch anything. Do you see the yellow-striped handle in front of the seat?"

"Yes."

"If we have to get out of the jet while flying, press your back and head against the seat and pull that handle. I'll let you know with the command 'BAILOUT, BAILOUT, BAILOUT.' Don't stick around for the third one because I'll be gone."

"Then what?"

"Then you'll get a kick in the pants and pop out underneath a parachute a second or so later."

"Oh, yellow-striped handles. Got it."

He could tell the way her voice wavered, she was scared.

SENIOR AIRMAN JEFFERSON stood in front of the F-2000 waiting for the signals from the pilot during the engine start. It had been his first time seeing the flirtatious major on the flight line, but he had heard the stories about her from the other crew chiefs. It was unusual she wore her helmet to the jet, but some of these pilots were quirky. He had been told she wasn't very pretty anyway; her body was her main attraction. The guys would be envious when he told them how she grabbed his ass. No, they wouldn't believe him.

The pilot gave him hand signals, and Jefferson went through all the standard motions for the engine start. Airman Jefferson noticed the fire bottle cart was too close to the taxi line and went to move it. As he rolled it in place, he looked back at the hangar. There was some kind of commotion taking place. He turned his attention back to the jet, jogged back out front, and stood at parade rest.

JASON RAPIDLY MOVED through his flows. When he finished, he noticed the crew chief relax his stance, focusing behind the aircraft. The crew chief looked at him, then back behind the jet again. He started pointing and gave the "cut off engine" sign, pointing toward the hangar.

Jason quickly checked his engines and noted nothing wrong. He adjusted the mirrors on the side of the canopy and saw behind him several sets of headlights racing toward the jet.

"Damn."

"What's wrong?" Sherri asked.

"We've got company. Hang on. The jig is up. They found Jennifer." Jason pushed the throttles up on the jet, but it didn't budge.

"Why aren't we going anywhere?"

Jason noticed the crew chief frantically waving his arms.

"The chocks are still in place." He pushed the throttles farther, forcing the powerful jet over the small wooden chocks. Once over the chocks, he kept the power up as he engaged the nosewheel steering, and the jet taxied rapidly to the parallel. Jason looked to the right where he needed to taxi as a truck pulled onto the parallel blocking his path. He elected to go to the left and accelerated as the vehicles trailing him started to catch him. He figured they would try to get in front of him to keep him from taxiing or taking off.

As his speed approached seventy knots, the jet pulled away from the maintenance trucks. He kept his cross-check going back and forth from the taxiway in front of him to the mirrors, checking on his pursuers. He wasn't worried until a couple of vehicles with flashing blue lights pulled out about a half mile in front of him.

82

May 30, 2001

WELLINGTON JERKED HIS HEAD upright, lunging forward in his seat. Did he hear that right? He adjusted the volume on the radio to monitor Edwards Tower.

"Unidentified aircraft on parallel taxiway, this is Edwards Tower on Guard," the voice said over the radio. "Hold your position on parallel taxiway. You are not authorized to taxi."

He glanced at his watch. *That dumb bitch is thirty minutes early. What the hell is she thinking?*

Waving to the lineman, Wellington signaled he was ready for engine start. Snapping his oxygen mask in place, he cranked the JFS, then started the engine on his single-engine jet fighter.

"ARE THOSE CARS heading toward us?" Sherri asked from the back.

"Yeah."

Jason glanced at his instruments. Still holding seventy knots indicated airspeed, it hit him. Grabbing his flap handle, he lowered the flaps to fifty percent, pushing the power up to MAX. The jet gave them a slight kick in the pants as the afterburner ignited.

"You're not going to try to ram them, are you?"

"No . . . better," Jason said.

The headlights were getting bigger fast as the two forces accelerated toward each other. At less than a thousand feet to go, the F-2000 had accelerated to one hundred knots. He reached for the nozzle thrust vector lever, moving it to the VSTOL position. The engine exhausts shifted downward as the large fighter jet lifted away from the ground.

The jet hovered a couple of feet, wobbling back and forth as he struggled with the flight controls, but it was smoother than the simulator. Gradually, it climbed high enough for him to raise the gear. Outside, the police cars slowed to a stop. Two security policemen exited the first vehicle, drew their weapons, and fired at the jet.

He applied right rudder and the jet pivoted on its lateral axis, pointing the exhaust nozzles at the SPs firing at him, their bullets bouncing off the futuristic jet. The landing gear sucked into the bottom of the aircraft and the jet climbed and crept forward with the reduction in drag. When he raised the flaps, he lowered the nose, and shifted the nozzle direction to the normal position. The F-2000 started to accelerate as he made a climbing turn to the east.

THE SUN PUSHED ITS WAY above the horizon. The sky was always its darkest before sunrise, but the visibility to the east would pose new problems as he scanned the horizon. In the sky toward the base, Wellington saw the rising jet over the airfield. The afterburners on the F-2000 were barely visible from the field twenty miles away, highlighted by the still dark sky high above the horizon. The unusual vertical movement on a clear black night gave it away.

Lowering his canopy, he ignored most of the normal checks. He needed to get airborne quickly. Turning on his VHF radio, he called Jennifer on their predetermined frequency with no response.

Signaling for the lineman to remove the chocks, Wellington pushed the throttle forward. He taxied onto the parallel and headed for the hammerhead.

"Tower. Tango India Niner-Five-Zero-Three-Niner-Niner approaching number one. VFR to the east. Ready for takeoff," Wellington said over the radio.

There was a slight pause, then the tower responded. "Tango India Niner-Five-Zero-Three-Niner-Niner, you are cleared for takeoff."

"Five-Zero-Three-Niner-Niner is cleared for takeoff," Wellington replied.

Wellington slowed his jet as he approached the turn into the hammerhead. He cleared the sky around his position for other aircraft and taxied across the hammerhead onto the active runway. He didn't stop, pushing the throttle into afterburner as his nose straightened in line with the runway for a rolling takeoff. Eight seconds later he was airborne, turning toward Edwards Air Force Base.

JASON PULLED THE THROTTLES out of afterburner and leveled off at 10,000 feet while he input the coordinates Caldwell gave him into the jet's navigation system. The jet cruised at three hundred knots, and Jason noticed the jet held its altitude very well.

"How are you doing back there?" he said.

"Fine," she replied. "I take back all the bad thoughts I've had about you. You really know how to show a girl a good time."

"Thanks," he chuckled, "but I'd rather try something different next time." Jason struggled to manipulate the multi-function display to input the coordinates and fly the jet simultaneously.

"Oh, we're going on a second date?"

"Only if we live through the first one. I didn't realize you had a sense of humor."

"I'm overcompensating for being terrified"

"That's fine," Jason said, focusing on his task while the aircraft sluggishly pushed through the sky to the east. He silently cursed himself as he remembered to engage the autopilot. This was a luxury he wasn't used to since the T-38 didn't have an autopilot. Once engaged, it reduced his workload to the point he could finish his data inputs. "There's a button on the right side of the helmet," he said over the interphone. "The lens on these helmets is a prototype that lets you see in the dark. Push the button and see what you get."

"Cool," Sherri said. "Everything is green. I'm seeing what looks like instrumentation thingies on my visor."

Jason chuckled again. "Yeah, those *thingies* are a heads-up display generator. It helps the pilot fly the jet while looking somewhere else."

"How does it work?"

"Smoke and mirrors. Some kind of new technology allowing you to operate electronics without a data cord attached. The sun is starting to come up, so you'll want to turn the night vision switch off. If not, your visor will be totally washed out and you won't be able to see."

Jason finished plugging in the coordinates. For the second time, he pushed the throttles forward into afterburner when suddenly the cockpit illuminated, red lights going off everywhere in front of him.

83

May 30, 2001

J ASON PULLED THE THROTTLES out of afterburner, and the lights went out when the throttles were around sixty percent. Scanning his engine instruments, they appeared to be operating normally as the EGT on both engines returned to the normal range.

"Is everything okay up there?" Sherri asked from the back. "I saw a bunch of red lights reflecting off the glass."

"There's a slight problem if I try to use the afterburner. Both engines overheat, but I don't think it's the engines," he said. "It's probably the software again, but I'm going to play it safe and not use the afterburners. How are you doing back there? Are you going to be sick?"

"I'm okay. Are those red lights going to be a problem?"

"We should be good. I've only got to keep this thing airborne for another hour."

LEVELING AT 10,000 FEET, he accelerated toward the lone jet. Wellington pushed his F-16 past four hundred and fifty knots indicated airspeed as he sped toward the F-2000. The sun showed itself slightly, the horizon slowly evolving into a gradual changing palette of light and color. The F-2000 would be difficult to see until the sun popped above the horizon. Until then, he could track her on his radar. The TRENCOR technicians insisted on reapplying the self-healing skin to the jet in one more attempt to test how much the experimental skin compromised stealth. It was significant. Wellington considered it a stupid concept. Stealth is far more important than this self-healing skin. But there was a reason Ming wanted the jet back with the skin in place. Perhaps the Chinese had another use for this technology?

Cursing under his breath, he watched his target on the radar screen. Where the hell was she going? She was heading east, not south.

At a half mile, he recognized the closure on the F-2000 was too great; he was traveling well over a hundred knots faster than the new jet.

Rather than jerking the throttle back to idle, he would fly his F-16 in front of the F-2000 so Jennifer could see he was airborne.

Streaking past the jet from its left side, he banked his F-16 forty-five degrees for a ninety-degree turn. He briefly pushed the throttle into afterburner so she would see him as he crossed her flight path. He pulled his nose up, turning his kinetic energy into potential energy as he pulled the throttle to idle. Fuel management would be critical tonight.

"UH-OH, WE'VE GOT company up here, too," Jason said.

"Who is that?"

Jason watched the jet fly in front of them, then pull up and out of sight.

"It's an F-16. I can't believe they had one ready to fly tonight. Maybe they've got a secret alert status for fighters."

Regardless, he knew it was time to go. He pushed the throttles forward as the jet shot past his position. The state-of-the-art SCRAM jet engines rapidly accelerated the F-2000. In seconds, he was traveling at four hundred knots. Scanning up and behind him, he saw the position lights of the jet coming over the top to roll back in behind him.

Jason turned on his radio suite. With both VHF and UHF radios on, he could monitor radio traffic on four different frequencies.

"This is Edwards Tower on Guard. Unidentified aircraft departing Edwards to the east, you are ordered to land back at Edwards immediately."

"They're on to us. I can't listen to this all night," he said.

Jason pushed his finger to the touch screen and turned off the GUARD frequency on his UHF radio.

Checking his six, he picked up the F-16 closing again from the left side. The F-16 established itself in route position about five hundred feet away and slid in closer to the F-2000 until they were four ships' width apart.

The pilot in the F-16 gave him the visual signal to push the UHF radio to "Winchester," frequency 303.0, or 30-30. This was an unused UHF radio frequency and popular amongst aircrew for unofficial conversation between aircraft. The pilots liked it because the frequency represented the caliber 30-30, hence the name "Winchester". As the two jets climbed through 15,000 feet, he switched his radio over to the frequency and gave the F-16 a big head nod. He noticed for the first time that the F-16 wasn't painted the combat gray of most F-16s. This one was an off-white color with the TRENCOR logo painted on the side.

"Jennifer, what the hell are you doing?" Wellington snapped over the radio.

Jason laughed. "I should have known," he said to Sherri over the interphone.

"What?" Sherri said.

"It's Wellington. I think they were going to steal the jet," he said.

"What makes you say that?" Sherri said.

"Because no one schedules a chase plane to move a jet to another field. They are up to something."

Jason didn't respond to Wellington.

"Jennifer, you're going the wrong damn way. You're supposed to be heading south. Did you lose the coordinates? We've only got about an hour and a quarter of fuel." Wellington barked over the radio.

Jason stayed silent, realizing his assumption was correct. Wellington pulled his jet closer to a three-foot fingertip position. "An hour and a quarter south? South is Mexico," Jason said to Sherri. "They were going to steal the F-2000 and fly to Mexico."

"Who the hell is in the back seat? You're supposed to be alone," Wellington said over the radio.

Jason keyed the radio microphone on the throttles with his left thumb. "Good morning, Jeremiah."

"Who the hell is this?" Wellington replied.

"Just your favorite fricking FAIP," Jason said.

"Conrad . . . where the hell is Jen—uh, Major Walton?"

"She was busy back at the hangar, if you know what I mean."

"You son of a bitch. What the hell are you doing in that jet? Conrad, turn that jet south now," Wellington said.

Jason looked at him and shook his head. "I don't think I can do that. That dark hole out there to the south, that's Mexico. And I don't have a passport."

The F-16 bolted up forty-five degrees nose high and dropped out of sight.

WELLINGTON ROLLED HIS JET inverted to keep the F-2000 in sight. The sun pushed its way above the horizon, and he was able to visually track the F-2000's outline. What the hell happened to Jennifer? Was she in the back seat? Did she cut a deal with Conrad? No, that was impossible. It didn't matter, he needed the jet to head south. If he couldn't get Conrad to fly to their rendezvous airport, his future consisted of jail or death. Neither was an acceptable solution for the retired one-star general.

He let the F-2000 slide ahead about three thousand feet, pulling the nose of his fighter below the horizon. Once there, he rolled the jet upright, accelerated, and placed himself in a position aft about a thousand feet, offset to the left.

"Conrad, I need you to turn your jet to a heading of one-eight-zero immediately," he said over the radio. The two jets now passed through 23,000 feet. He noticed the F-2000 start to level off and accelerate.

"You can say 'south.' They taught us FAIPs what the heading is for south. North, east, and west, too. But I think I'll do my own thing for now."

Gritting his teeth beneath his oxygen mask, he maneuvered his jet into firing position.

Pulling up his weapons selection page, he armed the 20mm Vulcan cannon and lined up his shot in the HUD. He had a tracer every fifth round. Wellington flipped the safety off, moving his pipper forward of the F-2000. His finger hovered over the trigger, then softly rested on top.

A moment later, he squeezed.

"HOLY SHIT," JASON SAID AS tracers flew in front of them.

"Is he shooting at us?" Sherri said.

"Yes," Jason replied. "I'm guessing he doesn't like my sense of humor. And I don't like being shot at."

Banking the jet one hundred-twenty degrees to the right, Jason rolled, pulling away from the F-16 in a diving, high-G turn. Wellington followed, and Jason pulled his jet back up to the horizon.

Glancing to his right, he saw the F-16 move into firing position. He rolled back to the left and jammed his throttles forward, using caution not to bump them into afterburner. Another set of tracers flew through the airspace behind him.

He managed a little separation with the maneuver, but Wellington was hot on his tail. Jason made a hard left turn, and Wellington dove below and pointed his nose in front of the F-2000's flight path.

The F-16 entered a maneuver called a Low Yo-Yo, forcing him to pull the throttles back to idle and pop the speed brake.

The F-16's firing solution degraded, and the tracers shot out front as the Falcon overshot his jet with too much energy.

Jason rolled right again, dumping his nose as he pushed the throttles forward, diving toward the black hole of the desert.

WELLINGTON CURSED AT HIMSELF zooming from the Low Yo-Yo into a High Yo-Yo. Both maneuvers used energy to its advantage. In the Low Yo-Yo, the pursuing jet dove beneath the target's horizontal plane without adjusting his power. While in the descent, the jet accelerated, thus creating kinetic energy to pursue the target above. In the High Yo-Yo, the pursuer climbs, trading his airspeed for altitude. Using the separation, he's higher and slower than the target below, creating potential energy that can be used to descend and accelerate toward his target. He didn't want to waste ammo if he didn't have a good shot. Even though he was shooting 100-round bursts, that only gave him twenty squeezes of the trigger. The buyer in Mexico would have to settle for less than a full drum of ammo.

He turned back and saw the F-2000 in a descending right turn. He rolled the F-16 back into a position of lead pursuit, closing the gap with Conrad's jet. Wellington saw the F-2000 roll wings level and pull.

Conrad was taking him over the top. Wellington smiled as the F-2000 exposed itself vertically in his windscreen. Conrad's inexperience placed him in an optimum position for a target. Seeing the opportunity for a quick shot, he squeezed the trigger as the F-2000 flew upward 3000 feet in front of his HUD. The 20mm rounds hit the F-2000's left wing as it flew out of view. Wellington pulled up in pursuit as the two jets climbed vertically.

84

S HERRI SCREAMED AS BULLETS impacted the left wing, sending sparks everywhere. Checking his altitude and airspeed, he rolled out when he reached the top of his maneuver. It was sloppy, but he was trying to avoid getting shot. He checked his instruments—his jet was at 25,000 feet with a slightly over three-hundred knots airspeed. He quickly glanced at the left wing assessing the damage. There were at least five holes, and he wasn't sure how the jet would take high-performance maneuvers.

Jason looked to the right. Wellington's F-16 hung in the air about two thousand feet away, its airspeed as slow as his own. Recognizing Wellington's mistake, he dumped the nose of his jet and banked hard into the F-16.

"Jason, what are you doing?"

"The only way I can keep him from shooting us is to get behind him," he said.

As soon as Jason flashed his wings, the stuttering F-16 rolled, dumping its nose and pulling into him. Jason pulled hard until the jet shook excessively, indicating it was close to a stall. He eased off the back pressure, and as soon as he crossed in front of the F-16, rolled back to the left.

Focusing on the F-16, Jason rapidly banked to the right as they crossed paths again, aggressively pulling into the F-16 about a thousand feet away.

Wellington was slow to recognize Jason's move and rolled inverted over the top of Jason's jet. Jason instantly rolled back to the left, persistently bidding for Wellington's six o'clock, or aft position. The constant pulling and high-banking maneuver killed his energy as the two aircraft used altitude to maintain their airspeed. They were falling *through* the sky to keep from falling *out* of the sky.

The yanking and banking went on for another four iterations before Jason saw some hope. A frustrated Wellington's fired a burst of 20 mm shot into an empty sky, the F-2000 nowhere in his gun sight.

He maneuvered the F-2000 behind Wellington's fighter, but the battle was half over. The F-2000 had no armament loaded, and even if it did, he had no experience in air-to-air combat. He could fly the maneuvers, but weapons delivery was another animal. Sliding the jet into a close trail position, he placed his jet behind and slightly below the F-16. Flying at two hundred thirty knots indicated airspeed, the noses of the two jets dipped as his airspeed began a gradual increase.

Wellington banked his F-16 to the left and right. *He's lost me! He's looking for my position!* Jason couldn't believe his luck.

"Wha-where . . . Does he know we're right behind him?" Sherri asked from the back seat.

"Not yet. He'll figure it out real fast."

"What then?"

"I don't know. I'm making this up as I go along," Jason said. Touché, Indiana Jones.

Taking advantage of the lull in action, he checked out his jet. The left wing still looked fine. He wondered if his imagination played tricks on him, then he remembered that one of the original specs on this jet was to have a self-healing skin. Could this be one of the reasons for the high cost overruns? TRENCOR and their Chinese scientists must have re-installed the advanced technology on the F-2000. Maybe that was why they wanted the jet back.

AT AN ISOLATED AIRFIELD outside the western edge of the Tonopah Test Range, a small group of men frantically tracked two jets across the California and Nevada skies. The airfield, with its ten-thousand-foot runway with a one-hundred-fifty-thousand-square-foot ramp on its northeastern edge, belonged to Century Aero-Bot.

Two King-Air turbo-props sat on the ramp. The first delivered Doctor Brian Foster and his team. The second brought in a team from Century Aero-Bot's weapons division.

The radar operator quickly picked up the F-2000 with the second aircraft in pursuit. A quick phone call, and the team figured out it was

TRENCOR's F-16 from the East Kern Airport District. They monitored the two jets as they constantly changed direction and altitudes. Their initial assessment was the F-16 attempted to shoot down the F-2000. Once the uplink was established, that was verified. The F-2000's computer told them every time a bullet hit the jet.

"What's Bowman's ETA?" Foster asked the lead contractor for the second team.

"Ten minutes," he replied looking up from his desk. "When does the package get here?"

"Five minutes before that," Foster said.

"It could be a fur-ball up there when he arrives."

"We're relaying everything to his pilot. He'll avoid any trouble."

The team lead gave Foster a grimace and returned to his work.

Doctor Foster stood by, watching the weapons technicians set up their equipment. He was out of his comfort zone with what he saw. He was a doctor. These guys had flown out here an hour ago to set up a weapon Century Aero-Bot was developing. A weapon that could change the face of modern warfare. A weapon simply referred to as the LEEMA Protocol.

WELLINGTON SEARCHED BOTH sides of his jet but couldn't see the F-2000. The 20mm hits on the left wing were clearly visible when Conrad went vertical. Perhaps the high-stress maneuvering had been enough to cause it to crash. Conrad could have overstressed the jet at cornering velocity like he did on his sim profiles. Most likely, the state-of-the-art jet had simply disappeared, escaping the battlefield.

There wasn't a fireball on the ground, so Conrad must have escaped. He continued his descent to pick up airspeed. Approaching three hundred fifty knots, Wellington pushed the throttle forward and climbed to 17,500 feet.

Checking his fuel, he knew his time was short and he had to make a decision. He could search for the F-2000 and shoot Conrad out of the sky, claiming he stopped him from stealing the jet. Or he could go to Mexico, sell the F-16, and disappear in South America, avoiding Hong Kong altogether.

He decided it was time to cut his losses. Wellington turned toward Mexico.

JASON WATCHED WELLINGTON'S F-16 make an aggressive

maneuver to the south, breaking away from the engagement. Jason rolled his jet to his right, twisting his body left, as he attempted to keep the F-16 in sight.

"AAAGGHHH!" Jason exclaimed as a sharp familiar pain in his neck riveted his body and shot down his right arm.

"What's wrong?" Sherri asked.

Jason's grip on the stick loosened as he rolled out of his bank.

"I just tweaked my neck," he said. "Hurts like hell." His breathing came in large gasps as his body struggled to function. His grip in his right hand was deteriorating rapidly—and that was the hand that flew the jet.

He visually picked up the F-16 still descending and turning south about a mile away. Recognizing his opportunity, Jason pointed his jet toward the east, coupled the autopilot, and lit the afterburners. He knew he shouldn't, but he needed separation from Wellington fast. The afterburners kicked in a, immediately setting off the cockpit's red warning lights. The jet accelerated to 1.3 Mach as he pulled the throttles back to sixty percent and he re-engaged the navigation system. The warning lights gradually went out as the F-2000 headed to its destination.

"Are you okay?" Sherri said. "Can you land?"

"Uh, I'm not worried about that right now." He shifted in his seat to ease the pain in his back, but nothing worked. His entire right side went numb; he couldn't move his right arm. Silently, he evaluated his condition and their situation. They might not have enough fuel to make it.

"So we don't have to eject?" Sherri asked.

Jason picked up on the concern in her voice, but he didn't want to think about it. He knew the result if he ejected with his back in this condition. If it didn't kill him, he'd be crippled for life.

"I sure as hell hope not," he said.

The jet climbed, leveling at 25,000 feet as it flew to their unknown destination. He hoped he would get feeling back into his right side before he had to land the jet—providing they had enough fuel to make it that far.

85

May 30, 2001

THE PAIN RADIATED through the right side of his body. Being confined in the F-2000 didn't help his spinal column. His right arm was numb; he had no ability to grip the stick, and could never land the jet safely.

His flight computer told him his destination was sixty miles away. The jet's computer deduced his flight plan would run him low on gas, so it adjusted his altitude.

As he struggled for a solution, he realized Sherri didn't speak much. He'd been wrong about her. She was tough. For someone afraid to fly, she was having a hell of a night.

Reviewing the navigation track in the Flight Management System, Jason realized the location sat a hundred miles west of Las Vegas. Could it . . . no. Not Area 51; that would be too weird. He pulled up the digital map and checked the coordinates. It wasn't Area 51, but it was close to the Tonopah Test Range, and just as isolated.

When the jet reached the field, it slowed to its max endurance airspeed and rolled into a holding pattern, waiting for instructions. He needed to figure out how to get the jet on the ground.

"What's wrong?" Sherri said.

"We've reached our destination. The jet is holding overhead, waiting for me to take over and fly it to the runway."

"Well, what are we waiting for?"

Jason paused, "I can't move my right arm."

"What?"

"Whatever I've tweaked in my neck has me jacked-up. I can't move my right side."

"Can you land the plane?"

There was a moment of awkward silence; like when you get caught with your hand in the cookie jar and have an internal debate about whether to admit you were stealing a cookie. "Not right now."

"Don't you have some kind of autopilot thingy that can land the plane?"

"Sort of. The autopilot will get us on the approach, but it doesn't have auto-land capability. At least as far as I know."

"Oh," she said. He knew she felt helpless back there.

"Sherri, listen to me. I want you to stay with me as long as you can. The jet will keep circling until it runs out of gas. When you hear the engines stop running, I'll blow the canopy off the aircraft. You need to pull your ejection handle to leave the aircraft, okay?"

"What about you?"

"I'm going to stick with this as long as I can," he said as his vision started to blur. He couldn't focus. He tried to use the left side of his body to stretch his back, but it was useless. His mind wandered, as if in a dream. He could hear Sherri talking . . . the jet slowed and started a descent . . . he felt the large clunk of the landing gear . . .

Jason smiled under the oxygen mask. His father's team had come through. The jet line up with the runway when tracers flew from behind on the left and moved closer and closer toward his canopy.

IT HAD BEEN A TOUGH DECISION for Wellington to re-engage with the F-2000, but it was a decision made quickly. He was first and foremost a fighter pilot. He built a career on making quick decisions. After reassessing his fuel, he realized he didn't have the gas to make it to his secret destination in Mexico. Even if he did, the Chinese would find him and kill him for losing the F-2000. Fortunately, he could easily track the jet on the radar. The stealthy capabilities of the F-2000 were great, but not with the self-healing skin attached.

He hoped the US government would buy his story about stopping Conrad from stealing the jet. He'd worry about the illegal attributes of his F-16 later. Always better to beg for forgiveness than to ask for permission.

Conrad had the jet in a holding pattern at 5,000 feet about thirty miles ahead of him.

The F-16 descended to 17,500 feet as he tracked the F-2000 in his

HUD. He closed the distance between them to get within gun range. As he flew closer to the F-2000, Wellington eased off the airspeed. Trying to maneuver at too high a speed might lead to a G-Lock. Then he'd truly turn into a "lawn dart," as the jet had been nicknamed decades ago. He shook his head trying to stay focused. Never before had he thought that in the jet. Never.

Leveling at 6,000 feet, he armed the 20mm cannon. He gimbaled his radar both vertically and horizontally searching for the F-2000. The jet was two miles away, and he still couldn't see it as the sun blinded him rising halfway through the horizon. He slowed to three hundred fifty knots indicated airspeed. At one mile, he made visual contact. At a half a mile, he had the jet lock up; at a quarter mile, he broke radar lock.

Moving the pipper back onto the F-2000, he squeezed off a quick burst of the cannon as the F-16 zoomed overhead its target.

"DAMN," JASON MUMBLED as tracer rounds flew ahead of his flight path. He struggled to keep an eye on him as the F-16 flew overhead.

"Is he back?" Sherri said.

"Yeah, it's him."

"What can we do?"

"I don't—"

He stopped speaking as the gear began to retract into the jet and the throttles moved forward. The flaps retracted as the jet accelerated toward the east.

"What just happened?" Sherri said.

Jason grinned. He wanted to shout with joy, but he hurt too much.

IN THE CLIMBING TURN following his overshoot, Wellington looked back to see the F-2000 accelerate and turn east underneath him. Reversing direction, he acquired the state-of-the-art jet and continued pursuit. With Mexico no longer an option, the only thing left was to kill Jason Conrad.

The F-2000 was in the weeds now, utilizing the terrain-following radar. Another one of the extra features TRENCOR had provided, although not an initial requirement.

Two miles away, he searched desperately for an opportunity to take a kill shot. He had about ten minutes of fuel, maximum, before he'd have to take the silk elevator back to Mother Earth.

THERE WAS NO ACTIVITY in the small room except for the lone contractor who guided the F-2000's movement through the mountainous terrain. Foster and his team had the role of tapping into the RPA and taking control of the jet. Once their equipment gained the satellite uplink and logged into the F-2000's computer system, he confirmed the ITCS couldn't be used because there were no sensors attached to the pilot. However, the jet still could be controlled through the RPA system.

The team gathered around his desk and monitored the jet's actions. The two previously separate teams now acted as one. Across the room, the weapons techs were feeding the RPA controller coordinates to send to the jet.

Light spilled into the room as the door opened and the vice president of Century Aero-Bot, Jonathan Bowman, entered the room.

"Nice to see you, sir," Doctor Foster said.

"Doctor," Bowman said, nodding his head. "What's our status?"

"We have control of the jet. Unfortunately, there's a threat out there attempting to shoot him down."

"Who?"

"We don't know who it is, but it's an F-16. He's squawking 1200," Doctor Foster said. Twelve hundred was the code used for aircraft flying under visual flight rules.

Bowman thought for a moment. TRENCOR used an F-16 as a chase plane. It must be Wellington.

"Did the F-16 fire yet?"

"Yes, sir," replied the tech controlling the jet. "The F-2000 was on final approach at 5,000 feet when the F-16 made a gun pass at them."

"No missile shot?" He was concerned about his son, but the kid seemed to be holding his own against the aging fighter jock.

"No, sir."

"What's the situation now?" Bowman asked.

"We've initiated the LEEMA Protocol. It should be active now," the tech said, referring to Laser-Enhanced Electro-Magnetic Acquisition, a precision, laser-guided electro-magnetic pulse about to be used for the first time today.

86

May 30, 2001

THE F-2000 ACCELERATED to three hundred knots, hugging the terrain two hundred feet above the ground. The jet plowed east effortlessly, dodging mountains and rock formations. Jason assumed there were no power lines this deep into the desert, but he was well aware of the prohibited airspace his jet was headed for— the Tonopah Test Range.

"What's going on?" Sherri said.

"Whoever . . . is controlling us . . . detected Wellington . . . taking defensive maneuvers," Jason replied. Helpless, he struggled to hold his head up as it fell listlessly to the right.

THIS LITTLE SHIT CONRAD tried to screw his mistress and steal his jet. Wellington hated to destroy the jet he spent so much time and money developing, but this was about survival. Over the past few minutes, while he pushed his jet to catch the F-2000, he formulated his cover story. This could work. His bank account was empty, stolen by the Chinese. The same Chinese who ripped off the US government with a faulty jet. Jason Conrad, who had brought a Russian agent into the fold at Edwards AFB, stole the F-2000. The only option Wellington had left was to chase him and shoot him out of the sky. It was thin, but it was a start. All he needed was plausible deniability.

In the distance, he saw the F-2000 heading for the saddle in the ridgeline, a low spot in the mountainous terrain. He knew the jet would use the saddle to clear the ridgeline, and if done effectively, would be a quick pop-up maneuver before it returned to terrain following. That's where he'd take his shot.

Descending to 5,000 feet and closing within a quarter mile, Wellington lined the F-2000 up in his HUD. A quick check of his ammo in the HUD showed he had only two hundred rounds left. A good two bursts if he was careful. He accelerated to decrease his range. Ahead of the F-2000, he saw a mountain range that would require Conrad to make a ridge crossing. It would be the ideal location to take down the jet. Wellington positioned the F-16 for the shot. He'd shoot when the jet rolled to descend on the backside of the ridgeline.

JASON GLANCED AT THE FUEL GAUGE. They couldn't keep this up much longer. He hoped whoever controlled the F-2000 had the fuel in their crosscheck.

"Are you . . . okay back there?" Jason asked.

"Yes, but I'm ready to go home now," she replied. She didn't sound so good.

Jason grimaced under his oxygen mask. Both of them were trapped in the jet, helpless to do anything except go along for the ride. The jet bobbed and weaved through the terrain. The F-2000 turned toward a saddle in the ridgeline. Jason realized the jet would need to execute a pop-up maneuver, exposing him to Wellington's F-16.

WELLINGTON WATCHED PATIENTLY. Predictably, the F-2000 popped up over the saddle in the ridgeline. It rolled inverted, immediately pulling down toward the terrain. His angle was good as he armed the gun and placed his finger over the trigger and squeezed.

The F-16 vibrated with a buzzing noise as the 20mm Vulcan cannon spit its fire. Wellington watched the tracers dance all the way to the F-2000, again hitting the left side. The rounds impacted the fuselage ahead of the cockpit and worked their way aft, just above the wing root. He was certain he saw rounds impact the canopy. Banking to the right in lag pursuit to prevent another overshoot, he followed Conrad over the ridgeline as the F-2000 quickly rolled upright again and descended toward the flat terrain.

SPARKS FLEW AS THE F-16's 20mm bullets riddled the right side of the inverted F-2000. Sherri screamed as the rounds impacted the side of the jet with a series of loud plinks. Jason didn't move—at this point he couldn't, his right side totally numb. The canopy absorbed a few rounds; Jason, happy that at least that performed to spec. It might not survive another impact, however. The right side resembled a spider web as cracks emanated from three distinct impacts.

The jet quickly rolled upright again as it hugged the terrain. Once through the saddle, the jet descended into what resembled a flat bowl as mountains surrounding the area stretched at least forty miles across.

He couldn't see outside, but he assumed the self-healing skin properties of the jet were doing their thing. The titanium lining surrounding the cockpit kept the 20mm rounds from damaging the internal systems of the jet.

CURSING, WELLINGTON ROLLED back to the left. He maneuvered into position to get his final shot, from the right side this time if the F-2000 remained airborne. His last shots hit the only place on the F-2000 protected by the titanium shell and the reinforced canopy. Damn, he thought, we built a good airplane. It's a shame I've got to destroy it.

In the HUD, his pipper moved gradually around the target until the radar locked on the F-2000. Wellington took a deep breath and moved his finger over the trigger.

JASON STARED AT DISTANT LIGHTS on the ground, unsure of who or what would be located this deep into the desert. The longer he watched them, the more they appeared to moving. Autokinetic Illusion, nothing more than a trick the eye plays on the brain when staring at a bright light for too long on a dark night. But it was daytime . . . and these lights really did appear to be moving.

GRADUALLY, THE F-2000 slid into the gun sight in Wellington's HUD. This would be his last shot, and he lined it up carefully. His F-16 now 2,000 feet away with textbook alignment of the two aircraft. Smiling at his skill in air combat, he felt pleased with himself. An aging fighter pilot who could still kick the crap out of a young, snot-nosed jet jockey flying the latest and greatest state-of-the-art fighter. Skill overcomes technology every time.

Confirming in his HUD the rounds of ammo left, he laid his finger over the trigger when his peripheral vision picked up bright flashes outside. A line of tracers flew past his canopy at a steady rate. Anti-aircraft fire! Damn! He broke contact with the F-2000 and dove toward the ground, his hands instinctively deploying chaff and flares that didn't exist.

"SIR, BOTH JETS ARE CLOSING. The triple-A was right on time and created the separation we need. LEEMA Protocols are in place, ready to go live," the tech said to Bowman.

"Sensors indicate the F-2000 took approximately twenty-six rounds to the right fuselage. All systems are functioning normally. Fuel state is critical," a second tech said behind him.

Bowman glanced at the second tech briefly before returning his gaze to the screen tracking the jets.

"Execute the LEEMA Protocol," Bowman said.

"Roger," the tech said, picking up a red phone. "LEEMA Protocol, execute, execute, execute."

"Roger, LEEMA Protocol in progress," a voice said on the other end.

Bowman focused on the screen. The damn Chinese thought they were getting away with something. Well, they would have if it weren't for Jason and his friend. It was a good plan except for the fact they needed Century Aero-Bot's tech.

The blips on the screen edged closer and closer to the center. Bowman watched with trepidation. His newest and most innovative project would soon be tested.

"WHAT'S THAT?" SHERRI SAID when the tracer rounds raced from the ground toward the F-16.

"We must have some friends here," Jason said. "That should scare him off."

Suddenly, the jet rolled into a forty-five-degree climbing left turn.

"Uh-oh," Jason said.

"What's wrong?" Sherri was a trouper, but she wasn't stupid. Jason was aware she knew their situation.

"I'm . . . not sure . . . but it looks like," he said, gasping, "we're climbing back . . . toward our original destination."

"But won't that make us vulnerable to that asshole out there?"

Jason thought for a moment; the answer obvious.

"Yes."

HE HADN'T KEPT TRACK of his location, but experience told him they must have drifted too far east, into the prohibited airspace of the Tonopah Test Range. They approached the no-fly area, and he wasn't responding to their radio calls. Their orders no doubt, were to shoot down the jets if they entered their airspace.

Wellington instinctively checked his six in an effort to find the AAA location. He received no radar warning because the threat warning controls and azimuth indicator gear didn't work on his decommissioned A-model. He never considered updating it when he had the radar re-installed. Returning his attention to the front, his windscreen filled with terrain as he approached a small hill. He instinctively pulled back on the stick, and his jet climbed skyward. Checking his altimeter, he saw the F-16 had climbed to 6,000 feet above the ground. He rolled the jet inverted and pulled the nose below the horizon to get back in the weeds and create a tougher firing solution for the gunners.

His eyes were distracted by colored lights on the ground that danced around, but abruptly came together as one.

Lasers?

Then his jet went dark, his displays, lights, and buttons shut down. No Master Caution Warning light. Nothing. His jet lost all power.

"SIR," THE TECHNICIAN SAID. "The LEEMA Protocol functioned as advertised. Programming for a second shot."

"Standby," Bowman said. "Where's the F-2000?"

The radar operator stared at his screen. "Separation is good. Over a mile and six thousand feet altitude separation."

Bowman turned back to the tech manning the LEEMA Protocol. "Hold off that second shot. I want to see how this plays out."

"But Mister Bowman," Doctor Foster interjected, "isn't that your son up there?"

Bowman never looked up from the screen. "Yes."

SOMETHING HAPPENED TO the electrical power in his jet. The cockpit went dark and his HUD blanked out. Wellington checked switches for the Main AC, Alternate AC, Main DC, and the battery for electrical power with no results. He made the control inputs to roll the jet upright.

The jet didn't move.

Fear worked its way into his consciousness as he again attempted to roll the jet upright. He couldn't see his instrumentation to tell how high above the ground his jet flew, but he knew he needed to eject.

Not sure of his airspeed or altitude, he did the quick mental math. His canopy filled with nothing but the rapidly rising desert floor and he realized, with the acceleration of the jet from that seat-of-the-pants feeling, it didn't matter. Even with a zero-zero seat, he wouldn't survive the ejection. He was done.

They say your life flashes before your eyes before you die. All Wellington saw was his hands around the throat of Jason Conrad while Jennifer lay nude on the bed on a pile of money as he killed Conrad. Those things never happened, but he wanted them to. He smiled at the thought.

The jet plunged inverted toward the desert floor for three more seconds before impacting the ground and erupting into a huge orange, yellow, and red fireball.

THE EXPLOSION WAS CLEARLY visible from the F-2000 as they turned and climbed back to the west.

"Oh, my God," Sherri exclaimed. "What was that?"

Jason struggled as the numbness of his arm continued to work its way into his head, but the billowing black smoke a mile away got his attention.

"That was . . . that guy . . ." he mumbled. He couldn't tell if Wellington ejected or not. Relieved from the immediate threat, Jason succumbed to his body's struggle with consciousness letting blackness overcome him.

The F-2000 leveled at 10,000 feet and flew west toward its original destination.

EPILOGUE

September 10, 2001

The Boston Park Plaza Hotel stood wedged between Columbus Avenue, Park Plaza, and Arlington Street. Built in 1927, it was the gold standard of hotels. The first hotel in America to have a radio in every room, it also introduced the concept of utilizing the same plumbing for two rooms with their backs to each other. Thus, it became the first hotel in America to have a bathroom in every room, as well. Today, the refurbished hotel housed over 900 guest rooms and suites in its fourteen-story setting.

Jason paid the cab driver and stepped onto the sidewalk. A group of young men across the street yelling "Go, Sox, Go!" staggered toward their favorite bar to watch the Red Sox-Yankees game on television. Roger Clemens was scheduled to take the mound against the Bronx Bombers in an effort to sweep the series. Red Sox fans were drowned out by the occasional cab honking its way through traffic.

Over the entrance, The Boston Park Plaza Hotel and Towers, was emblazoned on the deep brown overhang hovering above the front door. Jason entered the two-story lobby, stairs to his left and the front desk ran the length of the wall on his right. Two huge crystal chandeliers hung centered in the lobby over an intricate floor design.

Jason walked through the lobby to the restaurant. His directions to McCormick and Schmick's were simple: through the lobby, a right, and then a left. Jason took a deep breath and walked through the door.

She sat right where they told him she would be. He had no idea how they knew she would be here, but there she was. And she was beautiful. The quaint wood table was flanked by high-backed wooden benches, as cozy and private as you could get in the bar area. Black-

and-white photos of Ted Williams and other Red Sox players hung on the wall on each side of the lamp sconce at the table. Sherri hadn't seen him yet as she typed away on her laptop.

In fact, she didn't notice him until he stood by her table.

"Oh, my God!" she exclaimed. Sherri jumped out of the booth, wrapped her arms around his neck, and kissed him. As quick as she did, she released him and backed off. "I'm sorry, I let my emotions get the best of me."

Jason grabbed her and gave her a big hug. "It's okay," he said, gazing into her eyes, "I kind of liked it."

"How did you find me?"

He paused, he couldn't tell her the CIA sent him here. "Let's just say I'm a very committed person."

"Have a seat," she said with a smile, motioning to the opposite side of the booth. "We have a lot to catch up on. Where have you been?"

"Hospitals, debriefings, training. Uncle Sam's keeping me busy."

Sherri closed the laptop, sliding it to the side. Reaching across the table, she grabbed his hands and held them in hers.

"I never had the chance to thank you for saving my life. Twice."

"I'm just glad I was there. When we landed . . . did they treat you okay?"

Sherri told the story of their landing at the remote desert runway in the F-2000. Men in black with ski masks put ladders up to the jet, climbing up to unstrap her. She climbed out of the jet and looked up at Jason one last time before they placed a black hood over her head. The initial treatment was rough, but for the next two weeks, her debriefs were spent under guard in a VIP suite at Nellis AFB. Steven flew in from New York to bring her back, but she stayed in the city only a couple of days before flying back to Missouri for two weeks. She was told by both the *New York Times* and the government, this story was off limits.

Jason told her of his numerous hospital visits, including his spinal surgery. Bulging disks in his cervical spine pushing against nerves shut down his right side that night in the F-2000. His days in jets with ejection seats were over. He had recently recovered and begun a physical therapy regime to get back in shape. He was on his way to Little Rock AFB for C-130 training, followed by more training at Kirtland AFB in Albuquerque. His next assignment was the MC-130P at the 17th Special Operations Squadron, Kadena Air Base in Okinawa.

He was going to Air Force Special Operations Command.

"Is your neck okay? The surgery worked?" Sherri said.

"Yes, I'm fine."

"So I've been wondering, how did we get back on the ground if you couldn't land the plane?"

"The F-2000 has a classified function called the Sensory Integration Package. It has a sub-system called RPA—Remotely Piloted Aircraft." Jason wasn't worried about discussing the classified aspects of the jet. He knew she signed nondisclosure agreements regarding the F-2000. Hell, she rode in the damn thing.

"That technology has been around for decades," Sherri said. "They use it, or at least a form of it, to fly drones out of Tyndall in Panama City, Florida."

Jason nodded. She'd been doing her homework.

"True. The interesting part is," Jason continued, "the F-2000 is tied to the pilot through an extensive sensor network so it can tell if the pilot is incapacitated. When it detects the pilot is unconscious, another sub-system called the Integrated Thought Control System takes over and automatically flies the plane home."

"But you didn't have any sensors attached."

"No, but the RPA can be flown from the ground," he said, impressed with her research. They sat in the booth, still holding hands across the table. Both seemed unaware because it felt so natural.

"Did you see your boss on TV today?" Sherri said.

Jason tilted his head, eyebrows raised.

"The secretary of defense? He had a press conference today and announced the Department of Defense cannot account for 2.3 trillion dollars. That's trillion with a 'T.'"

"Holy crap," Jason said. "Is it possible to even count that high?"

"Apparently. At least we know where the cost of the F-2000 is being hidden." Sheri paused. "I saw you on C-SPAN last month," she said, changing the subject again. "Looks like the congressional hearings were a nonevent. You had nothing to say."

"Trust me," Jason said, "more was said in the closed-door session."

They spoke for several more minutes, filling each other in on what they knew. Wellington, of course, was dead. His body was found in the F-16 wreckage. Jennifer awaited her court-martial. Kathy, as far as Jason knew, died in the TRENCOR explosion. Due to the intensity of the fire, no human remains were found in the building. The sarin gas kept the fire department at distance until fire burned itself out.

Ming and his wife were safely in China. The TRENCOR facility had a 1.5 billion-dollar insurance policy on the building. Ming's wife, the attorney Amanda Johnson Rieffelming, tried to collect the insurance while in Hong Kong, but Congress seized the insurance claim. The money the DOD paid to TRENCOR—gone.

The F-2000? It apparently never existed. All publications and documents now resided in a vault in the basement in the Pentagon. Dane's news report was written off as a hoax by the Air Force, the aircraft on tape explained away as an experimental model used as tactical deception for another secret project. The wing commander at Edwards, while not formally charged, was reassigned, then retired as a colonel following an extensive investigation.

They chatted for several minutes about what they had been doing since they last saw each other. The two sat lost in each other's eyes. He liked her. And it was obvious she liked him, too.

"Are you doing okay?" he asked.

"Yes, I'm fine. It took a while to wind down. I had to do some self-evaluation. Re-examine how I see some things . . . some people," she said, squeezing his hand. "I tried writing again, but it wasn't until a month ago I could really get back into the swing of things. They've killed my story. The one that took me out to California in the first place. About the Saudis."

Jason's eyes dropped to the table, then shot up again. "I know," Jason said stoically.

Sherri tilted her head inquisitively, releasing her grip on Jason's hands.

"You know? How do you know?"

Jason said nothing. Her eyes turned glassy as the disappointment began to show.

"Sherri, I—"

"The damn CIA sent you here?" she said, aggravated.

"Yes."

"Why? What the hell do they want with me now?"

Jason took a deep breath. He had been briefed on what to say, but he knew he wouldn't stick to their plan.

"This story . . . your paper killed it, but you're not letting it go. You've got to stop."

Her eyes grew wide, and she leaned back in her seat, shaking her head.

"Oh, no . . . hell no."

"Sherri, please listen to me—"

"No, you listen to me, Mister 'I'm a Jet Pilot.' That damn agency isn't going to stop me from pursuing this story."

"Sherri," he said, gently caressing the hand she pointed at his face. "They already have."

"What do you mean 'they already have'?"

As if on cue, her cell phone rang. She pulled from Jason's hands and answered her phone.

"Sherri."

"Steven, hi, what's up?" she said as her gaze fell on the wooden table.

"Sherri, I need you to come back to New York tomorrow afternoon."

"I can't, Steven. I'm flying to Los Angeles first thing in the morning."

There was a slight pause on the other end.

"Change of plans. I know we said we'd ignore the publisher and pursue this anyway, but it's dead. Sorry. I had travel change your reservations to fly back to New York tomorrow afternoon."

Sherri's head slowly rose toward Jason. She was no longer paying attention to Steven. Mumbling goodbye, she hung up and placed the phone back in her purse, staring at Jason the entire time.

"Why? Why do they want this story dead?"

"I don't know. I don't even know what you're investigating."

"You . . . you know something. Are you working with the CIA? Your buddy the president? How could you do this to me?"

"Sherri, it's not me. Please trust me. They asked me tons of questions about you. Questions I didn't have answers for. They said you were working on a story, and you had to back off. I asked them to let me be the one to tell you. Believe me, you wouldn't have liked the way they were going to stop you."

"Why did you come here?" Sherri said.

"I wanted to see you again. Personally. I mean, on a personal level."

Jason detected a smile, if only briefly.

"Well, the story is dead . . . for now," she said, draining the last of her Jack and Coke. She stared at Jason with a look he couldn't decipher. Was she angry? Sad? Interested? He couldn't tell.

After a minute or two, the waiter came by and asked if they needed anything.

"I'll have another Jack and Coke," she said, "and give him a Sam Adams. He's going to need it."

Jason eyes squinted as his head tilted to the side. He could not figure this woman out.

Sherri slid closer to the wall, smiling at him. Now he caught on. Jason climbed out of the booth, then slid in next to her. Their eyes locked for a moment. Sherri reached around and grabbed the back of Jason's head, pulling his lips to hers. They kissed long and passionately. Neither of them noticed their drinks arrive.

THE SHRILL RING OF HER PHONE woke her up. The morning rays pushed their way into her room. Moving the large, soft white pillow, she saw Jason sleeping next to her. She smiled as best she could at this time of morning, memories of the last twelve hours racing through her mind. The CIA might have stopped her yesterday, but there was no way in hell she was going to abandon this story.

She rolled over to her side, grabbing the phone from the nightstand. Flipping open the phone, she didn't recognize the number.

"Hello?"

"Sherri, it's me," said a familiar voice.

"Dane, how did you get my number?"

"Sherri, darling, I'm an investigative journalist. How else do you think I got your number?"

"You probably stole it, like you steal everything." Sherri was still furious about Dane stealing data from her laptop.

"Hey, babe," Dane said, "I thought we were a team."

Sherri rolled her eyes then glanced over at Jason to see if he was awake. He was out cold.

"We were never a team," she said.

There was a pause, as if he waited for her to say something else. She could hear background noise of something over the phone. It sounded like he was at the airport.

"Why are you calling me this time of morning, Dane? Hell, why are you calling me at all?"

"The story we're about to break, babe."

"Dane, if you call me 'babe' one more time, I'm going to come through this phone and rip your stomach out."

"Uh, sorry. Anyway . . . the story we've been working on . . . that's why I called."

"We are not working on a story—oh, my God! You stole my story from my laptop?"

"Like I said, it's *our* story. Clearly, you wanted us to work together on this."

"No, no, no," she spoke in hushed tones. "Dane, I will never work with you. Ever. Why are you calling me at seven in the morning?"

"Because, Sherri, I'm sitting on the plane waiting for you."

"What plane?"

"The plane you're scheduled on to Los Angeles. American Airlines Flight 11. You're supposed to be here right now. We're getting ready to push back. If you don't make it, I'll have to tail these guys myself."

"Dane, take my advice and drop this. Get off the plane and go back home."

"Sherri, there's no way in hell I'm getting off this plane. The American people have the right to know, and I'm not going to let them down."

Sherri gawked at her phone as if he could see her. Not only is Dane unethical, he's an idiot.

"Fine," she said. "You can have the story. Tail them yourself." Sherri hung up the phone and placed it back on the nightstand. Jason stirred and rolled over to look at her.

"Who was that?" Jason said.

"Nobody."

"Who's nobody?" he said, smiling at her.

Sherri crawled back underneath the covers, leaned over and kissed him softly.

"Hopefully, nobody I'll ever hear from again." She edged closer, curling up next to him. He wrapped his arms around her, and they both fell back to sleep.

THE END

Be on the lookout

for the further adventures

of

Jason Conrad

in

The

Crucible

Acknowledgements:

Writing a book is perhaps one of the most challenging endeavors one can embark upon. When I wrote my first book, it was a solo affair. I had absolutely no idea what I was doing; I had simply put a lot of blood, sweat, and tears into the effort. It paid off, sort of. I put together what I think was a truly entertaining yarn that showed quite a bit of promise.

Publishing a book is another animal altogether. It can be terrifying. The author exposes himself to the world and like Forrest Gump's box of chocolates, "You never know what you're gonna get." My initial goal was to get a copy of my work to put on the shelf for descendants to see one day. Feedback from early readers of the book was good so we jumped in using a strategy I liked to refer as 'running with scissors'. After winning three awards and reaching #1 Military/Thriller on Amazon with *SURLY BONDS*, it is easy to see what I would like to have done different.

Here we are with book number two in your hands. I would like to thank some of the people who made my journey with this second book possible. Scott Tyler, Mike Burton, JD Rudman, Terry Sears, Nick Beihl, Bill Walter, and my son, Derek Michael Jeter, thank you for your valuable insight.

Thanks to Bev Rosenbaum, Amanda Sumner, and John Briggs for your conceptual inputs, editing, proof-reading, and overall morale boosting.

Finally, I thank you, the reader, for making this journey possible. I hope you enjoy this book as much as I enjoyed creating it.

About the Author

Michael Byars Lewis, author of the award winning thriller, SURLY BONDS, is a former AC-130U Spooky Gunship Evaluator Pilot with 18 years in Air Force Special Operations Command. A 25-year Air Force pilot, he has flown special operations combat missions in Bosnia, Iraq, and Afghanistan. He served as an Expeditionary Squadron Commander for AC-130U combat operations in Iraq and spent his final assignment on active duty instructing and mentoring the next generation of gunship pilots at the Air Force Special Operations Air Warfare Center's schoolhouse for flight instruction, the 19th Special Operations Squadron. Michael is currently a pilot for a major U.S. airline.

Active in his community, Michael has mentored college students on leadership development and team-building and is a facilitator for an international leadership training program. He has teamed with the Air Commando Foundation, which supports Air Commando's and their families unmet needs during critical times.

While his adventures have led to travels all around the world, Michael lives in Florida with his wife Kim and their two children, Lydia and Derek.

Follow Michael Byars Lewis:

www.michaelbyarslewis.com
www.facebook.com/mblauthor
Twitter @mblauthor

Contact Michael Byars Lewis:

michael@michaelbyarslewis.com

Also from SATCOM Publishing

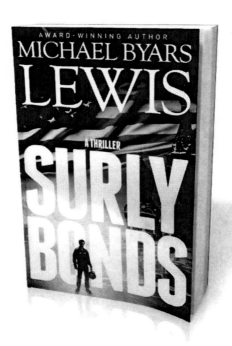

Available online in paperback and ebook from these fine retailers!

tolino

CPSIA information can be obtained
at www.ICGtesting.com
Printed in the USA
LVOW11s1345290617

539808LV00002B/113/P